Gifts For Our Time

ANNA JACOBS

Gifts For Our Time

HODDER & STOUGHTON

First published in Great Britain in 2017 by Hodder & Stoughton
An Hachette UK company

1

Copyright © Anna Jacobs 2017

The right of Anna Jacobs to be identified as the Author of the Work has been asserted
by her in accordance with the Copyright, Designs and Patents Act 1988.

A CIP catalogue record for this title is available from the British Library

Hardback ISBN 978 1 473 61638 7
Trade Paperback 978 1 473 61637 0
eBook ISBN 978 1 473 61636 3

Typeset in Plantin Light by Palimpsest Book Production Limited,
Falkirk, Stirlingshire

Printed and bound by Clays Ltd, St Ives plc

Hodder & Stoughton policy is to use papers that are natural,
renewable and recyclable products and made from wood grown in sustainable
forests. The logging and manufacturing processes are expected to conform
to the environmental regulations of the country of origin.

Hodder & Stoughton Ltd
Carmelite House
50 Victoria Embankment
London EC4Y 0DZ

www.hodder.co.uk

Dear Reader

I hope you enjoy this final story in the Rivenshaw Saga. The books have been very close to my heart because I was born at the beginning of World War Two and remember the post-war era with a child's eye*. I loved researching the era with an adult's understanding and writing about it.

I was four when the war ended and a few months later my father came home. I hadn't met him till then because he'd been serving in the Middle East. Imagine how happy my mother felt to get her husband back after four years apart! She had met him when she was sixteen and he was the sun in her sky for all the seventy-one years they were together.

I've read in history books that people in Britain were miserable after the war because of the ongoing post-war shortages of goods and food. Well, I don't remember anyone being miserable about life in my family.

I do remember the shortages, and one vivid memory is of eating my first banana quite soon after the war. The adults had managed to buy one, so they gave it to me and stood round to enjoy the sight of me eating it. They had to show me how to peel it first, and it must have been over-ripe, because I remember something squishy. I spat it out and refused to eat it, to their great disappointment. I still don't like over-ripe bananas!

I remember clothes being sold by one mother to another as children grew out of them. I had to wear things I didn't like the looks of, even as a child. Luckily, my father had

*My favourite picture of me as child with my mother in Falinge Park is on the back flap of the book!

brought a big flag back from the war and I was allowed to take it up to my bedroom and use it for dressing up. It was as big as a sari, so could be used in a lot of ways and I soon forgot what I was really wearing.

When sweets came off the ration in 1953, my father came home with an armful of bags of sweets of all kinds, laughing happily. He always did have a sweet tooth.

The big incident in my post-war life was the arrival of my little sister, who was part of the post-war baby boom. She was born at home and I was summoned into my parents' bedroom afterwards to meet her and be the first to put her down in the cot. I treasure that memory – and I still treasure her.

My sister grew taller than me, to six foot like our father. My husband is also the eldest of his siblings and both his brothers grew taller than him. I suppose that's the effect of wartime food shortages, though I was never aware of being hungry.

I've wondered a few times if the secret cellar in this series was inspired by the disued air raid shelters. We children played occasionally in the bigger ones, buy they always made me a bit nervous, and I never went into the dark parts.

I wasn't the boldest of children physically! I did a lot of my exploring and going on adventures inside my mind. I always did have a vivid imagination. No wonder I became a storyteller.

I hope my four Rivenshaw stories reflect accurately the way people interacted and lived during the post-war years. I've tried very hard to keep it accurate, but life was different in each part of the country, of course, and for each family, so mine is a northener's tale.

Happy reading!

Anna

*In fond memory of John and Vera Colgan, friends
and neighbours who are greatly missed.*

I

Christa's Tale
Germany: January 1939

Taking advantage of every shadow to stay hidden, Hans Sommer slipped into the block of flats, waiting to make sure he hadn't been followed before he entered his own home.

In the tiny hall, he sighed with relief and leaned against the closed door for a few moments to pull his thoughts together, then moved towards the bedroom.

No time to waste. He woke his wife and daughter and they all sat on the big bed to talk, as they'd done many times before. He ached at their dismay as he told them what had to be done.

'After the killings and mayhem of *Kristallnacht*, it has become obvious that freedom and justice have been openly set aside in our beloved country. We three are now in danger.'

'But we're not Jewish!' Christa protested.

'No, child, but Communists are also hated by our new leaders and I am well known as one who opposes their regime. This makes it too dangerous for my family to remain here in Berlin, so I've found a way to get you to safety, Christa.'

'Papa, no!'

'Yes, *Liebchen*. First we get you away to Britain, then your mother follows. After all, she is British, even though she came to live here as a child. I will join you later because there are still things I can do to help others. Not all the people managing our country are bloodthirsty in their solutions, thank goodness. Some of them just want problems like us to go away, as far away as possible.'

His wife nodded acceptance and put an arm round her daughter. 'We have no choice, *Mausi*. Getting you to safety in England will take a huge worry off our minds. Please . . . don't make it harder for us. It is better this way.'

Christa looked from one parent to the other, tears in her eyes. 'But it's so far away.'

'You will be safe there. I have asked a very big favour of my friend Andreas and he has found a way for you to join the *Kindertransport*. They are giving refuge to Jewish children in Britain and to a few children of dissidents, so you will pretend to be younger than your real age. Since you are small and slender, like your mother, you can become thirteen, not sixteen.'

'How can I feel like a child again here?' She touched her chest near her heart.

'You must find a way to keep up the pretence. Your life depends on it.'

'Thank goodness you can speak some English,' her mother said. 'I wish now that I'd made more effort to teach you. You must practise hard when you get there and learn quickly. They will accept you better if you speak the language properly. It's such a pity I've no close family left there for you to go to.'

Her parents spent the next two days packing and repacking the small suitcase which was all Christa would be allowed to take, cramming in anything they could. Her mother sewed the family's few pieces of jewellery inside a rag doll, even her wedding ring, brushing aside her daughter's protests.

'If I escape, my darling, I shall find this again. If I don't, it is better that you have it. But if you need money, you must sell any or even all of these valuables. Do not hesitate. Life is what matters most, not shiny baubles.'

'I'll write to you, let you know where I am,' Christa said.

Her mother sighed. 'No, *Mausi*. We must go into hiding, so you will not know where to send a letter.'

'But how will I know you're even alive?'

'You won't. No, shh. Don't cry. It's hard, I know, but *we* shall know you're safe. If we can, we'll escape later. We'll know how to find you after the war, because the Refugee Children's Movement will keep records. I can bear anything if I know you're safe.'

Such love shone in her parents' faces that Christa felt blessed to be their child. She swallowed further protests and did whatever they asked.

But when she was in bed, she wept silently . . . for them, for herself, for a world where families could be torn apart like this.

With everything happening so quickly and so much to do – and say – the hours flew past. Two nights later, her father took Christa to the rendezvous point under cover of darkness. Before she could say anything, he hugged her close, kissed her forehead and walked away.

By the time it sank in that this might be the last time she saw him, he'd vanished into the darkness. Oh, how she wanted to run after him! She stood straight and tried to be brave, as he would want her to. But she couldn't stop the tears welling in her eyes.

She was taken to a cellar where she waited for what seemed a long time with a group of children, all strangers. Many of them were taller than her, for all they were younger, so she didn't seem out of place. Her heart icy with fear, she kept a firm hold of her suitcase, which was all she had left of her family now.

Could you fit a whole life into a suitcase?

More children arrived and joined them in the cellar, some weeping quietly, others stony-faced. Most were alone like her, but a few had brothers or sisters. How lucky they were to have each other still!

No one spoke unless they had to. Christa guessed that, like her, they'd been told to keep quiet and do as they were told.

'Do not draw attention to yourself!' her father had repeated time after time.

When it was nearly morning, a plump lady who spoke mainly English with only a few halting words of German came down the stairs and beckoned to them. She put one finger to her lips to indicate silence, then they picked up their suitcases and filed out.

It seemed to Christa that sadness walked beside them like a ghost in the night as they stumbled along the poorly-lit back streets.

If she listened carefully, Christa knew enough English to understand what their rescuers were saying. They were worried that the Nazis might change their minds at the last minute about letting the children go. She'd overheard her parents sharing the same worries.

One boy watched her and asked if she understood what the grown-ups were saying. When she nodded, he said, 'Tell us. Please.'

The information was whispered down the straggling line of children, some of whom kept looking uneasily over their shoulders.

They arrived at the station and soldiers watched them pass in the grey, unreal light of pre-dawn. She held her breath as she walked along the platform, but none of the grim-faced men tried to stop them.

Oh, thank goodness! she thought as she climbed onto the train.

They were crammed into it and some fought for the window seats. Christa preferred to sit out of sight. She found herself comforting two younger girls who said they were eight and ten, each travelling on their own. That took her mind off her own troubles, at least.

At the Dutch border, they had to show their passports. Most of them had a red letter 'J' stamped on the front page. The guard examining Christa's passport asked her why she hadn't had the stamp put on. She struggled to reply politely, saying that she wasn't Jewish.

The guards didn't look as if they believed her, but they didn't stop her. They made jokes to one another openly about getting rid of rubbish, but they let all the children through.

The train stopped just across the border. Some Dutch ladies came on board with fresh orange juice, bread and butter for everyone. The bread was white and soft, the butter lavishly spread. Christa ate hers slowly, savouring every mouthful. It was months since she'd had food as good as this.

Then they were off again, moving slowly. The passengers had nothing to do but stare out at the dark countryside and, as it grew lighter, comment on the windmills.

Every now and then the train stopped for no reason that she could work out, but it didn't matter. They were in a free country now.

It was dark once again when the train arrived at the Hook of Holland. At Rotterdam they were led onto a ship. Christa tried to count the children walking up the gangway. About two hundred. So many families torn apart.

They were given more food and then shown to bunks. She put her suitcase under the thin pillow for safety, then lay down. The bunk was hard, the pillow even harder, but she was so tired she fell asleep.

They docked at a port in the cold light of a misty grey day. It had been a calm passage, but even so, one or two children had been sick.

Christa overheard a man telling one lad that they were now in Harwich on the east coast of England. She didn't remember ever noticing the name on a map and the mist prevented her from seeing what the town was like.

Some of the smallest children were still asleep and couldn't be woken. Since there were boys bigger and stronger than her, she wasn't asked to carry any of the little ones, thank goodness. She was finding it hard enough just to put one foot in front of the other.

The children walked slowly down the gangway into England and after their passports had been checked, they were taken to a hall next to a church. Food was provided and Christa ate it, even though she didn't feel hungry. She knew she must keep up her strength, stay alert and be ready to do whatever was necessary.

After they'd eaten, they were sorted into groups, their names called from lists. No one told them why they were going with one group or where they were going. The people organising things spoke pleasantly enough but were in a hurry.

Some children were sent off to the station and told they would be taken to London. She and several others were taken to a lorry at one side and told to wait for help to climb into the back.

Suddenly a man loomed out of the mist and tried to take her suitcase from her. She screamed and struggled, kicking him in that place her father had taught her was very sensitive for a man.

He yelled in pain and raised one fist, but a man wearing

an armband was already running towards them and her attacker fled, cursing. She didn't know the actual words, but curses sounded the same in any language, she felt sure.

'Well done, lass,' the second man said. 'Are you all right?'

'Yes, sir. Thank you for coming to my help.'

'You speak English?'

'A little. I soon learn more.'

'That's the right attitude. Hey, Mary! This one speaks some English. She'll come in useful. Some sod just tried to steal her suitcase.'

An older woman joined them. 'I hope he rots in hell! To steal is bad enough, but to steal a child refugee's only belongings is a vile crime.'

She turned to Christa. 'What's your name, dear? Yes, you're on my list. Let Herb help you into the lorry. Will you take charge of the food, Christa?'

'Yes, if you wish.'

'Give everyone a sandwich. Just one each, I'm afraid.'

As she passed a basket up, she added, 'There's water in that metal urn in the corner. Only half a cup each. You understand?'

'Yes. One sandwich and half a cup water each.'

'Good girl. And there's one blanket for *each person* as well.'

There were ten children in the back of the lorry in the end, sitting on the bare floor. Even with blankets wrapped round them, they were still cold, so they huddled together for warmth as they had on the ship.

Christa made sure they shared the food equally and didn't allow the two bigger boys to take any from the smaller children when they said they weren't hungry.

'You must eat,' she told the little ones.

'They don't want it,' one big boy protested. 'We wouldn't *steal* it from them.'

'No, but I'll tell the lady if you take the food,' she threatened. 'Then you'll start with a bad mark against you.'

To her surprise they stopped protesting and everyone, even the little ones who'd said they weren't hungry, ate the sandwiches, which seemed to have some sort of yellow jam in them. The bread was squashed and stale, but food was food. She made sure the youngest children ate every last crumb.

Most of them fell asleep after that. She leaned back against her suitcase and though she tried to sleep, she couldn't help worrying that something might go wrong.

The lorry didn't seem able to go very fast. It stopped twice and they were told to get down and relieve themselves by the side of the road, then given more food. Again she helped the little ones.

The next stop was to buy petrol. The grown-ups had cups of tea there, she could smell it. The children were given tin mugs of weak cocoa, but it was warm and sweet at least.

Would this journey never end? she wondered as they set off again. And would they really be safe here in England?

When she woke, it was dark again and cold. Well, it was winter, after all. Not the best time for a journey. The other children were still asleep, except for one of the bigger boys.

'What will it be like here?' he asked her.

'I don't know. I've never been to England before. My mother was born here but went to Germany when she was a child. She's the one who taught me how to speak English a little.'

'Are you glad to have escaped from Germany?'

She shrugged. 'Partly glad, partly not.'

'Me too. Even my father was crying.'

'Mine also.'

'Will you teach me a few English words?'

'Yes.'

She taught him *Please, Thank you, Yes, No, I don't under-stand.* But then the lorry stopped again and the man and woman let down the back, beckoning to the two youngest and helping them off it. The children cried out in terror as they were handed over to strangers and didn't understand what people were saying to them.

The lorry stopped three more times, leaving children at each place.

Christa was the only one left now. She wouldn't let herself show fear when they stopped for a final time, but she felt very apprehensive as she got down.

'Where is this place, please?' she asked the woman.

'Lancashire, dear, in the north of England. You'll be living near a town called Preston. A lady called Mrs Pelling has offered to take an older girl.' She looked round, frowning. 'Someone should have been waiting for you.'

Christa stood quietly, her suitcase on the ground between her feet. She wished she had a map, so she could see exactly where she was. She wished she was still with her parents, in spite of the risk. She wished all sorts of things as the slow minutes ticked past.

At last they heard the sound of a car in the distance. It seemed a long time till it came into sight. A man was sitting inside it, a dark silhouette against the dull evening sun.

He didn't get out immediately, and seemed to be studying them. When he finally came towards them, Christa saw that he was wearing a military uniform.

'Mr Pelling?' the lady asked and received only a nod in reply. 'Is your wife not with you?'

'I'm not married. It's my mother who wants the child. Last November she heard Viscount Samuel's broadcast on the radio appealing for foster homes and decided that she wanted to help. I'm away serving in the Air Force and she gets lonely.'

'Where is your mother tonight, then?'

'Recovering from a bad cold.' He fumbled in his pocket. 'Here, Mother said to show you this letter.'

The lady checked it in the light of a small torch and nodded. 'It's all in order. This is Christa.'

He studied her, his eyes narrowed. 'She's very small.'

'You were surely expecting a child!'

'Yes. But we asked for an older girl.'

'She's thirteen, old enough to look after herself and give little trouble. We've found her very helpful. And she speaks some English.'

'Ah.' This time he addressed Christa. 'I'm Thomas Pelling. My mother bids you welcome to England.'

'Thank you, Mr Pelling.'

'We have to get back to Harwich now,' the lady said. 'More children will be coming in soon – a private group.'

'Right. I'll put this in the boot.' He picked up Christa's suitcase before she'd realised what he was doing and she tried to snatch it back from him.

He looked at her in shock. 'I'm not stealing it.'

'It's all she has in the world,' the lady explained quietly.

He gazed at the shabby little suitcase and shook his head. 'Poor thing.'

Christa went with him to the car boot, then he opened the door for her on the passenger side, which seemed the wrong side of the car to her. But she got in, calling 'Thank you!' to the lady.

There was no answer. The lady with no name had already gone back to the lorry.

'Half an hour,' Mr Pelling said. 'We'll be there in half an hour. Do you understand me?'

'Half hour,' she repeated. 'I understand.'

He didn't speak again, just drove on and on through the greyness of the cold evening.

So she didn't speak either.

She never saw the other children again and she never knew their full names. That seemed wrong, somehow.

They could have been taken anywhere. Her father had said that people all over England had volunteered to care for refugee children until their parents could join them, or until they could be sent on to America or Australia.

She hoped she could stay in England till her parents joined her. America was much too far away.

Worried about being alone with a complete stranger, she made sure she was ready to run away. But he didn't look the sort to harm a child. Indeed, he'd hardly looked at her, let alone touched her. He seemed tired more than anything.

She was almost a woman, she hadn't felt like a child for a year or two, because in such difficult times her parents had talked openly to her, treated her as an equal.

Could she do this? Become a child again? She had to. Her father had said it was the best way of staying safe.

She wondered what life would be like in England.

She hoped Mrs Pelling would be a kind lady.

Christa's worries began to fade as soon as she met Mrs Pelling, who came to greet them in the hall, switching on the lights.

'She's called Christa Sommer,' Mr Pelling said abruptly. 'She's thirteen.'

Christa paused by the entrance, studying the older lady as closely as her hostess was studying her. The woman had silver hair, intelligent eyes and a kind expression.

She held out her arms and said, 'Welcome to your new home, child.'

And her expression was so sincerely welcoming that Christa

surprised herself by bursting into tears and running to her. Mrs Pelling held her, patted her shoulder and made soothing noises.

When the sobs died down her hostess spoke to her son, and Christa tried to understand what they were saying.

'Could you please make us something warm to drink, Thomas? Tea for me and hot milk for this young lady.'

'Yes, Mother. I'll bring her suitcase into the sitting room. She doesn't like to be parted from it. It's all she has left.'

Christa thought he hadn't paid her much attention, but he had noticed one thing at least and he was right: she did feel better when she could see her suitcase.

Mrs Pelling took her to sit on a sofa, saying quietly, 'You're safe here, child, and I'm very happy to have you.'

And she did feel safe there. Well, as near safe as was possible in such troubled times. Warm milk, a fire and two people who didn't fuss at her, who let her find her new self in peace.

Then a bedroom all to herself, with more drawers and cupboards than she knew what to do with. But she didn't unpack her suitcase. Not yet. She took out what she needed and put the case in the wardrobe, locking its door with the little key and putting it under her pillow.

Just in case.

The bed was so soft and cosy, she could feel herself falling asleep almost at once.

Safe, she told herself. It's safe to sleep now.

Christa was dismayed when she found out she had to go to school and have classes with younger children. To her relief, this had its good side. It quickly improved her English skills, and she learned a lot about the history and geography of Britain.

She was soon known as the quiet one who always sat at

the back of the room, and she made no attempt to change that.

Some children were hostile towards her because she was German, and it was no use telling them her mother was English because they didn't believe her. Others were friendly and clearly felt sorry for her.

She had thought long and hard and decided she didn't dare risk making close friends, because she might grow careless and give something away.

Anyway, they were so young, the children in her class, and she didn't have a lot in common with them. They hadn't known fear as intimately as she had, and she hoped they never would.

She envied them in many ways, but mostly for knowing where their parents were, though some had fathers serving in the armed forces.

She had no idea where her parents were now. That hurt a lot.

Several months passed and Christa settled in with Mrs Pelling. She cried sometimes at night, because she had still had no word from her parents, but she hid her anguish from her kind hostess. Then in September 1939 the war that Christa's father had been expecting began in earnest.

She knew her parents wouldn't be able to join her now, even if they were still alive. All she could do was pray for them every night; pray that they would survive, that she would see them again.

In May 1940 she heard that some German refugees who'd sought shelter in England were being sent to internment camps and went straight to Mrs Pelling. 'Will they take me away from you and put me in a camp?'

'No, dear. It's mainly the older male children that they're

taking and, actually, I think the authorities are panicking. There's simply no need for it.'

But Mrs Pelling did have to take her down to the local police station to register her as an 'enemy alien'.

A few weeks later, she was summoned to appear before the local investigative tribunal. She knew the two police officers who were on duty there and they knew her. Mrs Pelling had told her to keep quiet and say as little as possible.

The three-person tribunal was composed of two men and a woman. They were sitting behind a table and she was taken to stand in front of it. They stared at her coldly and questioned her.

She protested when one of the men said 'You Germans need to—'

'I'm half English. My parents were working *against* the Nazis. I am *not* an enemy.'

'*We* shall decide that,' the woman said sharply.

The man picked up a letter. 'This is from the lady who has taken you in, Mrs Pelling.'

'She is a wonderful, kind person,' Christa said at once.

The policeman standing at the door cleared his throat. 'If you please, sir, Mrs Pelling is waiting outside in case you want to question her.'

'Show her in.'

Mrs Pelling came in, leaning more heavily on her walking stick than usual, to Christa's surprise.

'Shall I fetch the lady a chair?' the policeman asked.

'Yes, please.'

He brought it in and helped Mrs Pelling sit down.

'You seem very concerned to keep this young woman with you.'

'I love her, but also I need her help because I'm not able to get around easily.'

One of them studied Christa in a different way, but didn't

address her directly. 'She's not very big for fourteen, is she? Wouldn't you be better finding a stronger girl to help you?'

'No. I've grown very fond of Christa. She's a good girl and knows my ways now. She works hard at school, too.'

'But she's still German.'

'Her mother was English. That surely makes a difference.'

'Hmm.'

'Now that my cleaning lady has gone off to do war work, I don't know what I'd do without Christa's help and—'

The younger official interrupted abruptly, 'Is she in touch with any other Germans?'

'No. Not even her family. They were in danger because they were working against the Nazis. We don't know what's happened to them.'

'Is the family Jewish?'

'No. Her father is a known Communist who has spoken out against Hitler many times. They had hoped to join her here, but she hasn't heard from them since she left, poor thing.'

The older of the two men sighed and said in a gentler tone, 'Eh, I've got a granddaughter the same age as her. I can't bear to think of my Liddy on her own in a foreign country. This lass is lucky to have you, Mrs Pelling, she is that.' He looked questioningly at his two companions. 'Category C, don't you think?'

The other man looked reluctant and Christa held her breath. Being classified as Category C would allow her to live freely in this country.

As the silence and frowning continued, the policeman cleared his throat. 'If it's any help to you, sirs, madam, I know the family and see the girl often on my rounds. What Mrs Pelling has said is true. She does need help and the girl gives it willingly. I always respect a hard worker.'

In the end, they agreed to Category C as long as the policeman continued to keep an eye on things.

Christa tried not to let her relief show. She went across to help Mrs Pelling stand up and retrieved her walking stick when she let it fall.

As they walked out, she felt nervous, half expecting them to change their minds and stop her. But they didn't.

'Thank you,' she said to Mrs Pelling as they were driven home in a taxi.

'For what in particular, dear?'

'For everything, especially the way you helped me today.'

'It's my pleasure. I've grown very fond of you, child. And it's you who is helping me much of the time.'

'I like to do that.'

There was silence for a few moments as Mrs Pelling looked out of the taxi window. Then she sighed, murmuring, 'I wonder when Thomas will get another leave? It seems so long since I've seen him.'

'I'm sure he'll get home to see you as soon as he can.' Christa patted her hand. Mrs Pelling and her son were very close, and because of that she felt rather left out when he came home. But she didn't complain, just tried to leave them together. They were family and she wasn't, however kind they'd been to her.

The rest of the time, she and her foster mother did nearly everything together. Christa now spoke quite good English and her teacher had praised her progress. She was known in the shops where she went on Mrs Pelling's behalf and in the library where she went every week to borrow books for them both.

She thought she was fitting in as her parents would have wished. She'd unpacked her suitcase within a month of her arrival.

She held the rag doll sometimes, remembering how her mother had sewn the few pieces of jewellery inside it. She didn't take the things out. They were safer where they were.

By 1943, Christa was allegedly seventeen and she was directed into war work, a job in a local factory making uniforms. Once again she faced hostility and suspicion but she got on with her work and didn't waste her time protesting or arguing.

As always, she didn't make close friends, but this time it was because Mrs Pelling wasn't in good health. Christa had to rush home from the factory to help her, and if their neighbours hadn't been doing some of the shopping for them, she didn't know how Mrs Pelling would have coped. She couldn't have stood in the queues for very long.

At least Christa could take over the heavier household chores and did so willingly.

She felt comfortable with Thomas, though she didn't know him as well as she knew his mother. He was a quiet person, and she heard him cry out in the night sometimes. He teased her that her slight German accent only came out now when she was upset or angry.

It was he who suggested she change her name to Summers. It meant some extra paperwork, but she explained to the officials that she wanted to be properly English and they clearly approved of that.

She'd managed to keep her real age a secret for several years but one day when she was very tired, she betrayed herself. She clapped her hand to her mouth and waited for Mrs Pelling to get angry.

'Don't look at me like that, child. I guessed quite early on that you were older than your papers said, though not how much. It doesn't upset me at all and I won't give your secret away. I'd have told you to do the same if I'd been your parents.'

She sat frowning for a moment or two, then added, 'I

don't think we should tell anyone else about your real age, though, not even Thomas. The fewer who know about it, the better. Anyway, he has enough to worry about.'

No need to explain that. Thomas was in the RAF, flying the bombers that were targeting German cities. Many fine young men were being killed daily in such dangerous jobs and he was doing well to survive so long.

But it hurt Christa to think that the people being bombed were German civilians like her parents.

His mother was always worried about Thomas being in such danger. How could she not be?

There was still no word from Christa's parents and she'd tried to resign herself to them being dead, like so many others.

But when one day a letter arrived from the people at the Refugee Children's Movement, saying that they'd been sent word from a trusted source that her parents *were* dead, she wept in her foster mother's arms. To know for certain was agonising.

After that she didn't talk about them any more, even to Mrs Pelling. But she still thought about them often and vowed to make them proud of her once the war was over.

Then her grief had to be put aside, because the terrible thing her kind hostess had been dreading all through the war finally happened. In March 1945, her son Thomas was killed during a bombing raid on Germany.

It was Mrs Pelling's turn to weep now and she did little else, because Christa could find no way to comfort her.

To add to her dear foster mother's distress, the war in Europe ended shortly after in May 1945.

'If only he could have survived a little longer,' Mrs Pelling muttered to herself over and over. 'It's cruel, too cruel to bear.'

Neither of them joined in the VE Day celebrations. The war had cost them both too much for them to want to participate in street parties.

It had been an all-out war to which, it sometimes seemed to Christa, civilians had contributed all their small personal freedoms, as well as their rights as individuals. She admired her adopted country greatly and was proud that Britain had won.

After VE Day, Mrs Pelling began to fade. Every month she seemed frailer and needed more help to get around. Fortunately, Christa was given permission to stop working and look after her dear friend.

It was heartbreaking to see such a fine woman become so thin, ageing quickly. Christa cared for her devotedly, but the deterioration gathered speed and by VJ day, when the war in the Far East ended at last, Mrs Pelling was little more than skin and bones.

The doctor said she couldn't live much longer and asked about relatives. Christa had to admit she didn't know of any. He suggested she search for information about other family members, but she could find nothing.

What was worrying her now was what she would do after Mrs Pelling died. She had no idea what would happen to this house.

In the end she went to see Mrs Pelling's lawyer and explained the situation to Mr Audley, asking how things stood and what she should do if her foster mother died.

He sighed and looked down at his hands. 'Thomas wrote a will, but of course he predeceased his mother. I'll come to see her and suggest she makes another will. Her son did mention that there were cousins and gave me their names, because he was well aware of the danger of his work. I'll get in touch with them if . . . *when* the worst happens. She looks . . . very frail now. Can you continue to look after her?'

'Of course. She's looked after me since I came to England as a child. I owe her a lot and, anyway, I love her.'

'She's lucky to have you.'

'I've been lucky to have her. Unfortunately I have to think ahead, so I wonder . . . could you write me a reference . . . for afterwards? I'll need to get a job then, you see.'

'Yes, of course. I'm happy to.' He gave her a smile. 'Now, we have to be practical. Are you all right for money?'

'Yes. She's been writing me cheques which I take to the bank. I've given up my job and I'm letting her keep me. I hope that's all right. I've kept careful accounts.' She handed a copy to him.

'Very sensible of you.' He studied them and nodded. 'Very reasonable amounts in the circumstances.'

That left Christa with a lot to think about. She could go out and find a job . . . afterwards. And she still had some money saved. But what sort of job? And where would she live?

What was she going to do with the rest of her life?

There was no one else she could turn to for advice or help, no one in the whole world.

For now though, all she had to do was make sure Mrs Pelling received the care she needed. After that she could think about herself.

2

Lancashire: October 1945

In the late afternoon Mayne Esher persuaded his wife to take a break and stroll with him round the grounds of Esherwood, the old manor house that had been in his family for hundreds of years. Parts of it dated back to the seventeenth century, just after the Civil War.

'I want to talk to you about something before I discuss it with the others,' he said as soon as they were away from the house. 'We've got so many people living at Esherwood now that it's hard to snatch time alone during the day.'

Judith smiled. 'And my children are among the worst offenders. Well, Kitty's developing a little tact, but the other two don't seem to realise that us two newly-weds would appreciate some time together.'

He stopped to give her a hug, then his expression turned serious. 'You know I love them dearly and I'm glad they feel free to chatter about what they're doing. Besides, Kitty's nearly grown-up now, and the others are at grammar school, so we must make the most of them while we have them.'

'You're a wonderful stepfather. Now, tell me what Councillor Blaxton was talking about so earnestly when he popped in for a chat.'

'He was sounding me out about erecting some prefabs on that scruffy piece of land at the back of the gardens.'

'And?'

'I thought it might be a good idea.' He saw understanding in her eyes. 'There's a housing crisis in this country, and I'm not yet in a position to build houses for returning soldiers. He said he'd send the new chap in charge of planning to talk to me and then I could show him the land in question. Thompson, he's called.'

'Well, that'll put off the time when you'll be forced to give up the big house and turn it into flats,' she said gently. 'I know how much you love Esherwood.'

'I get the impression you've become fond of it, too. You've been a tower of strength to me since the war ended, my darling.' He sighed. 'I still don't understand how my father could have lost so much of the family money, or how any commandant could allow his men to cause so much wilful damage in a house that had been requisitioned.'

She laid one finger on his lips. 'Shh. We agreed we'd try to put the anger about that behind us. Your father has no more idea about money than a child, because he lives in his books and historical research. As for the men who were in charge of Esherwood while it was requisitioned, they were focused on the injured men who were sent here to recuperate, not the house.'

He caught hold of her hand and cradled it for a moment against his cheek. 'You're right. It won't do any good rehashing the past. Only it's hard not to get angry when every day I can see signs of needless damage.'

'The men were probably bored and angry at being shut away in a small country town.'

'Maybe. Anyway, we'd already decided to ask the council if the town would like to buy that rear piece of land, and it's a scruffy part of the estate which never did get land-scaped. And if our new building company erects the prefabs, as part of the deal, it'll get Esher and Company started without us needing a large amount of capital. Prefabs can be set up quickly once the ground is prepared and the water and other services brought in . . . But that will only postpone selling the big house for a while. I know that.'

They walked along in silence for a few yards, then he added, 'With a bit of luck I can keep the Dower House for us to live in and modernise it, now that Ray Woollard has found some valuable small items among the general chaos. You and I can move in there with the kids when work starts on the big house – as long as you don't mind putting up with my father and his absent-minded ways.'

She gave his hand a sympathetic squeeze. 'Of course I don't mind. He might be absent-minded but he has a kind nature. There will be plenty of room for us all at the Dower House, even if we have to squeeze the Rennies in as well.'

As they started moving again, she said, 'Think how desperate people are for somewhere to live. And although prefabs are ugly from the outside, the photos of the interiors that I've seen in the newspapers show very comfortable modern homes. It'll be good to help people, won't it? So many have had to live with relatives during the war, but now it's over, it's only natural that they'd want to start a new life in their own places.'

'Is that how you feel about living with my partners and their families, wanting to live on our own?'

'No. Esherwood is so big, we can find some privacy if we really need it. Though we might find we huddle together near fires more often during the winter. Those spacious rooms take a lot of heating.'

'From what I hear, we'll be glad of the wood we gathered, because coal is going to continue being strictly rationed.'

'Everything seems to be rationed still. We won't know ourselves when that ends.' She smiled. 'Besides, I like your friends and enjoy their company. It's lovely to see Victor and Ros settling into marriage, and now that Francis has been reunited with his wife, he's so much happier.' She chuckled. 'Diana's doing her best to fit in. She even mopped a floor today.'

'*Diana* did?'

'Yes. She got Mrs Needham to show her how to do it, just to prove to Francis that she's changed. She isn't the spoilt brat she used to be, but oh, she hated every minute of the mopping and couldn't hide her feelings. Still, she made a good job of it.'

'I'm glad those two got back together. There are too many divorces these days.'

'People rushed into marriage during the war. Now they're finding that they don't fit together in peacetime. I wouldn't condemn anyone to a lifetime of unhappiness.'

She fell silent for a moment or two, remembering her own so-called marriage and the shock of finding that Doug was a bigamist. But there was no use dwelling on the past, so she banished the memories and said brightly, 'Let's walk round the land you'll be selling.'

They walked round the stable block and into the old gardens, which had low walls and little paths which must have been charming in the seventeenth century but which were sorely in need of some restoration work now. Their feet swished through piles of fallen leaves as they moved into the untidy part at the rear. The paths here were rough tracks only and, in some parts, all the vegetation had been destroyed because it had been used to train small combat units.

About a hundred and fifty yards before the rear perimeter wall, Mayne stopped. 'This is it. From here onwards I should think they'll knock the wall down. It's in a terrible state.'

'That'd be a pity because it's very picturesque. This area will make a nice little street and I should think people will fight to get one of the prefabs.'

As they turned back, she looked up at the trees and sighed.

'Winter's coming on fast. Soon most of the branches will be bare.'

'Councillor Blaxton emphasised that they want to push this project through quickly before the worst of winter.'

'If they do, it'll be the first time the Rivenshaw town planning section has done anything quickly since it was formed.'

'The new chap was apparently an officer in the Army during the war, so maybe he'll be more efficient.'

She let out a little snort of derision. 'And maybe pigs will fly. No department at that town hall has ever been efficient when I've had to deal with them. This Thompson is probably someone's cousin or son.'

'Well, we'll have to deal with him whoever he is.'

When they got back, Mayne and Judith found that the children had come home from school and tea was ready on the table. Ros was on tea-making duty this week so she must have worked quickly after she'd met her stepdaughter Betty from school.

Judith hugged her son, who was looking at her expectantly. 'I suppose you're dying of hunger. Goodness, you're growing fast. Just look at you! You're taller than me now.'

Gillian came up for a hug as well. 'He's always hungry, Mum. Mrs Needham says all boys are stomachs on wheels at fourteen.'

Judith laughed and hugged her elder daughter Kitty for good measure, keeping her arm round her shoulders as she turned back to Ben. 'Go on then, call everyone to tea.'

He rushed into the hall to thump the dinner gong and ran back to take his place at the table before the gong had even stopped reverberating.

All ten of them sat down at the big wooden kitchen table, like a big family. The only partner missing was Daniel. Once everyone had been served, Mayne told them about the prefabs.

'The government is urging towns to push anything to do with building houses through the planning stages as quickly as they can,' Victor said thoughtfully.

'And now they've switched from wartime production, the factories are churning out prefabs at an amazing rate,' Francis said. 'Most of the other stuff they're producing is for export, though. Anyway, we really need Daniel to come back now. He's—'

At a quick shake of the head from Mayne, who glanced meaningfully towards the children, Francis changed what he was going to say and finished, 'He's our architect, after all.'

All the adults knew Daniel was still troubled by his wartime experiences but that wasn't something they discussed in front of the children. Kitty considered herself grown up and acted like it most of the time since she'd started in the sixth form at school, but Ben, Gillian and Betty were still young enough to blurt out information to anyone and everyone and the other adults didn't want to risk upsetting Daniel as he was settling down into civilian life.

'What about this house?' Gillian asked. 'Are you going to start turning it into flats now, Mayne?'

'Once we've got the prefabs erected. We still need Daniel to draw up detailed plans for the conversion. I'd prefer to wait for him to do it before I take any steps.'

'And I haven't finished charting the electrics they installed here piecemeal during the war.' Francis sighed at the thought. 'They must have done the various extra circuits in a rush, and a right old mess they made of most of them.'

As they went on with their meal, Ben told them about a friend of his at school. 'His mother's furious because they got a parcel of food from her sister in South Africa and it weighed more than five pounds, so it's going to be taken off their food rations.'

'I don't think that's fair,' Kitty said. 'We're not at war now, after all. Why shouldn't relatives overseas send presents? I only wish we had someone to send us treats.'

'It's because the government still needs to share out what food there is,' Mayne reminded her gently. 'There are people starving in Europe, which is why rationing has stayed so strict.'

That led to a discussion about which food treats the adults were missing from pre-war days and how soon they could expect to see such items in the shops.

'I'd love a banana,' Diana said wistfully. 'They were my favourite fruit.'

'I can't remember ever eating one,' Gillian said and added, with her usual devastating frankness, 'We didn't get a lot of fancy things to eat when our father was living with us because he used to take the best of everything Mum bought and then spend most of his wages on booze.'

Kitty flushed in embarrassment, Ben jabbed his elbow in his younger sister's ribs to shut her up and Judith hurriedly changed the subject.

In their comfortable home near Preston, Daniel O'Brien and his recently widowed aunt were eating their evening meal together. He watched her as he spoke, trying to gauge how she was feeling about the changes ahead. 'The sale of this house will be going through in a couple of days and that removals firm I told you about can take our furniture across to Rivenshaw at the weekend. Are you ready to move?'

'Oh, yes. It'll be a relief to get it over with and there are only a few things to pack now. I can go whenever it's convenient with you. Only . . . are you really sure your friends will want me to live at Esherwood? I still worry about that. They've never even met me.'

He patted her hand, knowing how sad and lost she had been feeling since his uncle's death. He had no intention of leaving her behind. 'I'm certain they'll welcome you, and Mayne said there was plenty of room to store your furniture in the cellars. We four chaps are more like brothers than friends, after serving together on those special projects. We consider each other's relatives part of the adopted family.'

'I still can't get used to the war being over. Six years is such a long time that it's hard to change into a peace-time way of thinking.'

'Yes. Very hard.' He stared into space.

After a moment or two she said softly, 'You were calling out in your sleep again, dear.'

'Was I? Dammit! I thought I'd stopped that. I do hope our lodgers didn't hear me.' He saw how anxious she was looking and forced a smile. 'Still, I must be getting better because I didn't wake myself up. Haven't done that for a few weeks, at least.'

'Their room is further away from yours than mine, so I doubt they'll have heard anything. They've been good lodgers, haven't they?'

Daniel grinned. 'Perfect. I never saw a man so desperate to move out from his in-laws' house and so happy to move in with strangers.'

'Well, this house will belong to them soon.'

The telephone rang just then and he went to answer it, chatting for several minutes and once laughing out loud.

When he came back, he found that his aunt had cleared the table and was in the kitchen washing up.

'That was Mayne on the phone. Rivenshaw Town Council is going to build some prefabs on the scrubby land at the back of his grounds, and they want to start work as quickly as possible. It's lucky we're ready to go back. I'm really needed now. Oh, and Mayne said everyone's looking forward to meeting you.'

'Really? You're not just saying that?'

'No. He volunteered the information without any prompting from me.'

'What a relief!'

In a house only a few streets away, Christa looked at the district nurse, but she already knew what Doris was going to tell her.

'I'm sorry, love. There's nothing anyone can do to help her now. At least she died peacefully in her sleep. We'd all prefer to do that, wouldn't we?'

'I shall miss her so much. She's been like a second mother to me.'

'Well, no one could have looked after her more devotedly than you these last few months. People round here thought you were a relative and that's why she took you in.'

'No, I was one of the child refugees who came to England before the war. Mrs Pelling took me in out of sheer kindness. She was a wonderful woman.'

In spite of her efforts to hold them back, tears began to trickle down her face and Doris patted her shoulder.

Christa scrubbed at her eyes. 'What do you think I should do now? Should I stay on here? I don't even know who's going to inherit this place, her niece I suppose. Mrs Pelling always refused to discuss her will and I don't think she managed to make a new one after her son died, as her lawyer wanted.'

'Go and ask him about it. No need for you to move out yet. Someone has to take care of the house, after all. And perhaps one or two of your own relatives will have survived the war, love. It does happen. I know a family who were told their son had died and it turned out he was in one of those horrible concentration camps. He looks like a walking skeleton but at least he'll recover once he has enough to eat.'

Christa had faced the painful truth years ago. 'My mother or father would have found a way to send word to the RCM if they were still alive. The Nazis must have killed them. If my father hadn't got me out of Germany, I'd be dead too.'

'What was that RCM again?'

'Refugee Children's Movement.'

'Oh, yes.' After a brief pause, Doris changed the subject. 'Blackman's do a nice funeral. Shall I send our Jimmy to let them know she's passed away?'

'Are you sure you've time?'

'Of course I have. In fact, I can drop in myself on the way to my next call. You should stay with her till they take her away, then go and see the lawyer.'

Doris left almost immediately. She was a busy woman. Unlike Christa, she'd grown up in the district, had relatives and friends everywhere, as well as people she met on her nursing rounds, and was always needed somewhere.

The undertakers came an hour later. Once they'd removed the body, Christa sat for a few moments, still wondering what was going to become of her. Then she pulled herself together and went to consult the lawyer.

'You did the right thing sending for Blackman's,' Mr Audley said at once. 'They're well thought of. I shall have to inform Mrs Pelling's niece, because she's the closest relative left and she's named in the will Mrs Pelling made years ago in case her son was killed. It's the only will we have, but it seems unfair because the niece has never been near her that I've heard. Could you look after the house till she comes? She's called Grayton.'

'Yes, of course. Then I suppose I'll have to find somewhere to live.'

'I can't reimburse you for all your previous expenses until we get probate, I'm afraid.'

'What? Oh, that isn't important now. I just want to make sure Mrs Pelling has a decent burial and a nice headstone, remembering her and her son. Only someone else will have to pay for that. I don't have much money left.'

'Please go ahead and make arrangements. I'll deal with the finances.'

As she walked back home, Christa looked in the newsagent's shop window to see if any lodgings were advertised. But there were none. She did take down the address of a small hotel, advertised on a yellowed card. If she couldn't find anything permanent, she'd have to go there temporarily.

It was a good thing she didn't waste her money. With care, she could manage for a few more weeks, till she found a job.

Mr Audley felt sad as he watched Miss Summers leave. Mrs Pelling had been in the middle of making a new will, with her protégée benefitting. Now, the niece would get everything.

Sometimes life could be very unfair.

Mrs Pelling's niece turned up in the middle of the following morning, marching into the house without knocking.

When Christa hurried out from the kitchen to see who'd come in, she found a plump, middle-aged woman staring at her, arms akimbo.

'I'm Mrs Grayton, Mrs Pelling's niece, and I'm the owner of this house now, the lawyer tells me. And Mr Audley should know. He's been the family lawyer for years.' She gave Christa a dirty look. 'I suppose you're the German she took in, of all the stupid things to do. You're a scrawny little thing! You can't have been much use round the house.'

'I'm not a German. My mother was English and I've been allowed to take English nationality.'

'You were still brought up a German and that'll never change. I lost a son to you damned Huns.'

Taken aback at this unwarranted attack, Christa didn't know what to say or do.

'Well, you can pack your things and get out of the house this very minute. I'm not having you sleeping under my roof.'

'Very well. I'll go and pack.'

'*We* will go and do it together. I intend to check that you don't try to steal anything.'

'*What?* How dare you say that? I've never stolen anything in my life.' Christa glared at Mrs Grayton, who glared back at her. There was clearly no reasoning with the woman, so she turned and went up the stairs. The other woman followed her closely, to her annoyance.

The front door opened again. Mrs Grayton leaned over the banisters and yelled, 'We're up here, packing her things. Come and help me keep an eye on her, Harry.'

She tried to come into the bedroom, but Christa put her arm out to bar the way. 'You can see everything you need to from the doorway, if you insist on being so ridiculous about this. I'm quite capable of packing my own things.'

A man appeared behind Mrs Grayton.

'She's telling me what to do in my own house, Harry.'

'Only in my bedroom and these are *my* things that I'm packing.'

'The cheek of it! And her nothing but a charity case.'

'Calm down, Mavis. We can keep an eye on her from here. Hurry up, you.'

Christa started taking her clothes out of drawers and putting them on the bed. She had a big old shopping bag Mrs Pelling had given her, but it wasn't enough.

She addressed her words to Mr Grayton. 'I shall need something else to put the rest of my things in. When I was brought here from Germany as a child, all I had was a suit-case. It means a lot to me, the last thing I have left of my parents.' The mere thought of it gave her courage to face their hostility. 'I shall need to get that from the attic, and I'll need another suitcase as well, if you want me to take my things away today.'

Was it her imagination or was that a flicker of sympathy in Mr Grayton's eyes?

'How come you've got all these things, if that's all you brought with you?' His wife moved forward, hands outstretched as if to grab one of Christa's books.

Christa held out one hand to fend her off. 'Because I worked in a factory . . . *war* work . . . once I left school. And I stayed there, doing my bit for Britain, earning my own money and buying my own clothes until Mrs Pelling grew too ill and I had to give up work to nurse her.'

Mavis sniffed. 'So you say.'

'You can ask the doctor, the district nurse and the lawyer. They will all bear me out.' She waited a few seconds, then said, 'So how do you expect me to take my things away without anything to put them in?'

'Any way you can. If you don't, I'll throw them out of the door myself.'

'Mavis! There's no need for that,' Mr Grayton said sharply. 'Think how that would look to the neighbours. I'll go and look in the attic, Miss–er . . .'

'Summers,' she told him.

'Summers.'

'Right. Miss Summers. What's your old suitcase like?'

'Shabby brown leather, with some German labels on it from when my parents used to take holidays. It'll be with the other suitcases, probably on top. There are several cases up there. Surely you can spare another old one as well as finding mine?'

'Yes, all right. I won't be long.'

'She's trying to take more of our things,' his wife protested.

'Look, love. We have a whole house full of furniture and stuff. We can spare a suitcase as well as the one that belongs to her. After all, she did do war work for our country, you have to give her that.'

'Only because she had to.'

Christa held in her anger with difficulty and concentrated on taking her things out of the drawers and off their hangers in the wardrobe. As she made neat piles on the bed, she was aware of the hostile gaze on her the whole time.

'Where did you get that doll from? If it's from the attic here—' Mrs Grayton snatched it off the end of the bed.

Christa immediately snatched it back. 'Don't you dare touch that! It's the last thing my mother ever made for me before I left Germany. I never saw her again.'

'Another Hun!'

'Why will you not listen? I've already told you she was English. From Hertfordshire. But she married a German. He was a Communist, so Hitler probably had him killed and her with him.'

The man had re-joined them and heard that. 'Did you say your father was a Communist?'

Christa hadn't heard him come down. 'Yes. He was working against Hitler.'

Mr Grayton pushed past his wife and put two dusty, battered suitcases on the bed. 'That's a bit different, Mavis. There were some Germans on our side, you know.'

'Not as far as I'm concerned, there weren't. They didn't *stop* Hitler, did they?'

With a sigh, he turned back to Christa. 'We lost our son. She'll never forgive Germans or see any good in them. Here. This one's got a lot of rubbish in it. I don't know what that's about.' He opened the suitcase.

Christa looked at the bits of paper, newspapers, old clothes and other oddments and tears came into her eyes. 'Mrs Pelling got very secretive at one stage and started hiding things. I thought I'd found all her caches. There won't be anything valuable here.'

'Tip it out and leave that for me to decide,' Mrs Grayton said at once.

'Very well.'

Mr Grayton put his arm round his wife. 'Let's wait in the kitchen, Mavis!'

His wife shook his hand off, glaring at them both. 'No. I'm keeping my eye on her.'

He sighed. 'I'll help you carry the suitcases to wherever you're going, Miss Summers.'

Only then did it occur to her that she had nowhere to go. 'Oh dear! I'm afraid I don't know where I'm going because I didn't know when you would arrive. I shall have to find lodgings somewhere and come back for my things, if you don't mind. Mr Audley asked me to stay here to keep an eye on things till the heir was found.'

'And I have been found, so you can go away and never come back,' Mrs Grayton snapped.

'I just told you: I haven't had time to arrange anywhere to go.'

'No one will take *you* in,' Mavis said triumphantly. 'I'll make sure of that. I grew up round here. I know a lot of people.'

Her husband turned and grabbed his wife's arm, dragging her along the landing. Though he spoke in a low voice, his words echoed clearly. 'Stop that, Mavis. If she can't find anywhere to stay, we'll have to take her back here or people will talk. That lawyer said she looked after your aunt devotedly.'

Mavis's reply was too low to be heard, but Harry came

back to the bedroom on his own. 'Is there a wheelbarrow, do you know?'

'Yes. In the garden hut.'

'I'll go and fetch it. Then we'll put your things in the hut while you go hunting.'

While Mr Grayton was gone, his wife came back and leaned against the doorframe, scowling at Christa while she continued with her packing. She didn't have a lot of money, but she'd have to go to the hotel for a night or two, whatever it cost.

As she picked up her beloved suitcase, Christa looked at the sad pile of rubbish she'd tipped on the floor and tears came into her eyes. She felt as if she was being tipped out of the house like that rubbish would be.

'If you could let me know when the funeral is being held, I'd like to attend.'

'If you do, I'll have you turned away. You are *not* part of our family and you are *not* wanted.'

'I'm glad I don't have to live with your conscience, Mrs Grayton.'

'You cheeky young madam. I hope you wind up on the streets where girls like you belong!'

Christa turned and walked away sadly; the world was suddenly empty.

3

Christa spent an uncomfortable night on a hard, narrow bed at the hotel, unable to sleep for worrying. The owner, Mrs Salter, had been very sharp with her, seeming annoyed at being disturbed so late.

She needed to find proper lodgings first, then a job; that was the obvious way to sort things out.

Having decided on her plan, she told herself to go to sleep, but something inside her was wide awake and she couldn't turn it off. She tossed and turned, hearing the town hall clock strike midnight, then one o'clock, then two . . .

She finally woke at seven but breakfast wasn't till eight o'clock, so she lay waiting for the hands of her wristwatch to move slowly on. No use getting up because the room was cold.

The watch she kept looking at in the light from a street lamp had belonged to Mrs Pelling's son. It had been last year's Christmas present to Christa, given in his memory. She would always treasure it.

After a meagre breakfast of tea and toast served in a chilly dining room by an equally chilly Mrs Salter, she put on her only winter coat and hat, and went out job hunting.

First, she tried the factory where she'd worked before leaving to care for Mrs Pelling. But the men who'd been employed there before the war were gradually being demobbed and had priority for jobs.

'We'll give you a reference, though, if that's any use,' the manager said. 'You were a good little worker.'

'Thank you. I'd be grateful.' She waited while the secretary typed it up and felt pleased that they'd thought so highly of her. But that wouldn't find her a job, would it?

When she left, she bought a newspaper and went for the two jobs that were advertised, but other people had got there before her and there was a long line outside each place. It wasn't even worth waiting, there were so many others ahead of her.

After that she walked all over town looking for 'Help wanted' signs in shop windows and calling in at factories and workshops, but to no avail. When she returned to the hotel, exhausted, she was met by a grim-faced landlady.

'I didn't know you were a German or I'd not have given you a room.'

'But I'm not!'

'I was told that your father was German. Is that true or not?'

'He was, but he was fighting *against* Hitler!'

'They all say that. But I hate all Germans. They've been our enemies in two world wars now.'

'Who told you about my father?'

'None of your business.'

Christa could guess. 'Look, my mother was British and I've got British nationality too, now. I was a child when I came here as a refugee before the war. I've been doing war work, too. How could I possibly be an enemy?'

'Who can see inside another person's head? All I know is, half German is more than I'm having under my roof. I've my other guests to think of and a lot of them feel the same way.' She gestured to where Christa's suitcases were sitting in the hall. 'I packed your things for you.'

Christa was outraged that the woman had handled even

the few possessions she'd unpacked, but bit back her anger. 'How am I supposed to carry two suitcases and a bag on my own?'

The woman hesitated. 'Well . . . you can leave them here for now. I'll put them in the store room. But I want them gone by midday tomorrow at the latest.'

Christa decided to take her German suitcase with her and walked slowly outside, holding back the tears with difficulty. It was late afternoon now and people were hurrying home from work. She tried two nearby lodging houses, but they were both full.

She wondered if the lawyer could help her but when she went to his offices, there was a sign on the door saying they were closed until Monday 'due to family bereavement'.

There was a small public garden nearby and since her feet were aching from tramping around all day, she went to rest for a few moments on a bench. Idly, she watched an older lady stroll along one of the paths. She looked sad and weary too.

As the other woman stopped to stare down at some of the few flowers remaining from summer, a man suddenly sprang out from behind some bushes and tried to grab her handbag. She fought him off, shouting for help, and without hesitating, Christa ran across to her, also shouting at the top of her voice.

At the sound of her yells, the man froze for a few seconds then disappeared into the bushes. Christa glanced around, anxious about her own suitcase and called, 'I'll have to fetch my case.' She grabbed it then hurried back to check on the victim of the attack.

The woman had sunk down on another of the wrought iron park benches, clutching her handbag to her chest with both hands and looking terrified.

There were footsteps coming along the street, so Christa

yelled, 'Help! Help!' in case it was the thief returning. But it was two women and they turned off down a side street before they reached the gardens, even though they must have heard her calls.

She sat down next to the woman, keeping a wary eye on the bushes at the top of the open area. 'Are you all right? Did he hurt you?'

'No, thanks to you. But I do feel a bit wobbly. I need a minute to pull myself together.'

'I'm sorry I had to leave you for a second or two but I didn't dare risk my own suitcase being stolen. It's got almost everything I own in it. I'm Christa Summers, by the way.'

'Beryl O'Brien.'

Christa glanced at the woman's left hand and saw the wedding ring. 'We ought to move to somewhere with people nearby, in case he comes back, Mrs O'Brien.'

'I suppose so.' She tried to stand up, winced and sat down again. 'I must have twisted my ankle trying to fight him off. Please, could you stay with me till I can put some weight on this foot?'

'Of course.'

Another man came into sight on the street that ran along the lower edge of the gardens so Christa again yelled for help, waving her arms about. He stopped at once, staring at them, his whole body radiating shock, then ran up the grassy slope towards them.

'Oh, thank goodness!' her companion exclaimed. 'It's my nephew. I was going to meet him.'

He stopped next to the older woman. 'Auntie Beryl, are you all right?'

'A man tried to snatch my handbag but when this young lady ran to my aid, he left in a hurry.'

The newcomer turned to Christa, 'I can't thank you enough.'

'Anyone would have done the same.'

'No. Not everyone would help. Look, it's starting to get dark, so I think we'd better leave here now. We'll escort you home, in case he's still around.'

It was humiliating to have to admit it. 'I've nowhere to go. They turned me out of the hotel.'

He stared at her in shocked silence for a moment. 'Why did they do that?'

'Because my father's German. He fought *against* Hitler and I think the Nazis killed him because of it, but some people don't believe me when I tell them that. And my mother was English. She died too.'

Mrs O'Brien at once said, 'You poor thing. You must come home with us.'

Her nephew hesitated, then nodded agreement.

Christa burst into tears of utter relief and found the older lady's arms round her.

'S-sorry. I didn't know what to do, where to go tonight. I'm so grateful.'

'One good turn deserves another. Is that all your luggage?' He pointed to her suitcase.

'I have two other cases. They said I had to pick them up by noon tomorrow.'

'I'll take you and Auntie Beryl home, then go and collect them today. I don't trust people who treat others like that. For all we know, they might go through your suitcases and steal things.' Now he came to think of it, he had heard someone he knew criticising the new owner of that hotel for her grasping, sneaky ways.

'I'm very grateful. You're both so kind.'

Her voice was almost a whisper and he could see that she was struggling not to cry again. She was such a little slip of a thing, with lovely dark, wavy hair. Dark eyes, too, which at the moment were welling with tears of relief . . .

★　★　★

Daniel took the two ladies home, relieved to see that his aunt's ankle wasn't sprained as he'd feared, just a little sore from twisting it or, as she called it, 'cruckling'.

He immediately left again for the hotel, which wasn't far away.

Its front door was closed and the woman who came to answer the doorbell frowned at him. 'I'm afraid we're full. Didn't you see the sign?'

'I've come for Miss Summers' suitcases.'

'What? Oh, her. It'll take me a minute or two to get them. Please wait here.'

You'd have thought she'd have been glad to be rid of them, but for a moment there she looked almost panicked, which puzzled him.

When she didn't return within a couple of minutes, he began to feel suspicious. It didn't take this long to pick up two suitcases and he'd seen where the woman went, so he followed her along the corridor that started from one side of the desk, ignoring a big sign that said 'PRIVATE'.

He found the woman in a storeroom, feverishly stuffing clothes that had been strewn about the floor into two battered suitcases.

'What the hell do you think you're doing?' he roared.

She looked round, guilt written all over her face.

'I think I'd better call the police.'

'No, don't do that. There's no harm done. I was just checking that there wasn't anything . . . dangerous. You never know with Germans.'

'Miss Summers is English, not German. Now her clothes are rumpled and in a mess, and for all I know you might have stolen some of her things.'

'She hasn't anything worth stealing.' The woman clapped one hand to her mouth as she realised she'd betrayed herself.

He looked more closely. 'And you've torn the lining of that suitcase at the corner.'

'It was like that already.'

'I'm calling in the police. You were definitely out to rob Miss Summers. We'll get her back here to check that nothing is missing.' He marched back to the reception desk and picked up the phone.

The woman ran after him and slapped her hand down on it to cut off the call before the operator could answer. 'Don't! *Please* don't. It was just her being German that made me do it.'

'Even though her mother and father died fighting Hitler?'

'Are you sure about that? She could just be saying it. I was told differently by someone I trust, someone who knows about her.'

Two could play at that game, Daniel decided. He trusted Miss Summers as instinctively as he mistrusted this woman. 'Well, your *someone* is telling lies. I know about the organisation her father worked for. They were definitely on our side.'

'Oh.' She sagged against the counter.

He had an idea. 'She'll have to wash some of her things and iron others, at the very least. If you paid back what you charged her for last night, I might consider letting the matter drop. But if she finds even one small item missing, I'll insist she calls in the police.' He went back to the storeroom to finish packing the suitcases.

As he put in the last garments, he again said quietly, 'You're sure that's all? I mean it about calling in the police if anything is missing.'

She flushed and pulled something wrapped in tissue paper out of her pocket. 'Good thing you reminded me. I nearly forgot this. Um, I keep the money at the reception desk. I'll get the refund on the way out.'

She left the store room, so he fastened the suitcases and carried them back into the entry hall. He put them down and stared at her. His disgust must have showed because she turned a deep red as she took some money out of a drawer, slapping it down in front of him. 'Here. That should make up for the misunderstanding.'

'I don't think I misunderstood what you were trying to do. I hope I won't need to return here with the police.' He picked up the suitcases and walked out of the hotel without another word, hearing the front door slam shut behind him and the key turn in the lock.

He felt sorry for Christa. He was quite sure the poor girl wasn't a traitor. There was something innately decent and open about her face. He'd heard of a few people with German ancestry who'd been living in England for decades and considered themselves English, but they'd still been interned. Things had been done so hastily in the rush to protect the country from internal enemies.

That damned war had messed up a lot of people's lives! Not only because of the terrible things men had seen and done during its course, but because so many families had lost homes and possessions.

Even worse, to him, was the damage done by the violence and horrors to some men's very souls. He didn't feel it was exaggerating to describe it that way. He definitely felt his mind was damaged by all that he'd seen and been forced to do. His nightmares weren't as bad now, but they were still . . . horrible. He'd kill again to protect his country, of course he would, but he could never take a life and not regret the necessity.

It made him feel better to help people now that peace had come, especially someone like Christa Summers, who had helped his aunt and saved her from who knew what injury.

It was as if both he and Christa were putting good back

into the world, to balance the evil that had spread so widely. And if that was a fanciful thought, well, he didn't care. That was how it seemed to him. And that was a good thing to do, surely.

When he got back to his aunt's house, Daniel found the two women sitting together with cups of tea in front of them, chatting quietly, looking as comfortable as old friends.

'I got your suitcases, Christa, but I was only just in time.' He explained what the woman at the hotel had been doing.

His aunt was horrified. 'I knew that woman's father and he must be turning in his grave at her doing that, for a more honest fellow you couldn't hope to meet. When *he* ran the hotel, the king would have been able to leave the Crown jewels there safely!'

'You'd better check the suitcases, Miss Summers,' he said. 'I shan't hesitate to call the police if anything is missing.'

'Better take the cases upstairs for her, dear,' his aunt suggested. 'She'll have room to spread her things out on the bed and check them properly. What with our lodgers and packing my things ready for the move, I've had to put her in the attic.'

'I don't mind where I sleep, I'm just grateful to have a roof over my head tonight,' Christa said. 'I'll go out first thing tomorrow to look for lodgings.'

What a lovely voice she had, Daniel thought: low and musical. Surprising in such a tiny woman. She was pretty too, in a quiet way, which he preferred to flashy women, however beautiful.

'If we weren't leaving here ourselves in two days, you could stay longer,' his aunt said. 'I enjoy having company.'

The following morning, Christa was out of the house by nine o'clock, determined to find somewhere to stay. She was happy to leave her suitcases in their care because she trusted them absolutely.

In the late afternoon Daniel went to stand by the front room window, packing finished ready for tomorrow's move. He was feeling restless and eager to start work again.

He saw Christa coming down the street, her whole body radiating weariness, and called out to let his aunt know.

When he opened the front door, he gave their guest an instinctive hug, something he'd never done to a near stranger before. But the poor girl looked so downhearted, it upset him. 'I can see you've had no luck.'

'No, neither with a job nor with lodgings, because someone has been going round the town blackening my name, saying I'm not only German but a thief.' Her voice wobbled on the last word.

'Dear heaven, what is the world coming to when people tell such lies?' Daniel's aunt exclaimed from behind them.

'I'll just go up to my room and rest for a few minutes, if you don't mind,' Christa said. 'I need to work out what to do after you leave tomorrow. I think it may be necessary for me to move to another town. I doubt I'll ever find work in this one now.'

'No, don't hide away,' his aunt said. 'Take your coat and hat off and hang them on the hall stand, then join us in the kitchen. I was just going to make a cup of tea. We'll put our heads together and see if we can think of some way to help you.'

'I'll use the bathroom first, if you don't mind.'

When Christa had gone upstairs, moving slowly like an old woman, his aunt grabbed Daniel's arm. 'Come into the kitchen quickly. I've got an idea.'

On the Saturday morning the group at Esherwood met as usual and the adults split the day's jobs between them. Judith, who didn't believe in idle hands, gave her children chores to do that would last them well into the afternoon. Kitty preferred to work inside the house while tomboy Gillian always wanted to be outside with her brother and the men.

And since Ros felt the same way about her stepdaughter, even little Betty had tasks allotted to her.

Diana couldn't hide her relief at being allocated the task of shopping. 'Thank you,' she whispered to Judith.

'Someone has to go to the shops every day if we're to have enough to feed everyone and I hate queuing. One day we won't have to queue like this, but in the meantime, as you seem to prefer that job to the others, we're all satisfied. Actually, you're better at shopping than I am. You seem able to charm our dear grocer and his wife into giving you little extras from time to time.'

She smiled at Diana's blush, then sighed. Rationing might be in place, but shops didn't always have enough of the food people were entitled to, let alone the food they wanted, and the few luxury items that had reached the country were on sale at ridiculously high prices. They'd been able to eke things out with produce from the garden during the summer and autumn, but she dreaded trying to cope in winter.

'Get as many apples and pears as you can today. At least they're readily available at this time of year, and the dockers' strikes can't affect home-grown stuff.'

Diana nodded, sorting out some shopping bags – though the heavy things would be delivered, thank goodness – and set off towards the town at a brisk pace.

Judith watched her go, feeling much older than the decade or so between them warranted. Diana was beautiful and moved gracefully. *She* had never gone short of food. Men's eyes followed her in the street, though she never gave them any encouragement.

Oh, well. People were all different, weren't they?

Judith shrugged and went on with her work, trying to plan ahead on the catering side. There were some cooking apples left from the two trees at the Dower House, which had borne an excellent crop this year, thank goodness. The trees had been picked clean of apples – even those pecked by birds had had their good bits stewed and bottled. Picking them had been one of the jobs the children actually enjoyed.

Judith had stored the sound apples carefully on shelves in the cellars at the big house, where they would stay cool and last longer. She'd taken care the stored apples weren't touching one another in case one went bad. She intended to bottle some more when she had a free afternoon. At least the house was well supplied with Kilner jars.

She'd hoped Diana would be able to do that, but the younger woman had confessed that her parents had always supplied her with black market jam and bottled fruit, above and beyond her allotted ration, and no one had ever taught her to do the bottling herself. She added that she would be happy to learn.

Poor Diana was estranged from her parents and had even been forced to escape from her bedroom in their house down a ladder so that she could join her husband in Rivenshaw. Her father must be a horrible man to have kept her away from Francis like that.

Anyway, there was no time for worrying about such things. Acting in her unofficial role as the group's quartermaster, Judith had allocated some of the fruit to Mrs Rennie, the housekeeper at the Dower House, for Mayne's father and the Rennies.

The orchard at the big house had provided a smaller harvest, even though there were more trees, because they'd suffered what seemed to her like wanton damage. In spite of the government's urging people to 'Dig For Victory' and even scavenge the hedgerows for wild fruit like blackberries, the fruit trees at the big house seemed to have been used for target practice sessions by the groups of soldiers training in the grounds and had lost a lot of their branches.

Tomorrow she might send the children out to scour the grounds of the house, and if necessary the nearby country-side, to see if there were any late blackberries that had escaped other scavengers. She'd see if there was any sugar to be had and make some more jam. That wasn't her favourite task, but there you were. You did what was necessary to survive.

4

Once she'd sorted out the domestic arrangements, Judith turned her attention to her own day's work. She intended to join the three men clearing out the Nissen hut near the stables, because she often had a better idea than they did of whether items could be used in the big house or sold. Who'd have thought her years of scrimping and making small sales at a friend's stall at the market would be so useful now?

She found that the men had already started clearing a path down the centre of the hut's interior. They'd kept goods piled up there when the hut wasn't being used, to prevent anyone stealing them – and also to prevent anyone falling down the steps into the secret cellar. Now, some of these things had been moved outside.

She paused beside the hole in the centre of the hut; she didn't know why. It was pitch black at the bottom of the stone steps and it always made her feel uneasy.

Her son Ben thought a secret cellar very exciting. He seemed to regard himself as an honorary Esher now, and kept spending the odd hour with Mayne's father learning about family history or getting help with his history homework.

According to family legends, this secret cellar dated from the Civil War in the seventeenth century and had been concealed to prevent the theft of the family's valuables.

Judith felt rather cynical about this. For a start, how could they even tell whether there was still a cellar behind the heavy oak door? The original family house had been razed to the ground during the fighting between Roundheads and Cavaliers, and surely that would have included all the cellars. Mayne said he would investigate this one day – just in case – but he had enough on his plate at the moment without adding unnecessary tasks.

The men who'd dug the grave to hide a corpse had found the steps and exposed the big door but they hadn't even tried to break it down. It was supposed that they'd been in too much of a hurry.

Mayne had brought in an experienced locksmith recommended by Ray Woollard, the fifth partner in their newly formed company. The locksmith had become very excited because the cellar door was not only protected by a puzzle lock, in itself a rarity, but had been made by a locksmith nicknamed Crosskey, who had been famous during and after the English Civil War.

Such locks apparently slammed heavy metal bars across the inside of the door if tampered with, another reason for leaving it alone for the time being. They had found the big key needed to open the door, but not the special instructions on how to use it. Mayne's father was trying to track those down in the family papers and diaries.

Her husband didn't believe they'd find valuables inside, even if there was still a cellar behind the door, because his ancestors were more likely to lose such items than keep them safe.

Judith glanced round with a shiver, wondering why she'd stopped here yet again. She wasn't a fearful sort of person usually but in this part of the hut, she always felt as if someone was watching her.

Once or twice, she'd even thought – no, not thought,

imagined! – that she'd seen the faintly shimmering outline of a woman in a long dress at the far end of the hut. Which just went to show how foolish you could get about shadows.

Except . . . she'd remembered the style of the gown and had looked it up in a book in the big house's library showing the history of ladies' fashions. The apparition had been wearing a deep lace-edged collar and what seemed like ridiculously full sleeves to someone like Judith, who was used to the current war fashions, which used the minimum amount of material. The bodice of the woman's dress had been tight but the skirt was full and gathered at the waist. Even the apparition's hair had matched the illustrations in the book, with a crimped fringe and side hair.

That had made Judith's blood run cold. She'd known nothing about fashions of the seventeenth century, so how could she have dreamed this up? She couldn't have really seen a ghost, could she? And not just once but twice. She hadn't told Mayne, didn't want to make a fool of herself.

Unfortunately, this storage hut didn't have windows in the sides like the Nissen huts that were used for offices or accommodation, just one window at each end. So even with the double doors at the front left open, it was dim inside. The men were using an oil lamp, because the window at the far end had been covered on the inside by wooden panels to make the place more secure.

But most of the light from the lamp was hidden by some huge pieces of corrugated iron stacked near the end. Judith shivered and moved forward, heart thudding, to join her husband and Victor. They were manoeuvring another shaped section of corrugated iron away from the pile.

Mayne gave her a quick smile. 'Can you move those short metal struts out of the way, please, Judith? They're not heavy. Then Victor and I can lug this big piece outside. Francis nipped out a few minutes ago to phone the man who's buying his house, but he'll be back in a minute.'

'He'll be glad to have everything finished with at the village. Diana's still afraid her father will come after her, you know.'

'Even he won't dare cause trouble in Rivenshaw. Now, if you stack the small pieces on that trolley, one of us will wheel them out later. We're trying to put similar pieces together and count them. They just seemed to have been dumped in piles any old how.'

'Yes, of course.'

When the men came back, Francis was with them. He pushed the trolley of struts outside while the other two eased the last big piece of metal away from the wall and out of the hut.

Mayne stopped to ask, 'Can you manage one of those boxes of screws and hinges? Good. Bring it out with you and help us solve the jigsaw puzzle of the hut.'

She picked up the box and hurried after them, not looking behind her, though she still felt as if someone was watching her.

Oh, she was being so stupid today! *Stop it, Judith!* she told herself firmly.

They placed the final corrugated iron sheet at the end of a row of similar pieces, and everyone stood back, trying to assess exactly what they'd got and how the pieces fitted together.

Unfortunately, they'd have to carry the various parts inside and lock them safely away again before nightfall. Although looters had mostly been deterred from targeting the big house and its outhouses now, if word got round that prefab parts could be had there, people would certainly try to get hold of them.

'Have you decided what you're going to do with these two huts?' she asked.

'We can continue to use this first one as a store for the building equipment, and all the small stuff we've found around Esherwood that the Army left behind. I can't believe how wasteful they were.'

'And the second hut?'

'I'm not sure. Daniel will need a drawing office and we'll need somewhere for meetings. Once we start converting the big house into flats, we won't be able to work from the present office.'

She linked her arm in his for a moment. 'It's a good thing you're doing, even though you're losing your home. Families are desperate to get their own places to live in again. Any sort of a home.'

As the four of them walked up and down the row of metal pieces, Francis proved the most practical at mentally fitting them together. Perhaps it was his training as an electrical engineer in the Army that helped him visualise how it would look. He moved from one to the other, measuring and muttering to himself.

By early afternoon, he'd worked out that they probably had enough parts to build another quite large Nissen hut, with a few pieces of corrugated iron to spare. It wasn't immediately clear to any of them what the latter were for, however.

Francis looked at his friends and shrugged. 'I haven't been involved in erecting huts like these before. We really need Daniel. As an architect, he could probably sort it out in a tenth of the time it'd take me.'

'I'll give him a ring tonight and see if he can hurry up his return,' Mayne promised.

About an hour later they heard the sound of a vehicle coming slowly along the main drive. Ben immediately dashed off round the corner of the house, yelling, 'I'll see who it is.'

'I hope it's not the military police come back again about that damned corpse we found,' Mayne muttered.

A minute later Ben appeared again at the corner of the house. 'It's Daniel and there are two ladies in the car with him.'

Everyone immediately left what they were doing to hurry round to the front of the house and greet the fourth member of their original group.

Judith walked with her husband. 'The older lady must be his aunt. But who's the younger one? Did he say he was bringing another person?'

'No. But if she's a friend of his, she'll be made welcome.'

'I love the way you offer people somewhere to stay.'

'Is that all you love about me?' he teased.

She blushed, but fortunately they reached the others just then, so he stopped teasing her.

Daniel was already out of the car, beaming at them. 'My aunt and I had a sudden chance to move house this weekend, so we thought we'd surprise you. Our furniture and other things will arrive tomorrow.'

The men shook hands and pounded each other's backs, then Daniel turned to draw the ladies forward.

'This is my aunt, Mrs Beryl O'Brien, and this is Christa Summers who has been very shabbily treated and at the moment has nowhere to live. We'll explain over a cup of tea, if someone could be so kind as to rustle one up. We're all parched.'

Mayne was delighted to see his old friend looking so much better. And if it was this young woman who had put the sparkle back in Daniel's eyes, they all owed her a debt. 'Welcome to Esherwood, Mrs O'Brien, Miss Summers. I'll introduce the others once we're sitting down. There are a lot of us to remember . . . Ben—'

Kitty chuckled. 'He didn't need telling. As soon as he

heard you mention cups of tea, he ran inside to put the kettle on. My dear little brother is always ready to put something into his stomach.'

Judith moved forward, standing with her arm round her daughter's shoulders. 'Welcome to Esherwood, everyone.'

Mayne was studying the car. 'You certainly brought a lot of stuff with you, Daniel. How about we men unload the luggage into the hall and the ladies can go with my wife?'

In the kitchen Judith introduced Ros, Diana and the three girls to the newcomers, then asked, 'Are you hungry?'

'We stopped for a meal on the way here,' Mrs O'Brien said. 'But I'd kill for a cup of tea.'

'That bad, eh?'

'Tea gets me through, even when I've nearly finished my ration and have to use the same tea leaves twice.'

The four men made short work of unloading the car and joined them at the big table while the children took charge of brewing a big pot of tea and setting out the enamel mugs.

'Sorry about the mugs,' Judith said, 'but some were left behind when the Army closed the convalescent hospital and returned the house to Mayne's family. We use them because it saves washing up saucers and they hold more tea than cups. Anyway, most of the everyday crockery is chipped and the rationing rules don't allow us to buy any new stuff yet.'

When she paused, Daniel explained what had happened to Christa. 'So, if you can find somewhere for her to sleep tonight, even a couch somewhere, my aunt and I will help her get some lodgings in town and then, hopefully, a job.'

Judith looked inquiringly at Mayne and he said at once, 'No need for that. You sound like our sort of person, Miss Summers. If you'll muck in and help as needed, you can stay here and take your time about finding work. Though most of the jobs that become available in Rivenshaw are being given to returning servicemen, I'm afraid, as you've already found. Unless they're tasks only women can do.'

Judith dug him in the ribs and he grinned, amending his statement to, 'Jobs that are supposed to be women's work. We can offer you a small attic room, Miss Summers. Bare boards and very simple furniture.'

'I'm not fussy. But are you sure?' Christa asked. 'I don't want to be any trouble.'

'Of course I'm sure. Any friend of Daniel's would be welcome here automatically, and one who has the courage to help his aunt beat off an attacker will fit in well with our group, I'm sure.'

Ros leaned forward. 'We can ask our friend Ray later about jobs for you, Miss Summers. Nothing escapes his notice in our little town. Mr Woollard is our fifth partner.'

'Thank you. And do please call me Christa.'

'Good. We're all on first name terms here.' Ros looked at Mayne as if handing the conversation over to him again.

He realised Christa was struggling not to weep in sheer relief and changed the subject to take the attention away from her. 'Daniel, you couldn't have come back at a better time. We've found the parts for a Nissen hut but we need guidance in how best to erect it.'

'A whole Nissen hut?'

'Looks like it.'

'I could erect one of those in my sleep, I supervised so many during the war.'

'Oh, good. We've got the parts laid out behind the house but we'll have to store them away again before it gets dark. The other news is that the council wants to buy some land from me and erect a whole street of prefabs, which should be right up your alley too. That task ought to get our new company well and truly off the ground.'

Daniel brightened. 'As soon as I've finished my tea, I'd

like to see the parts. I'm dying to get back to work now my aunt's situation has been sorted out.'

'Christa and I can unpack for you, dear,' his aunt said at once. 'Unless Judith needs us to do anything. Please include me in your list of willing hands and people on first-name terms. I much prefer to keep busy. I particularly love cooking – when there's anything to cook.'

'That's settled, then. Children, I'll leave you to clear up the kitchen while Ros and I go and sort out bedrooms for our guests.'

Ben scowled at this and muttered something about 'women's work', but Judith gave him a stern look. 'How many times do I have to tell you that since everyone dirties the crockery, it's only fair that everyone helps with clearing up?'

He continued to mutter under his breath as he began to remove the dirty dishes from the table, so she turned back. 'You've been talking to those Garton boys again, haven't you? They seem to have some very old-fashioned views of the world.'

Ben looked at her defiantly. 'My teacher says the same thing: that there's women's work and men's work, whatever happened during the war.'

'If he says it in my presence, I'll give him a piece of my mind. And if the other children at school continue to infect you with their selfish, old-fashioned attitudes, I'll complain to your headmaster. I will *not* let you grow up like your father, treating women as slaves and worse.'

He lost his aggressive look and said quietly, 'Sorry, Mum. I never thought about it like that.'

As she led the two newcomers out, she sighed. 'That son of mine is getting harder and harder to handle.'

'They all do at that age,' Beryl said.

'I agree with you absolutely about sharing the work, though,'

Christa commented. 'My father always helped with the house-work.' She saw the unasked question in her hostess's eyes, and added quickly. 'My parents had to stay behind in Germany and they vanished during the war. I had word that they were dead.' She blinked furiously because she still felt like weeping whenever she had to tell someone about it.

'I'm sorry. I'm without parents too. My mother's dead and my father has remarried. He's moved to Wigan. Not that I was all that close to him.' Judith picked up a suitcase and gestured towards the stairs. She rolled her eyes as they heard Ben's voice all the way from the kitchen, raised in an argument with his sisters. 'Ben's wife will thank me for training him to do household chores one day. Unless he marries a meek doormat, of course.'

'My mother always said that if you want to be a doormat, first you have to lie down and let people walk all over you,' Christa murmured.

'Oh, I like that! I'll remember it.' She saw Beryl looking surprised and wondered if she'd been too vehement, so added quickly, 'I think our generation has changed the world in so many ways. We've had to, fighting such a long war. Things were different in your day.'

'In some ways,' Beryl agreed. 'During the Great War women did all the men's jobs, but my husband never offered to help with housework, even when I couldn't get paid help. Yet he was considered a good husband and I loved him dearly. But since his death I've been struggling to deal with the money, so I do think he ought to have at least taught me how to handle the money side of our life.'

They reached the bedrooms on the second floor just then and the conversation changed track as Judith showed Beryl where she'd be sleeping. 'We may have to keep changing rooms once work gets under way on converting the house into flats.'

'I shall be happy to fit in as needed,' Beryl assured her.

Judith hesitated, then added, 'I think you ought to understand the situation here. I know Daniel's explained about turning the house into flats, but we try not to talk about it too much, because it upsets Mayne. Esherwood has been in his family for hundreds of years, you see, and he loves it, but the house was badly damaged during the time the Army took it over and the compensation won't nearly pay for the repairs or the ongoing maintenance. The roof is in a terrible state.'

She frowned as she always did when she thought about the Esher family's finances. 'There used to be enough family money to manage on, but no one knows what happened to it. His father is hopelessly impractical and his mother must have dealt with it, but she's dead. The bulk of the money . . . well, it simply isn't there any more. Nor are some of the valuable family treasures which Mayne could have sold. So the only way he can see of saving the house from demolition is to divide it into flats and sell them.'

'That must be very painful for him,' Beryl said softly.

Daniel was surprised by how much the back of the house had changed since his last visit. The whole area was looking tidier, more organised. Well, it would with Mayne in charge, and Victor had a similarly orderly attitude to the world.

He walked along the row of corrugated iron pieces, smiling. 'These will make a decent-sized prefab. And I see there's a provision for windows too. That's what those spare pieces are for. If we can get hold of some glass to put in them, that is.'

Mayne nodded. 'Ah. I see. We couldn't work those bits out.'

'The extra pieces can be adapted according to the type of window wanted.'

'You know, there are various salvaged building materials lying around in the sheds and half-ruined buildings,' Victor said. 'They're one of the next things on my list to sort out. I'm sure I've seen some window frames with glass in them, maybe with one or two panes missing, or with the corners of some panes cracked. Quite a lot of pieces are potentially useful if we don't bother about neatly matching the windows we put in. We can replace them with proper windows when peace time production improves.'

Daniel stood frowning for a moment, then asked abruptly, 'What are the town council planners like? Will they want to tell us where to put the Nissen hut? Or requisition it for themselves, even, under the emergency regulations?'

There was silence for a moment or two, then Mayne admitted, 'I don't know what they're like. There's a new chap taken over, name of Thompson. I gather he was an officer in the Army but there's no word of where he served.'

Daniel stared at the extra pieces of corrugated iron then grinned at his friends. 'May I suggest, then, that we start work on erecting the hut immediately, so that we can present the council with a fait accompli and claim the Army erected it?'

The others looked at him in surprise, then turned to Mayne, who grinned and said, 'Good idea, Daniel.'

'And what's more, if necessary some of us should move into the hut, so that this fellow can't claim he needs it for his housing project,' Daniel added.

Mayne looked at him in surprise. 'Why do you say that?'

'Because I've heard other architects talking about planning wallahs they've had to deal with. They reckoned one of them didn't like people to breathe in and out without his permission, let alone erect what he considered to be unsuitable buildings in places he didn't approve of. I gave up a lot for my country, but I'm not putting unnecessary limitations on my work now that the war is over, however short of supplies we all are.'

'Nor am I.'

'Me neither.'

'Definitely not.'

All four men spoke at once, stopped together and laughed. This had often happened in the Army when they were working on projects together, they were so in tune with each other's ways of thinking.

'Anyway,' Victor added, 'we have Ray Woollard on our side. If anyone can get us what we need, including various permissions to build, he can. Talk about a Mr Fix-it!'

'How quickly do you think we can erect the hut?' Francis asked.

Daniel thought for a moment, head on one side. 'Within a few days. Sooner, if you can get hold of extra help. Nissen huts were designed to go up quickly. And no one will know what it's like inside if we put blackouts across the windows.'

'Al and Jan will help,' Mayne said at once. 'They've been doing odd jobs for us. As a displaced person, Jan is always glad of extra money and now Al's out of the Army, he's in the same boat. They're really good with their hands. Daniel, you haven't had much to do with them, but we've already decided to employ them permanently once our company gets going. You couldn't get better workers anywhere.'

'As soon as you're sure of the dimensions and how you want to use the hut, I'll work out an electrical plan for it,' Francis said. 'In the meantime, I've been trying to trace some electrical wiring that seems to vanish into the floor of the attic. When you have a moment, Mayne, perhaps you'd come and look at it, see if you know why it was done like that?'

'I'd like to have a look, too.' Daniel sighed happily. 'It feels good to have the four of us together again, doesn't it? We can really get things moving now. I've never worked with a better team of chaps.'

Mayne was delighted to hear his friend speak so enthusiastically. All of them had been mentally scarred by the war, but it had upset Daniel most of all.

'Where shall we put the hut?' Daniel asked. 'We might have to act quickly, but we can still think long-term about what will be going where. Whatever the authorities say about the prefabs being designed to last for only about ten years, no one really knows how long such temporary housing will be needed for. And from what I've seen, they're sturdy enough to be used for far longer. Better a prefab than some of the nineteenth century slums I've seen.'

He stopped for a moment, as if remembering something, then asked, 'Where do the water and sewage supply lines come on to your land, Mayne?'

And they were off, working for as long as it was light, measuring, calculating, discussing, then locking the pieces of the new hut away.

When Judith glanced out of the window, the group of men looked so happily busy, with Ben bobbing to and fro helping whomever needed an extra hand, she didn't go outside to join them as she'd intended.

Instead she went into the kitchen, where Diana was studying their food supplies, looking more than a little worried.

'Something wrong?'

'I'm not very good at dealing with meals. Francis used to say I didn't give him enough to eat.'

'We can do it together.'

'Can I help as well?'

They turned to see Beryl hovering in the doorway.

'It occurred to me that I can probably be most useful to you in the kitchen. I used to work in the WVS canteen during the war, you see, and I miss it. I'm used to catering for large numbers. If I'm not treading on anyone's toes, that is. You may already have a head cook on board, in which case I'll do whatever else is needed.'

'I thought you'd want to unpack and have a rest after your journey today.'

Beryl waved one hand dismissively. 'I can unpack the rest of my things later and rest when I go to bed.'

'It'd be good to have someone used to catering for larger numbers,' Judith admitted. 'There will be thirteen of us from now on.'

'We catered for a lot more than that in the canteen.'

'Then I accept your help willingly. In fact, if you want to take charge of the catering once you get used to the shops in town, I'd be delighted. We'll supply you with willing labourers. No one's a fussy eater, though milk makes Kitty feel sick, so I don't force her to drink it.'

'I'd love to take charge. You're sure you don't mind?'

'Good heavens, no! I'm not at all fond of cooking, but someone had to do it. And I have a son who is permanently hungry.'

'I'd be happy to help, too.'

They all turned to see Christa standing by the door, looking unsure of her welcome.

'I've no experience of cooking for large numbers, but I can learn. Or do anything else you need.'

'Come in. The more the merrier,' Ros said cheerfully. 'It's getting dark, so I'd better tell those men to lock up for the night and get their evening meal.'

'It's just sandwiches and fruit, I'm afraid,' Judith said. 'There are plenty of apples, though. We're eating the damaged ones and cutting off the bruised bits. I have to bottle some before they go off.'

'I can take charge of that, too,' Beryl said at once.

'You're going to be a godsend.'

'Well, you people are a godsend to me. I wouldn't know what to do with myself now . . .' Her voice faltered for a moment, then she took a deep breath and continued, 'Now I'm on my own. I can't depend on Daniel staying with me. He has his own life to live. And Christa is so young that—'

'Um . . . I'm not as young as I seem. I'd rather start here with the truth. My father knew the Nazis would be after him and his family, and was desperate to get me out of the country. As I'm rather short with a bit of a baby face, we pretended I was three years younger and I came to England with one of the *Kindertransporte*. I'm actually nearly twenty-three now, not nineteen.'

'Your parents must have loved you very much.' Ros gave her a quick hug.

'Don't you have any other relatives?' Beryl asked.

'Not that I know of.' She put up her chin. 'I'm lucky to be alive and it's thanks to the British people who organised the *Kindertransporte*. I'll always be grateful to them.'

There was silence for a few moments, then Beryl patted Christa's back. 'All right. Let's get started on this meal.'

5

The following Tuesday, Steve Rennie, who lived at the gatehouse, was taking an early morning stroll round the grounds of Esherwood, as he often did, when he came across a chap measuring out the area right at the back by striding to and fro across it, making notes.

'Oi!' he shouted. 'This is private property.'

The trespasser turned and scowled at him. 'I'm from the council planning department, so I have every right to be here.'

'Not without informing the owner, you don't. I've worked for the council too and I know the rules.'

The man simply looked down his nose at Steve. 'I'm going to call on the owner later. I just need to work out something here before I discuss it with him.'

'You can come back and work it out once you've got Mr Esher's permission to trample about on his land.'

'I won't need his permission to come here and do what is needed.' He smirked as if that thought pleased him, then he stared at Steve with narrowed eyes and added sharply, 'What business is it of yours, anyway?'

'I'm one of Mr Esher's night watchmen. It's my *job* to check for trespassers.' Steve folded his arms and stared right back at the man. He wasn't going to let a fat little bully like this intimidate him. And how had the fellow got hold of enough food to become fat with wartime rationing, eh? That said something about him, by hell it did.

The intruder stopped trying to outstare him, muttered something under his breath that sounded suspiciously like a threat and left.

Steve didn't move till the fellow had disappeared from sight down the back road.

He remembered hearing a friend of his at the pub complaining about an officious sod called Thompson who had just taken over the planning section at the council. The fellow had apparently managed to put everyone's back up within a few days, only he was pally with Councillor Draper, so no one dared complain.

Steve felt fairly sure he'd just witnessed this Thompson in action. And he didn't like what he'd seen. He automatically mistrusted people who wouldn't give you their name, and he wasn't usually wrong. Thompson, if that was him, hadn't come here openly, had he? No, he'd sneaked in the back way. That said something about him, too. He'd bear watching, he would indeed.

Suddenly Steve realised he was standing staring when he should be going up to the big house to tell Mr Esher what had happened.

Maybe they'd better lock the big chain across the front entrance day and night, to stop folk driving in without being checked. At the moment he was only putting it across and locking it in place after dark. It had been a lot easier before the war, with wrought iron gates, but they'd been taken for scrap early on.

When he opened the kitchen door, Mayne was surprised to see the usually jovial old man look so angry. 'Come in and tell me what the matter is, Steve lad?'

He listened to the explanation. 'Well done! You did exactly

the right thing. Forewarned is forearmed. You keep your eyes on that area and let me know if you see anything else going on. I shall look forward to meeting our new planning manager.'

'He sounded like he was coming to see you today.'

'Hmm. Well, we don't want him coming round the back and seeing the new Nissen hut till we've got it finished.' Mayne decided Christa could most easily be spared, checked with his wife, then asked Christa if she'd mind keeping an eye on the front drive for the next hour or two in case they had a visitor. He passed on Steve Rennie's description of a 'fat little sod'.

'I'm happy to help in any way.'

'Come and fetch me as quickly as you can if you see anyone approaching, on foot or in a car. I'll be working on the new prefab.'

'I'll do that.'

Half an hour later the sound of running footsteps heralded the arrival of Christa and Mayne went out to see what was going on.

'A man's approaching the house on foot. He keeps stopping to stare at it and make notes. He's short and fat.'

'Must be Thompson. I'll walk round the side of the house and pretend to run into him by accident. I'm a bit dirty to come inside, anyway.' He glanced back at the new Nissen hut which had been erected now, but hadn't been fitted out inside or had any window glass fitted. 'Can you chaps keep the noise down till Christa tells you our visitor has gone? We're repairing this hut, remember, not building it, if anyone asks.'

Al made a mocking gesture of touching his forelock.

Smiling, Mayne beckoned to Daniel. 'Might be useful to have you with me.'

'Fine. I'd like to meet the ogre.'

The two men strolled round the house and arrived in time

to see the visitor start to mount the stone steps that led to the front door.

He turned round at the sound of their footsteps on the gravel. He had thinning grey hair cut very short, as if he was still trying for a military look, with a little brush of a moustache which lent him an unfortunate resemblance to Hitler – only he was plumper and had crooked teeth with one missing.

Mayne stopped walking and called, 'Can I help you, sir?' He deliberately spoke with a bit of a local accent, and let the visitor come right up to him without saying another word.

The man looked scornfully at his scruffy clothes. 'I doubt it. I'm looking for the owner, Mr Esher.'

Another silence during which Mayne studied his visitor equally openly. 'Then you've found him. I'm Esher.' He didn't introduce Daniel. 'And you are?'

'Captain Thompson. I need to speak to you. In private.' He looked questioningly at Daniel, but Mayne didn't take the hint and introduce him, just continued to wait him out.

'If we could go inside, Mr Esher, it might be more convenient? I have certain matters to discuss with you and some paperwork to go through before you sign it.'

'Not today, I'm afraid. I'm in the middle of something. You should have rung for an appointment.'

'I'm here on behalf of the council, since I'm now manager of the town planning department, so I think you'd do better to listen to what I have to say.'

He spoke pompously and confidently, as if quite sure the world revolved around him and his needs.

After waiting until the man looked ready to burst with irritation, Mayne said quietly, 'I don't care who you are. I'm in the middle of a job which will take all morning and

I have appointments for the whole of this afternoon, which I don't intend to cancel. You can phone my assistant and she'll let you know when I'm free. Now, if you don't mind leaving us to get on with things . . .' He gestured towards the drive.

Thompson gaped for a moment, looked at the steely, unflinching expression and turned round, muttering to himself as he walked away.

'What a nasty little creep!' Daniel said.

Mayne chuckled. 'I love some of this modern slang the Yanks brought over with them. *Creep!* That word describes Thompson accurately, don't you think? And he's arrogant with it.'

'Nonetheless, if he's in charge of planning, I think we're in for trouble.'

'Well, he'll be in for trouble with me if he tries to push me around. This is England not Nazi Germany.' Mayne took a deep breath. 'But I'm glad you advised me to have that Nissen hut erected quickly.'

Even before the unwelcome visitor had got to the end of the drive, a car turned into it, passing him so closely, he had to skip hastily to one side.

'What next?' Daniel muttered.

'It's all right. It's only Ray. He doesn't usually drive so carelessly, though. I wonder if he knows what Thompson's like and deliberately drove close enough to make him jump. If we're in for a few battles, I shall be glad to have Ray on our side.'

Daniel looked at him shrewdly. 'You weren't so sure about that when we first discussed letting Woollard invest in our business.'

'Let's say I had to be persuaded to take him on board, and if I hadn't been certain he'd more or less wound up his black market operations, I'd not have done it, whatever anyone said. But I'm glad to say there's a lot more to him than meets the eye. He's turned out to be very knowledgeable about antiques and ornaments, and he's already sold one or two items for me privately, at a higher price than I'd expected. He even bought a couple of pieces for himself. He loves old things.'

'Good for him.'

The car stopped and its driver, a slender young woman, got out and went round to open the door for her passenger, who was grinning broadly.

'His niece stayed here, then,' Daniel murmured. 'I wondered if she would when we travelled up together from London.'

'She's become his assistant. Seems highly intelligent. I was surprised you weren't interested in getting to know her better. She's pretty enough.'

Daniel shrugged. 'I don't know why, but she didn't even register as an attractive female in that sense when I helped her escape from the fellow who was hounding her at the station.'

'You never know when Cupid will strike. My Judith thinks you're rather taken by Christa.'

Daniel let out an involuntary spurt of laughter. 'Your wife never misses a trick, does she? I certainly like Christa and I find *her* attractive. But she's too young. I'm not into cradle snatching. Why, I must be more than ten years older than her.'

'Does that matter?'

'I think it does. If I ever get married again, I want to be sure it'll last.'

Mayne was just about to explain that Christa was older than they'd assumed, when Ray took a briefcase from the back seat of the car and started across to join them. 'Good morning, Esher. Good to see you back, O'Brien. I think we may be needing you. I reckon we're going to have a fight on our hands.'

'With Thompson?'

'Yes. He's already got my back up with his officiousness about some business properties I own in town.'

'I just joined the same anti-Thompson club. He expected me to drop everything, pay attention to him and his paper-work, then sign it on the spot.'

'Make no mistake about it, we do need to pay attention. From what someone told me, I suspect he's going to try to seize your whole property.'

Mayne looked at him in shock. '*The whole property?*'

'Yes. We're all aware that the government has a push on to get homes built. What if one man in a small town could work near miracles? He might be up for a decoration, or even a knighthood. The fellow is already flashing his army rank and insisting on being called Captain Thompson.'

Ray let that sink in, before adding, 'I hired a chap this morning to look into his past. Thompson doesn't seem to have a wife or family, and won't talk about where he comes from. He doesn't have a northern accent and for all his posh way of talking, I'm wondering if I've picked up a hint of London – not quite Cockney but thereabouts.'

'Is all that necessary?'

'I didn't get where I am now by underestimating the oppo-sition, and I can smell a rotten fish a mile off. How about contacting your Army friends and asking them to find out about his service record?'

'I'll bear that in mind but I won't trouble them till I'm sure it's important enough.'

'Your choice. In the meantime, I've got people interested in a few more of your ornaments and one of your paintings. Do you want to deal with it or shall I talk to Judith? Your wife has a fine business brain.'

'Deal with her, but I must put it on record that we're grateful for your help.'

'The company needs money. I enjoy making it. Don't ask me to sell anything you love, though. Not unless it's hugely valuable and you're desperate for a big chunk of money. Our little company can make a good start with what you chaps have agreed to put in and for you, as the major partner, we can add to that the proceeds from smaller valuables you don't care about.' His tone lightened. 'Now, what are you up to today? You look like you're working with your hands.'

'Come and see.'

'All right if Stephanie tags along? I'm employing her as my assistant from now on, so she'll be available to work with Esher Building Company on my behalf as well as me, if that's all right with you chaps.'

'Fine by us.'

As they started walking, Stephanie fell in beside Daniel, but beyond giving him a nod, she didn't say a thing. He'd never heard her waste words, but he was sure she didn't miss much of what was going on. Intelligence shone in her eyes, sadness too sometimes.

Mayne took them round to the back of the house, across the yard and round behind the outbuildings. 'Voilà!' He raised his voice. 'Make as much noise as you like, lads. The enemy has departed.'

'I don't remember seeing this hut before . . .' Ray said.

'That's because we've only just erected it. We found the parts in the other Nissen hut.'

'You've erected it quickly, then.' Ray went to the doorway of the new hut and peered inside. 'Goodness! I thought it was just about finished from the plants growing outside, but it isn't, is it?'

'No. It was Jan's idea to plant them and he's made them

look as if they've been there for a while. It will be finished soon.'

Ray began to grin. 'And if the Army left it here, it didn't need planning permission, so it won't be on the council's books. Clever. Do you need some furniture?'

'I don't think so. Daniel's aunt brought some with her and we have plenty of spare pieces in the big house. We still have some of the hospital beds that were left behind, as well.'

'Good.' Ray turned back towards the main house. 'If I can look through those ornaments now, I'll report back to my buyer. They'd fetch higher prices if we waited, I'm sure, but you need working capital now to start your business off, because you can be sure customers will take their time about paying you what they owe you.'

'I know.' Mayne waved one hand in a permissive gesture. 'You go ahead and talk to Judith. I'd join you, but I'd only tramp mud all round the house. Anyway, she knows where the pieces are better than I do.'

Before they went into the house, Ray turned to his niece: 'I don't think Mayne fully realises how awkward that fellow in the planning department can make things for us. The damned government will have regulations about how to blow your nose if they go on like this and that Thompson looks the sort to take advantage of every little sub-clause.'

'He reminds me of someone.'

'Does he? See if you can remember who.'

Steph shrugged. 'I may be imagining it, but if any details come to mind, I'll tell you.'

'Good lass.'

Just as Ray was about to enter the house, Sergeant Deemer rounded the corner, so he paused to see what was going on.

The elderly policeman was looking a little less strained

these days, without quite so much emphasis on the enforcement of war regulations. He'd agreed to go on running the local police station until new men were found to take his place, then he'd return to the retirement that had been interrupted by the needs of war.

Deemer paused, sighed, then walked across to Mayne. 'I've got some bad news for you, Mr Esher.'

'Oh?'

'Yes. That fellow who led the gang that stole from you when they were stationed here, Sam Newton. He's escaped from prison.'

'How the hell did he manage that?'

'I don't know the details, but he was always a very clever chap. Pity his mother couldn't afford to let him go to grammar school. It might have knocked some sense into him. She even got permission for him to leave school early and work in the market café with her.'

'When did he escape?'

'Two weeks ago. We've been keeping quiet and watching out for him coming back to Rivenshaw, but there's been no sign of him.'

'He'll have gone overseas, I should think,' Mayne said. 'It's what I'd have done.'

'You could be right. Only he talked in his sleep in prison sometimes, and he was near enough the guard station for them to hear him. It was always about getting hold of his stuff again. Kept mentioning a cellar too, apparently. The guards didn't think much of it at the time and laughed at him when he told them he'd be rich one day.'

'Going to be rich, eh? By stealing my possessions?'

'Yours and the Army's. He was stationed here for a while, but then his unit was transferred suddenly and things started to go missing from time to time.'

Mayne let out a growl of anger. 'There are other valuables

I remember, but we can't find any sign of them! Quite frankly, my family's possessions are in a mess.'

'Well, good luck with your searching. I thought I'd better come and warn you to keep your eyes open for intruders.'

'I'm grateful. We'll certainly do that. How about a cup of tea, Sergeant?'

'If it's no trouble.'

Daniel checked on progress at the new hut, then left Al and Jan to deal with it. They were as skilled at the practical work as he was and didn't need anyone standing over them to do the job properly.

A couple of times, he thought about the news Mayne had passed on about the thief who'd escaped from prison, and didn't dismiss the idea that the fellow might return to Rivenshaw. During the war, men had been taught to move silently and without being seen. They'd acquired all sorts of stray skills.

Who should know that better than he and his friends?

Already there were tales of some men putting their new skills to bad use once they'd been demobbed. He had a feeling they were about to experience that first-hand. He vaguely remembered a lad called Sam but couldn't remember what he looked like as a man.

Oh well. They'd have to wait and see, and, as the sergeant said, keep a sharp eye out for intruders. In the meantime, Al and Jan had enough to keep them busy for the rest of the afternoon, then they'd all confer before finalising the placing of inside walls.

Daniel said they should get the women involved in the interior design. He'd found that they could add another dimension to the details of how rooms were set out and, unlike some architects he knew, he was more than willing to listen to their ideas and needs.

Appearance wasn't the only thing that mattered. A building had a purpose and should fulfil that purpose before everything else. One of his friends had a phrase to describe pretty but inefficient buildings: all show and no go. Well, no one was going to say that about Daniel's work.

The new hut was a small matter, but he'd enjoyed sorting it out. What he was eager to do now was to get on with his main job and obtain a clearer picture of where everything inside the big house was located, measuring it exactly this time. Then work out how to turn it into flats, with as little destruction of the beautiful, remaining features as possible.

Mayne and the others must have worked very hard while he was away, because they'd cleared out an enormous amount of clutter. You could see the bones of the building clearly now in most areas, and work out in which era the various parts of the house had been added. There were a few anomalies, though, and—

It took him a moment or two to realise that someone had spoken to him. 'Sorry. What did you say?'

'Judith sent me to ask you if I could be of any help.'

He watched Christa stare round, her eyes lingering on the exquisite plasterwork of the ceilings. In need of some care here and there, but still remarkably well preserved after all the old building had gone through.

'I'd love this house,' she confided. 'I've never been inside a private house this big before. Yet it's still a home, isn't it?'

'It is. Partly because it's not too big. And I'll be very glad of your help to note down any measurements, not to mention holding the other end of my tape when I'm dealing with the longer stretches of wall. I have a spare notebook and pencil.'

She took them from him, beaming with pleasure.

'I already have a rough outline of the overall layout in my

mind, but not with accurate details, and, as various architects have said over the centuries, "The devil's in the detail" or "God is in the detail". Take your pick.'

'Details are very important in all parts of life, I think.'

She was so eager to be part of everything, he thought. She must feel very alone in the world, poor girl.

'Where do we start?'

'I always prefer to start at the top and work my way down.'

He quickly sketched an outline of the attic in his notebook and then they swapped books and he began measuring exactly, telling her which figures to enter where.

He soon noticed that she didn't need telling anything twice. 'You pick things up quickly. Not everyone can work from diagrams.'

She looked down in surprise. 'It all seems very clear to me.'

'You must have a natural gift for this sort of work.'

He could see her go a little pink. Not used to compliments, he'd guess. Well, he wasn't lying. She was far quicker than some of the chaps he'd trained with.

After another hour or so, he stopped, took the chart and its measurements from her and studied it carefully, shaking his head. 'It doesn't quite fit.'

'I was wondering about that. But you didn't get the measurements wrong. I'd have noticed.'

'Well, even taking into account the secret room, there's still space unaccounted for.' He turned as footsteps sounded on the wooden stairs.

'I heard you were up here.' Francis came across to join them. 'I forgot to remind you that I found a couple of anomalies when I was trying to sort out the various electrical circuits that have been added over the years. There's one cable that leads nowhere that I can work out. I daren't cut it off because there might be some hastily-made connection behind the wall. But we can't just leave it there when we turn the place into flats.'

'Certainly not. Only you can't go knocking down walls in old places like this without reason, either, to find out what's behind them.'

'It won't make much difference how you divide the space into flats up here, but you'll have to chop up some of that lovely wood panelling and plasterwork downstairs, and it'll hide the bigger patterns.'

Both men sighed in regret at that thought, then Daniel said, 'Show me the cable.'

Francis went across to a big cupboard full of boxes. 'These boxes weren't here before. What have they got in them?'

'They look like old curtains and blankets to me,' Christa ventured.

'It won't matter where they're stored. If I pass them out, can you two stack them nearby?'

When the cupboard was clear of junk, he pointed to a cable that came out of the bottom of the wall at the back. 'That one doesn't make sense electrically. I've racked my brain and I can't work out where it comes from or goes to.'

'It looks hastily put together.'

'Yes. But I don't want to be too hasty about pulling it apart.'

The cable ran along the bottom edge of the back wall for a couple of feet, after which it went down into the floor at the adjoining side of the cupboard. It was a clumsily done job that made both men shake their heads in disgust.

'Perhaps it's been done that way to avoid a joist or heavy beam?' Daniel suggested, and knelt to examine the floorboards more carefully with his torch. He tapped them with a small hammer, frowning. 'No, that isn't it. There isn't a joist here or we'd see signs of it. What the hell is it connecting?'

Christa had a sudden thought and left them pointing and arguing. She walked across to the window and stood on tiptoe, but was still too short to look out. With a mutter of annoyance she began pushing one of the boxes across to it.

Daniel came across to join her. 'Here, let me.' He positioned the box under the sloping window and helped her get up on it. 'Be careful.'

'I will. Thank you.'

She felt so warm and feminine against him. He hurriedly let go. 'We'll have to feed you up so that you can finish growing,' he teased, trying to lighten the moment.

Her head was higher than his now. She looked down at him and laid one hand on his shoulder as if to help herself balance. She didn't even seem to notice that she was touching him. But he noticed. He definitely did.

'Before we go any further, you should know my real age. The other women know already.' She summarised her escape from Germany, ending up, 'Everyone here has been so kind, I don't want to lie to any of you. I'm twenty-three now, a grown woman.' Then she looked down at herself ruefully. 'If you can call barely five foot grown. I don't think I'll get any taller, either. My mother didn't.'

'Oh. I see.' He couldn't think what to say to that.

Their eyes met for a moment, then she flushed again and turned away to stare out of the window. 'I, um, wanted to check something, Daniel. I think that cupboard with the cable in it is over the bathrooms on the floor below this, don't you? The one the ladies use.'

He joined her at the window, peering out at the drainpipes. 'Yes.'

'The ceiling is very low in that bathroom, much lower than the ceilings in the nearby bedrooms. You won't have been in there to notice it. I've wondered a few times why it's like that.'

He stepped back, resisting the urge to touch her, only too aware of Francis standing nearby. 'I'll have a look at it next time I go downstairs. Maybe they've put in a false ceiling to cover up the pipes.'

'If so, there are no pipes coming out in the rooms next to the bathroom on either side. I was puzzled so I had a quick peep. And their ceilings haven't been lowered at all.'

'That *is* strange. You'll have to show me.'

He tapped the notebook. 'Let's make a list of anomalies. Could you start a new page for that, please? We'll do a complete survey then start investigating the anomalies one by one.'

He caught Francis's half-smile and guessed that his friend had noticed his reaction to Christa. He was trying to think how to change the subject when Francis saved him the trouble.

'I never saw a house modernised so haphazardly. I suppose the Eshers did it piecemeal over the generations, according to the current owner's whims, and then the Army did it even more haphazardly during the war. I gather that teams were transferred in and out, so they wouldn't always know what had been done before or why.'

'You're probably right.'

'It's a good thing we'll need to rewire the whole place to set up the flats, because otherwise I'd have been trying to persuade Mayne to do it anyway. I know it's difficult working in a very old house, but whoever put in the latest sets of electrics could have been, *should have been*, a lot more careful.'

The gong for their midday meal rang out just then, echoing clearly up the stairwell.

'Is it that time already!' Daniel looked at his wrist watch in amazement. 'Now I come to think of it, I'm ravenous. After you, Christa. We'll look at that bathroom later.'

She ran lightly down the stairs in front of the two men.

'You're allowed to find a woman attractive, you know,' Francis murmured.

'Not until I've sorted my head out.'

'Still having nightmares?'

'A few. Not as bad as before. I'm hoping things will continue to get better now I've got work to keep me occupied. I'm a bit worried about Mayne, though. He looks so sad when we talk about the changes needed.'

Silence, then Francis said, 'He has no choice, so I try not to comment, and I think Judith does the same.'

'I for one won't be able to avoid mentioning it.'

'Poor chap. Do you think he'll get enough money from the sales to keep one wing of the place for himself?'

'He will if Ray is as good as I suspect at spotting valuable items and selling them. And I could design Mayne a very pleasant residence from either of the wings. But he might not want to live there and see the rest of the house changed so much. I'd put my money on him moving into the Dower House and building a high wall between him and his old home, once everything's finished and sold.'

They left it at that.

What can't be cured must be endured, Daniel thought. He knew about that sort of thing. He'd been upset that his marriage had fallen apart so quickly. That was one of the reasons he didn't share with his friends for not hurrying into another relationship. He intended to take great care before getting attached to someone again.

As he reached the kitchen door, he saw Christa talking animatedly to his aunt, who looked flushed but happy, and his breath caught in his throat. Who was he fooling? He liked Christa more every day, and even his aunt had hinted at what a good wife she'd make for some lucky man.

Some things in his little world were starting to tick along

nicely. He'd take his time about the other possibilities, but perhaps one day . . .

You didn't get over years of warfare easily.

And that thought made him wonder suddenly how Christa's wartime experiences had scarred her.

Ray Woollard's secretary wasn't there, so his niece Stephanie picked up the telephone.

He looked up from his desk, but she shook her head and mouthed, 'It's for me.'

'Yes, Stephanie Woollard speaking.'

'I believe you know Anthony Giffard.'

'Yes. I used to be engaged to him.'

'Ah, good. I've got the right person then.'

She listened and looked so shocked, her uncle put down his pen.

'*He's alive?*' she whispered. '*Anthony is alive?*' Tears began to roll down her cheeks. 'Just a minute till I find something to write with.'

She fumbled around, her hands trembling, so Ray picked up his own pad and pencil and took them across to her.

She was holding back sobs with difficulty.

'You say the words and I'll write them down.'

She nodded. 'Why didn't you *tell* me, Mrs Giffard?'

Someone was sobbing at the other end and as the woman, it was definitely a woman, went on speaking, Steph seemed to pull herself together.

'Tell me the details.' She took the pencil from her uncle and started writing. 'Yes. Got that. Yes, I can meet him. I'll bring him here. We have plenty of room. Mrs Giffard, I love your son. I'll look after him with everything there is in me, I promise.'

When she put the phone down, Ray thrust a handkerchief at her and she mopped her still-wet cheeks.

'Well?' he prompted.

'Anthony's alive.'

'Your fiancé?'

'Yes. But . . . he was a prisoner in Japan and the Army sent him back via Egypt to recuperate. He—' she gulped and fought to keep from weeping again. 'He only weighed seven stones when they got him out of the prison camp. And him six foot tall. They . . . weren't sure he'd survive. He had tropical abscesses and all sorts of problems.'

He frowned. 'When was this? The war in Japan ended in August!'

'The Army contacted his parents. They weren't sure he'd survive, so they didn't tell me. Mrs Giffard said they didn't want me grieving all over again.'

Then she lost herself in tears and let her uncle pull her into his arms and hold her close till she'd finished sobbing.

He took her across to sit on the sofa. 'So . . . why did she ring today, then?'

'Mr Giffard isn't well. He's had a stroke, luckily a fairly mild one, but she can't leave him. Anthony's arriving in London in two days' time. Someone has to meet him at the station there. She can't leave her husband. The rest of the family are all over the place and none of them are able to house an invalid, let alone nurse him.'

She blew her nose, then blew it again. 'Anthony's mother wasn't best pleased when he and I got engaged. She'd wanted him to marry the daughter of a friend of hers. Whatever she says, *I* think she did this on purpose. Not telling me, I mean. She was trying to break us up, Uncle Ray, I'm sure she was.'

'That's jumping to conclusions a bit, Steph love. Surely Mrs Giffard wouldn't be so cruel to her only son?'

'Oh, wouldn't she? She always did like to boss him around. She has her husband right under her thumb. When I wouldn't be bossed, she took against me as a future daughter-in-law, but Anthony loved me and wouldn't change, or even wait to get engaged, so she couldn't stop us.'

'Well, what do you want to do about meeting him? Of course you can have as much time off as you need, but if I can help in any way, you've only to ask, you know that.'

'I told her we could look after him here. We can, can't we? You know how hard it is to find accommodation. I'll do everything he needs, won't be an imposition on you and—'

'Steph, you're my niece and you seem like the daughter we never had. We've got plenty of room in this house, so of course your Anthony can come here. And welcome, too. I'll make sure I find him some light, nourishing food, even if I have to get it on the black market. He won't be able to eat much, even now, from what I've been reading about returned prisoners of war who've been starved for years.'

'No. And there will be other problems, I do understand that.'

'So . . . What do you need to do first?'

'Go to London and meet him off the train. Then, if he's well enough, I'll bring him back here. Otherwise we'll speak to doctors about what to do.'

She watched her uncle frown and didn't speak. She recognised that expression. He was thinking and planning.

After a few minutes, he said, 'I'll give you some money to use in London. I'm rich, love, and what's that worth if I can't help my own family? So don't even think of refusing.'

She flung her arms round his neck. 'I'm so glad I came here. You're the best uncle in the world.'

Then she paused. 'But what are you going to do about an assistant?'

'I managed without one before you came here and I can manage again. There are plenty of people around looking for work and your aunt is a lot better now, so perhaps she can help a little.'

'Neither of you can drive, though.'

'I'll find someone who can. Go and tell your aunt, then get packed. I have some phone calls to make. I've a friend who can find you a hotel room and—'

'Two hotel rooms. Anthony won't want to share at the moment, not if he looks like those men we've seen on the newsreels.'

'Two hotel rooms, then. We're going to get that lad of yours better, whatever it takes.'

6

That evening, when she served up the first meal she'd cooked on her own at Esherwood, Beryl watched her companions anxiously. People started eating then stopped and looked at their plates in surprise. Was something wrong?

Suddenly she realised they were smiling and nodding approval to one another, scooping up big mouthfuls of stew. Oh, thank goodness! They were enjoying it. You couldn't mistake that look.

Before the war she'd have made enough for seconds all round. Nowadays, you had to just about measure each mouthful so there was only a little left, mostly lumps of potato and carrot in gravy, because she'd taken it upon herself to serve them, trying to share out the meat fairly. Well, at least there was extra bread to fill up a growing boy and hard-working men!

Ben beamed across the table at her. 'You're a good cook, Mrs O'Brien. Much better than Mum.'

Kitty dug her elbow into her brother's side. 'Don't be so rude.'

'Well, she is.'

Judith laughed. 'It's all right, Kitty. I don't enjoy cooking. Mrs O'Brien does and it shows in this delicious food. You can't be good at everything and I'll be delighted to leave our meals to someone else more capable from now on. Which doesn't mean you children get out of setting the table, helping where needed and clearing up. Mrs O'Brien, they usually peel the potatoes if they're not at school. Or prepare other vegetables. Whatever is needed. Don't hesitate to give them jobs.'

Mayne had eaten everything on his plate almost as quickly as his stepson. He put down his spoon and fork with a happy sigh. 'That was really delicious, Mrs O'Brien.'

'There's a little more left. Would anyone like a second helping?'

Ben was on his feet in an instant, plate clutched in his hand. 'Yes, please.'

'We'll wait till everyone else has finished and share out what's left among those who want more,' Judith said firmly. 'Sit down and wait for the others, Ben.'

He didn't protest, just let out the plaintive sigh of an ill-treated lad.

'And you have to leave room for the pudding, don't forget,' Mrs O'Brien said.

'There's pudding as well?' Ben beamed at her even more broadly.

'It's only bread and butter pudding.'

'Only! That's one of my favourites.'

'Any pudding is your favourite,' Gillian mocked. 'Boys will eat anything.'

Christa watched wistfully as the children bantered and teased one another. To her surprise they next began discussing the new international organisation that was being formally inaugurated that week. The United Nations, it was to be called. Would the members all remain 'united'? She doubted it. But at least some nations were trying to work together again. She hoped they'd do better to maintain world peace than the old League of Nations had. Her father had been very angry about its fumblings and hesitations.

'My teacher says there are 51 countries in the United Nations this time, so they should be able to do better at keeping the peace,' Ben insisted.

'China isn't keeping the peace,' Kitty argued. 'The Chinese are fighting each other now, Nationalists versus Communists. Haven't we had enough wars in this world?'

'Well, at least our country isn't involved in that one,' Judith said soothingly.

'That's not the point, Mum. China is a big country, so it's a big struggle. A lot of people are dying. We've been learning about it at school. I think I'm going to become a pacifist.'

'That's a cop out,' Ben scoffed.

'It is not!'

Judith didn't try to stop them arguing. They were intelligent children who had grown up during an all-out war, and it wasn't any wonder they were taking an interest in developments which might affect their future. As any mother would, she prayed there wouldn't be a third world war to snatch her children away and put them in danger.

Later the talk turned to the men who'd been prisoners of war in the Far East. They'd all been horrified by the photos in the newspapers of the men returning to Britain. How thin and weak they'd looked still, even after months of recuperation!

The photos had emphasised to Christa how lucky she'd been personally, in spite of losing her parents, and she ventured to say so. *She* hadn't been held in a so-called work camp, or killed with masses of other poor souls in one. She'd heard a man saying on the news that it looked like several million Jews had been slaughtered.

She hadn't felt so bleakly alone since she'd come to Esherwood, at least. It seemed like a haven of sanity. Yet these people didn't ignore what was going on in the wider world. And the adults encouraged the children to join in and think about the new world their country was building.

What must it be like to have brothers and sisters? Or any family at all? She could remember her parents clearly, of course she could, but there had only ever been the three of them.

Someone touched her arm and she turned to Daniel, who was sitting next to her.

'Are you all right?' he whispered. 'You were looking sad.'

'Yes. Just feeling a touch of envy. It must be wonderful to have a family. All of you have someone you belong to.'

'Well, Ros has no actual family now.'

'She has a husband and step-daughter, though.'

'Give it time. You're making friends. This is a wonderful group of people. You'll soon feel part of our big family, I'm sure.' He grinned. 'Though not as rapidly as my aunt has. She's an amazing cook. That's the quickest way to people's hearts.'

Christa squeezed his hand without thinking. 'Thank you for thinking of me.'

He captured her hand and kept hold of it for a moment or two under the cover of the table, staring down at it, frowning.

When he let go, he didn't continue the conversation with her, but concentrated on his food.

He was still frowning. Was he regretting holding her hand? She couldn't help wondering and hoping she was wrong.

She didn't know why she'd reached out to him first, except that sometimes she hungered for another person's touch.

After the meal, Christa reminded Daniel about the need to check the bathroom ceiling. 'We'd better go and look at it before the girls start using it.'

'I'll come too,' Francis said. 'How about joining us, Diana?'

'I'd love to.'

Ben would have followed them but his mother tapped his shoulder and pointed to the table.

With a grunt of annoyance, he began clattering the used crockery together.

She watched for a moment then said sharply, 'If you break anything through careless handling, I'll dock the cost of replacing it from your spending money.'

Since regular weekly spending money was a new thing to all her children, instituted only since her marriage to Mayne, and much treasured, Ben started taking more care. But he still sighed loudly at intervals.

Upstairs the four of them crowded into the bathroom and looked upwards. 'Won't take us long to measure it,' Francis said.

Afterwards they went into the room next door, which was where he and Diana were sleeping at the moment, to measure the height of the ceiling there.

'It's a full three foot lower in the bathroom,' he said. 'Why the hell do you think that is? There shouldn't be any electrical circuits going through it.'

'It could just have been done to make the room easier to warm up,' Diana offered.

'I doubt the Army would have bothered about that. They *like* people to toughen up by taking cold showers.'

Both men laughed at the memories this brought.

'Well, we can't keep stopping and starting our main job to chase anomalies,' Daniel said firmly. 'I intend to do this properly and get a master diagram with exact measurements before we start investigating the bits that don't fit.'

He stared down at his notes, then looked around. 'It's a strange old house, isn't it? The whole of English history from the Restoration onwards seems to have left its mark on the architecture. And even though this isn't one of the huge stately homes, it still has quite a few secrets. I wonder what the big houses like Chatsworth are hiding.'

'Secrets that will probably never be discovered,' Francis said.

Ben came pounding up the stairs and broke the spell. 'The electricity has suddenly stopped working in the kitchen. Mum says can you please have a look at it, Francis?'

'Coming.'

Diana followed him down, so Daniel and Christa spent the next hour on their measurements, working together smoothly as a team.

'Do you want to stop now?' he asked. 'I don't want to work you to death.'

'I'm happy to continue. I find it interesting seeing the house as a pattern like this.'

He was still a little surprised at how well she'd taken to this sort of work, but pleased. It was yet another thing he liked, yes and admired, about her.

By the time the girls came up to get ready for bed, there were only the cellar and the area near the kitchen still to be measured, though they all knew the cellars would take a while, because there were a lot of different side rooms and storage cupboards down there, not to mention the secret room.

'We've done far more today than I'd have thought possible,' Daniel said. 'Thanks to your help, Christa. You seem to have a talent for this sort of work.'

He smiled as she blushed scarlet at his compliment.

'Thank you. I've really enjoyed doing it.'

'Let's go and lay out the pieces of paper on the library table, then tomorrow we'll put them together.'

She paused in the doorway of the library, staring round. 'We only ever had a small flat. I love the feeling of space here, all sorts of different spaces for different purposes.'

'We had a comfortable middle-class house, with a daily maid, but the rooms were small compared to this. It's very special, isn't it, Esherwood? At least Mayne had the privilege of growing up here, even if the poor chap can't keep it.'

That night, while others slept, two men moved carefully through the back streets of the town.

'It's good to get outside in the fresh air after being shut inside Mum's attic.' Sam Newton took a deep breath and stopped to gaze up at the stars.

'They'll catch you in the end and put you back in prison,' Cuthbert said sourly. 'Then your ma will be in trouble as well for harbouring you, and I will too if they catch me with you.'

'Well, they won't catch me unless someone gives me away. It's a clever hiding place in Ma's attic and it's fooled them on a couple of surprise searches, though it's damned uncomfortable to squeeze myself into. I'll be off to Australia as soon as I've got hold of those things we stashed away. We took a lot of risks to nick them while we were in the Army. We've *earned* our reward.'

'And the dear old officers never guessed what we were doing. What about the others? They'll want their share of the profits when they come out of prison. How are we going to manage that if you're in Australia and I'm living somewhere else?'

'Sod the others. They're still sitting in prison awaiting trial, haven't even been sentenced yet. I had the wit to escape. They didn't. And you're the only one who managed not to get caught.'

'Don't you think we ought to give something to their families once we get hold of the stuff?'

'No, I damned well don't. It could lead the police to us. Now, make sure you keep quiet from here on, Cuthbert lad.

We're getting close to the big house. You always did natter too much. And watch where you tread. We don't want to give ourselves away.'

'I haven't forgotten how to move quietly.'

They stopped speaking as they entered the grounds of Esherwood, two dark silhouettes keeping to the shadows. The terrain was familiar to them after the months they'd been stationed here. Both of them stopped in surprise, though, when they saw the new Nissen hut that had been erected next to the old one.

'They didn't waste any time putting this up, did they?' Cuthbert murmured softly.

'I wouldn't have, either, in their place. Never mind that. You're the locksmith. See if you can undo those padlocks and get us into the old Nissen hut.'

But when Cuthbert checked, he found that new padlocks had been installed, damned good ones too, and he'd need better tools to pick those locks without anyone knowing. He cursed under his breath. The whole point of tonight's exercise was to get the locks open without anyone finding out and check out that secret cellar because they were both curious about what lay behind the big, fancy door. He might be a locksmith, but even they needed the right tools and you couldn't carry everything you owned in your pocket just in case you needed it.

The sound of footsteps coming in their direction sent both men swiftly into the bushes, from where they watched a man walk by and pause to check the door they'd just been studying.

When the fellow had moved out of their hearing, Sam said, 'They've still got a night watchman, damn them. My mum said they'd stopped all that.'

'Well, she was wrong.'

'Can't you do anything about those locks?'

'Not easily, Sam lad. I'd have to break them to get in tonight because I need some other tools to open them without it showing, and that'd make a noise. Besides, we agreed that we wanted to keep this first visit secret and just reconnoitre. These are really good padlocks. Someone knew what they were doing and didn't mind how much they spent.'

'Where would they have got them from?'

'It was probably Reston who supplied these, damn him. My boss is good at his trade and he's been seeing a lot of Esher and Woollard lately. Hasn't taken me along, hasn't told me what he's doing, either. Next time I'll bring the proper tools.'

'Do we want to check the passage that leads to the cellar?'

'Not with someone keeping watch. We've learned a lot from coming here tonight and we'll do the thing properly next time. We don't want to leave signs that we've been in that old garden, which we might if we open up the tunnel.'

'Let's get out of here, then.'

They made their way back through the grounds as carefully as they'd entered and stopped for a moment before separating.

'You all right for money, Sam? If not, I can let you have a bit.'

'I'm fine. I didn't spend the first lot of money we made. Mum hid it for me. She's all right, my old lady is. Have you still got your money?'

'Most of it. The wife poked through my things and took some of it, but I told her the rest belonged to a friend who'd beat her up if she took it, so she left it alone. She's still suspicious, though, so I keep it better hidden now.'

After a pause and a scowl, he added sourly, 'I'm going to Australia too, but I'll be leaving *her* behind.'

'Well, you'll be all right there, be able to open your own locksmith's. You were put into a good trade.'

'I wasn't asked, though, and I get fed up of fiddling around with locks. Most of the work's boring everyday stuff. And it's shown me how rich folk live. I want the same sort of life.'

After a short pause, he continued, 'I'll send a message through your ma once I've worked out how to do it next time.'

'Come and see me. It's safe to walk around at night now the war's over and there are no wardens patrolling the streets. But check with Ma first that I'm still there. I need to slip out of town and find out how to get hold of Army uniforms for us and steal an Army lorry.'

'Bit risky, isn't it?'

'It's all risky. But I did hear in prison that they can be got hold of. I think our best chance of retrieving our stuff is just to drive it away openly.'

'Sounds a good idea.'

7

The adults sat down to a more peaceful midday meal the following day, with the children at school.

When everyone had finished, Mayne tapped his spoon on his mug to get their attention. 'Well, the outside of the new Nissen hut is finished now, except for a pane or two of glass. Jan's coming back this afternoon to look through the bits and pieces we've salvaged. He's sure he's seen some window glass that can be cut to size.'

Mayne let them nod approval then went on, 'If he doesn't find anything, I'm sleeping in the new hut to keep an eye on things. Steve Rennie found footprints in the woods this morning and showed them to me. They looked freshly made, probably last night, because he's pretty sure he hasn't seen them before. They weren't on any path that people use regularly, so I'm suspicious too about why someone would be walking round in that area.'

'Collecting wood for bonfires?' suggested Judith.

'There is no fallen wood left in our grounds. We've gathered it all for firewood.'

'Perhaps . . .' Victor broke off, frowning.

'Perhaps what?' Mayne prompted.

'Perhaps it's the thieves, checking things out, ready to finish the job they started. Ever since we heard that Newton had escaped from prison, I've been wondering if he's going to be stupid enough to try for the hidden cellar again. He won't realise that he needs the key *and* a good locksmith to get inside it.'

'None of the fellows we captured were locksmiths and the only ones in town are Dick Reston and his employees.'

'One of whom, Cuthbert Blane, was demobbed recently,' Victor said. 'I asked around. He went straight back into his old job and has never been in trouble with the police. I rang up a pal in his regiment and he was considered a good soldier. Got on well with the other fellows, did what was asked of him. *But* I only had to ask who his friends were and my contact named Newton and a couple of the other fellows who broke in here and are still in jail.'

'I don't like the sound of that,' Francis said. 'Who's to say we got them all when they attacked the house? They were very stubborn about not talking and even when they come up for trial, I don't think that'll change. They'd served together during the war, and as we all know, that means a lot in comradeship.'

It was Ros who said what the others were thinking. 'Who would be wandering round our woods, if it wasn't them? The whole town knows by now that we've got everything carefully locked away, and even the kids out hunting for wood for their bonfires didn't come here.'

Mayne shook his head. 'I'm stumped. I don't think it's Thompson, because why would he be wandering through the woods? That's not the part of the estate he's interested in. Anyway, these prints looked more like those made by boots than by his bright, shiny new, I'm-the-boss shoes.'

'We'll have to keep our eyes open, then,' Daniel said.

'In the meantime, Thompson has made an appointment to see me this afternoon.' Mayne bared his teeth in a tiger's grin. 'I think we should greet him in force, to make sure we all get an idea of what he's like. Can you all be there? You too, Judith. And Ros, you're welcome to join us.'

'I'm not as involved in the building company as the rest of you, so unless you want me for some specific reason, I'll get on with the sewing,' Ros said. 'Diana and I had planned to make a start on some curtains for the new prefab this afternoon. We've found some old ones we can cut down. But it's kind of you to invite us.'

'I didn't want anyone to feel left out.'

Both women smiled at him. 'We don't, Mayne,' Ros said.

'I hadn't realised there were bosses who involve their staff in decision making like you do,' Diana added. 'My father would as soon die as ask any of his staff for advice, and he doesn't care about their feelings, boasts he can sack a man in two minutes flat.'

Christa waited a moment, then, when no one spoke, asked, 'What can I do this afternoon? I want to make myself as useful as possible.'

'Oh, sorry, Christa!' Mayne said at once. 'You were hidden behind Ros.'

Ros turned to her. 'Are you any good at sewing?'

'Only at mending and hemming, things like that. And only because I had to do it.'

They chuckled. 'It's a rare woman who hasn't had to learn to patch and darn during the war years,' Diana said. 'Come and join us. We'll find work of some sort for you. We're going to measure the windows in the new hut and see if we can come up with any ideas about the inside layout.'

Mayne took over again. 'I'm hoping today we'll find out exactly what Thompson wants. Ray suspects the fellow intends to take over the whole of my land in a forced purchase, but I find that hard to credit. I'm not letting the council take Esherwood.'

'I can't believe they'd go so far!' Francis exclaimed.

'Well, just let them try. My family and I could see the need during the war for the government to take over

Esherwood, so we put up with it being requisitioned without a protest. But I'm *damned* if I'm giving away my house and land now. I've offered to sell the council the back part for prefabs at a very reasonable price, and that must suffice as my contribution to rebuilding our country.'

But it'd all be a lot easier if he could trace the family money. Had his father lost it or was it his mother? She'd stolen and sold quite a few small family heirlooms as she slipped towards dementia. At least, he hoped it was her failing mind that had made her do that. Was she also to blame for the missing money, guided by his ex-fiancée who had also stolen countless pieces?

He hoped his mother hadn't done it all before her mind failed. He had more than enough bad memories of her to cope with.

At two o'clock precisely, everyone gathered in the dining room, where the big mahogany table had been cleared and polished, with its matching chairs set round it for the meeting.

Ray had just arrived, but he'd come in the back way, as he always did now that he had been fully accepted into the group. He took a seat on the left side, with his back to the window. 'Mayne, you need to be aware of something. I've been talking to a chap I know. He's pretty certain Thompson really does intend to take over the whole of Esherwood.'

'*Why* is he so set on that?'

Ray had no chance to explain further because they all heard a car turn into the drive. 'Damn!'

Judith looked out of the window. 'It's Thompson, on time to the minute. And he's brought a woman with him. After he's gone, I think you should have the chain barrier at the front entrance put into place and locked.'

'Good idea.'

As agreed, Christa opened the front door and showed Thompson and his companion into the dining-room.

Mayne nodded his thanks and she went off to join Diana and Ros in the hut.

'Good afternoon, Mr Thompson.' He stood there, waiting for an introduction to the woman, but all the visitor did was wave one hand and say, 'My secretary will take notes.'

The woman looked steadfastly towards the ground as if trying to attract as little attention as possible. But when Francis went to fetch her a chair she had to look up. She was starting to whisper a thank you when Thompson snapped, 'Not there. She can sit to one side and use that little table. She has no part to play in the discussion. Now, if you don't mind me taking a seat, I'd like to start by—'

'*I* would like to start by finding out your secretary's name, as a matter of simple courtesy.'

While Thompson was still gaping in surprise, the woman said quickly, 'It's Mrs Vickers.' She then moved her chair to the very edge of the room, as if disassociating herself from any involvement in the proceedings.

Judith drew her miscellaneous sheets of scrap paper closer and picked up a fountain pen, unscrewing the top, ready to take notes which would later be entered into the new company minutes book.

'Mrs Esher will be taking the minutes for us today, but this doesn't preclude *her* from taking part in the discussion,' Mayne said pointedly. 'Now, Mr Thompson, you were saying?'

'I'm here on behalf of the council to give you notice that we'll be taking over the rear half of your land as from next week.'

Dead silence greeted this remark and after a few seconds, he repeated, 'I said, I'm here on behalf of—'

'We heard you the first time, but I think I speak for my colleagues when I ask at which council meeting this was decided? And did you say *half* my land? There has been no previous mention that I would be willing to sell so much to the council.'

'In troubled times like these, one has to act decisively, and I have Councillor Draper's permission to go ahead with this project in accordance with the Government's policy of providing as many houses as possible, and doing it as quickly as possible, to replace those destroyed in the war. The Councillor oversees the planning of the town's buildings.'

Mayne leaned forward. 'Wait a minute. Let's get this absolutely straight, for the record.' He nodded towards Judith, sitting with her pen at the ready. 'This matter hasn't gone before the council itself yet?'

'It will do so, but that's merely a formality.'

'May I be told when it'll be going before council?' Mayne asked.

'No, you may not. And may I say that I'd have thought someone in your financial circumstances would be glad to sell his land quickly and set his finances in order. *You* can't afford even to maintain this crumbling old house.'

There was a gasp from several people at this rudeness. Mayne raised one hand to stop anyone replying hastily. Again he waited, noting Thompson's colour rising as the silence seemed to pulsate with anger around them.

'I'm sorry, Mr Thompson, but I decline to discuss this matter with you until it's been referred to the council, after which I will need to be officially notified of the projected actions and given time to appeal, if I don't agree with them. Now, Mr Thompson—'

'*Captain* Thompson, if you please.'

'I don't please. Military titles are out of place in civilian life for those no longer serving in the armed forces and I have no intention of clinging on to my own Captain's title.'

'As an officer, I—'

Mayne's voice became steely. 'There are several other

ex-officers in this room as well as myself and we're all in agreement. Mrs Vickers, for your records, please note that I decline to discuss this matter of resumption of my land in such an informal way or to allow anyone to act without due authority. The meeting is over.' Mayne stood up.

Thompson stayed where he was. 'With or without your approval, the surveyors will move in next Monday.'

'They will not,' Mayne said quietly.

'You can't—'

'Let me show you out, Thompson. This meeting is now at an end. I've had my say and I don't intend to argue with you.'

'I'm not stirring from here until I've made you realise that we need to start work on these homes as soon as possible. Indeed, patriotism alone should make you do your bit.'

Victor said sharply, 'For your information, Mr Thompson, Mr Esher more than did his bit during the war years, and were it not for the Official Secrets Act, it'd be my pleasure to enlighten you about how.'

'Leave it, Vic,' Mayne's voice was still quiet and emotionless.

Everyone had stood up by then, except Thompson and Mrs Vickers, who was hastily putting her papers together.

Mayne walked along to where Thompson was still sitting, making no attempt to move. 'I'm asking you to leave my house now, sir.'

'But we have to—'

Mayne took a step forward. 'Do you need help getting up from the table?'

All hung in the balance for a moment, then their unwelcome visitor grabbed his papers, stalked across the room to dump some of them in front of his secretary, and turned towards the door. 'You haven't heard the last of this, Esher.'

'Allow me to show you out.' Mayne moved to the door and held it open.

Completely ignoring his secretary, Thompson strode out of the room behind his host, his face dull red with fury.

Mrs Vickers jumped up to follow him, but dropped her folder. Loose papers from it scattered across the floor.

'Let me help you.' Francis knelt down and began to pick them up.

Since there wasn't room for her on the floor behind the chairs, she stood waiting for him to finish.

'Very difficult situation for you,' Francis said. 'Here you are.'

She took them from him, glanced towards the door and said in a low voice, 'I'm so sorry.'

'Not your fault.'

A voice yelled from the hall, 'Mrs Vickers, will you please hurry up.'

She hesitated, then deliberately selected one piece of paper and let it fall back on to the floor.

'*Mrs Vickers!*' Thompson yelled again. '*I am waiting.*'

She hurried out without picking up the paper.

8

Jasper Audley looked up with a smile as someone tapped on the door of the inner sanctum at his legal practice. He knew that firm double knock. 'Come in.'

His chief clerk opened the door and stood in the doorway. 'Just to let you know that I'm back, sir.'

'Glad to see you. And may I say that you look a lot better for your two weeks by the seaside.'

'Yes, sir. I was fair run down after that influenza, I must admit.'

'Well, make sure you don't overdo things and undo all the good work.'

'Thank you, sir. I'll be careful. Um . . . I was sorry to hear about Mrs Pelling dying.'

'Yes, very sad. She declined rapidly. Unfortunately she didn't finalise the new will we'd been discussing.'

Stackpole stared at him in shock. 'But she did, sir. She brought it in while you were away dealing with Sir Matthew's problems. I knew the will was simple and straightforward, and since you'd already approved the draft, I checked with young Mr Roberts, and he said to go ahead. I found a suitable witness – Mr Hardcastle from the ironmonger's – and he and I witnessed Mrs Pelling signing it, which Mr Roberts checked afterwards before he went off to get married. He won't be back till next week or you could ask him.'

'The young woman looking after her didn't know anything about this will?'

'No, sir. Mrs Pelling wanted it kept secret till after she was dead.'

'You're sure she understood what she was doing?'

'Oh yes, sir. She repeated her wishes several times. And it was all very straightforward, if you remember.'

'What happened to the will then?'

'Mrs Pelling took her copy away with her and I was feeling pretty sick by then, so I gave our copy to the office boy to file. He'll know where it is.'

Audley thumped his hand down on the desk. 'I fired that young devil when I returned a couple of days after you'd gone off to recuperate. He'd been stealing from the petty cash.'

'*No!* His family must have been shocked.'

'He ran away without telling them about being in trouble. No one knows where he's gone, but my secretary says he was always talking about emigrating to Canada to join his cousins, now that the war is over.' He frowned. 'We did look in the Pelling box but there was no sign of any new will.'

'I'll go and search for it straight away, sir. That lad was always misfiling things. I was going to speak to you about his suitability.'

'I wonder what happened to the copy of the will the old lady took with her?'

Stackpole spread out his hands in a helpless gesture. 'Who can say? If it had been anywhere obvious, her relatives would have found it. I blame myself. If I hadn't been so careless . . .'

'Nonsense. You couldn't help falling ill. Unfortunately, not knowing about the new will, I contacted Mrs Pelling's cousin, who had been named in her son's will in case his mother pre-deceased him. She came the very next day and immediately threw poor little Miss Summers out in the street. I was away at my uncle's funeral so didn't know about this till afterwards, by which time Miss Summers had left town.'

The clerk looked at him in shock. 'Threw that nice young woman out, after all she'd done for Mrs Pelling? Why, that's shocking!'

'Yes. Says something about what sort of woman Mrs Grayton is, eh? She came to see me as soon as I got back and I didn't take to her at all, I must admit. She seemed a very grasping woman. But I thought she was the rightful heir so I started the process to get her named the legal heir and probate granted.'

He lowered his voice, to add, 'Between you and me, Stackpole, if *she* found the will Mrs Pelling took home with her, I'd guess she would have destroyed it.'

'It's not often *you* take a dislike to someone, sir.'

'Well I did to her.'

'What can we do to remedy matters?'

'I'm not sure. I don't think we should get in touch with Miss Summers until we have the final will safely locked away. I don't want to raise false hopes because if we can't find it, we can do nothing.'

'Where did the young lady go, sir?'

'That's another thing. I don't know where she went. If I'd realised she'd be thrown out of her home so abruptly, I'd have sent my housekeeper to offer her temporary accommodation at our house. I have a great deal of respect for Miss Summers. She cared for Mrs Pelling as if they really were mother and daughter.'

'Would you like me to make enquiries in the town, see if anyone knows where Miss Summers has gone?'

'Yes, please. And we'll put a halt on the probate proceedings until we've sorted out the situation and found both her *and* the new will. That stupid office boy must have put it somewhere, for heaven's sake.'

He stopped and looked at his chief clerk in sudden dismay. 'You don't think the boy deliberately hid it, do you? Out of spite at being dismissed. There have been a couple of other documents mislaid.'

'Surely not? Oh, my goodness, what is the world coming to?' Stackpole squared his shoulders. 'But if it's here, be assured that I'll find it.'

Francis bent to pick up the piece of paper that Thompson's secretary had let fall as she left Esherwood. 'You've dropped something!' he called after her.

She didn't turn. If anything, she speeded up and almost ran out of the front door to where Thompson was waiting for her in the car.

Francis looked at the document in his hand. Clearly she'd intended them to keep it. As he caught sight of the heading on it, he gasped in shock and began to read it.

The others were still watching Mrs Vickers.

'She looked terrified of that horrible man,' Judith said.

Daniel nodded agreement. 'Yes. I wouldn't have believed anyone could behave so rudely to someone who works for them. And in front of others too. I feel sorry for anyone who's answerable to such a boor.'

Judith let out a scornful snort. 'He probably couldn't even tell you what she looks like. I've cleaned houses for people like that. They called me "Mrs—um".'

Daniel was still frowning. 'What I can't understand is why Thompson is so confident that the council approval for compulsory purchase is merely a matter of rubber stamping and—'

Francis cleared his throat and everyone turned towards him.

'What's the matter?' Judith asked.

He waved the paper at them. 'Mrs Vickers dropped this

deliberately. It's a letter from Bentinck's Building Company, thanking the council for contracting them to erect prefabs on the rear part of the Esherwood estate. And not ten prefabs, either, but fifty.'

'But fifty won't fit on that piece of land we're selling,' Judith protested.

'Precisely. And Bentinck's are a small firm, have only done minor jobs, mostly repairs and extensions. They don't have a good reputation in town and are usually scrabbling for work.'

'Thompson must feel very sure a compulsory purchase will go through,' she said slowly. 'And if it does, they won't pay us nearly as much as we'd get if we could sell plots of land and build houses on them.'

There was dead silence, then Francis frowned. 'What I don't understand is why on earth Thompson would risk bringing the file with him.'

'He probably wants to prevent anyone in the office from looking at it without his say-so,' Ray said.

'He could have locked it away somewhere safe in the Town Hall.'

'There must be duplicates to all the keys there and as a newcomer, he'd not be sure who could get into his cupboards.'

'I've met men like that before,' Francis said. 'Can't delegate. But that still doesn't explain why Mrs Vickers deliberately dropped that particular piece of paper from the file.'

No one spoke until Judith put in quietly, 'You can push someone too far and he treated her very rudely in front of us. He won't know she's done it, won't even know it's missing until he goes looking for it and then he'll not think it's her. I'm sure we won't tell anyone who it was that let us see the letter.'

'She's not only done us a very big favour but confirmed what someone else hinted at to me.' Ray looked round. 'I didn't have time to tell you before Thompson arrived. Look, I'll send a message to Mrs Vickers that I'll help her if she needs another job. Her husband hasn't been demobbed yet, has he, so she may need the money.'

Judith looked at him approvingly. 'That'd be a kind thing to do. None of us has such good contacts as you.'

They all turned round as Mayne came storming in, looking furious.

'I have never met such an arrogant fellow in all my life. I stood just inside the front door and watched him go right down the drive. He had the unmitigated gall to stop and get out of the car to stare across at the Dower House, as if he was planning something for that as well.'

'He probably is.'

'You were right, Ray. I do need to check up on his background. I wonder what exactly he did in the Army and *why* he got demobbed so quickly.'

He broke off as Judith touched his arm.

'We found something out while you were gone.'

Francis explained about the letter and handed it to his friend.

Mayne read it then looked at him in shock. 'But we've been assured that we'll be the ones to erect the prefabs in return for voluntarily selling the land to the council at a reasonable price.'

'Who by?'

'Councillor Faulkner.'

Ray's voice was harsh and his northern accent suddenly stronger. 'We'd better check him out as well, then. Because I reckon someone's been pulling the wool over your eyes, Mayne lad, using delaying tactics while they made their plans. Now they seem to be putting them into operation before you can stop them. That must have been put in train well before Thompson came to work here. In fact, that might be *why* he was appointed, because he was prepared to do the deed for someone.'

'I can't believe this is happening in Rivenshaw, of all places.' Mayne's voice was tight and strained, and for once his anger was barely under control.

'I don't think you chaps understand how much bribery and corruption has been let loose among civilians by the continuing shortages,' Ray said. 'It's going on everywhere, not just in our little town. People who wouldn't have done this sort of thing before out of patriotism are doing it now that the war's ended, because the country's survival is no longer at stake.'

'Well, I still refuse to act illegally,' Mayne said stiffly.

'No one's asked you to. But my chap is already checking Thompson out. There isn't anything illegal about that. In the meantime, you really should consult your lawyer about your rights. If you don't, that Thompson chap will have people swarming all over your grounds and digging up your woods before you can blink an eye so that Bentinck can put up the prefabs.'

'They'll have to knock the perimeter walls down first. I'll put up a new gate. We have enough wood to make a solid one and—'

'The perimeter walls won't take much knocking down. They're in a sorry state. And that fellow wouldn't hesitate to bring in a bulldozer, even if they were in perfect condition.'

'They can't really take so much land off me, can they?' Mayne asked in a near whisper. 'Not . . . the whole of the back area?'

Ray sighed. 'I don't know. All sorts of rules and regulations were set aside because of the war and they haven't been reinstated. We have to find out whether the council still has the power to trample all over people.'

He thought for a moment, then added, 'However, the

council would probably be required to get estimates before undertaking any big tasks. I wonder if they did that.'

'They certainly didn't contact us,' Judith said at once. 'And they knew we had set up a building company.'

'Do you have a good lawyer, Mayne lad?'

'Not one who's well informed about council and government regulations, Ray. I don't think there is one with that expertise in Rivenshaw. Maybe in Manchester, but I wouldn't know who to go to. I've never needed that sort of lawyer.'

'Then I'll see who I can find to represent you.' He waited a moment or two, then said in a gentler voice, 'Don't let it get you down, lad. There's always a way.' He grinned and added, 'Even if one is forced to act honestly, which makes it much harder.'

That drew a reluctant smile from everyone.

People started to get up but Ray held up his hand as a sign to stay where they were. 'There's another thing we should deal with. My locksmith friend wants to know whether your father has found the instructions for the puzzle lock yet or whether we should start planning a break-in.'

'Not found them yet, I'm afraid. Let's give him a little longer.'

'There's no desperate hurry, though I must admit I'm fascinated by it myself. Your ancestors wouldn't have taken such care with the lock if there wasn't something valuable to be guarded.'

'No. I suppose you're right.'

'Dick's managed to get his foreman demobbed early, so he's planning to take things easier now. But he's still dealing with the puzzle lock and is absolutely itching to have another go at getting into your cellar.'

Mayne sighed. 'The cellar will have to wait till we've sorted out Thompson and the council.'

'You could ask your father to hurry, though. Or I could ask him on your behalf. Yes, why don't I do that?'

Mayne looked at him in surprise. It wasn't like Ray to press a point so stubbornly. The older man was still treading carefully with the other four original partners in the company. 'It's rather low on my list of priorities, I must admit, and I thought it would have been on yours.'

Ray shrugged. 'I can turn my mind to more than one thing at a time. It's a bit of a long shot, but it might be useful to have a valuable historical site in your grounds, don't you think?'

'You surely don't think Thompson will care about history!'

'Of course not, but I know some folk in Rivenshaw who take the history of our town very seriously indeed.'

'Oh, all right. Why don't *you* ask Dad if he's had any luck finding the instructions? But even if he has, I'm not prepared to put much effort into the cellar. Whatever's in it won't make a difference to our present problems, I'm sure. My ancestors were not noted for their financial acumen.'

Ray opened his mouth to argue then shut it again because he could see how upset his younger companion was, beneath that rigid control. This was not the time.

Mayne took a deep breath. 'Now, if you'll excuse me, I'd better go and help Judith write up those minutes. If there's one thing I learned in the Army, it was to document everything you do. Even when the documents were covered by the Official Secrets Act, they came in useful sometimes behind the scenes.'

'You'd better keep that letter Mrs Vickers dropped somewhere safe, lad. Or better still, let me look after it for you, then if anyone asks, you can swear you've looked and it's not on these premises.'

That won a reluctant smile from Mayne. 'We'll get Christa to make some copies of the minutes for everyone then I'll give that letter to you. We may need to refer to them at some stage. The way Thompson introduced the question of the council taking over my land was highly improper for a start. I think I can still remember his exact words.'

Ray watched him go, then looked at Daniel. 'I've never seen him so upset. He usually has iron control over his emotions.'

'He loves this house more than he shows. It's breaking his heart to think of selling it off piecemeal.'

'Who wouldn't love it?'

'He was making a lot of plans to restore it during the war – till he found out about the family finances. And then he started working out ways to save the building, at least. Said buildings like this one are the nation's history as well as his family's history. Now . . . who knows what they'll do to it? I wouldn't put it past Thompson to knock it down.'

'Not if I can help it, Daniel. There was something else: I heard that you and Francis have both found anomalies in the structure of the building. Mind showing me what's puzzling you?'

'Happy to. We can either go up to the hiding places in the attic – there are more than one – or down to the anomaly I found this morning in the cellar, or there's another little puzzle in the ceiling over one of the bathrooms.'

'That's a damned strange place to put a secret hiding place.'

'There may be nothing there. The different ceiling height may be just to make it easier to keep the bathroom warm.'

Ray frowned. 'Hmm. I thought they'd already found the secret room in the cellar.'

'They found one, but the measurements still don't fit, so there may be another. Only I can't see any signs of false walls or hidden doors. The walls nearby are all solid brick and old-fashioned bricks too, not modern ones. I want to ask Mayne if everything is as he remembers down there, but after what he found out today, I think it might be better to wait to do that.'

★ ★ ★

When Mayne came into the office they shared, Judith took one look at his face and walked into his arms, pulling him close. For a few precious moments they held one another, saying nothing. If he'd been any other man, he might have shed a tear or two, but he just shuddered and breathed deeply, holding her tightly all the time.

Then he pulled away, keeping one arm round her shoulders. 'For once, I can't think what to do.'

'About what Thompson said?'

'Yes.'

'Then we'll start with a smaller job. We'll get the minutes done. After that I think a walk in the fresh air would do us both good, clear our heads. We could figure out exactly where the land you've already agreed to sell to the council ends, even put up some rough markers to show which part it is.'

'Yes. You're right, love. One small step at a time till I can— till *we* can see our way more clearly.'

'I agree. But I think . . .' She hesitated. 'I think this is a time when you should listen to Ray's advice. He's more aware of the ins and outs of cheating behaviour than you are. He was in the thick of it during the war years, after all.'

Mayne stiffened. 'You think he's cheated people?'

'No. Actually, I don't. Skipped around the laws and regulations, yes, but cheated individuals, no. I don't think he's that sort of person.'

'You always did have faith in him, didn't you?'

She smiled. 'Yes. Because I was living among ordinary people and I never heard anyone complain about being badly treated by him. In fact, he's well liked. Come on, my darling. We'll do those minutes, then we'll get some fresh air. I've re-filled my fountain pen. Here are the notes. You dictate the final version and I'll write it down.'

9

Ray followed Daniel and Christa down into the cellar. Victor decided to go and chat to Jan and Al, who were rather more than lowly employees. Or would be once the building company took off. Their futures were involved in it as much as anyone else's, so he felt they had a right to know what was going on.

And you never knew where helpful ideas would come from if you were facing major problems. Jan in particular was a very clever man, who sometimes offered solutions to problems that no one else had even considered.

Victor sighed. When they planned their new company, they had expected to start building the prefabs more quickly than this. He mentally changed the age-old saying to: *Man proposes, local council disposes.*

He found Jan in the kitchen chatting to Mrs O'Brien. There was a bunch of some sort of spinach, well, he thought it was spinach, on the draining board. Jan had real 'green fingers' where plants were concerned and had coaxed a late harvest from their garden.

'Do you have a minute, Jan?'

Both people stared at him as if they could read trouble in his face.

'You'll hear all about it at teatime, Mrs O'Brien, but if you don't mind, I'd like to discuss something with Jan privately first.'

She smiled and made a banishing motion with one hand. 'I'm a newcomer, so I don't expect to be told every detail of what's going on here.'

'I think you'll find Mayne usually keeps people well informed.'

She nodded and turned back to her work.

Outside Victor said abruptly, 'Let's go and study the rear part of the estate as we talk.' On the way there, he explained quickly what had happened.

'I've seen that man Thompson,' Jan said. 'Heard about him too. He's not wasted any time making himself disliked in certain quarters. Miss Peters next door to us can't stand him.'

'She's the best judge of character I know. Pity she couldn't go into the law like her brother. She'd have made a good lawyer.'

'I've seen many like Thompson during the war, bullies and grabbers of other people's food and possessions.' Jan's voice was almost a snarl.

'Pity chaps like that survived the war when so many good men were killed. Not that I'd wish anyone killed.'

'There were some I would wish killed.' Jan's expression was sad with memories. 'I have seen women and children murdered as well as men, and not just by soldiers. Very brave women, too.'

They walked along the wall of the estate at the rear of the grounds, studying it carefully. It was more or less intact until they came to the pillars where wrought iron gates had once hung. They'd been taken for scrap during the early war years. Mayne didn't intend to replace them, had expected to knock down the pillars and put a short new street in here, lined with prefabs.

'The wall is in bad condition,' Jan said. 'But it still makes a barrier for bigger vehicles. If the council intend to bring heavy machinery in here, they'll have to knock some of the wall down as well as the gate pillars to get it inside.'

'If we let them do it,' Victor said.

'How can we stop them?'

'I don't know yet. Let's go and talk to Al about the situation.'

As they set off again Jan looked at him. 'What are you thinking of doing?'

'I'm not thinking anything yet. But I get the impression Thompson's trying to act quickly, so that he can present the world with a *fait accompli*. And if that means knocking down the rear wall, he won't hesitate to do it.'

'Well, if I can help Mayne, I will, so don't hesitate to ask me. I've only known him for a few months but he is a good and generous person.'

Victor clapped him on the back. 'Good man! Now, let's go and talk to Al, then consider our options.'

In the Dower House, Reginald Esher sighed and pulled yet another ancient text towards him from the pile on one side of his desk. For weeks he had been hunting through shelves and boxes of old books from the seventeenth century for diaries he thought might contain the instructions for opening the puzzle lock, and getting nowhere. He was feeling very disheartened about his lack of success.

He knew he wasn't a practical man, but he was usually good with books. If he could supply this information, his son would know how to act on it. And he wouldn't feel so useless.

He reached for the next book, exclaiming in surprise when he opened it. He'd thought he was dealing with an old printed book, but this looked like a hand-written diary. He studied the outside cover again. It had been carefully bound to match a set of similar books, same colour of leather binding, same gold lettering on the spine. How intriguing!

He began to read, quickly finding out that it had been written by his ancestor, Lawrence Maynard Esher. He knew about the life of this many-times great grandfather, of course he did. The man had been the first to be called 'Maynard', old English for *hard strength*.

He had first found out about Lawrence when he was looking through the family tree for a name for his own child. During the English Civil Wars, unlike his younger brother Carolus, Lawrence Esher had fought for the King, going off to fight and leaving his very capable wife, Margery, in charge of his estate.

She had run it extremely efficiently, by all accounts, but in the end the Parliamentarians had captured the small manor house and razed it to the ground. No one knew what had happened to Margery, but it was assumed that she'd been killed during the attack on the house and her body buried in an unmarked grave because she'd never been seen again after the house had been destroyed.

No one knew what had happened to the second son Carolus, either; he was presumed to have been killed fighting for the Parliamentarians.

After the Restoration, Lawrence was given back his family's land and married again. Elizabeth was much younger than him and brought a large dowry. She gave him three sons and a daughter. Since the old house had been totally destroyed, Lawrence decided to build a fine new one. Fortunately, he proved to be one of the few Eshers to have the gift of making and keeping money.

One of his former servants always said Margery was buried somewhere on the site of the old house, but though they'd searched, they'd never found her body.

In the end, Lawrence gave up the hunt, resolving to let her lie in peace, ordering that the remaining piles of scattered stones from the old house were to be used for garden walls. That area was still very pretty and was known as the 'old garden'.

The new house had been built closer to the centre of his land and he'd created a new entrance from there and a street running down to the town centre along Parsons Mead.

Legend said that Lawrence Esher never fully trusted anyone, and had had one or two hiding places constructed in case fighting ever broke out again in England, since King Charles the Second didn't seem able to provide a legal and indisputable heir, and who knew what would happen when he died?

But no further wars were started in his lifetime and the succession was settled reasonably amicably, for a time at least, with Charles II's brother taking the throne as King James II until he was deposed in 1688.

Some of the secret rooms and hiding places had been found, but there might be one or two others, for all anyone knew.

Various owners added to the building, not every generation, but every now and then. It was as if Lawrence's love of building appeared occasionally in his descendants, as it seemed to have done in Mayne.

Reginald mentally chided himself. What was he doing, thinking about family history when Mayne needed him to find the instructions for the lock?

He intended to write a proper history of the family but not till all the present troubles were settled. It would be his second major gift to his family. The first and best one was producing a son like Mayne. Surely if anyone could find a way to keep Esherwood, it was him?

The worst thing Reginald had done, he admitted to himself, was failing to control his wife as she started to lose her senses. As usual he'd been lost in his books and, since they weren't close as a couple, he'd left her to her own devices, not realising how far she had slipped mentally.

They still hadn't found everything she'd stolen and then hidden or sold, valuable Esher possessions which Reginald mourned the loss of. He wondered if they ever would be found.

No use dwelling on that. He settled down to read the diary with such intense concentration that Mrs Rennie had to shake his shoulder good and hard to make him realise the day was ending and he needed to eat.

What he'd found was the most promising information so far, but there was one big problem.

At Jasper Audley's rooms, his chief clerk searched through the papers in all the family boxes near the Pellings' box in the storeroom, to no avail.

Just looking round the big storeroom, Stackpole felt overwhelmed. Every wall was covered in shelves right up to the ceiling, and all the shelves were full. In fact, there were so many boxes after three generations of Audleys had served their little town as lawyers that he could search for weeks and find nothing.

He'd have to be more clever about it, work out how that dratted office lad might have thought. In the meantime, he would search for Miss Summers. If she'd been thrown out of the Pelling house, she'd have had to find somewhere to stay.

He didn't want anyone in town to know what was going on, especially Mrs Pelling's so-called heir, so he didn't intend to go round town openly asking questions himself. He'd ask the new office boy to do it for him.

Jimmy Clark was almost seventeen, too young to have served in the war, though he'd acted as a local messenger boy and fire watcher, and people in charge of him had spoken well of his hard work and enthusiasm. He was going to go far, that one was. Stackpole could always tell. Unfortunately, the lad would still have to go into the forces before he could settle into a job.

He reckoned that through this concept of 'national service' the government intended to have a well-trained force of civilians to fall back on in future, and he agreed with that. Mind you, he didn't want to see coming generations of lads going off overseas to get themselves killed in other wars. No one did.

Whatever shortages people still had to face, at least they wouldn't have to cope with the deaths of more fine young men and women. Stackpole himself had lost a nephew only last year, and he'd lost a distant cousin, a woman in her forties, at the beginning of the war, in the London Blitz.

He had been dubious about the previous office lad's suitability and had said so to Mr Audley, but there had been few choices during the war, because as soon as a lad reached eighteen – some of them even before then – off he'd go and enlist or else be called up.

Cuthbert was feeling restless after yet another quarrel with his damned fool of a wife, so decided to go and visit Sam to see if he could hurry him up about retrieving their loot. He left word with his friend's mother that he'd be coming round that night.

Just after midnight he tiptoed out of his own house, leaving his wife sound asleep. He doubted she'd wake up, the way she was snoring.

He hugged the shadows as he made his way across town. The back door of the house had been left open for him, and when he opened it a voice whispered from the darkness, 'Over here.'

He sat at the kitchen table next to Sam in the dark. 'How are you doing, lad?'

'Going mad from being shut up in that damned attic. I come down here in the night sometimes.'

'It's better than prison, though.'

'Yeah. But only just. At least you had company in prison. Ma says she's too busy to come up and chat to me in the daytime and if she keeps leaving the café, people might wonder why.'

There was silence for a few minutes, then Sam said, 'Well, out with it. Why did you decide to come and see me?'

'I'm fed up of waiting to get our stuff,' Cuthbert told his friend. 'Old Reston's turned into a real martinet now the war's over. He's a first class locksmith but he's getting older and he wants me to do most of the work while he takes most of the money.'

'Is he still talking about that fancy puzzle lock?'

Cuthbert sighed. 'Yes. It's the main reason I'm being so helpful. He's a shrewd old sod. If *he* thinks there's something valuable inside the cellar, he's probably right. Only . . . is it worth us waiting? We'd be able to get away quickly if we didn't bother with it.'

'I'm going to look inside the cellar if it's the last thing I bloody well do. And you'd better help me, or you'll be sorry.'

Cuthbert didn't argue any more. When Sam got that tone in his voice, it was best to do things his way. 'All right, all right. I'll break open that fancy lock for you. I'm good at puzzles, always have been, and I quite fancy having a go at it. We'll take a quick look inside the cellar but if there are any problems, any problems at all, we'll leave it be. Any road, for all we know, that Mayne Esher may have filled in the entrance to the cellar for safety.'

Sam shook his head stubbornly. 'He's not daft. He's short of money so he'll want to see what's inside, just in case. And so do I.'

'Well, don't wait too long. I'm eager to leave Rivenshaw. I'm going when you do.'

'It might be easier for us to escape one at a time.'

'No. We go together.'

'You don't need to rush. They don't suspect you of being involved. Everyone was captured and arrested last time we tried to get our stuff except you. You were damn lucky to get away.'

'It wasn't luck. I was careful, had an escape route planned for every step of the way. That's why I don't like the idea of going down to that secret cellar under the Nissen hut. If they came after us, we'd be trapped down there, with no other way of getting out.'

'Ah, stop worrying. We'll both be doubly careful this time and do the thing quietly. They won't even know we're there.'

Cuthbert gave in. 'Next time I'll take the right tools with me and get them padlocks on the outer door open easily. I'll close 'em again once you're inside and you can open a window down the other end of the hut to let me in. We can get out through the window, too, once it's unlocked and them padlocks won't look as if they've been touched.'

'Good idea.'

Cuthbert was silent for a moment or two, then admitted, 'Actually, if it weren't for the risk we're taking, I'd be looking forward to having a go at that puzzle lock. Mr Reston is afraid of tackling it, but I'm not.'

He chuckled. 'Reston let slip a couple of days ago that Esher has found the key to the cellar. He gave it to him to check against some pictures in his old books. Reston made a copy of the key while he was at it, without telling them. I know where he's put it so I'll make my own copy one day when he's out.'

'What are you worrying about the puzzle lock for, if you have the key?'

'It's not just a key that's needed. There's a special way of using it. Do it wrongly and the door slams shut. Reston reckons Esher's ancestors will have hid the instructions for using it somewhere and old Mr Esher at the Dower House is having a good old look round. If anyone can find them instructions, that one can.'

'That all sounds promising, then.'

'It is. I'm turning into quite an actor these days. You should hear how excited I get when Mr Reston tells me about puzzle locks. Though not nearly as excited as him. He's got a bee in his bonnet about that lock.'

'Well, keep fooling him. I'll have an Army lorry waiting just outside town on the night we choose to break in.'

'Are you sure you can manage to get one?'

Sam laughed. 'Oh, yes. They're easy enough to pinch these days. There are lines of 'em parked in depots all over the county, now that they're not being destroyed and replaced all the time. The police won't look twice at me if I'm dressed as an officer and driving an Army lorry.'

'You, an officer! And pigs might fly.'

'I only have to *look* like one. I won't be the only officer what doesn't talk posh, after all. They promoted a lot of ordinary fellows during the war.'

They were both silent for a few moments, then Cuthbert sighed. 'I'd better be going home now. I don't want *her* waking up and screeching because I'm not there.'

Sam hated the thought of more long hours spent on his own. 'Aw, you can stay for a bit longer.'

'Well, just a few more minutes.'

'You're quite sure they haven't found that other entrance to the main cellars in the big house? We'll be best getting in that way.'

'I'd have heard from Reston if they had. After all, it was only by sheer chance we found it when we were on manoeuvres here.'

Sam sought for a way to keep his friend with him. 'Let's go over it all one last time, every last bloody detail. This time it's got to be foolproof. I'm not going back inside again.'

'Was it bad in prison?'

'Aye. It was. But I managed to hold my own. You had to be tough, though. And I do *not* like being locked up. I had a bit of a fainting fit the first time they shut me in a cell. I felt such a fool.'

They went over the basic plan again, step by step. But when the town hall clock struck two, Cuthbert stood up and said firmly, 'I really do have to get back now.'

Sam watched him go, then paced to and fro across the kitchen, sighing. He was sick of waiting around. He'd hated being in the Army, had waited all through the war for the fighting to end so that he could get his own life back.

He was waiting for Cuthbert now, because he wouldn't be able to open that stupid puzzle lock himself. Once Cuthbert had played his part, Sam would be out of Rivenshaw so fast, they'd never have a chance to catch him.

Tomorrow night, Sam intended to take a big risk. He'd leave Rivenshaw and go into Manchester. There was a fellow he knew who'd be able to get hold of an officer's uniform. And on the way back he'd pinch an Army lorry.

Things were coming together. The waiting was nearly over now.

Just be patient for a bit longer, lad! he told himself and as a yawn caught him out, he went reluctantly back to his hiding place in the attic, to dream of what he'd do with all that money and what it'd be like in Australia. He'd read a book about it, seen the pictures. Sunny all the time, it was there.

Mayne found that he was unable to see Councillor Faulkner to find out what the real situation was with Esherwood. The woman at the front desk at the town hall even refused to make an appointment for him to see the man later. She said Mr Faulkner was too busy just now and had told them not to make appointments.

The shop assistant at Faulkner's haberdashery looked embarrassed as she said the same thing. It seemed obvious they'd both been told to deny Mayne access to Faulkner. It was no use sounding off at her, she was only doing as ordered, so he left.

When he turned round in the street to look at the building in which Faulkner's shop was located, he thought he saw a face at the window of the office, which was above the shop. It was a man's face with a bald head and rather large ears. Faulkner, without a doubt.

Now there were two bad 'uns on the council, Faulkner and Draper. What was the world coming to?

After a moment or two's hesitation, he decided to call on Ray and ask his advice.

In great contrast to his reception elsewhere, the cheerful elderly maid he'd met before opened the front door and greeted him with a smile. She showed Mayne straight into Ray's big, comfortable office.

His secretary began gathering up her papers. 'I'll leave you gentlemen to chat and I'll get on with typing these letters in the other office. Would you like a pot of tea sending in, Mr Woollard?'

'Good idea, Jen.' He quirked one eyebrow at Mayne. 'Thirsty?'

'I could murder a cup of tea. Where's Stephanie?'

Ray explained about her trip to London. 'Unfortunately the POWs' arrival was delayed, so she's hanging about there waiting to hear. At least she's managed to get herself listed as the next of kin, the one who'll be caring for her fiancé.'

'She'll be in for a shock. I've seen the photos.'

'So has she. But she's not a weakling and she loves Anthony dearly, so if anyone can cope, it's her.'

While they waited for the tea, Mayne explained how he'd been treated that morning, unable to conceal his indignation and concern.

'They'll know they can't keep you at arm's length for ever,' Ray said thoughtfully. 'So it's my guess they're planning an early move on your property. We have to be ready for them, Mayne lad, whatever it takes, or they'll win hands down.'

'You mean . . . you think they'll just turn up and start building without having taken the necessary legal steps to obtain my land?'

'Yes. And once they make a start, you'll never get rid of them, because in times of housing shortages, no one's going to make people pull houses down, especially if they're offering the owner compensation for the land.'

He nodded. It made sense.

There was a knock on the door and the maid brought in a tea tray, leaving them to pour for themselves.

By the time Mayne had taken a sip or two of some very excellent tea, he was starting to calm down a little. 'I think I should pull out some of my wartime skills,' he said abruptly. 'Though I swore I'd never get involved in deception and cheating once I was demobbed. I'd had a bellyful of it during the war. It was one of the things my team specialised in.'

'Sometimes you need to use whatever weapons you have to prevent people cheating you. I don't know what exactly you four did during the last year of the war, but I gather it was very hush-hush.'

'So hush-hush that we've had to sign the Official Secrets Act and I daren't even tell Judith the details. But it helped the war effort.'

'Bletchley Park?'

Mayne looked at him in shock. 'How did you know?'

'I didn't *know* but I guessed. I, um, supplied items to people there from time to time, for which I too had to sign the Official Secrets Act, items that couldn't be got hold of easily but I'm proud to say that I managed it in the given timeframe.'

He held up one hand. 'And I only charged costs for the expensive items. I paid for some of the cheaper ones myself. I might have been too old to fight for my country, and I might have been working on the black market, but I did what I could.'

Mayne was looking at him with a wry smile. 'I think I've misjudged you in several ways.'

Ray shrugged. 'That's good, really. It means secrets are being kept by all concerned. We'll say no more about that. We need to start working out some way of protecting your land till we can deal with it legally and officially.'

'But how?'

'First, we'll build a gate at the back. Very off-putting a gate, to council workmen especially. I know a couple of fellows who'll make you one quickly. You said you had some wood.'

'We do. We locked every piece we salvaged in the outhouses and old stables, big stuff and small. There's some good solid stuff that will make a strong gate.'

'Great. I'll get in touch with my chaps as soon as you leave. And what if I could get hold of some heavy duty barbed wire? I know someone in Army stores. Would you be prepared to lay it outside and on top of your rear wall?'

Mayne didn't hesitate. 'Yes. And what if I put up signs warning people about hidden obstacles being in place along the perimeter? We could say they were put in during the war. I have enough friends in this town for people to agree that it happened, if I ask them to.'

'Obstacles such as?'

'Whatever we care to invent. Concrete block, rocks, hard stuff that would damage machinery if they tried to use a mechanical digger. Stick a corner of a rock out of the ground and you can arrange it to look like it's part of a bigger rock, the sort vehicles avoid. We want to make them reluctant to try to enter forcibly.'

Ray let out a hearty bellow of laughter. 'I'd like to see that happening.' He drank his tea, poured himself another cup and offered his guest a scone.

Mayne accepted one.

'Take two, lad, then go and sort out the wood for that gate. I'll bring my two carpenters round later, if that's all right with you. They'll drop what they're doing if I ask them, especially if it's for you. You're well liked in this town. People don't forget past kindnesses and favours.'

Mayne flushed slightly and didn't reply to that, but it made him feel good.

Mayne walked home briskly, feeling far more hopeful. He approached his land from the rear, wanting to study the lay of the land. At the house he found a message waiting for him from his father, asking him to go to the Dower House as soon as he could. The word URGENT was written in capitals and underlined.

He looked at Judith. 'What's this about? Did Dad give you any idea? Has he found something?'

'He refused to explain, but he seemed very excited. I've never seen him quite like it. I'm hoping he's found the instructions for the puzzle lock.'

'That would be too much to hope for.' He sighed. 'I think I'd better go down and see Dad. He wouldn't get that excited for nothing. But first, let me tell you what happened today, then I'll ask Victor to sort out some wood for me.'

Reginald started in shock as Mayne came into his study at the Dower House. He hadn't even heard him come up the stairs, he'd been so lost in his reading. 'Ah, there you are at last, son. I need you to get all your friends on to this.'

'On to what exactly?'

'Finding the next volume in this series. There are books everywhere, here and at the big house, and it'll take weeks if I have to hunt for it myself. It's really important and—' He stopped to gasp for breath.

'Slow down and explain what's going on, Dad.'

'Oh, yes. Sorry. I found a clue about the puzzle lock but the actual instructions for opening it are in the next diary, only that's missing. It must have got packed in another box. So we need to find it as quickly as we can.'

'We'll have to do that later. I'm a bit busy stopping the council men knocking down the rear wall of Esherwood and building on the back area of land: not just the strip I told you about, but everything up to the outbuildings and the Nissen hut they erected during the war.'

Reginald looked at him in horror. 'They can't do that! The entrance to the secret cellar is under that Nissen hut and the cellar is probably somewhere behind it, so they may destroy it.'

'I know. But I doubt the officious fellow now in charge of the Planning and Building section of the council will care two hoots about that. Thompson is determined to seize our land and erect fifty prefabs to show what a wonderful fellow he is at getting things done.'

'He must be stopped.'

'Exactly. So your cellar will have to wait.'

His father got a stubborn look on his face. 'I'm not having that. If I hire some people to go through the books, will you pay them?'

'How much?'

His father looked bewildered, then brightened. 'Mrs Rennie will know. She says she knows people eager for work of any kind. Demobbed soldiers who can't get their old jobs back and women who've been widowed. She says she can find me as many as I need, and they'll be people she trusts.'

'I'll talk to her on the way out. I'll pay for a few days' work.' It'd be worth it to stop his father pestering him.

'Good. I knew you'd be able to sort it out. Now, I have to finish searching through the books in my office and then start on the ones in the attics here. And those are all packed in sealed boxes. Oh dear, and I mustn't get them muddled up. I do need help with this.'

Mayne left his father muttering to himself and went to find the housekeeper.

Mrs Rennie talked a lot more practically about the quest to find the next book, explaining it more clearly than his father had. They agreed that Mayne would pay three people for a week. It'd keep his father quiet – and Ray Woollard too.

But he didn't feel optimistic about the outcome.

10

Jimmy whistled as he walked along the street, pleased to have caught a sunny period between showers. He enjoyed his new job working for a lawyer, and his mum was really happy that he'd got a foot in the door there, but sometimes he missed being out in the fresh air.

Today Mr Stackpole had sent him to see if he could find out where Miss Summers was staying without being too obvious about it. It was just like the detective stories he loved to read. He squared his shoulders as he walked along, taking bigger strides and imagining himself to be following in the footsteps of Hercule Poirot or Albert Campion. Today he would think of himself as James Clark, private detective, not Jimmy Clark, office boy.

His mother had known Miss Summers and Mrs Pelling well enough to speak kindly of the young woman with her sad past. Because of that, he'd got permission from the clerk to ask his mother's advice about his search. Together they'd made a list of boarding houses in the town. She said he could tell people he'd come on her behalf and pretend she had two books belonging to Miss Summers that she wanted to return.

He drew a blank at the first few boarding houses. Because they knew his mother, the owners were polite to him, but they all said they hadn't had a spare room for weeks, what with demobbed soldiers coming back and families who'd been bombed out in London looking for somewhere to live in the north. They didn't even bother to ask the names of most people who knocked on their doors looking for rooms.

He went back at midday to report his failure to the head clerk.

'Oh, dear. Have you got some other places to try, Jimmy?'

'Yes, Mr Stackpole, but only a few.'

'Then go home for your dinner and carry on asking around this afternoon.'

About three o'clock, just as Jimmy was nearing the end of his list, a woman said, 'I do remember her. But I was glad I hadn't taken her in once I found out about her past. Your mother should be more careful whose books she borrows in future.'

'Found out what, Mrs Tosley? I'd, er, better warn Mum.'

'That young woman was a German and I don't know how she'd wheedled her way into a decent British family, but she wouldn't get into my house, not after what they did to my husband.'

He was shocked at the vehemence in her tone. 'Who told you she was German?'

'Mrs Pelling's niece, and she should know, shouldn't she? She was very upset about her aunt taking that young woman in.'

'My mother says that when Mrs Pelling grew frail Miss Summers looked after her as if she were her real daughter.'

The landlady frowned. 'Your mother said that?'

'Yes, and she knew the Pelling family. She said the niece never once visited the old lady, let alone helped her, so how would Mrs Grayton know anything about Miss Summers?'

A man spoke from behind her. 'I told you not to believe that woman, Mary. I didn't take to her at all. Spite, that's all it was. Just spite. You could see it in her face.'

The man must be an ex-soldier, because he had lost an arm and his unused shirt sleeve was pinned neatly up against his chest. This explained his wife's hatred of Germans, Jimmy guessed.

Mr Tosley continued, 'I'll walk along the street with you, lad. I'm just going out to stretch my legs and it'll be nice to have a bit of company.'

Jimmy guessed he had something to tell him. This was all very exciting. It really was detective work.

Once they were away from the house, Mr Tosley said, 'I've seen you around, delivering messages and doing little jobs during the war, haven't I?'

'Yes, Mr Tosley. I started when I was twelve, because we were only at school half-time and I had a bicycle. But I'm working at Audley's now that I'm not needed. I won't be eighteen till next year, you see, so I don't have to go into the Army yet. I'm the office boy and it's a big chance for me, Mum says, because if I work hard, I can get to be a lawyer's clerk like Mr Stackpole.'

'Good for you.' Mr Tosley looked sideways at him and added, 'Is this really about your mother returning some books?'

Jimmy could feel himself flushing and didn't know what to say.

'That lawyer of yours is looking for that nice lass, isn't he?'

'Yes, but please don't tell anyone, Mr Tosley.'

'I'm not a gossip. But tell me one thing: Miss Summers hasn't done anything wrong, has she?'

'No, she hasn't. She's well thought of by most people. Mr Audley is trying to *help* her.'

'You might ask at the Park Hotel, then. I did hear that Miss Summers stayed there for one night. I hear a lot of things while I'm out job hunting.'

Jimmy sighed. 'Mrs Salter at the hotel wouldn't talk to me. She's a bit, um . . .'

'I know. Sharp-tongued. How about I ask her for you? I don't like to think of that lass needing help. I've seen her with Mrs Pelling. She has a nice, kind face.' He winked at Jimmy. 'You wait for me down the street and leave Mrs Salter to me.'

'You won't tell anyone else about this? Mr Stackpole would go mad at me.'

'No. I won't tell anyone. I wouldn't like to mess up your big chance in life.' He glanced down at his missing arm as he spoke and sighed.

The Park Hotel always looked unwelcoming to Jimmy. At this time of day, the front door was locked and the blinds pulled down over most of the windows. Mr Tosley had to ring a bell to get inside.

Jimmy went to stand behind the post box further down the street and wait for his unexpected ally to come out again.

It was only a few minutes before Mr Tosley appeared and he looked so angry, Jimmy's heart sank. What had Mrs Salter said to him?

Mr Tosley marched along the street and said abruptly, 'Get moving. I'm coming back to your office with you to tell Mr Stackpole about it myself. *That woman* is even nastier than I'd remembered. She wants to watch out or she'll cut herself with that tongue of hers, saying such vicious things about people.'

'You'll get me in trouble if you tell Mr Stackpole. I wasn't supposed to let anyone know what I was doing, except for Mum.'

'Don't worry. I'll make sure Mr Stackpole understands that I *guessed* what was going on.'

He did this so well that the head clerk offered Mr Tosley

a seat, listened intently and then told Jimmy to make them all a cup of tea because it looked like rain was setting in again. 'I'll just have a word with Mr Audley about what to do next if you can spare the time to wait, Mr Tosley.'

'Call me Barry. Most people do.'

'Barry, then.'

'I can spare as much time as you need, Mr Stackpole. I've not had much luck finding any work with this.' He jerked his head towards his missing arm.

'Does it impede you much?'

'Well, it does and it doesn't. There's no denying it makes some jobs difficult, but luckily it was my left arm so I can still write and do smaller jobs without much trouble.'

'I daresay you can lift a cup to your mouth easily enough too, can't you, Barry?'

Jimmy stared. It was rare that Mr Stackpole made a joke but he seemed to like Mr Tosley and the two men were smiling at one another.

'I can indeed, Mr Stackpole.'

When he came back from speaking to his employer, the clerk asked Mr Tosley to come and tell the lawyer what Mrs Salter at the hotel had been saying about Miss Summers, and who had started the rumours.

After a moment's hesitation, he said to Jimmy, 'You'd better come and hear this, too, lad. Stand just inside the door and don't interrupt unless you have something important to say.'

Mr Audley looked horrified as his visitor told him of the terrible gossip being spread about Miss Summers.

'And,' Mr Tosley ended up, 'Mrs Grayton has even hinted that the young lady must have got into bed with Mr O'Brien in order to find another protector so quickly.'

'Slander, that is,' Mr Audley said. 'I shall have words with her, whether we find the missing will or not. I won't stand by and let a decent young woman be unfairly maligned. Did Mrs Salter know where Miss Summers had gone?'

'No. Only that she'd left town with Mr O'Brien and his widowed aunt. And she said good riddance to them all, Mr Audley.'

'His *widowed* aunt?' Mr Stackpole cleared his throat to gain their attention. 'If she's also called O'Brien, we may be able to find out where they went from our records here in the office, sir.'

'Really! How is that possible?'

'One of our customers, a Mr O'Brien, died a few months ago and his widow recently sold her house. We did the necessary legal work for the sale. There's bound to be a forwarding address. If it's the same woman, and *I* haven't met any other O'Briens in our little town . . .'

Mr Audley beamed at him. 'What a lucky coincidence!' He turned back to Mr Tosley. 'I'm sure if you go and wait in the outer office, Jimmy here can give you a fresh cup of tea.'

'See to it, lad,' the clerk said quietly. 'I'll join you in a few minutes. I just need to have a word with Mr Audley about another matter, then I want to ask Mr Tosley something.'

When they'd gone, he said, 'I wonder, sir, if you'd consider employing Barry Tosley in the office? We're going to need some more help once your son is demobbed and comes back to work. These office lads can be very chancy sometimes, plus they have to go off into the armed forces when they're eighteen, so we have to keep training new ones.'

He seemed to be talking to himself when he added, 'I wonder how long this national service is going to go on for?' After a moment's pause, he added, 'Not that Jimmy has been anything but reliable. He's one of the better lads, that one is. I'd welcome him back again after he comes out of the forces. However, a nice stable, older clerk – and Tosley is likely to stay with us for obvious reasons – might make a useful addition to our staff. I know the family. The Tosleys are decent folk.'

His employer smiled. 'And if I say no?'

Mr Stackpole's smile grew even broader. 'I doubt you'll do that, sir. You're as grateful to those who've made sacrifices for us during the war as I am.'

'Make any arrangements you like about Tosley. I trust you implicitly to judge whether he can do the work or not.'

Back in the outer office, Mr Stackpole accepted another cup of tea from Jimmy and whispered to the lad to get himself a refill and take it into the storeroom. 'I need a few moments' privacy with Mr Tosley.'

When the two men were alone, he waited till his guest had put down his cup and asked, 'Are you still looking for a job, Barry lad?'

'Yes. I'll not stop looking, neither, not if I drop down dead still trying, I won't. But the more men who get demobbed, the more there are applying for each job that comes vacant, so it gets harder all the time. If you ever hear of anything . . .'

'We're looking for a man here, actually.'

Barry had picked up his cup again, but as the implications of this sank in, his hand began to tremble and he dumped the cup down abruptly in the saucer, sending splashes of hot tea across the desk. He snatched his hand back, hiding its trembling in his lap.

'Does that mean . . .' He couldn't finish.

'It means we'll give you a try for a week or so, see how we all get on. We don't pay high wages, just average. Three pounds a week to start with, and it'll go up to three pounds ten shillings, once you know the job. Higher later when you're fully trained. And once Mr Audley learns to value your work, you can have a job for life because his son is getting demobbed soon, and he's a lawyer too. You couldn't find a more considerate employer.'

It was no use. Barry couldn't stop the tears from pouring out as he said in a husky voice, 'I'll work hard, I promise. You won't regret this, Mr Stackpole. I have ways of coping with only one hand and I'll figure out others when I see what's needed. I'm clever that way and my friend makes me little gadgets to help.'

'Then you can start tomorrow. I'll just, er, go and find Jimmy.'

He went into the storeroom, leaving the poor young man to recover in private. He could see that Jimmy had been listening in, so said severely, 'Not a word to anyone about this. Mr Tosley lost his arm in the service of this country and in my book that makes him worth twice as much as a man who just shoved papers around during the war.'

'I should think so, too!'

'Good. Now, lad, see if you can find your way around our filing system and get out the papers about the sale of Mrs O'Brien's house.'

He went to the storeroom door and peeped into the office, relieved to see that Barry was looking more in control of himself.

As he went to join him, he said briskly, 'I'm glad that's settled. We've been needing more help. I'll get young Jimmy to sort out a desk for you, and you can have a think how you'll manage with the papers.'

'Yes, Mr Stackpole. The teacher always said I wrote a neat hand. I still do. And I'm good at figures as well.'

'Good, good. Go home now and tell your wife you've got a chance of a permanent job. I'm sure she'll be pleased for you.'

'She'll be over the moon. I can't thank you enough.'

'And give my regards to your father when you see him.'

'I will, sir.'

'Oh, just a moment. Do you have a dark suit and a white shirt?'

Barry looked at him in dismay. 'Only my demob suit. Horrible stripy thing, it is! Most of them are like that. Everyone can tell them a mile off and you wouldn't wear one unless you had to. Sorry, but it's all I've got. I'll save up money and my clothing points for a better suit if I get the job, I promise.'

'There's no shame to wearing a demob suit. None at all.' Mr Stackpole held up one hand to stem more gratitude. 'Now, I must get on. I'll expect you at nine o'clock sharp tomorrow.'

He made up for his softness by being especially stern with young Jimmy for the rest of the afternoon, but he had to give praise where praise was due when Jimmy quickly found the files about the sale of Mrs O'Brien's house. That lady had gone to a new address in a small town called Rivenshaw, it seemed.

Unfortunately, he couldn't be sure that this woman was related to the Mr O'Brien who had taken Miss Summers away, even though it seemed likely. But if they turned out to be the same people, Mr Stackpole would have bet five whole pounds, and he was not a betting man, that Miss Summers had gone there with the lady and not as the paramour of this Mr Daniel O'Brien.

Mr Audley had asked to be reminded to draft a letter to Mrs O'Brien the following day. Which Mr Stackpole wouldn't forget to do. He didn't know when he'd felt so angry about what that spiteful Grayton woman was doing. He hated gossipmongers, had once been the target of them himself.

Christa slipped outside as the children started to clear up after the evening meal. Everyone at Esherwood seemed to have someone to spend time with but she felt very alone when the day's work was done.

She had no relatives now, no one in the world who belonged to her. And though these people had been very kind to her, three of the four partners in the building company were recently married and still at the love bird stage. This was lovely to see, but it only emphasised her own position.

Daniel was part of the team and had known the other men for years. She'd been surprised to hear that he was divorced. When someone had mentioned that, he'd gone very tight-lipped, as if it upset him. Could he still be in love with his former wife? Surely not!

Tonight everyone had been more serious than usual, discussing how to stop this Thompson person from sending in the council bulldozer and workmen to start clearing the land.

As she stood near the back door watching the moon rising, a man approached the house from the rear, walking quietly along the uneven drive, and glancing over his shoulder as if he didn't want anyone to see or hear him. She stiffened, worried that this might be an intruder.

She was wondering whether to run inside and warn the others when he saw her. He stopped and took off his cap, nodding politely. She could see now that he was an older man with a lined, worried face. He didn't seem like someone to be afraid of, unless she was much mistaken. Anyway she was close enough to the kitchen to call for help if she needed to.

He came a little closer and stopped again, asking in a low voice, 'Is Mr Esher around, love? I've got an urgent message for him.'

'I'll go and find him.'

'I'll wait in the shadow over there, if you don't mind. The fewer people who see me here tonight, the better.'

'Oh. All right.'

No one was in the kitchen now except Kitty, who had finished her chores and was sitting close to the fire reading. Christa could hear Gillian and Ben working in the scullery, and see little Betty carefully carrying some plates across to the crockery shelves there.

'Do you know where your father is?' Christa asked. 'There's a man outside with an urgent message for him.'

'I'll go and tell Dad. I know where he'll be.' Kitty ran out of the room, trailing the last few words behind her.

Christa went outside again and joined the man. 'Mayne won't be long. One of the children has gone to fetch him. Run actually.' She smiled. 'They're always full of energy.'

'I'd love to be young and carefree again,' the man said wistfully.

'So would I.'

'Eh, you are young, lass.'

But not carefree, she thought. Not for a very long time.

Before she could say anything else, she heard footsteps from inside the house and the outer door opened.

Mayne came across to join them, nodding to her but looking at the man. 'You have a message for me? Dennis, isn't it?'

'Aye. Mr Woollard said I should tell you myself, Mr Esher. I wasn't here tonight, think on, because it's as much as my job's worth if that new chap at the council finds out I spoke to you.'

'I won't say a word about your involvement.'

'Thank you. It's just, well, I can't bear the way they're doing this. It's not fair, and after you fighting for us in the war, too. That Thompson was only in charge of stores somewhere in Scotland, never even left the country.'

'Was he now? How do you know that?'

'My cousin served under him. Said he was a lazy sod, never lifted a finger himself but took all the credit for the work done and was a right old yes-man, so got hissen promoted even though he didn't deserve it.'

Mayne made a mental note of that. 'Well, thank you for taking the risk and coming here to see me. Who are "they" and what exactly are they planning?'

'As I telled Mr Woollard, when I heard he'd been asking around, them from the council have let Thompson arrange to start work at the back of your house tomorrow as soon as it's light.'

'How do you know that, if you don't mind me asking?'

'I reckon he's a bit deaf because he allus talks in a loud voice. Me an' my mates keep our ears peeled so that we know what he's up to. We don't want to be caught out doing something that upsets him and get sacked like poor old Walter was. Nasty piece of work, that Thompson is.'

'I see. So what exactly is he intending to do?'

'He's planning to take you by surprise, like, and start clearing the land without your permission, just barge in the back way and start knocking the trees and bushes down. Even if we hadn't overheard him talking, we'd know something was up, because we had to get the equipment ready this afternoon and were told to be at the depot by seven o'clock in the morning. Seven o'clock! What kind of a starting time is that for an honest day's work? It's not even light then at this time of year.' He waited, looking anxious.

Mayne closed his eyes for a moment as the ramifications of this sank in. 'Oh, damnation! And we've not finished our first-stage preparations yet. We haven't even got a gate to stop them coming on to Esherwood land.'

'Mr Woollard said he'd send someone tonight to finish the gate and I'm to tell you the other stuff you wanted will be delivered in an hour or so.' He held up one hand. 'Don't tell me what that is. Better if I look surprised tomorrow.'

'Very well.'

'Mr Woollard said if you and your folk can work all night, he thinks you'll get enough finished to keep them out, at least for tomorrow, and then you can bring in the lawyers. He'll find one for you during the night if he has to go and hammer on someone's door.'

He added with a grin, 'Not that I'll know anything about all that, mind. I shall go home now and take over in my workshop. The wife's put the light on out there and she's inside pottering around, wearing my old cap and jacket, keeping her face away from the window, so that the neighbours think I'm out there.'

'Thank you for doing this and please thank your wife as well.' Mayne shook the man's hand.

'I hope you win, Mester Esher. We all do.'

Mayne smiled as he turned away because the word 'Mester' had been spoken in a broad Lancashire accent that reminded him of his boyhood. But his smile faded quickly. Could he do it, keep them out? He had to.

Christa had been standing to one side and hadn't been able to help overhearing what they'd been saying. As soon as the man had gone, she said, 'If there's anything I can do to help tonight, you only have to ask. I'm stronger than I look.'

'Thank you, yes. I think everyone here will pitch in and I'll be grateful for your help. Come over to the house and we'll get the others together to start planning who does what. It's going to be a sleepless night, I'm afraid.'

He looked up at the sky. 'Thank goodness the clouds have passed and the moon will be shining for a good part of the night. Third quarter moon only, but even that much light will be a help, because we don't want to use electric lights where people can see us. It's not detailed work, thank goodness, just rough work along the back edge.'

'You can't work without making a noise, so the neighbours are bound to hear you,' she pointed out.

'Well, let's just hope people nearby don't go running to the police.'

'If anyone comes to see what's going on, we could tell them it's a burst water main being repaired,' she suggested. 'My father did that once when he wanted to keep watch on what some Nazis were doing. He started digging up the street openly and no one tried to stop him.'

'Excellent idea.' He looked round. 'Would you mind standing outside the kitchen door while I talk to the others and making sure no one else approaches the house? I'll leave the door open, so you'll be able to hear what we say inside, but you know most of it already.'

'As I said, I'm happy to do anything you need.'

As she stood waiting for the others to assemble in the kitchen, Daniel came out to see her. He too stared at her, but his expression was different from Mayne's. He was looking at her the way a man did when he liked a woman in that special way. She hoped she wasn't reading the situation incorrectly. Perhaps he didn't want his wife back.

He took her hand. 'I can tell you worry about being an outsider here, but after tonight, you'll be fully one of us, Christa. Baptism of fire, eh?'

He drew her towards him and surprised her by kissing her cheek, his lips lingering there, soft, warm, comforting. '*I* haven't thought of you as an outsider since we travelled here to Rivenshaw together. Nor has my aunt.'

She was sorry when he moved away, but the warmth of that kiss seemed to linger on her cheek. What he'd said made her feel hopeful that she was reading the situation accurately. She certainly felt attracted to Daniel O'Brien. Very attracted.

The kiss gave her hope that perhaps . . . just perhaps . . . he might be learning to care for her.

Was that possible? Oh, she did hope it was.

11

The carpenters arrived at the back door and continued the work they'd begun on the gate, which had been partially assembled but not completed. They grumbled about the difficulties of working by lantern light and warned Mayne that it wouldn't be neat work.

Luckily the other planks had already been cut to size and were lying ready in one of the former stables behind the big house, so he could leave them to it.

Steve Rennie appeared in the stable yard just as Mayne was about to leave for the rear entrance to await delivery of the barbed wire. 'Ben said you wanted to see me, Mr Esher.'

'Yes, I do. Thanks for coming. I know it's late but I desperately need your help.'

When he explained what was happening, Steve said at once, 'You know I'll do what I can, Mr Esher.'

Mayne clapped him on the shoulder. 'Good man. I'm grateful. Now, what I particularly want is someone to keep an eye on the grounds at the front of the house, to make sure no one is creeping in that way.'

'Me an' Nellie can do that.'

'I'll give you young Ben and his trusty bicycle to act as a messenger boy and fetch me if I'm needed. Perhaps you could park my car across the drive? And can you drag that chain across and lock it in place?'

Steve chuckled. 'It'd be my pleasure.'

'You might get into trouble with the law.'

'You gave me and my wife a home. If I can help you keep yours, I will. You stop Thompson getting in the back way and we'll keep him out of the front drive.'

'Thank you.'

He grinned. 'What's more, if anyone tries to get in by force, my Nellie will send them off with a flea in their ear. When her temper is roused, she's afeared of no one, and she'd speak her mind to the devil himself.'

'I'd like to be a fly on the wall if she has to put Thompson in his place. Thank you, Steve. You seem to have it all figured out.'

'I fought in the Great War. I was a sergeant and I learned a thing or two about planning for confrontations, Mr Esher. I didn't manage to save all my lads, but I saved some of them.'

'I bet you did. Well, I'll leave the front entrance in your capable hands, then, and I'll send Ben back to join you.'

He found his stepson in the disused stables, watching the carpenters.

Ben straightened up and beamed at being given this task. 'I can do that.'

'I'm relying on you, son.'

'I won't let you down . . . Dad.'

It was the first time the boy had called him 'Dad' in that tone of voice and emotion clogged Mayne's throat for a moment or two.

Then he got back to his planning.

By the time Mayne reached the rear gateway again, a lorry had driven up and two men, their heads and faces covered by balaclavas to hide their identity, were unloading rolls of barbed wire.

He shone his torch briefly on the wire. It was rusty in parts and had obviously been salvaged from somewhere else, but it was the larger sort that could rip smaller tyres if you drove on it. He wasn't sure it'd keep the bigger vehicles out, but it'd slow them down, because new tyres were hard to get. You had to go on a waiting list unless they were for government services.

Anyway, how many big vehicles did the council have? Not many, he was sure. They'd have to take care of them, too, because you couldn't easily get replacements.

If he and his friends managed to dig a few strategically placed trenches and make it look as if there were objects buried there to stop people passing – something he'd done before with good effect – he reckoned they'd be able to keep people out of his grounds the next day and after that it'd be up to the law.

Ray Woollard had promised to find a lawyer for them, and he would do that, Mayne was sure. They'd learned to value and trust their fifth partner's word.

As the empty lorry drove away, he showed his helpers how to unravel the wire and lay it in position. 'Don't try to do this bare-handed,' he warned. 'Only the ones wearing these heavy leather gloves Woollard sent are to handle it.'

Yet another thoughtful touch from Ray, those gloves. The man had a brilliant understanding of the details needed to get all sorts of jobs done.

Mayne left the women and children in Victor's charge. They'd be able to do smaller jobs under his guidance. And if anyone could keep them from getting hurt as they worked, it was Victor, who had served under him as a sergeant for part of the war. Who knew better how to hold back youthful enthusiasm and replace it with both an understanding of a task and also some idea of how to do it safely?

When Mayne had been moved to a special project,

organised out of Bletchley Park, he had asked for Victor to be assigned to him, and his friend had proved invaluable in some very tricky, not to mention downright sneaky operations to fool the enemy.

Together they had built a team with an amazing collection of skills which had great, if secret, value to Britain.

Mayne realised his mind was wandering. Well, no wonder. By this hour he was usually in bed asleep. He straightened his shoulders, jogged on the spot and swung his arms about, breathing deeply. He must keep a better focus on this job, because it was now as vital to his personal life and happiness to keep the council men out, as it had been vital during the war for the nation to defeat the Germans.

And if it was selfish of him to think that way, well, he'd done his bit for his country and surely now he was entitled to do his best to keep his home?

He beckoned Daniel and Francis across. 'Right lads, let's make a start on the trenches. We have two wheelbarrows and a small handcart. We'll dump the soil we dig out from the trenches behind the wall, so that they can't use it to re-fill them.' He picked up a shovel and began digging.

'What sort of machinery does the council own?' Daniel asked Francis.

'Whatever they own, it's not well maintained. I was talking to a chap only last week who said their machines break down regularly and limp along in fits and starts at the best of times. They're a bit of a joke in the town. Held together by string and glue, people say.'

'Well, let's hope that will work in Esherwood's favour now. Come on. Mayne's getting ahead of us.'

Although they dug with a will, they had to take regular breaks from the work. And all the time, the moon was moving inexorably across the sky and the hours were ticking past – so few hours, so much to be done before dawn.

When Mayne saw three people coming along the street towards them, he stopped work for a moment, wondering who the hell they were.

The two girls and Christa came out of the shadows, where they were keeping watch on the nearby streets and stopped the new arrivals, talking earnestly.

One of the men chuckled, the sound floating clearly through the still night air. He gestured to the girls to move out of their way and they did, which surprised Mayne.

Mayne watched them approach, wondering what they were doing there. He and his friends didn't need interruptions. They desperately needed every minute of the night to put his plans into operation.

The figures turned out to be two men and a woman. They stopped in front of him, seeming familiar but they were outlined against the moon, so it was difficult to see them clearly and it would have been rude to shine his torch on their faces.

One of the men saluted him smartly. 'I've dug more trenches than you've had hot dinners, Mr Esher. I reckon I can get on with this more quickly than you. Give me that spade and I'll finish this one, then you can tell me where to dig next.'

'If someone finds me another spade, I'll help too,' the other man said.

'There's one here. We can take turns with it.' Daniel passed his spade over and used his forearm to wipe the sweat from his brow.

The woman was left on her own. 'I was in the Land Army, Mr Esher. I may not be as strong as a man, but I know how to dig.'

Mayne swallowed hard. 'I can't ask you to—'

'You didn't ask. We volunteered. Though we'd rather not be seen doing it, so we'll have to leave before daylight.'

She went across to Francis, who'd also been taking a break. 'I can spell you for a while.'

'I can't ask a woman to do this and—'

She smiled, her teeth showing pale against the darker tone of her skin, and took the shovel from him.

'You need to cover your faces.' Mayne beckoned to Kitty. 'Can you lay your hands on some scarves for our kind helpers?'

'I know where there are some. I'll go and fetch them.'

'Wait!' He grabbed her arm. 'You don't go anywhere on your own tonight. We have no idea whether anyone is sneaking round Esherwood and there aren't enough of us to guard the whole perimeter. Thank goodness there are houses with fenced gardens along the longer sides of the land. Thompson won't be able to get in that way, at least.'

He let go of Kitty's arm. 'Stay with your sister. I don't think you'll meet anyone who shouldn't be there, but if you do, no heroics. Just scream loudly and run for your lives. Don't even wait for each other. It's more important to warn us. We'll do any rescuing needed, though I don't think they'll bother with you.'

Both girls nodded solemnly.

'Off you go, then.'

The girls were back a few minutes later with scarves.

With the new helpers, the digging went on more quickly, with everyone taking turns and working furiously for as long as they could. Before long, trenches were in place behind the barbed wire near the weakest parts of the perimeter walls.

Jan arrived a short time later, not saying much, but helping the two men to hang the huge, heavy gates on the pillars that had been there for several hundred years.

'Al's at the front gateway helping the Rennies and someone called Tommy,' Jan said. 'That chain is heavy, but they've got it locked in place now. Thompson will have to saw through it to unblock the entrance, and it'll take more than an ordinary saw to cut heavy steel.'

Mayne was deeply touched by the help he was getting from folk in the town. He was a lucky chap to have grown up in Rivenshaw, damned lucky.

Judith waved across at him and he raised one hand briefly to the love of his life, warmed by her smile, then he went back to work.

He felt better now that the gates were fixed in place.

At six o'clock in the morning, Mayne sent the girls back to the house, refusing to let them get involved when the men from the council arrived. 'You ought to get some sleep. You're in no fit state to go to school today. I'll write a note tomorrow explaining your absence.'

When Kitty continued to protest that Ben was still helping and she could perfectly well carry on for a bit longer, her mother said sharply, 'Do as you're told.'

Mayne suddenly thought of something else that needed doing. 'Just a minute. When you get to the house, you can do a job for me. Make sure all the downstairs doors and windows are locked and kept locked. If you really can stay awake, you can watch for anyone trying to get into the house.'

Kitty beamed and gave him a salute, a proper one too. Like many children, boys and girls both, she must have practised that action during the war. Mayne didn't allow himself to smile as he returned the salute smartly.

But he lost any inclination to smile as he gathered the adults round him.

He turned first to the three townsfolk. He knew who they were, but hadn't let on. 'Thank you for your help. You've made a big difference. But you'd better get off home now. You don't want to be seen here.'

'No, sir. Glad to be of use.'

They gave back the scarves and slipped away through the last shadows of the night.

Mayne turned to his friends. 'Well, the council men will be here soon. I don't think we should go back to the house for a cup of tea, even though you must all be dying for one. Can you—'

'Mr Esher!'

He spun round.

Mrs O'Brien was carefully pushing along a rusty iron wheelbarrow containing what looked like a tea urn wrapped in a ragged piece of quilt. There was a lidded metal container, presumably of milk, a basket containing their tin mugs and the biscuit tin.

'I thought you'd be ready for a hot drink,' she said cheerfully. 'We carried hot drinks around this way when I was in the WVS serving in our mobile canteen. Lucky you had this wheelbarrow in the old stables, eh?'

'You're a lifesaver!' He gave her a big hug, which made her smile and pat his cheek in a motherly way.

Daniel came across to pass out the mugs of warm liquid as she ladled it out.

'Better drink up quickly,' Mayne warned them. 'I don't know exactly when they'll arrive, but I want to be ready to confront them.' He bit off half a biscuit as if to lead by example.

'Here.' Judith was by his side, pressing a mug into his hand.

He took it, automatically raising it to his lips and sighing with pleasure at the comforting warmth.

'I'm going to meet Thompson and his men outside the gates,' he said as he handed back the empty mug.

'We'll all stand outside the gates with you,' Francis said firmly. 'They need to see that they're not just dealing with one man.'

'If you're facing them, so am I, Francis Brady.'

Mayne was amused to see Diana stare at her husband, hands on hips, as if daring him to tell her not to stay with him. Since they'd got back together after their marital troubles, she'd changed a lot, and for the better.

But there was one way she hadn't changed. As usual, Francis's elegant wife had somehow managed to tidy herself up in spite of working hard physically, while his Judith had a smear of dirt on her forehead and her hair tied back any old how. Well, no woman had ever looked more beautiful to him than his wife. Being pretty was no substitute for character and hard work, as Diana had found out.

It wasn't yet seven o'clock, but it was getting light and he stiffened at the sound of a car approaching. 'Here we go!' he called.

As they went outside the gates, he moved to the front of his little group of supporters and waited, arms folded, until the car came close enough to identify who was in it.

12

To Mayne's surprise, no other vehicles were following this car. Then he realised it was not someone from the council. Ray got out of the front passenger seat and the stranger sitting in the back opened his own door.

The vehicle was being driven by Stephanie's temporary replacement, a man Mayne knew by sight but hadn't dealt with before. He sighed in relief though he knew the confrontation with Thompson was only postponed.

'Nice of you all to come out to meet us,' Ray joked. 'I see you've been doing a little gardening.'

'Just a little light digging,' Mayne agreed.

Although everyone had relaxed somewhat, they were still keeping an eye on the bumpy potholed road, expecting several council vehicles to turn up any minute and workmen pile out.

The stranger came to stand slightly behind Ray, giving the group a thoroughly assessing stare. Mayne looked him over equally carefully as he waited for their partner to explain who this was. The man seemed even older than Ray and was well-dressed with sparse silver hair, spectacles and an air of quiet confidence. The very way he stood said this was a person who would expect and get respect from those he dealt with.

Could this be the lawyer Ray had promised to find for them? Mayne very much hoped so. He'd much prefer to deal with this problem legally. Though how his partner could have found them a lawyer in the middle of the night, he couldn't think. The scene was like a sepia photograph, he thought, with no real colour in the landscape till the sun rose, and that added a sense of unreality to the scene.

Ray gestured to the gate, visible now in the pre-dawn light. 'Those lads did a good job on that. It looks really solid. I'll see they get a bonus.'

'Should be solid,' Mayne said. 'It's mainly oak. Some of those planks are well over a hundred years old, if not older. They've really hardened up. You should have heard your chaps cursing when they had to drill holes in them.'

Ray turned to the man behind him. 'Edward, let me introduce you to my good friends and partners in the Esher Building Company. Mayne, everyone, this is Edward Forrester. He's a lawyer specialising in civil and business matters. He's about to retire for a second time now that the war is over, but is going to take on a few cases now and then out of interest. He's agreed to represent our company.'

The two of them exchanged quick smiles.

Mayne moved forward and shook hands. 'I'm extremely glad to see you, Mr Forrester. We're expecting unwelcome company any minute now and I hope not to break the law, but I don't intend to let them on to my land without proper authorisation, as no doubt Ray has explained.'

'He did go over what's been happening. It sounds interesting and—'

Before the lawyer could say anything else, there was the sound of vehicles approaching, more than one it was clear, with heavy engines chugging loudly in the still early morning air. Everyone turned to watch them come to a halt.

'Well, those are nearly all the lorries and heavy vehicles the council owns,' Francis said. 'They've certainly come out in force.'

Forrester spoke in a rapid undertone. 'Say as little as you can, Esher, and if I signal to you to be quiet, please stop talking at once. Even when you do speak, keep what you say to the minimum. You want to give them every opportunity to put their foot in it, legally speaking.'

Mayne nodded, his eyes on the car at the head of the small group of vehicles. It was the large Wolseley Landaulette usually used by the mayor, but the mayor wasn't in it today. Instead, Thompson was sitting stiffly upright on his own in the back.

He told Forrester in an equally low voice, 'That fellow in the front car, acting like an arch-duke on parade, is Thompson. We think this – this *invasion* is his idea.'

'Sounds like it, from what Ray told me.' Forrester took a step backwards and waited.

Mayne scowled across at the big black car. He might not know Thompson well, but he'd known others like him during his Army career, and despised their arrogance and ruthless, cheating ways.

He glanced briefly at the other vehicles. He knew several of the people who were squashed into them. These chaps were ordinary council workers, some of whom he'd played with as a lad. Most of them were avoiding his eyes, looking embarrassed, as if they didn't want to be here.

He folded his arms and waited for Thompson to get out of the big car, making no attempt to move forward or speak. Let the fellow come to him.

The others stood quietly behind Mayne, taking their cue from him, watching and waiting for as long as it took.

Christa was still standing on her own behind them, looking uncertain. She hesitated and would have gone to join the end of the curved line of people, but Daniel gestured to her to squeeze in next to him, giving her a welcoming smile.

Minutes ticked by and Mayne continued to stand motionless.

At last Thompson seemed to realise that he had to take the first step, so got out and moved forward. 'Kindly open those gates and move out of our way, Esher,' he said loudly. 'As I've already informed you, the council is taking possession of this land in order to build much-needed houses for our brave soldiers returning from war.'

'Do you have the legal authority to requisition my land?' Mayne spoke more quietly, but his voice carried not only to everyone there, but to the people who had come out of the nearby houses to see what was bringing all these vehicles to the area so early in the morning.

Thompson flapped one hand dismissively. 'That's a mere formality. You'll be supplied with the paperwork in a week or two, as I also told you on my last visit.'

'I'm afraid you'll have to wait for the paperwork and legalities to be completed before you do anything. Until then, I can't allow you take over *my* land.'

'This matter is urgent and if you don't move out of our way, we'll have to force an entry.'

A hand on Mayne's arm stopped him responding and Edward Forrester stepped forward.

'I'm the lawyer representing Mr Esher and I have advised him, as I now advise you, to wait for the legalities to be sorted out before anyone tries to take this land. He is within his legal rights to keep his gates closed and locked until such time as that is done.'

Thompson's eyes flickered towards the walls, crumbling in parts. 'There are other ways on to the land.'

'If you're considering knocking down those walls, or any other structure belonging to my client, I must inform you that such an act could constitute malicious damage and we would definitely bring a suit against you for it.'

'I'm acting on behalf of the council.'

'You haven't produced any authority from them, so we would be bringing our suit against you personally.'

'Who the hell are you to tell me what to do, anyway?'

'Edward Forrester, from Manchester.'

Thompson mouthed the word 'Forrester' so clearly that he might as well have spoken it aloud. It was obvious from the sour expression on his face that he recognised the name, if not the man, and didn't welcome this intervention. 'I had been hoping that Mr Esher would not try to prevent us from doing this, if only out of sheer patriotism.'

'My client's patriotism is not in doubt, sir. And were his war service not covered by the Official Secrets Act, you would understand why. But *your* right to seize his land is very much in doubt. Now, if you'll call off your men, we can all get on with our day.'

Thompson looked beyond him to Mayne. 'I'm not going anywhere. I shall give you a few minutes to reconsider, Esher, then I shall order my men to act. And if you think that flimsy barbed wire is going to keep us out, you can think again.'

Mayne managed to keep his voice even, though he was feeling a desperate urge to punch Thompson in the face. 'The barbed wire is there for the safety of you and your men. There are obstacles along the outside of this wall, not to mention trenches and pits which could be dangerous for your vehicles. Esherwood was requisitioned during the war and the Army left a lot of debris and earthworks, some of which still need to be cleared and levelled. I wouldn't like to see any of your men get injured.'

Thompson seemed to puff up with rage. 'That barbed wire was not there before, sir.'

'Of course not. I wasn't afraid for anyone's safety until today.'

Again a touch of a hand on his arm prevented him from embellishing this statement.

'You will hear from the council's lawyer, Esher.'

'You should get him to address any correspondence to me, Mr Thompson,' Forrester put in. 'As I've already told you, I'm acting on behalf of the Esher Building Company.'

'It's *Captain Thompson*!' he corrected automatically.

'We don't recognise temporary wartime ranks in peacetime, sir.' Forrester moved forward. 'Here is my card. Remember, the council's lawyers should contact *me*, not Mr Esher.'

'They will do no such thing.' Thompson flicked away the card and it fluttered to the ground.

Forrester shook his head with a pained expression, took out his notebook and began to write in it.

Even in the dim light of a cloudy morning they could see Thompson's face go dark red with anger. 'What the hell are you writing?'

'I'm noting down your injudicious remarks verbatim, sir, in case I need to refer to them in court. I shall then get two impartial bystanders to witness them.'

'There are no impartial bystanders in a small town like this!' Thompson snapped.

A man moved forward from behind the council vehicles. 'I think I'd count as impartial. I'm one of the new teachers at the boys' grammar school, recently demobbed, and I only arrived in Rivenshaw last week. I've never met Mr Esher, though I knew someone of that name owned Esherwood, of course.'

'I don't believe you. They must have got at you already.'

'I don't tell lies about important matters and I resent your remark.' He turned to Mr Forrester. 'I'm at your service, sir.'

'Could I have your name and address, sir? Perhaps you'd write it down for me.'

'Happy to. Like Mr Esher, I fought for this country's freedom and this doesn't look like a fair or democratic action to me.'

A woman walked forward to join them. 'I'm here visiting my sister, so I'm not involved in Rivenshaw matters, either. But I too did my bit in this war, and I don't believe in dictatorships, so would be happy to act as an impartial witness for you.'

Mr Forrester passed her the notebook. 'Thank you, madam. If you'd kindly write your name and address . . .'

Thompson growled under his breath, spun round and waved his hands at the men waiting nearby. 'Get into your vehicles and follow me. I shan't give you your instructions until we're out of earshot of this unpatriotic fellow. Follow my car and stop when I stop.'

He turned back to Mayne. 'This matter is only postponed, Esher.'

Mayne didn't even attempt to reply, just folded his arms again and waited. The way Thompson spoke and looked at the men was also arrogant. Several of them had been giving him dirty looks.

As they drove away Mayne turned back to Forrester. 'Thank you for your help.'

'My pleasure. A colleague of mine had to deal with Thompson during the war. He'll be interested to hear about this contretemps.'

'I doubt that fellow will agree to send you any copies of his paperwork, so perhaps you can give me your address, Mr Forrester?'

'That's easy. My wife and I will be staying with the Woollards for the time being. He and I are old friends. This is a golden opportunity to get our house in Manchester repaired. It was damaged in the war, not too badly but enough to make it uncomfortable to live in. We've had to sleep in the dining room. So you can pass any paperwork on to me easily enough.'

'That's going to be very useful.' Mayne took the hand Forrester was offering in farewell and shook it heartily.

Ray turned towards his car, then turned back again and snapped his fingers as if something had just occurred to him. 'Have you got someone guarding the front entrance, Mayne?'

'Yes. And the big chain was being put in place across it when I left this morning, the one the Army used during the war. But I'm glad you've reminded me. I'd better go and check that Thompson isn't trying to tear it off the bollards. I wouldn't put anything past him after seeing how he behaved today.'

'I think we'd better come with you,' Forrester said. 'Just in case.'

'We can fit another two people in the back of the car,' Ray offered. 'It'll be quicker for you to drive round with us, Mayne lad, than walk across your grounds to the front entrance.'

The car slowed down as it drove up the side of Parson's Meadow. They passed the group of council vehicles, now parked along the side of the small park and its wartime allotments.

Thompson was standing on a slope, waving his arms and looking as if he was haranguing the group of men standing slightly below him. They looked sullen and fed up.

The Planning Officer turned round when he heard their car, realised who it was and ran towards his own vehicle.

'I suppose he's going to follow us. Couldn't the idiot even walk the hundred or so yards from there to the gates?' Mayne wondered aloud.

'He doesn't give up easily, does he?' Forrester murmured.

'He's even more pig-headed than I'd expected. How on earth did someone like him get to the rank of captain?'

'Who can tell?' Mayne directed the driver into the parking space at the front of the Dower House and got out quickly. 'OK. Here we go again.'

Steve Rennie hurried towards them from the front doorway of the house, grinning and gesturing towards the council vehicles which were now moving the short distance up the hill towards them. 'Look at them lot. They won't get in here. The chain's all fixed up and locked in place again, Mr Esher.'

One of the lorries seemed to be having trouble with its gears, which were making grating and clashing sounds as the man driving it struggled to double declutch.

'That gearbox won't last much longer,' Victor muttered.

They saw Thompson gesticulate and shout something to the driver of his own vehicle. The car drove quickly to the entrance, swung in, then the driver braked hard, sending his passenger sideways across the rear seat. They stopped just short of the big chain stretched across between the two bollards. It had links bigger than a man's hands and would have done serious damage to any vehicle running into it.

Mayne watched with quiet satisfaction as Thompson erupted from the car and strode forward towards the group of people in the garden of the Dower House.

'Who gave you permission to put up that chain?'

His voice was loud and shrill, rather a high voice for a man, Mayne thought. He waited a moment to reply, praying for patience, 'The Army put it up. I wasn't aware that they bothered to seek anyone's permission for what they did.'

Thompson was almost bouncing with rage as he turned to his driver. 'You can bear me out. This chain wasn't left in place after the war, was it?'

The man spoke slowly, his face expressionless. 'I couldn't say, sir. I don't often come to the big house.'

'Well, you drove me here the other day and there was no sign of this chain then.'

'It was being cleaned and mended,' Ray said. Can't let good iron rust away, can we? As the government keeps reminding us: *Waste not, want not.*'

'Don't be ridiculous. You can't possibly need a barrier here in peacetime. The council will not allow it. Take that chain down this minute.'

Forrester moved forward, saying quite audibly to his client, 'This is getting tedious, Esher. It's hard to put up with such rudeness without losing one's temper, is it not?'

He strode across to Thompson, not stopping until he was so close to him that the other man moved back a step involuntarily. 'I had thought from what you said during our last encounter that you were trying to take possession of the *rear* part of this estate?'

'You know we are. For much-needed housing.'

'Then why are you trying to tell people what to do at the front of Esherwood?'

'Because we need to gain access.'

'Not without the legal paperwork, you don't. *As I have already informed you.* Now, kindly go away and leave my client to get on with his day. This is harassment and you have no justification for it, none at all. At this rate, I shall have to advise Mr Esher to take out an injunction to prevent you from coming on to any part of his land, whatever the alleged reason.'

Thompson's face was still that unhealthy shade of red. He took a deep breath, hesitated as he looked up at the lawyer and met his steady gaze, then turned to the men standing beside their vehicles. 'Return to the council workshops for the time being. You can always count on lawyers to delay necessary work.'

He got into his car, but not before giving Mayne a look that said he wasn't finished yet.

'You've made an enemy there,' Forrester said quietly. 'You should watch your step from now on.'

'Is he likely to acquire the legal paperwork to take away half my land?'

Forrester spread out his hands in a gesture of helplessness. 'I doubt it. But they might still take the smaller rear area that you agreed to sell. Have you changed your mind about that?'

'No. It's a piece of land the family has never used, just scrubby woodland. I'd be glad to see houses built there for returned soldiers.'

'Then that might give us a useful bargaining counter.' He thought about it for a moment or two. 'I can't see any judge insisting the council be allowed to take away so much of your family's land, especially after your distinguished war service, but you never can tell.'

'I don't think there are any local judges, just a couple of Justices of the Peace. I'd offered to sell them the small area at the rear on condition that our company erected the prefabs. Daniel has some experience of those. But they've already given the contract for far more prefabs to a minor building company in town, a company with a reputation for shoddy work, moreover.'

'Well, I doubt they'll allow you to do any erecting of prefabs now.'

'That's obvious. Pity, though. It'd have given us a start as a building company, taught us a lot, I dare say, and allowed us to start assembling a team of tradesmen.'

'Well, there are enough building projects in Lancashire for you to find another job or two to get your hand in. I understood the need to dictate to people during an all-out war, but now that's over, I intend to help re-establish the rule of law in this country.'

Ray joined in. 'Unfortunately the council has certain elected officials who are open to bribery. That could make things difficult because it's hard to prove. I shall do my best to keep an eye on them but you can't catch every villain. Like my friend here, I've seen things done during the war which sickened me. Some judgements were given and carried out which were utterly wrong. I won't put up with it in peacetime, if I can help it. And I can afford any legal fights that might be needed.'

Forrester looked down the hill as the sound of the lorry's gears clashing echoed from a distance, so still was the air. 'I think they've done their dash for today. When things are quieter I'd love to see the inside of your house, Esher. One of my passions is the history of Lancashire. And I've heard that you've found a cellar with a puzzle lock that's causing some excitement.'

'I'll be happy to show you round the house. And yes, we do have a door with a puzzle lock. My father is looking for the instructions to open it. If he can't find them, we'll have to break in.'

'I'd love a ringside seat for that.'

'It's a very small space, but I'll make sure you're invited to join the bystanders above the cellar.'

Ray turned to walk away. 'I'll get going now, lads. Let me know if you need anything else, Mayne.'

'Yes. Thanks for your help. Oh! Just a minute. Any word from your niece?'

'The ship bringing the ex-POWs from Cairo was delayed but she's expecting Anthony to arrive any day now. She's still staying at a hotel my friends in London found for her. Like everyone else they've got a house full of relatives, no place for a man in fragile health. She'll have a lot on her plate with Anthony, however much she loves him. Some of the men are never going to recover from how badly they were treated.'

'I've seen photos in the newspapers of returned POWs. They looked like walking skeletons.'

'Yes. Those who ran the prisons and work camps in the Far East have a lot to answer for. But if anyone can nurse Anthony back to health, it'll be Steph. You've only seen her since she thought she'd lost him. She used to be a lively lass before that, not quiet and reserved as she's been lately. And if I have my way, she'll be happy again. Anything I can do to help her young man recover from his experiences, I shall.'

They were both silent, then Mayne said it. 'Well, good luck to him. War leaves a mark on us all, even though we haven't faced what he has. I hope she understands that.'

'I'm sure she does. We'll do our best for him. That's all anyone can do in this life, their very best. Now, you go home and take things easily, and so will I. We need to gather our energy and resources to fight another day.'

As Mayne started to walk back through the grounds to the big house, his father came rushing out of the Dower House.

'Mayne! Wait a minute.'

With a sigh, he stopped.

'Can you let my team of helpers into the big cellar?'

'Can't it wait?' He regretted the words as soon as they'd escaped him, because his old man was only trying to help in his own way.

His father clapped him on the shoulder. 'I know you've got a lot on your plate but we've found a couple of clues and I think we're very close to finding out how to get into that secret cellar. There is one more diary to find.'

'Do you really believe you can find it?'

'Of course I do. I've read Margery's other diaries. She was a very powerful, determined woman and she wrote that she wasn't going to let the family treasures fall into Parliamentarian hands, whatever it took. We don't even know what family treasures she was talking about. What if she managed to hide some valuable things in the secret cellar, eh? They won't have been touched since. We might even be able to sell enough for you to keep Esherwood.'

'I'm not going to rely on something as tenuous as that, Dad, and you shouldn't either.'

'It's worth a try, son. Don't say you wouldn't be glad of a pile of money!'

Mayne bit back a sharp response. No matter how many setbacks his father faced, he remained childishly optimistic. 'About the cellar. Yes, you can bring your helpers into it, as long as they don't get in our way. When do you want to bring them up to the big house?'

'Tomorrow morning.'

'We might be busy fending off Thompson and the men from the council.'

'All we shall need is letting into the cellar. I even know where the final diary is likely to be. Well, I know of one or two *likely* places. The family diaries are all packed away in boxes, of course. If they aren't down there, we shall have to continue searching until we do find them. There may be something up in the attic. I believe some boxes were taken up there, out of the way of the soldiers.'

'All right, then. See you tomorrow.'

Mayne walked away, back to the common sense of his wife and the realistic view of the world held by his team. He had always had trouble coping with his father's unfounded optimism about life. Indeed, there were times when it depressed him.

At the moment, with the rest of his life full of crucial problems and the approaching loss of his beloved home, it seemed even harder than ever to get excited about academic trivia like diaries – or even rare puzzle locks.

13

Mr Audley and his clerk took tea together to discuss what to do next about the Pelling inheritance.

'With the best will in the world, I don't have the time to search all the boxes for our copy of the document,' Mr Stackpole said gloomily. 'We have three generations of that family's records in the store room. And who's to say the will is in there anyway? That lad may have destroyed it out of sheer spite. I wouldn't put anything past *him*.'

'I think we should get in touch with Miss Summers, whether we find it or not. I've decided that morally she has a right to know about it.'

'Yes, I've come round to that conclusion myself.'

'Telling her is something better done in person than by letter, don't you think? But I can't get away, not with Mrs Rawley's case coming up. Would you mind going to Rivenshaw on my behalf and having a little talk with Miss Summers? She may even have an idea where we could hunt for the other copy of the will.'

The clerk considered this for a moment or two, then said, 'I believe you're right about it being better dealt with person to person. And yes, I'll be happy to go and speak to her.'

The following day, Stackpole put on his best suit and took the earliest train to Rivenshaw, which meant going via

Manchester and changing trains there. He intended to enjoy this outing, because it hadn't been possible for most people to travel for either pleasure or business during the war.

Besides, he had always been fond of the moors and part of his journey lay near them. It stirred something inside him to see such big open spaces stretching towards the horizon, uncluttered by humanity and its debris.

Today he was thoroughly enjoying sitting in the train and looking out of the window. The train wasn't crowded with soldiers standing or lying in the corridors for hours on end, as wartime trains had been, so it was the perfect opportunity to think about the new life the British people were building. A life of peace.

It was good to have a quiet think without being interrupted. At home his dear wife, bless her, was rather a chatterbox.

A couple of days ago, he'd read an article about the United Nations that had given him a lot of food for thought. The organisation had come into formal existence last month, on October 24th, after 29 nations had ratified the Charter.

This new international organisation would surely be able to keep peace in the world better than the previous League of Nations had? Maybe not always between smaller nations in distant lands, but peace between the major world powers and above all, as far as he was concerned, peace in Europe. Two World Wars had nearly torn the continent apart.

His thoughts turned next to the Beveridge Report, which had made a big impression on him and which everyone was talking about. William Beveridge had identified five 'Giant Evils' in society, and Stackpole agreed with him about them. Yes, he definitely did. Squalor, ignorance, want, idleness, and disease had no place in the modern world. Everyone in Britain had fought in the war, rich and poor alike, so everyone deserved to share in the fruits of peace.

Surely the new Labour government would be able to implement the report's recommendations and set up what some people were calling a national health service? He did hope so. People shouldn't die simply because they couldn't afford to pay a doctor, nor should they end hard-working lives in the shame of the poorhouse, as one of his great-uncles had.

No, better times were coming for his country, Stackpole was sure of it. He had a great deal of respect for Mr Churchill, but only as a war leader, and felt Mr Attlee would care more for the welfare of ordinary people like himself now that the war was over.

He gazed out of the train window again, enjoying the rhythmic rattling of the wheels on the track. Of course, at this time of year the landscape looked rather bleak, but he still found the rolling, dull green undulations attractive and restful on the eye.

He didn't attempt to chat to his fellow passengers and they kept their thoughts to themselves, thank goodness, though two ladies opposite him did have a little discussion about the coming festive season.

As his dear wife had reminded him, it would be Christmas in a month or so. The first Christmas after the war. Those who'd lost loved ones would be sad, and the shortages of food and goods were just as bad as ever, but still . . . it was peacetime and Christmas. That meant a lot. People would find ways of celebrating, if only by listening to the wireless or having a sing-song.

His wife wanted to buy one or two delicacies on the black market. They hadn't done this during the war, because he felt it was unpatriotic. But now? Well, maybe they'd allow themselves one or two foods they'd enjoyed in the old days. A piece of ham, perhaps. He licked his lips at the mere thought of that.

He suddenly became aware that they were slowing down

at a small station, and when he saw the name Rivenshaw on a sign he jumped to his feet. Good heavens, he'd spent the whole journey lost in thought! He hadn't even taken his library book out of his briefcase.

He got out of the train, pausing outside the station to admire the big paved square of which the station buildings formed one whole side. This was presumably the town centre. It looked a nice little place.

Well, he'd indulged himself in his own thoughts for long enough. Now he had to concentrate on the task that had brought him here. Raising one hand, he hailed a taxi and asked to be taken to Esherwood.

To the taxi driver's surprise there was a big chain across the gateway to Esherwood. He stopped the car and apologised to his passenger. 'Danged if I know why that thing's been put back. I'll nip across to the Dower House and ask.'

'I'll come with you. I can ask about the person I'm here to see at the same time.'

Nellie Rennie opened the door. 'Oh, it's you Ted.' She looked beyond him to his companion then raised one eyebrow in a mute question as to who this was.

'This here gentleman has come all the way from Preston to see Miss Summers and now I can't get into the grounds to take him to the big house.'

'It's thanks to that Thompson fellow at the council. He's trying to take Mr Esher's land away from him, and Mr Esher a war hero, too. So they've had to put up barriers to keep him out. My cousin works for the council and he says he and his mates don't want to do this, but they're frightened of losing their jobs. They remember what it was like after the Great War when there was so much unemployment. I'll give that Thompson an earful if he ever comes anywhere near me, you see if I don't. He's caused more trouble than a cage of monkeys, that one has.'

'Well good luck to you, Mrs Rennie. I suppose I'd better drive my passenger round to the back.'

'They've got big wooden gates up there now, and had to lock them too. It's a crying shame, that's what it is.'

She turned as her husband joined her at the door. 'Steve love, this gentleman is here to see Miss Summers. What's the best way for him to get to the big house?'

'If you don't mind walking, I can take you up to the big house. It's only a few hundred yards, Mr . . .?'

'My name's Stackpole. Will someone be able to call me a taxi afterwards? I do want to get home today and it's a bit far for me to walk back to the station.' He looked at them apologetically. 'I'm not as young as I was.'

'They've got the phone on up at the big house and if they call the station, someone will send the taxi. That all right with you, Ted?'

'Yes. I'll come for you as soon as I hear, Mr Stackpole. They can tell me where to meet you when they phone, here or at the back gate.'

'Thank you. How much do I owe you?'

Money changed hands, including a very reasonable tip, and Ted Willis smiled approvingly. 'I won't keep you waiting, sir.'

Steve led the way along the drive and they walked briskly enough not to feel the cold. When they came in sight of the house, Mr Stackpole slowed down to study it. A pretty little manor house but in great need of renovation, as were many places after the scarcities of the war years.

'Ah, there's Mr Esher. He'll know where to find your lady.'

Mr Stackpole found himself being introduced to the owner, then taken inside the house and left in the kitchen which was a good deal warmer than the big, echoing entrance hall.

While he waited for someone to fetch Miss Summers, he was given a cup of tea, but refused the scone, not wanting to take someone else's rations.

Judith found Christa in the attic, helping to move some boxes and old suitcases so that Francis and Daniel could check out the area whose measurements didn't seem to match the overall dimensions of the upper storey.

'There's someone to see you, Christa.'

'Who on earth would be coming to see me in Rivenshaw?'

'It's a Mr Stackpole. He says he works for Mrs Pelling's lawyer.'

'Oh, yes. I've met him a couple of times. He's the head clerk there, a very nice man. But I can't understand what he would want with me. It's a long way to come.' She felt uneasy and turned to Daniel. 'Do you mind . . . Could you spare the time to come and talk to him with me? I don't always understand the English legal system.'

'Yes, of course.'

As they started down the stairs, he squeezed her hand. 'Don't worry. You haven't done anything wrong.'

She stopped for a moment and Daniel was looking so sympathetic that for once she confessed her greatest fear. 'I can't help worrying. I'm always afraid they'll find a reason to send me back to Germany. Mrs Pelling's niece might have told more lies about me.'

He took her hand and kept hold of it. 'We won't let them take you away.'

'You won't be able to stop them if that's what they decide. I have no relatives in this country, no compelling reason to stay here.'

He frowned, not moving for a moment or two, then said slowly, 'If necessary, I'll marry you, then they won't be able to send you away. Does that set your mind at ease?'

He'd meant well, she was sure, but the way he'd said it upset her in another way and she blurted out, 'Thank you, but I don't intend to marry except for love, like my parents did.'

He stared at her, his brow crinkled in a frown, then tugged her forward again. 'Well, I doubt anyone will try to send you away from England, but the offer's still there.'

She didn't reply. The calm, emotionless way he'd talked of marrying her had upset her. Not a word about affection, or even liking her. And she'd been beginning to hope that he . . . Oh, she was a fool.

Mr Stackpole stood up as they entered the kitchen. 'Ah, Miss Summers. We have met before.'

'Yes, I remember you.'

'Is there somewhere we can talk privately?'

All her worries came back in force and she couldn't utter a single word.

Daniel moved forward, hand outstretched. 'I'm Daniel O'Brien, a friend of Christa's. She's asked me to stay with her, if you don't mind.'

'Oh, I don't mind at all.' Mr Stackpole smiled at her in a fatherly way. 'It's nothing to worry about, my dear.'

She pulled herself together. 'We can go into the library. It's a bit cold, but you can keep your coat on, and we're both well wrapped up.'

'Big houses must take a great deal of heating.'

At the library door she stopped and checked. 'I was right. No one is working in here this morning. The children are at school, the women are shopping or doing housework, and the other men are making regular tours of the grounds keeping an eye open for trespassers.'

She gestured towards a small table to one side of the big room. 'We could sit there.'

Mr Stackpole and Daniel waited till she was seated then

pulled up two other chairs. The lawyer cleared his throat. 'I need to tell you about Mrs Pelling's will.'

He explained the situation then asked, 'She, um, didn't give you a copy of it, did she?'

'No. I didn't know anything about it.' Christa took out a handkerchief and blew her nose, trying to wipe away a tear without them seeing how moved she was by her foster-mother's generosity.

'We feared not. If we can't find the final will, then I'm afraid you'll not be able to inherit and *that woman* will keep everything.'

'Even to know Mrs Pelling cared about me enough to make me her heir is . . . wonderful.'

'I'm sure it is,' the clerk said gently. 'You don't have any idea where she might have hidden the will?'

'No. She used to go up to the attic and look at her old things. She said they brought her memories of happier times. If it's anywhere I'd guess it'd be there. But Mrs Grayton would never let you inside the house to search up there.'

'No. I fear not.'

'I was afraid I'd done something wrong and you'd come to tell me they were going to send me back to Germany.'

Daniel squeezed her hand under the table but she pulled hers away, ignoring his look of surprise.

Mr Stackpole gave her an understanding glance. 'I can see that you must always have that fear at the back of your mind, but I'm sure it won't happen. And even if *that woman* tried to stir up trouble about you, my employer and I would be able to bear witness as to how well you cared for your foster mother and what a model citizen you've been.'

And the tears did overflow then at the kindness of this offer.

★   ★   ★

Daniel waited for Christa to stop weeping. He didn't dare take hold of her hand because he'd obviously offended her with his offhand proposal of marriage. That had been stupid of him. Any woman would want more than that, of course they would. And Christa wasn't just any woman to him.

Even he hadn't realised quite how precarious she felt. He'd been so lost in his own depression about the war that he hadn't taken as much notice as he should have done of the people round him.

As if he was the only one to have suffered!

He'd helped his aunt when she'd been suddenly widowed, but he'd still expected her to be supportive about his emotions. He'd let down his business partners, too, delaying his work for their new company to brood on his troubles.

This wasn't good enough. He must pull himself together.

He turned to the visitor. 'If you find the will, Mr Stackpole, I'll do all I can to help Christa claim what's due to her.' He looked down at her clasped hands on the table. They looked so small next to his larger ones.

He'd made a mess of things this time, but next time he proposed he swore he'd do it properly. He'd tell her how he really felt then, and would ask her if she could bear to spend her life with him, put up with his moods, share his joys . . .

A strange feeling filled him – a warmth, a rightness. He felt as if the sun had come out from behind some clouds, and though he knew there would be other cloudy days, when he'd feel down in the dumps again or experience nightmares, he just knew there'd be more sunny days as time passed.

Christa had such a warm, wonderful smile. There were times when that alone was enough to brighten his day. Why had he taken that for granted for so long?

As Mr Stackpole stood up, he turned away from them,

and on an impulse Daniel took her hand to his lips, giving it a quick kiss.

She looked at him in shock.

He gave her hand a squeeze before he let go and whispered, 'Later on we'll talk properly.' Then he raised his voice again. 'Let's get Mr Stackpole something to eat and then phone for his taxi.'

In the warmth of the kitchen they all had some sandwiches. As he was finishing, the clerk frowned. 'Are you *sure* you have nothing with you from Mrs Pelling's house, Miss Summers? You've checked every single thing you brought?'

'Quite sure. I didn't have time to do anything but pack quickly and get out. Mrs Grayton and her husband were watching me the whole time.'

'It's not like your foster mother at all. She was usually most careful where she put important documents, careful about everything. Her husband used to boast about her tidiness.'

'Towards the end she was rather quiet, poor lady. She'd lost her son, then her husband, and I don't think she wanted to live.'

'That damned war!'

They looked across the table at the speaker.

Daniel realised he'd spoken too forcefully. 'Sorry. But the war messed up a lot of lives, didn't it? You can't get over it in a few weeks, or even a few months.'

'But we *will* get over it and make something of this fine country, which took in thousands of children like me and did so many good things in spite of having to fight the Nazis,' Christa said firmly. 'If we don't make the most of the peace, Hitler will have scored a victory of sorts in spite of his personal defeat.'

It wasn't surprising, Daniel thought, how the war still coloured their thoughts. Six years was a long time to struggle.

★ ★ ★

After they'd phoned the station for the taxi, Christa walked down to the Dower House with Mr Stackpole, and Daniel went to help his partners. They had completely forgotten to come to the house for something to eat at midday and Daniel's aunt had asked him to remind them that they still needed to eat.

Since there'd been no more signs of Thompson trying to invade, Mayne was surveying the rear part of the grounds with Victor, marking out accurately the area he would be happy to sell and discussing how he would place the prefabs if he were building them. He looked up and waved to his friends.

'Everything sorted out with Christa?'

'Yes. How's your father getting on in the cellar? He hasn't come out of it since early morning, though the ladies came for a cup of tea mid-morning.'

'When he's concentrating on something he forgets the rest of the world completely. I've no idea what's going on. He drives me mad with his optimism, so I left him and his two lady friends to it.'

'Out of sight out of mind.'

'Out of sight, maybe, but not out of mind. He's even got me wondering if there's something valuable hidden inside that secret cellar.'

Hiding a smile at Mayne's ongoing irritation with his father, Daniel took the sketch of the area from him and studied the measurements and then the land around them. 'You know, if we keep a dead end to the street, we could fit an extra prefab in.'

With quick, sure strokes he started a new page in his pad, sketching out the area in more exact proportions, according to the scribbled measurements, and marking where each of the prefabs might stand.

He handed that to Mayne. 'It's more than time I got to

work on the conversion of the big house into flats, but this is how you should place the prefabs. I'll draw the plans up properly after we get the contract.'

'The council won't give us the contract to build. It's already promised to someone else.'

He was shocked. 'You never said you'd tendered for it.'

'I wasn't given the chance. No one was.'

'What? Didn't they even put it out to tender?'

'Not according to the letter a kind person let me see.'

'We can fight every step of the way about that.'

Then Daniel saw that his friend's expression was stricken with grief, so he stopped talking for a moment to give Mayne time to pull himself together. The situation was getting him down and no wonder.

'We could give you one wing of the big house,' he suggested after a few moments. 'You'll have enough money left for that from selling your remaining valuables, surely?'

'No. It'd rub salt in the wound to see the part of the house I can't have every day, especially if the new tenants don't look after it. I was left on my own a lot as a child, and the house became like a mother to me, always something to see, something to do, something to find.'

He paused, then said harshly, 'It's better to make a clean break, I feel. Judith and I can move to the Dower House and concentrate on that. Though we'll have to work out what to do about the Rennies.'

'You could turn the garage and shed into a flat for them quite easily. It'd be slightly smaller than the one they have now, but they'd still have somewhere to live, which is a problem these days.'

Mayne sighed. 'I feel guilty about even thinking of turning them out. Mrs Rennie's been wonderful. There aren't many people who can cope with my father's absent-minded ways as she does.'

'They'll understand that you too need a home.'

'I suppose so. I'll talk to Judith about it when things settle down, then you and I can have a planning session and discuss modernising the Dower House.'

'I'll get back to work on the big house then, drawing up proper, detailed plans.'

'Yes, please.'

His friend's voice sounded choked, so Daniel left it at that. He needed to finish sorting out the details of the measurements. He'd known enough to draft some rough plans, but you couldn't design the interior of a building properly when there were spaces that didn't fit the measurements. Well, you couldn't if you took a pride in your work.

Thompson left the office, telling his secretary he'd be about an hour but not saying where he was going. He didn't ask for an official vehicle but went on foot, feeling he'd be more inconspicuous that way.

He'd met a man in the pub last night who had seemed to offer a solution to his problem of getting access to that damned Esher land. At a price, of course. Everything came at a price.

Today he was going to see if Rusty Warner had been telling the truth.

He scowled as he saw the rear gates of Esherwood at the end of one street he passed and vowed that the land behind them would be covered in houses one day soon. What's more, he'd see that the shabby old manor house would be knocked down too. Easy to find several good safety reasons to condemn it.

He hated rich folk. They had no right to have more than their fair share of possessions, especially land. And why should they be brought up in houses with dozens of rooms, when some people, himself included, had to share two miserable rooms with five other people as a child?

He'd made good though. Once he'd got away from his family, he'd joined the Army, years before the war started. He'd worked hard and shown his superiors that he could get things done. Most of them didn't seem to care how he managed it as long as it reflected well on them.

The war had been a big bonus for him and he'd made sure he found a niche that didn't lead him into danger but did offer the possibility of promotions.

This building project at Esherwood was going to continue pushing him up in the world. Oh, yes.

As he turned the corner, he scowled again at the roof of the big house showing over the trees. It dominated the neighbourhood. But not for much longer!

Rusty answered the front door so quickly he must have been waiting for him. He took Thompson out into the garden. 'Let's do this while the wife is out shopping. I'll tell her once you've come to a decision. No use stirring up trouble till it's needed.'

They walked round to the back garden, which was in the middle of the side of Esherwood furthest away from the town centre. The same crumbling perimeter wall marked the boundary and was, as Rusty had said, just about ready to fall down behind his house.

Thompson studied the side of the house. Fortuitously the garden had once been a farm vegetable patch and was twice as big as those of the nearby houses. Yes, plenty of room for large vehicles to get through from the street to the wall and push it down. And after that, they'd drive straight through the gap and take possession of the land.

See how you like that, Esher!

'Well?' Rusty prompted.

'What? Oh yes, you were right. We can use this as a way of getting through. And I'd make sure the council compensated you for losing that piece of land at the side of your house.' He glanced quickly sideways, estimating what it would take to buy this man. 'At least fifty pounds, I should think.'

Rusty beamed at him.

'What I'll do is wait till Esher goes out and then bring my chaps in to do the job before he can stop us.'

He slipped a five-pound note into Rusty's outstretched hand. 'Just a token of the council's intentions.'

'Thank you, Captain Thompson. You're a gentleman.'

'I'll get back to work now. I don't know when exactly we'll be coming to do the job. Depends on Esher.'

'Come any time. Any time at all.'

Thompson smiled as he set off back. He was going to make his own luck again, as he had before.

Just wait, Mr Maynard Bloody Esher. He who laughs last laughs longest.

14

Francis and Daniel began by measuring the attic again, just to be doubly sure that they hadn't made a mistake last time. They seemed to have done a lot of measuring in this complex old building, which had been modified for use as a hospital so haphazardly by the Army that they were still trying to sort it all out.

'No. There's still a discrepancy.' Daniel pointed to the rough sketch he'd made. 'There's a narrow area about a yard wide running along part of one side of the attic from the secret room, but it doesn't run the whole way.' He tapped the short wall near one of the ceiling beams. 'Ah. Now, this sounds hollow, don't you think?'

Francis went to tap it. 'Yes. Could be. There are other discrepancies, like the electricity cable that runs down into the floor from the secret room Mayne found over there. We should investigate that as well.'

'We can't just tear the walls down without Mayne's say-so, even though most of the ones round this open storage area are made of thin planks and will be easy to put back.'

They both smiled at this feeble joke, then he asked, 'Why *are* these walls made of planks, though? The rest of the house has the usual plastered walls.'

They stared at one another.

'A wartime rush job, perhaps?'

'There's only one way to find out. I'd better fetch Mayne and show him, get his permission to dismantle part of the wall.'

'He'll be glad of a break,' Francis said. 'He told me he had to work on the accounts after he'd checked the rear gates, and accounts aren't his favourite task. He was going to leave Jan in charge of the rear entrance today with Al patrolling the grounds. He's worried that Thompson will try to break down the walls and get the council machinery in by force, then we'd have the devil's own job getting them out again.'

'Good thing the council doesn't own much heavy earth-moving equipment or they wouldn't need to be so careful about how they get into the grounds.'

'I rigged up a siren near the rear gate,' Francis said, 'so that whoever's on duty there can call for help if they need it. Good thing the main electricity supply goes into the house that way. I put a siren near the front gate too, on the side wall of the Dower House.'

'I heard you trying it out. Horrible noise it makes.'

Daniel went to find Mayne.

He returned to the attic a few minutes later with not only Mayne, but Victor as well. The latter was carrying a canvas tool bag that clinked as he walked.

'Thought you might need some of these,' Victor said cheerfully.

'I already brought a few basic tools up.' Francis pointed to them. 'But I need something like that to carry my tools in. I left a really good civilian tool bag at my parents' house during the war and I lost it when they were bombed out. I haven't been able to replace it with a decent one yet. I've ordered one, but you know what it's like getting new equipment these days. You have to wait months for it, even when you're working in a priority area.'

'I met a man who's ordered a new car. He has to wait over a year to get it,' Daniel said. 'I know the government needs to send nearly everything overseas for the export drive, but these shortages make life damned inconvenient. No wonder people snap up second-hand cars.'

He dropped a couple of his tools and cursed under his breath as one glanced off his foot.

'Why don't you use one of those old suitcases for the time being?' Victor pointed to a pile of them in the corner. 'Unless they're family heirlooms, Mayne?'

'They're nothing to do with me. My ancestors never threw anything away, however worn it was, and those are just gathering dust. Choose whichever you think will be best. In fact, take as many as you need.'

'One will be enough.' Francis went across and picked out a small suitcase, which was scuffed but looked sturdy. 'This will be big enough and it looks newer than the others, not as dusty.'

Daniel looked at it. 'No, wait a minute! Could you choose another one? This is Christa's suitcase, the one she brought with her from Germany on the *Kindertransport* just before the war. It's one of the few things she has left from her former life, so it's got great sentimental value to her.'

Francis searched through the pile and found a leather Gladstone bag that was more suitable anyway. He put it down beside his pile of tools, before going back to study the wall. 'What do you think, Mayne? There's no way of seeing what's behind this except by removing some of these planks.'

Mayne frowned at them. 'Actually, that wall of planks wasn't here when I was a child.'

'Are you certain?'

'Oh, yes. I often used to play up here. Maybe whoever built it installed an opening system.'

He checked it for a secret catch, tapping and pressing in

the likely places, then stood back, shaking his head. 'It's not like the other secret rooms in the house. It's much more crudely built. Go ahead and remove some of the planks and we'll look inside. It may have been done to reinforce a weak part of the roof, for all I know. How about starting at the end nearest the old secret room?'

'Fine.' Daniel began to lever off the planks and found what looked like an old blanket behind them. Working carefully, doing as little damage as possible to the planks that made up the wall, he eased the corner of the blanket out of the way.

'Looks like the back of a chest of drawers. No wonder there was no echo when we tapped the wall. They padded it carefully. I'm not sure there's room to move it out of the way so that we can get in. Let's take away the planks from further along. It may be easier to get in from there.'

But those planks too revealed padding and another large piece of furniture.

It wasn't until the men got to the third and final section of the wood-clad wall that they found the way inside clear.

Daniel handed a torch to Mayne. 'You're the owner. You take the first look.'

His friend pushed his head and shoulders inside, shining the torch to and fro, whistling softly in surprise. He moved back out and studied the hole. 'If we remove the lower planks, I should be able to get inside. I don't think this wall is structural, so why the hell did they build it?'

Daniel removed more planks, piling them carefully to one side. 'Right. That should do it.'

Mayne bent his head and twisted his body slightly to get inside, but it was a tight fit.

'Watch where you're putting your feet,' Francis warned.

Their friend disappeared from view but his voice echoed back to them. 'As the measurements showed, it's a narrow space nearly four yards long and about one yard wide, with two cupboards placed along the other wall – well, tallboys really. One looks familiar. Yes, I remember it now. It used to stand in my mother's bedroom. There are a few paintings piled on top of them. Smallish ones. It's too dark to see what they are. I'll open one of the drawers and see what's inside.'

There was the sound of a long, soft whistle of surprise. 'It seems to have ornaments in it. The whole house is full of damned ornaments. Did my mother do nothing but buy them?'

'Why would she have put stuff up here?'

'I don't know.' Silence then, 'Unless . . .'

'Unless what?' Daniel asked impatiently.

'Unless she and my ex-fiancée got together on this. Caroline would be much more likely to know someone to make this secret space than my mother would.'

There was the sound of drawers being opened and shut, then the crackling sound of paper being unwrapped.

'Well, this ornament came from my mother's side of the family, so I suppose she could do what she wanted with it. She always said it was very valuable, a seventeenth century piece. That settles it. *She* must have put it there because she'd have noticed if it was missing and kicked up a fuss. She knew every single ornament in the house, how old it was, how valuable. You'd think *she* had been born an Esher, instead of my father.'

'Look, I'll explore a bit further.' After a couple of slow, shuffling footsteps, he let out an exclamation of surprise.

'What's the matter?'

'There's an extremely narrow circular staircase leading down, more like a curved ladder. You have to step across the hole it goes down to get to the other end of this space.'

'Don't try to go down it till we've checked where it leads,'

Daniel said sharply. 'Not to mention whether it's safe to take your weight.'

'I think I'm too big to get down that and I'm not even going to try. I'm coming back now. I'll pass out a few ornaments then we'll close this place up till Ray's had them valued for us. Good heavens!'

'What?'

'This piece of rag has a brooch inside it.'

When he brought three ornaments and the brooch out, they gathered round to examine them.

'Looks like gold to me,' Francis said. He squinted at the back of the brooch. 'That's a hallmark, surely?'

They stared at the pretty little piece, which had a large ruby at the centre surrounded by diamonds.

'I don't recognise that,' Mayne said. 'I know most of the Esherwood jewellery because my mother was always playing about with them and often wore several pieces at a time.'

'Do you suppose there's other jewellery hidden there?' Daniel asked at last. 'It could give you a nice little nest egg.'

'The two chests of drawers look to be full of stuff, all wrapped up. I can't understand why she would have put them up here. You'd think she'd have taken them down to the Dower House with her.'

'Perhaps there were too many to fit in there, or perhaps she was playing safe in case one of the houses got hit by a bomb. Everyone saw on the newsreels how badly London got hit.'

Mayne spoke slowly, thinking aloud, 'I bet Caroline got involved at first because she was engaged to me and thought it'd save the family treasures. And I suppose she began stealing things outright later on, after I broke up with her. She was always saying how short of money her family kept her, making a joke of it, but you could see how angry that made her.'

He stared at the delicate objects for a moment or two

longer, then put them on a small table which had a roughly mended leg. 'Let's get those planks back in place, eh, and stack a few boxes against the wall to keep people away. Then I'll check the grounds and if everything looks peaceful, I'll go and visit Ray, show these to him.'

How many more surprises had his mother left for him? he wondered. She had grown very strange during the latter years of the war, her behaviour erratic and unreasonable. It had turned out she was developing senile dementia, so even if she'd still been alive now, she couldn't have told him why the hiding place in the attic had been made. And he wasn't going to ask Caroline, didn't want to go near that lying bitch again.

His mother had always been an unhappy woman. Even as a child, he'd understood that. As he grew older, he realised she'd married for position not love. His father was, after all, an Esher of Esherwood. Only, she'd chosen badly. Reginald was an absent-minded, studious fellow, who didn't give two hoots about social position, and she'd been unable to persuade him to join in the county set's social life at all.

Oh well, you couldn't change the past and perhaps the contents of these tallboys would add something to his finances to help him make a comfortable home and life for Judith and the children.

It suddenly occurred to him that he should mention this find to his father and see if Reginald knew anything about the secret cache. And what better time than now, when his father was searching through the cellars?

As Mayne went down the last flight of stairs he met Judith, who had just come back from the shops and was looking for him.

'What will we do with our time when we no longer have to queue for everything?' she asked cheerfully. He kissed her cheek and then had to kiss the other cheek to match, a silly little joke of theirs, before he explained what they'd found.

'I'll come down to the cellar with you. I'd like to see if they've located that old diary.'

They found Reginald sitting by an open box of books, not searching through them but squinting by the light of a dim electric bulb hanging from the ceiling as he tried to read.

Mayne breathed deeply, pushing back his irritation because it was never any use getting annoyed with his father, who only seemed to remember the things he found in books. 'Did you find the diary, Dad?'

'What? Oh.' He stared down at the book in his hands and sighed, putting it down in a small pile to one side. 'I was just renewing my acquaintance with some old friends.' He patted the books. The box I'm looking for seems to have gone astray, but we'll keep looking. The ladies are being very thorough.'

One of the ladies in question came across to Mayne and asked in a low voice, 'Is it all right if we keep nudging Mr Esher to continue? He keeps forgetting about the search, bless him. He does love those old books of his.'

'I think one of you should work *with* him or he'll keep getting side-tracked and never get through the boxes.'

'So you won't mind us, um, taking control a bit?'

'We don't mind at all,' Judith put in. 'In fact, we're counting on you to do that.'

'That's all right then. The search will go more quickly from now on. I'll make sure of that. It's quite exciting, isn't it, to think we may be helping to find your buried treasure?'

Judith dug her elbow into Mayne's side to stop him saying he doubted there was any treasure in the hidden cellar. 'Very exciting,' she said gravely, then dragged her husband away.

'Leave them to it, Mayne. And let them dream of finding

treasure. Now that you've given them permission to nudge your father along, I'm sure the search will go as quickly as is possible, given your father's nature.'

He gave her a wry smile. 'Dad's hopeless, isn't he?'

'He's . . . different. I couldn't marry a man like that. He'd drive me crazy in no time.'

At the top of the cellar steps Mayne stopped to put his arms round her and give her a proper kiss.

When they broke apart, someone cleared their throat and he realised Gillian was staring at them. A quick glance sideways showed him that Judith was flushing and he felt a little embarrassed himself.

'Isn't young love sweet?' Gillian teased.

'Not so young,' her mother said ruefully. 'Are you back from school already? I can't believe how the day has flown.'

'Kitty and I are back, because school ended early today for a teachers' meeting. Ben's school isn't out yet. We walked past the council workshops on the way home as you asked us to, and all was quiet there, so I don't think they can be planning another attack tonight.' She frowned. 'I think one or two of the lorries were missing, but they'll probably be out on jobs.'

'Thanks for checking that. You can never be sure what an enemy will do. We'll all stay on high alert till this matter is sorted out.'

'I hope they don't take your land away,' Gillian said. 'It'd be so unfair . . . Dad.'

'I'll do my best to stop them, I promise you.' She was the second of his step-children to call him Dad and it made him feel very happy.

'Well, if I can help in any way, you only have to ask. I'm getting very fond of Esherwood, too. Now, I'd better go and change out of my school uniform then get my homework done.'

From what Gillian had said about the council workshops, Mayne decided it would be safe to go and show Ray their new finds.

The minute Mr Esher left the grounds by the front entrance, a man who'd been sitting behind one of the huts on the allotments stood up, ready to follow him. He watched carefully and it was soon obvious that his quarry was heading towards the town.

He moved out from behind the hut, muttering to himself. He hated having to do this, but he didn't want to lose his job, so took great care not to be seen by Mr Esher as he followed him.

He slowed down to watch Mr Esher turn the corner at the lower end of Parson's Meadow but when he got to the corner in his turn, he saw that Mr Esher had stopped about fifty yards along to talk to his stepson. Edging carefully backwards, he waited out of sight until they each went on their way.

He pretended to be tying his shoelace as the two separated and Ben walked briskly past him on his way home.

Mr Esher was still in sight when he turned the corner, thank goodness.

In the bedroom of one of the houses along the side of Parson's Meadow, Veronica Peters was standing watching the world go by. It was annoying to be as old as she was. She couldn't believe she was in her eighties. It often surprised her to look in a mirror and see a wrinkled old face. Only it wasn't her grandmother staring back at her, it was herself.

Her mind was still as active as ever, well, *she* felt it was and hoped others agreed, but her body grew tired more quickly than it used to even a couple of years ago, so she couldn't walk around the town as much as she'd have liked to.

When she had to go upstairs for something, she quite often stood and watched people from her bedroom window. She used her father's binoculars, not to be nasty and spy on them, but simply to feel as if she was still part of the world.

When she caught sight of a man who was obviously hiding behind one of the huts, she wondered what on earth he was doing among the nearly bare winter allotments. It wasn't until he turned his face fully towards her house that she realised she knew him. 'Willie Hawsworth!' she muttered.

She was acquainted with the whole family and had known the man himself from childhood. A decent fellow, she'd always thought. Why wasn't he at work in his council job at this time of day, though? And why was he skulking about in the allotments?

Puzzled, she continued to watch, hidden by her net curtains.

A man passed her house, heading into town. Mayne Esher.

To her surprise, Willie came out from behind the hut and set off after Mayne, taking care not to be seen, it seemed to her. She had to wonder why he would be following her friend. No, she was letting her imagination run away with her. It was just coincidence.

Willie went in the same direction as Mayne, but when he started to turn left as Mayne had just done, he suddenly stopped dead and began edging backwards, pressed against the hedge.

Her guess had been right, then. He *was* following Mayne.

He bent and fiddled around with his shoelace as a lad came into view.

It took her only a few seconds to put the pieces of the puzzle together. There could only be one reason for this unusual behaviour: that nasty new chap at the Planning Department was up to something. Only he could have given Willie permission to leave work during the day.

She smiled grimly. It paid to keep your eyes open. If she

could find out something that would help Mayne, she would. She prided herself on still being able to help her fellow human beings.

As soon as Ben had passed him, Willie went round the corner again and disappeared from sight. Oh, if only she could run after him and see what he was doing!

Ben was approaching her house.

She hurried down the stairs and flung open her front door. 'Ben! Come here! I need your help.'

The lad stopped dead then ran to join her by the door, looking surprised. 'Is something wrong, Miss Peters?'

'I think so.' She explained about Willie following his stepfather and Ben's eyes lit up.

'Leave your schoolbag here and follow them, see what Willie does and where he goes. I'd do it myself but I'm too old.'

'What do I do if Willie just goes back to the council workshops?'

'Use your initiative. See whether you think your father should be told about this, because make no mistake about it, Willie was definitely following him. And don't go home without letting me know what happens.'

'I'll have to come back here anyway to pick up my schoolbag,' he pointed out.

He hurried off and she waited impatiently inside the house, walking to and fro from her front door to her kitchen. What was happening?

She dared to use one of the swear words that had been forbidden to women in her youth.

'Damn old age! Damn it to high hell!'

Ben ran down the street, stopping at the corner to look for his father. The only person he could see was Willie Hawsworth, a big man with a shiny bald head, easy to spot in a crowd.

The lad strode forward, not even stopping to say hello to a friend who went to another school, so eager was he to find out what was going on.

Mayne turned left before the town centre and Willie followed suit, hesitating for a moment at the corner.

So Ben turned round and edged into a shop doorway. It was a good thing he did so, because Willie was scanning the street behind him, as if afraid of being observed. Ben could see that clearly through the glass.

How strange!

Then they were off again. From his hiding place behind a tree, Ben watched Mayne go into Mr Woollard's house. Willie walked past, head averted, then stopped and hung around at the next corner.

When Mayne disappeared inside the house, Willie hesitated then set off again, retracing his steps, going toward the town.

Ben followed him, but all Willie did was go into the Town Hall. No use trying to go after him or even wait outside. They didn't encourage children to hang around and someone would come out and ask him what he wanted.

But then, by sheer good luck, the lad saw Willie's head pass behind a window on the second floor, then pass behind the next two windows as well. He giggled. That bald head did shine. That was the corridor where the Planning Department was situated, surely? Well, it always had been before.

Something told him this whole thing was to do with that horrible Thompson fellow.

He waited a few minutes, wondering if Willie would come out again. And he did. This time from a side door that led to the workshops, following Mr Thompson, who was marching along as if he were on parade.

Should he go and tell Miss Peters about this? Ben wondered. No, he'd better tell his stepfather first, just in case

Mr Thompson was planning to do something else to try to get hold of Esherwood land.

He ran headlong through the few streets and hammered on the front door. 'Got to see Mr Woollard! It's urgent.'

The maid took him straight to her master. His stepfather was there and the lawyer. 'Miss Peters said to tell you.' He gasped out what he'd seen.

'Sounds as if they're planning something,' Mayne said. 'You'll have to excuse me, gentlemen. I'd better get back.'

'I'm coming with you,' Ray said firmly.

'We'll *all* go,' Mr Forrester said even more firmly.

'Can you drive, Mayne lad?' Ray asked. 'I'm missing my niece being here when I need her. I tried to learn to drive, but it was no good.'

'Yes, I can.'

Ray turned to Ben. 'How about you go and tell Sergeant Deemer we think they're planning another attack on Esherwood? Ask if he's free to join us.'

'Yessir!' The lad was off immediately, his face bright with excitement.

Mayne sighed in relief when the car started first time. He waited impatiently for the other two men to get in, then drove off as fast as was safe.

No one was going to steal his land if he could help it.

15

Once Willie had reported that Mayne Esher had left Esherwood and gone to see Mr Woollard, Thompson didn't wait for the big official car and its lazy driver, who was always off having cups of tea when you wanted him. He hurried out to the workshops and crammed into the cab of one of the council lorries with the men. Speed was of the essence now, not dignity.

He directed the driver to where the bulldozer and other lorry were parked. The sight of the workmen lounging around reading newspapers annoyed him, but he'd had to leave these men on standby, so he could hardly complain about that.

'Follow us to Pexton Street!' he yelled. 'And be quick about it.'

When they arrived, he knocked on the front door of a house in the middle of the street and it was answered by Rusty Warner, who was yawning and stretching as if he'd just been taking a nap.

'We need to do the job now,' he said. 'We'll have to knock down your front hedge to get through, I'm afraid, but you'll be compensated for the damage.' He saw the man hesitate, so added, 'On top of the fifty pounds.'

'Go ahead. But do it quickly, before the wife gets back.'

Thompson gathered the men together, gave them further instructions then went round to the rear of the house.

He was rewarded a few moments later by the sight of the bulldozer chugging forward, covered in bits of privet hedge. It drove past and attacked the first part of the wall. That went down easily and he couldn't help smiling in triumph.

As the driver backed away ready for a second push there was a scream from the front of the house, so Thompson held up one hand to stop him. He didn't want to be responsible for anyone knocking down a child, something he'd once seen happen and never wanted to see again.

He hurried round the house in the direction of the scream and found a large woman, who looked to be more muscular than half the men he employed. It could only have been her who'd screamed and he guessed she was Mrs Warner. Surely her husband had told her what was going to happen?

But he couldn't have because she was staring open-mouthed at the mess where her hedge had been.

Rusty didn't come out of the house until Thompson got there.

'What in tarnation is going on here?' she shouted at the top of her voice when she saw Thompson.

'Your husband has agreed to give the council workers access to Esherwood so that we can start building the new prefabs.'

'Oh, has he? What stupid idea have you got into your head now, Rusty Warner?' She didn't wait for an answer but marched round to the rear of the house, stopping half way to screech again at the sight of her apple tree, which had been in the way. Its branches were lying on the ground, crushed, and the trunk was at an angle.

She came across to plant herself in front of Thompson. 'Explain to me again what you're intending to do, mister? And if that machine of yours moves by so much as an inch while we're talking, I'll throw you under it.'

'Your husband can tell you about this, madam. We need to get on with the work.'

'Don't you dare do anything till you've explained. *You*, not Rusty. He can never get a tale straight, that one. I want to hear every single detail from you, mister.'

So Thompson explained as quickly as he could what had been agreed, then glanced at his wristwatch. He'd be having to pay the men overtime if this went on for too long.

Her voice was shrill enough to make him wince. 'You mean, there's a road going through here?'

'Yes, madam.'

'*Over—my—dead—body!*'

She turned to her husband. 'Get them out of here, Rusty, and give me whatever they paid you. It won't compensate for the trouble we're going to have putting the garden to rights, but it'll be a start.'

'I'm afraid we can't stop now, madam,' Thompson said. 'Your husband and I have an agreement. The nation needs new houses and it's our duty to build them.'

'And I have six children who need room to play out, or they'd get under my feet all the time. Not to mention a seventh on the way. I also need my garden to grow vegetables in or they'll go hungry.'

She thrust her face closer to his. 'And what's more, this is *my* house and land, not my husband's. *I* inherited it and I intend to keep it.'

He gaped at her. 'But I just told you, we can't stop now.'

Another voice shouted, 'Hey!'

He spun round to see Mayne Esher standing in the gap where the wall had been knocked down. Damn the woman!

Behind him, she repeated loudly and clearly, 'The money, Rusty. I know they'll have slipped you something. Give it to me, then at least it won't be spent on beer!'

Silence, then she took the five-pound note from him and spoke more quietly, 'And don't you dare go out. You're going to be busy setting my garden to rights once these people have taken away their nasty old machinery.'

Thompson could have been sick, he was so furious.

To add insult to injury, the lawyer moved forward. 'Mrs Warner! A moment if you please.' He handed her a business card.

She stared at it. 'I've never been given one of these before. I suddenly seem to be rather important.'

'Yes, you are. I suggest you keep my card somewhere safe and if you don't get a satisfactory amount of compensation from the council for the damage they've just done, please get in touch with me. I'll help you get payment and there will be no charge. I'm staying with Mr Woollard.'

'Why would you do that?'

'From time to time I like to help ordinary people who can't afford to pay lawyers' fees get justice, especially when certain people are acting in an . . . unorthodox manner.'

He ended his speech with a little bow and she looked flustered. 'Oh, well. Thank you.' She turned to Mayne. 'Just look what they've done to your wall, Mr Esher.'

'I'll send someone to make it good. Don't let your kids take any of the bricks away.'

'I'll have to find something to block that hole till then. My kids like exploring and you won't want them let loose in your grounds.'

Al had run up to join them. 'I know where there are some old gates we can prop across the hole till we can rebuild the wall, Mrs Warner.'

'That'd be a relief.' She looked round but her husband had slipped into the house so she turned her anger back on to Thompson. 'Get off my land, you. And don't come back again. The very idea of it, knocking down a family's front hedge and back garden wall, not to mention ruining a good apple tree. I've a good mind to complain to the mayor. I know his mother well. She was a close friend of my mother. In fact, I *will* complain to the mayor. *And* I'll talk to that nice lawyer.'

Thompson had had enough. There was something about the woman that told him she hadn't been lying when she said the land belonged to her. And if she knew the mayor . . .

Drawing himself up to his full height, which was still less than hers, and ignoring everyone else, he walked away, gesturing to the men to follow him.

One of them mouthed 'Sorry' to Mayne as he turned to leave.

Mrs Warner let out her breath in a long whoosh. 'What next, Mr Esher? Eeh, I've heard tales of that Thompson fellow and I can see now that they were all true. I'll give that lazy husband of mine what for when I get inside. How dare he give my land away?'

'Luckily, we got here in time to stop it.'

'Yes. But I was fond of that apple tree. It gave us a lot of fruit. And it was a nice old wall, that one. I like them narrow old bricks.'

'Perhaps the apple tree will grow again.'

'I hope so. Any road, I'd better unpack my shopping now and get dinner started. Al, I'd be grateful if you'd block that gap as quickly as you can.'

She looked round to see a row of children watching from the back of the house. 'Little devils,' she said fondly, then yelled in quite another tone, 'Get inside, you lot. *This minute!*'

They scattered, pushing and shoving to get into the house quickly as she walked towards them.

Mayne grinned at Ray. 'I'd back Mrs Warner against a whole troop of soldiers.'

'So would I. Salt of the earth, she is,' Ray agreed. 'Which is more than I'd say for that lazy husband of hers.'

'I'll go and fetch the gates to put across the hole.' Al hurried off towards the old stables to look for them.

Ben came running across towards them. 'Oh. I missed all the fun.'

Mayne tousled his stepson's hair. 'Fun, you call it. Thompson nearly got on to my land this time. What took you so long? And where's Sergeant Deemer?'

'He's off on a case. That new constable said he'd been forbidden to leave the police station for anything less than a murder.'

Mayne couldn't help chuckling. Deemer kept firm control of new young policemen, who trembled at the mere thought of upsetting him. But he trained them well.

'After that I had to go and tell Miss Peters what was going on. She's the one who noticed Mr Hawsworth following you in the first place. If she hadn't, they might have got right into Esherwood.'

'I must thank her myself later. And now, I've promised your mother we'll discuss how we're going to celebrate Christmas. We really ought to do something special for our first peacetime Christmas, don't you think?'

'We never used to do much at Christmas,' Ben said. 'Except for my stupid father getting drunk, of course.'

'Well, this year we're *all* going to celebrate in style and no one's going to get drunk.'

And, Mayne decided as he turned to trudge back to the house, during the festive season he would try to forget about the problems with his land and take Christmas for himself and his family. The wider world would get on without him. They'd still need to keep a careful watch, but even council workers got holidays at Christmas.

And then, after the New Year's festivities, he would steel himself to start on the conversion of his beloved home into flats. And start watching world events again. These were memorable times, after all.

* * *

When Ray got home he found that his wife had taken a phone call from their niece, who was still waiting to meet her fiancé in London.

'How is she? Has she heard about Anthony?'

'Yes. He'll be arriving in London by train tomorrow. If he's fit enough to be discharged, I've told her again that she's to bring him here.' She looked at the Forresters and explained, '*His* family were bombed out and Stephanie said they're living with his sister and her children, so none of them can take him in.'

Edna shook her head sadly. 'It won't be easy for her looking after him. I've seen photos in the newspapers of men who've been in the Far East prison camps, and read guidelines about how to help them adjust. As if anyone who hasn't been there can understand what it was really like!'

'We can only do our best to help Anthony,' her husband said bracingly. 'What else would we do with our money but help our family? Does Steph have enough money? Did you ask?'

'Yes. I checked that, Ray love. She sounded a bit nervous, though.'

'Well, she would be. First she got used to him being dead. Now she finds he's alive, but has been badly treated.'

'If anyone can cope, it'll be our Steph. She's doing well as your assistant, isn't she?'

'Very well.' He paused to study his wife's face. 'How are you feeling today, Edna? Really?'

'I'm fine. Getting better all the time.'

His wife said that every day, and she was, but so slowly. If he could have taken her away to somewhere sunny, he would have done, but Europe wasn't in a state yet to let people go holidaying on the Mediterranean.

In London, Stephanie at last got the news she'd been longing for. Anthony would be arriving by train from

Southampton the following day. This time it really was going to happen.

Last time she'd been informed of his arrival date, it had been changed suddenly because he'd fallen ill en route. He'd been removed from the ship repatriating prisoners of war to Britain from the Far East and admitted to hospital. They hadn't said why.

The next message said he'd recovered but had to convalesce in Cairo for a couple of weeks. How galling that must have been for him, to have to wait yet again to get home, even more frustrating than it was for her.

Only . . . perhaps he'd been too ill to waste energy on being upset. She'd read about the survivors, whom people were calling FEPOWs. She had to keep telling people that was short for Far East Prisoners of War because it wasn't generally known as an abbreviation. She'd seen photographs of groups of FEPOWs and many had looked just as bad as the prisoners being released from Belsen and other concentration camps in Europe.

Would she even recognise Anthony now? That worried her a lot.

Anyway, she was to be at the station today at two o'clock in the afternoon to meet him and she intended to get there well before that time to find a good place from which to view the men getting off the train.

Of course, she'd woken up far too early in the comfortable hotel near the station. She'd had her hair washed at a hairdresser's the previous day, wanting to look her best for him, and she'd paid the hotel extra for a bath before she went to bed. Thanks to her uncle Ray's generosity, she wasn't short of money.

She'd booked a second room next to hers for Anthony for a few nights because she doubted he'd want to travel on immediately. They could stay on in London for a while or go back to Lancashire, or find somewhere quiet in the country. Even in winter, some hotels stayed open. She'd do whatever suited him.

Her aunt and uncle were being wonderful about this. She got on far better with them than with her own parents. Had two brothers ever been as different as her father and her uncle? She wondered about it sometimes. Her father was an old stick-in-the-mud. Uncle Ray was one of the most intelligent men she'd ever met and very open to new developments and inventions. She loved working with him. He'd said he could find a job for Anthony as well later.

The morning passed with agonising slowness. She went out for a walk to pass the time, making her way along the streets of central London without taking anything in, let alone entering any of the shops.

She went to a British restaurant for an early luncheon because she happened to be passing one. She paid her ninepence and was served a simple meal of meat, peas and potatoes, followed by a small square of sponge cake with a few stewed plums (more juice than fruit) and thin custard.

The food was quite tasty but she had no appetite. However, she told herself she needed to keep up her strength to look after Anthony, so forced it all down, every single crumb. The war had taught them all not to waste food.

Then at last, at long last, it was time to go to Waterloo Station to wait for the train.

Even though she got there early, the part of the station to which she was directed was crowded already. It was a quiet crowd, more women than men, faces solemn. Anxiety seemed to hang in the air around them. They were all listening intently for the sound of a train and watching the track, even though the train wasn't due yet.

She could see a big station clock, but its hands seemed to be moving far more slowly than usual.

After what felt a long time, things started to happen. Some officials moved forward into the space that had been kept clear to provide access for getting people off the train. Stretcher bearers followed them and people pushing wheelchairs. Nurses in pristine uniforms, doctors, orderlies.

They too stood waiting, hardly saying a word to one another.

Finally, there was the distant sound of a train approaching and a whisper ran through the crowd. The noise grew louder and the train came into sight, chugging slowly into the station and – thank goodness! – towards their platform.

Faces were pressed against most of the train's windows. Pale, thin faces. Unsmiling. Where more than faces could be seen, the men seemed to be wearing uniforms that were too big for them.

The train stopped and officials converged on it, one or two calling to the crowd, which seemed poised to surge forward as well, 'Keep back please, everyone. Let them get off the train. We don't want to knock them over.'

Most of the first group of men had to be helped down, and if they gestured to those waiting to let them manage on their own, an orderly usually continued to hover nearby.

Cries began to echo in the crowd as people here and there recognised a loved one.

Stephanie recognised no one. But she did recognise the look, what she thought of as 'the famine look'. She'd seen it several times on the cinema newsreels.

The crowd grew sparser as more and more men got off the train and moved off the platform. The new arrivals were taken or directed to a meeting area and followed there by family members, though the latter were still behind a barrier. They could have pushed it over easily, but they didn't.

Stephanie's heart clenched. *What if she didn't recognise Anthony?*

Then one man stopped in the doorway of a compartment further along to stare at the crowd. He looked familiar, like a thin, twisted shadow of the man she loved.

Was it him? Yes, of course it was.

Hesitantly she raised one hand. He scanned the crowd again and just as she thought he'd not noticed her, he stiffened and looked straight at her. After a moment he nodded a greeting, but didn't raise his hand, keeping hold of the door as he waved away an offer of help and slowly stepped down on to the platform.

She waited to see him off the train, then moved along to the meeting area behind the other families.

It seemed a long time till Anthony came through. It was definitely him. She hadn't been mistaken.

Oh, thank goodness!

She moved forward towards him.

He was standing still now, watching her, waiting.

'Anthony?'

'Yes. More or less.'

She waited but he made no attempt to put his arms round her.

Someone came past and bumped into him. He staggered slightly and she reached out to steady him.

He patted her hand quickly then let go, moving further away from where people were walking. 'I'm not . . . used to . . . being among crowds of people.'

The silence was uncomfortable, so she looked round. 'Are you allowed to just leave or do we have to go through some formalities?'

'You have to sign me out. I've been told it's all right to leave as long as I have someone to help me.'

'Fine. I've booked rooms for us both in a hotel.'

'Good. I'm . . . tired.'

A man in an orderly's uniform came up to them. 'Ready to go, old man?'

Anthony's voice was suddenly harsh. 'Hell, yes.'

'This way.'

When all the formalities had been completed, they joined a queue for a taxi.

Beneath the remains of his tropical tan, Anthony's skin seemed pale, almost translucent. She thought he must be hanging on by sheer willpower, because he looked ready to collapse.

Luckily they didn't have to wait as long as she'd feared because there were a lot of taxis, coming one after the other.

Once he'd eased himself into it, Anthony leaned against the back of his seat, eyes closed.

Gathering his strength, she thought, and let him sit in peace. But she watched him, so happy to see him alive she felt as if she could burst.

At the hotel, she paid the taxi driver and he refused a tip. 'I wish I could afford to take them free,' he told her quietly. 'Only I have a family to support so I have to cover my costs. But I'm not taking tips, not from them.'

In the hotel lobby, she said brightly to the receptionist, 'I've brought my fiancé as I said I would. He's just back from Japan.'

The woman looked at him with pity in her eyes and when he glared at her, she hurriedly took a key from one of the pigeon holes and handed it to him.

The horrid cage-like lift, which Stephanie had avoided until now, was a godsend because his strength looked to be ebbing by the minute.

When she opened the door to his room, he stood there for a moment, clutching the door frame.

'Can you open the window, please. I know it's cold but I
. . . hate to be shut in.'

'Of course.'

When she turned round he was making his way to the
bed. She didn't offer to help but she was poised to jump to
his aid if he looked like falling.

She wasn't needed. He made it to the bed.

'Aaaah.' He lowered himself slowly sideways, to half lie
on the pillow and then didn't seem able to complete the
action by raising his feet on to the bed.

'Let me help you, darling.' She didn't wait for his answer,
but swung his legs up and helped him wriggle into a more
comfortable position on the pillows. Only then did she shut
the door and turn to him.

She'd heard the phrase 'devouring someone with his eyes'
but had never seen it before.

'You look older, but you look really well,' he said in a
thread of a voice.

'I am well.'

Silence, then. 'I gather you'd been told I was dead.'

'Yes.'

'Did you not think of finding another man? I was locked
away for a hell of a long time.'

'I didn't want one. It's you or no one, as far as I'm
concerned. Keith came after me again, but I moved away
from home to live with my uncle Ray and he made sure
Keith wouldn't bother me again.'

There was the faintest hint of a smile at that, so she continued,
'You'll like my uncle Ray. He and my aunt have offered you a
room, if you'd like. They have a very large house and your
parents can't take anyone else in because they were bombed
out and are living with your brother and his family. They want
to come over to see you, but I said we'd phone when you were
ready.'

'I'm not . . . ready yet.'

'I know. I'll just make a quick phone call to let them know you arrived safely, if you don't mind.'

'Yes, do that. You always were a good organiser.'

Was that a slight edge to his voice? She couldn't even tell whether he was being sarcastic or complimenting her. But she could recognise her own feelings. She still loved him.

'I need to sleep, Steph. Just an hour or two. I'm still . . . weak as a damned kitten.'

'I'll get you a jug of water and leave it by the bed. I'm next door at number—'

But he'd fallen asleep between one word and the next.

She took a few moments to study his face. Suffering was engraved on it, showing clearly even in sleep, and there was a scar on his chin. He was thin, far thinner than a human being should be.

But she'd look after him now, do whatever it took to help him get better. He had to get better. They had a lot of time to make up for.

As he slumbered on, she allowed herself to shed a few tears. Tears of relief, of joy, of sorrow for his troubles. Then she left him to sleep. But she took the key to the connecting door with her in case he needed something.

When Steph lay down on her bed, she too fell asleep, tired now after a poor night's sleep and the stress of meeting Anthony.

She woke to hear someone moaning and calling out nearby, recognising his voice almost immediately.

Instantly awake, she jerked to her feet, hurrying next door.

He was thrashing around, calling out, moaning.

She didn't know how best to help him, so sat on the edge of the bed and took his hand, raising it to her lips and kissing it, then holding it against her cheek.

He seemed to feel her loving touch and murmured some-thing. So she kept hold of his hand and prayed as she'd never prayed before that she would do the right thing – for him, for them.

As he opened his eyes and stared at her, she waited.

'It wasn't a dream. You are here.'

'Yes. Always, darling.'

'Did I call out?'

'Yes. So I came in and you quietened.'

It was his turn to raise her hand to his cheeks, then to his lips. 'I'm not much of a prize now, Stephie.'

'You are to me.'

'I . . . get moods. The doctor said—' He broke off and gulped as if in pain. 'He said we wouldn't be able to father children after the privations of camp life.'

'How can he possibly know that?'

The faintest hint of a smile crossed his face. 'You never did kow-tow to doctors, did you?'

'No. They do their best, but they're only human and they can make mistakes as easily as the next person.'

'They don't believe that.'

'Well, too bad. I believe it.'

His voice was the merest whisper. 'Ah, that's my Stephie. I really am home again.'

And he fell back to sleep.

She lay down beside him and pulled the quilt over them as best she could, determined to keep watch over him.

He snuggled against her and she held him even closer.

She could feel sleep overtaking her again, so gave in to it, smiling as she felt his hand so warm and soft in hers.

16

At Esherwood, they ate another of Beryl's evening meals, making her blush with their compliments about how tasty it was, even with the limited ingredients available these days.

After that the children went off to read in bed or chat, not seeming to notice how chilly it was by this time of the evening, how impossible it was to heat all the rooms. Kitty promised to send little Betty to bed 'soon'.

Auntie Beryl said she had letters to write and stayed in the kitchen, where it was still warm, instead of joining the other adults in the sitting room where a log fire had been lit to take some of the chill off. Mayne used the poker to make the fire burn more brightly and held his hands out to the flames before sitting down to one side of it next to Judith.

'Nice to feel warm for once.' She took his hand.

He leaned back and smiled at her. 'What a fraught few days these have been.'

The others settled in their usual places and inevitably the discussion turned to Thompson and what he might do next. Gradually each couple withdrew into a low-voiced, private conversation, leaving Daniel and Christa sitting together on a small two-seater couch in the bay window.

The maroon velvet curtains were drawn to keep out the

night and it felt cosy there, as if they were in their own little world.

He wished they too were a couple and gestured towards the others who were murmuring happily to one another. 'Just you and I left to chat, eh?'

'I like that.'

'You do?'

'Yes, of course.'

'So do I.' He took her hand and she didn't protest or pull away, but gave him one of her hesitant smiles, as if she was unsure of what he meant by his gesture.

Suddenly he couldn't hold his feelings back any longer. 'Oh, hell! I'm fed up of pussy-footing around. I know I'm older than you, but Christa, I've grown very fond of you and well, I wondered whether you . . . um, you might—'

She let out one of those soft chuckles that always charmed him. 'You're stammering like a schoolboy asking his first girl to go out with him.'

'I am, aren't I? And I should know how to do this better by my age. Christa, could we try . . . would *you* like us to try courting one another?'

Her reply came without hesitation. 'Yes, please. If you don't mind courting a refugee without a penny to her name.'

'Whether you have money or not makes no difference to me.'

'It makes me feel like a beggar.' She sounded fierce.

'Don't let that upset you. I've never cared about money. But your Mrs Pelling left you some so perhaps if you find the will, you'll feel more comfortable about money.'

'If we don't find the will, her horrible niece will have everything and that's wrong. Not because I hunger for her money, but because it isn't what Mrs Pelling wanted. She was such a kind lady, like a mother to me, and she deserves to have her final wishes honoured.'

He ventured to put an arm round Christa's shoulders and she snuggled up to him as if she'd been born to fit there. 'Perhaps you should look through your things again to see if you've missed something. The old lady might have slipped the will in among your clothes. It can't have been very big.'

'What's left to look through? I don't own all that much, Daniel. I only brought a small suitcase with me from Germany, and because of the war and clothes rationing, there hasn't been a chance to buy many other things. Anyway, I've searched through all my clothes, shaken them, shaken every book too.'

He sat up abruptly as something that had been teasing his mind suddenly clicked into place. 'The suitcase! Have you looked in that suitcase you brought from Germany?'

'There wasn't anything left in that except my rag doll.' Which had her mother's wedding ring sewn into it still, to keep it safe. The stitches hadn't been touched since.

'There might be something hidden in the lid or the lining of the case. You ought to check again, if only to be absolutely sure.'

'I suppose so, but I don't think I missed anything. I put the case in the attic after I got here. I'll go and look for it tomorrow.'

'Where was it kept at Mrs Pelling's house?'

She looked at him without speaking, frowning slightly. 'In the attic there as well. I never went near it from one month to the next after I settled in. Why should I?'

'No reason. But it wouldn't hurt to take another look.'

After a long silence, she spread her hands in a helpless gesture. 'I emptied the case completely and I'd have *seen* it if the will had been there.'

'Humour me. And there's no time like the present.' He pulled her to her feet and called to the others. 'Christa needs to get something out of that old suitcase of hers.'

Mayne stared at him in surprise. 'The one in the attic?'

'Yes. There's a document missing.'

'Better look in the case before my father starts hunting up there, then. Papers seem to vanish when he gets hold of them.'

'We'll go up right now.'

Surprised, Christa let Daniel take her hand and lead the way up the stairs. On her own she'd have felt nervous coming up here after dark. The electric lights were few and far between in the upper storeys of the house, giving only dim pools of light, and a couple of the bulbs were no longer working. To add to the eerie atmosphere, the old house occasionally creaked and groaned for no reason that she could work out, and that always sounded especially loud on the top floor.

She pressed closer to him. 'Shouldn't we wait until daylight?'

'No. Mayne's right. His father has already started hunting up here and anything could get messed around. Reginald Esher is not only the most impractical person I've ever met but the untidiest as well.'

'He does seem to live in a world of his own, doesn't he? But he's very kind.'

'When he thinks of it.'

As they went into the attic Christa shivered. It was much colder up here and the huge space was lit by only two bulbs. They were swinging slightly in the draughts, which created the illusion that things were moving round the edges of the room.

'I put my case over there.' She went to look but the case wasn't where she'd put it.

'I think I saw it at that far end.' Daniel pointed. 'In among a pile of old suitcases.'

As he moved forward she quickened her pace so that she stayed closer to him.

He seemed to realise she was feeling nervous and put an arm round her shoulders to give her a quick hug. When she looked up at him, he felt like kissing her, but this wasn't the time.

'Watch how you go.' He kept hold of her hand as they threaded their way slowly around untidy piles of furniture and boxes. It was even darker at the far side, away from the light coming in from the stairwell.

'There it is!' He let go of her to pounce on something and then showed her the case. 'This is yours, isn't it?'

'Yes.' She reached out to touch it, feeling tears rise in her eyes.

'Wait! Let me wipe some of the dust off with this rag. Every time we move things, dust rains down on other objects. There you are. We'll not open it here, but wait till we have more light, shall we? Careful how you go back.'

They paused for a moment on the landing and she took her suitcase from him, staring at it, feeling hungry to see every inch. It wasn't very big and it looked old and shabby but oh, it brought back so many memories that more tears welled in her eyes.

Something moved about inside when she shook it. 'That must be my rag doll. I've been too old for dolls for a long time now, but I didn't want to give it away because my mother made it for me. And anyway, her wedding ring is sewn inside it.' She hadn't told anyone else that, not even Mrs Pelling.

'How sad that she should do that.'

'I think she guessed they'd not be able to join me in England.'

He waited a moment till she managed a shaky smile, then he gave an exaggerated shiver. 'Brr. Let's take the suitcase somewhere brighter and warmer before we examine it.'

He took it from her and they went down to the next floor.

'Do you want to go back to join the others in the sitting room?'

'No, let's go into the kitchen and open it privately. I think I heard Mrs O'Brien go up to bed a short time ago.'

But when they got downstairs they heard voices in the kitchen and saw that the sitting room was empty, so they went in there instead.

'I can wait for my cup of bedtime cocoa.' He switched on the lights again and led the way over to the dying fire, putting the case down on the rug, gesturing to her. 'You do the honours.'

She opened the lid and took out the rag doll. 'Trudi, I called her.' She had a sudden desire to hug the doll close, but didn't want Daniel to think her foolish, so put it down and turned back to the case, holding the lid wide open. 'See. It's empty.'

'But it has a lining. Humour me. Let's check every inch.' He started examining the seams down one side, then the other. 'Hey, there's a gap here where the stitching has come undone.'

'That's strange. It wasn't like that before. I'd have noticed.'

He began to pat the lining round the gap. 'Nothing there.'

She turned away, trying to hide her disappointment, but swung back as he exclaimed, 'No, wait! It feels as though there's an envelope inside the lining. It must have slipped along from the hole. Darn! My hand is too big to reach it. Your hand's much smaller than mine. I wonder if you could do better. If not, we'll have to cut open the seam.'

She knelt down and slid her hand inside. She wriggled her fingers along till she could just touch the edge of an envelope, but she couldn't get close enough. Taking her hand out, she managed to unpick a couple of stitches in the seam, then tried again.

This time she got hold of the envelope and slid it along

carefully towards the hole. Pulling it out, she held it up to him.

'No, you read it, Christa.'

The envelope wasn't sealed. She pulled out some pieces of paper, moved closer to a nearby table lamp and began to read aloud the words on the covering page, '*Last will and testament of Elsa Catherine Pelling . . .*'

She couldn't read any further because the sight of her foster mother's name made tears gather and try as she might to stop them, they escaped her control. She reached out to touch the name written there with her fingertips, because it was as close as she could now get to the second mother she'd lost.

Then Daniel's arms were round her and he was kissing her face, wiping away the tears with his handkerchief and holding her close. Safe in his embrace, she let the dam she'd carefully built to contain her emotions burst and began to sob.

Someone peered in through the doorway and he shook his head at them. He didn't even notice who it was, only knew that he and Christa needed some time together. When she calmed down, he would help her read the will and decide what to do.

It took a while for her to stop crying and look up at him. 'I'm sorry.'

'What for, Christa? Weeping for the woman you loved? For all that you've lost?' He pulled her into his arms again.

A few minutes later they read the will together. It was very simple. Mrs Pelling wished to make it plain that she had no relatives left who mattered, because none of them had helped her or even come near her after her son died. She was therefore leaving everything to her foster-daughter Christa Summers, who had been like a true daughter to her.

There followed a list of the main assets: the house, any

money left in the bank, some stocks and shares, and Mrs Pelling's jewellery, most of which was stored in the bank.

'I can't take all that,' Christa whispered.

'Of course you can. But before we do anything else, we need to get this will witnessed by a lawyer in Rivenshaw and then have a copy made for Mr Audley. We'll do that tomorrow. In the meantime we must put it somewhere safe.'

She thrust it at him. 'You keep it.'

'Are you sure?'

'Yes.'

'We'll show the will to Mayne and Judith as well, if you don't mind. The more witnesses there are to its existence, the better. Come on! No time like the present.'

In the kitchen Daniel explained what they'd found and everyone read the short will before he put it safely in his pocket.

Once that was done, he gave Christa a nudge. 'Go to bed now. You look exhausted.'

He nearly called her 'darling' but it was too soon to make that public. He thought of her as his darling, though.

Sam had stayed away for several days and been tempted not to return to Rivenshaw at all, because he was more at risk of being recognised there. But that would mean giving up the things they'd stolen and hidden in the big house during the war, and he couldn't bear to do that.

He drove back openly in the small, ex-Army lorry he'd stolen, wearing an officer's uniform. No one stopped him or questioned where he was going.

He'd thought long and hard about how to hide the lorry and intended to ask the cousin of one of the other men now languishing in prison to help him. There would be a small risk in that, but he didn't think anyone from that family had much time for the police.

The cousin had a farm just outside Rivenshaw and was probably not averse to making some easy money, so Sam intended to offer him a weekly amount to keep the lorry hidden at the farm. He'd stay there with it today until after midnight then make his way into town and hide out at his mother's again.

His plan worked like a dream; the cousin was happy to help and Sam's spirits were high as he crept through the dark streets of the little town. He only had one close call but luckily the other man had been drinking and didn't even see him pressed back in the shop doorway.

At his mother's he let himself in with the back door key which she would insist on leaving hidden under a stone, and tapped on her bedroom door.

'It's me, Ma. I'm back.'

He heard a faint cry of surprise then the creaking of springs as she got out of bed. She appeared in the doorway, still dragging on her dressing gown, and gave him a big hug. 'Eh, our Sam, I've been sleeping badly, worrying about you. Come and tell me what you've been doing.'

'Planning my escape.' He told her about the details and where he'd left the lorry.

She looked at him. 'You won't change your mind about taking me out to join you in Australia.'

'No, love, I won't. You're the only one who visited me in prison and you've given me shelter here at some risk to yourself. I won't forget that. Anyway, I can't face life without my old Ma.' He gave her another hug to prove it.

She listened to his tale of what he'd been doing, then sighed. 'I hope it continues to go well.'

'It will. I learned my lesson last time. I shan't be going at it like a bull at a gate this time. And Cuthbert's a cautious sod. That's why he got away before. He and I will plan out in detail how to get the loot back, and it'll go off as smoothly as clockwork. You'll see.'

They chatted for a while in the cosy darkness of the kitchen, then he couldn't hold back a yawn.

'Bed,' she said firmly. 'And don't wander round the house during the day. There are customers popping in and out all the time. I'll bring you up some food when the coast is clear.'

As they parted and he turned towards the attic stairs, she pulled him back and framed his face with her hands. 'You *will* be careful, son, *really* careful.'

'Yes, Ma. But just in case . . .' He reached into his inner pocket and pulled out the envelope. 'I've put some money in here for you. I don't want you going short while you wait to join me in Australia. There's more than enough there to pay your fare.'

The following morning, before it was even light, Reginald Esher walked in through the back door of the big house. He smiled round at the people having breakfast. 'Good morning to you all,' he said cheerfully, 'I couldn't sleep so I thought I'd start work in the attics.'

'Good thing we sorted out your suitcase last night,' Daniel whispered to Christa.

Mayne frowned at his father. 'I thought we'd agreed that you'd only work with your two helpers so they can keep things in order?'

Reginald flapped one hand at him. 'Oh, I can't wait for them. They said they'd be a little late this morning and I'm raring to go. I've been wide awake for two hours already, seeing that box in my mind's eye, the one I think the diary will be in. I couldn't get back to sleep for thinking of it, so Mrs Rennie made me an early breakfast and here I am.'

Mayne exchanged a long-suffering glance with Judith, then looked at Christa. 'If you've not got anything planned for this morning, perhaps you could help my father in the attic till his ladies arrive?'

'I'm happy to help. We're not going to see the lawyer till later.'

'Your main jobs will be to put things back once my father has checked them and stop him reading instead of carrying on with the search.'

Reginald grinned at her. 'I do get a bit lost in a book when I find something interesting. Just give me a nudge. It won't upset me.'

'I'd better help them as well,' Daniel said. 'Neither of them can lift the really heavy boxes.'

'I'll come too and we'll find out where that cable leads while they're searching,' Francis said at once.

Daniel clapped him on the shoulders. 'Good idea. When that's all sorted out, I'll go with Christa to the lawyer's then come back and get on with finishing my scale diagram. Then finally I'll be able to start on the preliminary sketches of how we could fit flats into this house.'

Mayne's face twisted with sadness for a moment or two, then he took a deep breath and said briskly, 'Very well. I'll stay outside with the others this morning keeping a watch out for Thompson. He'll try again to get hold of my land, I know he will.'

'Unfortunately, I think you're right.' Judith turned to the other women. 'Let's plan out the meals and the shopping duties. Whose turn is it to qucuc today?'

Ros groaned.

'I'll do it,' Diana offered.

'Are you sure?' Ros said. 'It's definitely my turn.'

'I think I get better supplies when I go.'

Ros grinned at her. 'You just flutter those long eyelashes and our dear grocer reaches under the counter.'

'I do not flutter my eyelashes at him.'

'You don't mean to, I know. But a woman as beautiful as you only has to look at a man for him to feel special.'

'Oh. Well, as long as you know that I'm *not* encouraging him.'

Judith gave her a quick hug. 'We know you're not. Ros was just teasing. So we'll leave you to do the shopping for us, eh?'

'I'll keep my eyes open for extras.'

'You do that. We're all sick of queuing, but we don't want to miss anything that might have come into the shops now that shipments are starting to get through from overseas. You know how quickly a queue can form once word gets out that something's arrived.'

Diana nodded. 'Last time I went I heard rumours that bananas might be available for Christmas. Just imagine that.'

'If more of those stupid dock strikes don't prevent them getting unloaded,' Ros said bitterly. 'Betty can't even remember eating a banana, poor little love.'

'It was always a rare treat for my children, but that was for financial reasons,' Judith said quietly. 'One day life will get back to normal. We've come so far, winning the war. Now we have to wait just a little longer for peace and plenty.'

17

Christa followed Reginald up to the attic. 'What does the box we're hunting for look like?'

'It's about this big.' He gestured with his hands. 'And two of the top corners have been crushed. The soldiers were very careless about moving my boxes of books when my wife and I had to get out of the big house. I was angry about that but the officer in charge didn't care, just said there was a war on and told the men to hurry up with my rubbish.'

He stopped dead in the attic doorway and blinked in shock. 'Oh, dear! I didn't realise how much stuff had been put up here.'

She stared round, but she'd seen it before.

'Where do I start?' he asked helplessly. The grey light of the winter morning added enough to the feeble electric lights to show him very clearly what a mess the attic was in.

'We could walk round and check where the main piles of boxes are. You might even see the one you're looking for.'

But a tour of the attic, winding in and out of the untidy piles, showed only a jumble of furniture, old luggage and boxes whose contents were anybody's guess.

Footsteps running lightly up the stairs heralded the arrival of Daniel.

Reginald greeted him with, 'We've walked round to take a look, but I'm afraid I don't know where to start.'

'How about we pile all the boxes we can reach to one side and check whether any have battered corners? You're quite sure about that, Mr Esher?'

'Oh, yes. It's the one thing I am sure about because I remember clearly how angry I felt.'

The most easily reachable parts of the attic yielded no boxes with battered corners and as they were about to start moving things around to get to other piles, Francis came up to join them.

'I got delayed by a crisis in the kitchen,' he announced cheerfully. 'I had to put a new fuse wire in. Really, it should all be rewired. Now, where are you up to? What can I do?'

With his help, they tackled the next section more quickly, but with no better result, then they nipped downstairs for a cup of tea. Mayne came in from the grounds and joined them in the kitchen.

'It's going to take forever,' Reginald told his son gloomily. 'And all the books in the boxes really ought to be checked for mould.'

'That will have to wait, Dad,' Mayne said firmly. 'We're looking for one particular book, remember.'

The two women helping his father arrived to join them as they were finishing their snack, so they went back upstairs feeling sure they'd get on more quickly now.

The trouble was, his helpers insisted on opening each box for a quick check of the contents, because they didn't trust old Mr Esher's memory.

'I should have thought of that,' Daniel muttered. 'They're right. He can be very vague about details.'

'Never mind. I—'

Christa broke off as there was a scream from one end of the attic and when they swung round, they saw that one of the women had put her foot through a rotten plank and her calf was bleeding.

'I daren't pull my leg out in case the sharp ends of broken planks cut me.' She was clutching a nearby table and she winced as she looked down.

Testing the floor carefully and trying to put his full weight only where the planks were screwed to beams, Daniel went to her side and asked Francis to hold her from behind in case the floor around the hole started to give way. 'I think the roof has been leaking a little above this part.'

Between them they got her out and as the leg seemed to be badly scratched but not in need of stitches, they left the other woman to help her downstairs and bathe her wounds in the nearest bathroom. If they thought it needed a bandage, they'd have to go to the first aid box Mayne had insisted on putting in a prominent position in the kitchen.

In the meantime, Francis had gone to stand as close as he dared to the hole and was shining his torch into it. 'Hey! I think this is the space into which that stray cable leads.'

Daniel and Christa peered over his shoulder but didn't go too near.

He looked round to estimate where they were in relation to the rest of the house. 'I'm right, aren't I? This is the area above the bathroom?' At their nods of agreement, he said thoughtfully, 'We wondered about the false ceiling, didn't we? Well, we're looking right into it. I can see now that it wasn't put there to make the bathroom easier to warm; it was to hide something.'

'It's galling to be able to see so little,' Daniel said. 'How do we get into it?'

Francis stared towards the narrow secret area at the side of the attic, one end of which was close by. 'Perhaps that makeshift ladder we saw behind that false wall leads into this. Only I don't think any of us chaps can get down it. We're none of us exactly skinny because the Army put good muscles on us.'

'I'm much smaller than you are. I bet I could get down,' Christa offered.

Daniel shook his head at once. 'No. Definitely not. It's too dangerous.'

'I could tie a rope to something and fasten it round my waist. It'd be safe enough if I tested the ladder rung by rung and—'

'*No!* I'm not letting you risk your life, Christa.' He lowered his voice to add for her ears only, 'You're too precious to me.' Then he peered down the hole again, borrowing the torch from Francis and shining it to and fro. 'It looks like . . . I think those are paintings. Big ones, too, judging by their corners. With such a narrow staircase, the only way they could have got those paintings in was to put them there *before* they added the false ceiling.'

Francis blew out his breath in surprise. 'My goodness, they did go to some lengths to hide these things, didn't they? It must have taken days to construct.'

'I can't see the Army looters doing that. Someone would have noticed what they were up to.'

'I agree. And anyway, why would looters steal big paintings? They'd be impossible to sneak out of the house. Besides, looters would be unlikely to have any expertise in judging their worth, let alone knowing how to sell them.'

'Who else could have done it?' Christa wondered.

There was a silence as the two men exchanged glances.

'Tell me!' she insisted.

It was Daniel who answered. 'Apparently Mayne's mother stole things and well, she grew very strange towards the end because she was suffering from senile dementia.'

'But this didn't happen towards the end of the war.' Francis frowned. 'I've heard Mayne say there was a lot of family money unaccounted for even before the war started. Could she have been buying antiques with it, do you think?'

'Why would she do that? She already had a home full of them.'

'Well, if her husband died, everything would pass to Mayne and she'd have to move to the Dower House. He told me once that she was furious she couldn't live in the style she'd expected, and that everything had to be left to her son under an entail. Mayne and his father refused to break the entail in her favour. She might have been ensuring she had money of her own in the future.'

'This is only conjecture,' Francis objected.

'I know. But something happened to the family money and Mr Esher would have been very easy to hoodwink.'

They all moved back a bit, leaning against whichever piece of furniture was nearby as they contemplated the hole.

'Only one way to find out,' Francis said at last. 'Someone will have to go down into it.'

'Me!' Christa insisted.

They heard Reginald's two helpers returning and Daniel put one finger to his lips, sliding a big empty cardboard box across the hole with his foot. 'Don't move that,' he told them. 'How's the leg?'

'It was just a few scratches,' the injured woman said. 'They bled a lot at first but that's stopped now. They'll heal more quickly if I let the air get to them, so let's get back to work.'

As they turned to look for him, Reginald yelled at the top of his voice, 'It's here! I've found it. I *told* you I'd recognise the box.'

They all went to look and sure enough there was a battered box with two corners crushed and crumpled.

Beaming, Reginald lifted it to a lower position and tore back the cardboard lid to examine the books, pouncing on one. 'There you are! This is the missing diary.'

He clutched it to his chest. 'I have to go home and start reading through it straight away. I'm sure it contains the information we need to get into that secret cellar, and the sooner we do that the better.'

'Just a minute, Mr Esher.' One of the women grabbed his arm and the other took the book from him. 'Mr Mayne said he wanted to see the book if we found it.'

'But there isn't any time to waste.'

'Mr Esher, your son has been paying us to help and we have to follow his instructions. It won't take long. Let's go and find him now.' She winked at the others. 'I don't suppose we'll be back if this is the book. Unless you want us to tidy up?'

Francis smiled back at her. 'No need. We'd only make it untidy again as we sort through the boxes.'

The minute the three of them had gone, with Reginald still protesting, Francis went across to the secret room and started moving the boxes away from its entrance.

As Christa went to join him, Daniel pulled her back. 'Darling, I don't want you to take this risk.'

'I'm sure we can find a safe way for me to do it.' Christa gave him a very determined look. 'I want to help the Eshers in every way possible. I owe them a lot for taking me in. Besides, I'm the smallest adult, so it seems obvious I should be the one who investigates the hole.'

Francis looked from one to the other. 'I can get inside the narrow room, even if I can't get down that ladder. How about I make sure the footing is secure and give her a safety harness to wear in case one of the rungs of the ladder gives way?'

She spoke before Daniel could protest again. 'Good idea. Let's do that.'

When the wooden wall panels had been removed again, the narrow space was revealed more fully by the light of a couple of lamps rigged up by Francis to shine along the inside. At least they could now see well enough to check that the floor was sound in that part of the attic. Francis was thinner than Daniel so could edge inside the area more easily, but when it came to twisting his body down the hole, he just couldn't do it.

As he came out again, he gave them a rueful smile. 'I'm not even sure *you* can get down there, Christa. It's very narrow.'

'Who could it have been built for?' Daniel wondered. 'Mayne's mother wasn't a very active sort of woman and I've seen photos of her. She was quite plump and would definitely not have got down that hole.'

'Mayne said she was very friendly with his ex-fiancée, Caroline,' Daniel said thoughtfully. 'I met her a couple of times when she came to visit Mayne in London, didn't you?'

Francis shook his head.

'Well she was so thin she looked as if a puff of wind would blow her away. Pretty, but no warmth in her eyes. I didn't take to her at all. He caught her and his mother stealing pieces of the family silver and other small items after the war, so perhaps they were involved in creating this hiding place, too. Pity his mother is dead. No one will ever know now what she did with the money she stole.'

'Would they really have arranged to hide things down there?' Christa asked. 'It seems such a strange thing to do.'

Daniel frowned. 'Those were strange times. They'd have had to find someone who could do the fixing, mind, and it wasn't very well done. There's only about a yard of space above that false new bathroom ceiling. Silly place to choose if you ask me. They must have thought those pictures very valuable to go to all that trouble.'

'Well, let's get on with it.' Francis hurried off down the stairs and came back shortly afterwards with a safety harness, which he fitted on to Christa before attaching it to the chunky ball feet of the heavy mahogany tallboy standing nearby. Then he fastened one torch round her neck and shone another down the hole as he watched her start down slowly and carefully.

'Is she all right?' Daniel called from outside in the attic.

'Shh.'

A bright light came on suddenly down in the hole.

'What the hell did you do, Christa?' Francis called in shock.

'There was a light switch, so I tried it. I'm surprised it worked at all. It's covered in dust. I don't think anyone's been down here since the beginning of the war. Hmm. This is strange.'

The two men waited, but she didn't explain what was puzzling her.

'For heaven's sake, keep talking, Christa, then we'll know you're all right.'

'Sorry. The ladder comes to a stop here and I don't think anyone is meant to go further. In fact, I'd guess this was built to help take the weight of the paintings off the ceiling once they'd been put in. They're sort of strapped to the walls and the foot of the ladder. You were right, Francis. The paintings can only be taken out by removing the bathroom ceiling.'

'Come back up, then.'

'All right.' She let out a little squeak.

'*What is it?*'

'Just a big spider running up my arm. Ugh! It had horrible hairy legs.' The light went off again and she twisted her body round to climb slowly out of the hole.

When she came back into the attic, Daniel let out an inarticulate cry and dragged her into his arms. 'You're not going into that hole again. I died a thousand deaths thinking you might get hurt or trapped.'

'Did you really?'

'Of course I did, you little fool.'

Francis allowed them a moment or two of this then said in a matter-of-fact voice, 'We'd better fetch Mayne. We can't tear his ceilings apart without his permission. How much could you see, Christa?'

'I couldn't see what the paintings were like, because they were wrapped in some sort of canvas. But one corner was torn and I could see the frame. It was fancy gold and looked expensive, even though it was dusty. I do hope they're all valuable, for Mayne and Judith's sake.'

'Sounds hopeful. Let's go and tell him what we've found, then. I could do with a breath of fresh air.' Daniel studied her face and teased, 'You might want to brush the cobwebs out of your hair first, though, not to mention washing the dirty smears from your face.'

She gasped and fled down to the bathroom.

Once she was out of hearing, Francis nudged his friend. 'You've got it bad, haven't you?'

'Very bad. And I'm a decade older than her.'

'What does that matter? If I'm any judge, she's got it bad, too. And I think her experiences have probably made her mature for her years. Well, they would, wouldn't they?'

They found Mayne striding up and down the back strip of land like a caged lion.

'Nothing going on out here today?' Francis asked.

'Nope. But I bet Thompson is plotting his next attempt.'

'Did you see the diary your dad found?'

'Yes. I had a hard time reading the handwriting from that era, but he seemed to find it easy. He's gone off to read it and transcribe anything important.'

'Good. We have other news for you, Mayne. Christa went into that hole in the narrow secret room and found out why the ceiling in the bathroom below is so much lower than the others.'

After they'd explained about the paintings, Mayne actually managed a wry smile, then as Jan came strolling towards them, he exclaimed, 'Just the man I need!'

He left Jan keeping watch and hurried back to the big house with them. 'We'll take that ceiling out straight away. I want to see what's hidden there. Judith, could you phone Ray please and ask him to join us here? He'll know better than anyone if the paintings have any value.'

'Of course I can. I hope they're worth a fortune.'

'So do I.' For a moment or two he allowed himself to dream. It would make such a difference to his future life.

'Would you mind if Christa and I go out now, Mayne?' Daniel asked. 'It's nearly time for that appointment I told you about with the lawyer.'

'What? Oh yes. I'll open the safe and get Mrs Pelling's will out for you.'

After making a copy of the will, Christa and Daniel strolled into town hand in hand, with the documents tucked safely in his inner jacket pocket. They were hardly aware of anyone else as they walked, though Daniel did wave to Miss Peters as they passed her house and saw her smiling at them from the bedroom window.

The local lawyer, Stuart Melford, was waiting for them at his rooms.

Daniel had explained the situation when he phoned and now produced the will, before sitting back and leaving it to Christa to answer the lawyer's questions.

'Could you phone Mr Audley and work out how best to formally verify the will for us?'

'First *we* have to be sure that it's genuine,' Stuart said.

'Apparently his clerk draws up all the wills,' Christa said.

'Mr Stackpole will know exactly how it's phrased, I should think, and who signed it. He's a very helpful man, and kind too. Mrs Pelling thought the world of him.'

'Perhaps you two could leave the will with me and wait in the outer office while I speak to Mr Audley?' Stuart said.

'Yes, of course.'

Ten minutes later he came out, smiling. 'I spoke to both him and his clerk, and they both feel this will sounds genuine. Mr Stackpole will be coming to Rivenshaw tomorrow to verify it himself, since he supervised its creation and is one of the signatories.'

'Oh, that's good. He's a very . . .' she hesitated and sought for a word, as she occasionally did in English, 'a very *honourable* man, the sort you'd trust instantly.'

'And will you trust me to keep the original will safe until then? You'll have the copy.'

'Yes, of course.'

As they left the lawyer's rooms, she chuckled. 'How could you not trust someone with as open a face as Mr Melford?'

'He's well thought of in Rivenshaw, though he's only been here a short time.'

As they strolled back towards Esherwood, she sighed happily. 'It is right that Mrs Pelling's wishes shall be carried out.'

'And you must feel better to have the prospect of money of your own?'

'I do. Daniel, I'd like to use it to buy a house. Is that possible? It seems so long since I've had a real home of my own.'

'It's likely to take several weeks to get probate, and houses aren't easy to find since the war.'

'I can wait. Maybe you can design one for me and your company can build it?'

'For us, don't you mean?' He pulled her closer, heedless

of who might see them. 'Let's not wait too long to get married. I'll put up half of the money if we can find a house to buy.'

'Your money is for the business. Let me buy the house.' She gave him a wry smile. 'Such plans and that will we found hasn't even been verified.'

'Never mind the will. I want us to agree and tell everyone that we're going to get married.'

'If you really wish it.'

'I wish very much to marry you. Christa darling, what have I said? You're crying.'

She blinked away the tears. 'This time I'm crying out of happiness.'

'But surely you understood where we were heading?'

'I was afraid to hope for too much. You've talked about love but not really about marriage.'

He took her face in his hands and kissed her mouth firmly. 'You should be very sure indeed that I want to marry you, my darling.'

As they set off again, he said, 'We'll try to find my aunt a house near us, if that doesn't upset you. She's not the interfering sort.'

'That'd be wonderful. She's so kind, reminds me of my dear Mrs Pelling in some ways and in others, of my mother.'

Happy simply to be together, Daniel and Christa continued to stroll back from town, only to jerk abruptly back to reality as they reached the top of Parson's Mead.

Mrs Rennie was standing outside the Dower House, arms akimbo, confronting Thompson, who was dripping water. He seemed to be trying to shout her down. Two workmen were standing nearby looking embarrassed, but though he was gesticulating vigorously at them to join him, they didn't move to his aid.

'What's he been trying to do now?' Daniel exclaimed as

they both broke into a run. 'And how did he get so wet? It's been fine all day.'

Only then did he notice the small lorry parked out of sight behind the clump of trees at the top of Parsons Mead. 'Ah. He's trying to sneak in. But how can he expect to get past the chain?'

'Oh, Mr O'Brien, I'm so glad to see you!' Mrs Rennie cried as soon as she saw them. 'This nasty man is trying to break into Esherwood again. It's a good thing I was pegging out my washing because Mr Esher doesn't notice a thing going on outside the house once he's got his head in a book.'

'I've just told you I'm not trying to break in anywhere, woman!' Thompson yelled. 'And if you'd have given me the key to this padlock, as I asked—'

'Don't you "woman" me! You're perfectly well aware of my name.'

Ignoring that, he carried on yelling. 'I have authorisation from the council – *from the council* – to make a start on the prefabs, and that's what I intend to do. You could have let me in. I'm sure you have a key.'

'The prefabs are at the back of Esherwood not the front, so why you want to break our lock and chain here, I do not know. Vandalism, I call it. Sheer vandalism. And I'm sure it's against the law to destroy other people's property.'

Daniel walked across to examine the huge padlock, which held the big chain in place across the drive and saw a scratch across it where someone had tried to saw through it. He looked down at a hacksaw lying nearby and let out a snort of amusement. They'd need a better saw than that to succeed! The padlock left by the Army was of very high-quality steel, like the chain.

'Lucky I had my watering can nearby,' she said to Daniel and Christa. 'I called out to him to get back but he brandished the saw and yelled at me to mind my own business.

So I poured the water over him. That made him jump back all right.'

Daniel had difficulty controlling a laugh. He wished he'd seen that.

Thompson glared at them all impartially. 'I'll be reporting you to the police for that attack on my person, woman. And you mind your own business.'

Mrs Rennie pointed one forefinger at him. 'We can go and see Sergeant Deemer together, *fellow*, and I can report you at the same time as you report me, only you really were trespassing and attempting to destroy Mr Esher's property, while I was just doing my job.'

Thompson was so dark a shade of red from suppressed anger that Daniel wouldn't have been surprised if the man had a seizure. 'I think you'd better leave now, Thompson. And if you attempt to break in this way again, we really will go to the police.'

After a moment's hesitation Thompson spun round and stormed across to the lorry. 'Hurry up, you two!' he yelled to the workmen. 'I haven't got all day to waste. If you'd done as I'd told you and kept her away from me, we'd have been inside by now.'

'It feels as if we're under siege,' Daniel said. 'I wonder why he thought he'd get away with it today.'

After a moment's thought, Christa suggested, 'Could it be . . . do you think he'd arranged a diversion for the rear of the estate? It's what I'd have done.'

'Dammit, I bet you're right. Come on, Christa. Let's see if we're needed at the rear.'

He set off along the drive at a run, and was pleased at how easily she kept up with him. In fact, everything about her pleased him.

18

Since the day was passing with no sign of Thompson, Mayne decided this was a good time to help Al replace one of the rusty hinges on the hastily constructed gates with a more solid one. Ray wasn't coming round till later, when they'd have got the paintings out of their hiding place.

Suddenly a council lorry pulled up at the rear of the grounds and three men jumped out. One of them was carrying a crowbar and he pointed it towards the gate, then strode forward, heavy boots thudding on the ground.

'Damnation!' Mayne muttered and immediately rang the warning siren, pushing the gate shut and standing in front of it because he couldn't lock it with the old hinge off and the new one not yet screwed in place.

Al came to stand by his side. 'Thompson doesn't give up easily, does he?'

The men stopped just in front of them.

'Three of us, two of you,' the leader jeered. 'If you have any sense, you'll get out of our way.'

Mayne didn't answer. He'd not seen this man before and felt pretty sure he didn't work for the council, though the other two looked familiar.

Before he realised what was intended, the leader grabbed him and tried to drag him away from the gate. He fought back using all his wartime skills, and not only prevented his attacker from using the crowbar but made him drop it. Unfortunately, this was a strong man who was also an expert fighter and Mayne couldn't get free of him.

The other two were still hesitating, eyeing Al, who had snatched up the crowbar and was looking more than ready to use it.

'Get the other one out of the way,' the leader yelled. 'What the hell are you waiting for? You're two to one.'

Just as they began to edge slowly forward, looking anything but eager for a fight, another voice yelled, 'Oi! What do you think you're doing?'

They stepped hastily back.

The leader glanced towards the voice, cursed at the sight of a policeman and let go. As Mayne shoved him further away, he made a threatening fist, as if he was going to start the fight again.

'Stop that at once, you!' the policeman yelled.

As Mayne stood up, Al dropped the crowbar and came to stand by his side, saying in a low voice, 'It's the new policeman, Waide I think he's called. At least the numbers are equal now, even though he's not up to their weight.'

The tall, spindly young constable placed himself between the two groups and addressed the leader of the attackers. 'I asked what you were doing.'

'Trying to get inside this gate on lawful council business.'

The leader moved as if to pick up the crowbar, but Waide put one foot on it. 'You can collect this from the police station tomorrow. And you still haven't answered my question.'

'We've been told to start work here and not to let anyone stop us, and that's what we're going to do.'

'Sergeant Deemer told me about this situation . . . *sir.*' The way the young constable said the last word showed clearly whose side he was on, however politely he spoke. 'The council has no legal authorisation for this work and if you three try again to get into the grounds of Esherwood, I'll have to arrest you for trespassing.'

His voice wobbled slightly on the last few words and Mayne felt sorry for him. Waide had only been working as a policeman for a short time. He wouldn't have been let out on his own before the war, but they were short of men in the police force till former officers were demobbed.

'Who ordered you to do this?' the constable asked when no one spoke.

'Mr Thompson did, and he should know what's right.'

'Well, he's wrong this time. As long as *you* go away, it's him I'll be reporting to Sergeant Deemer not you, for . . . for inciting damage and trespass. Now, go away and don't try this again, whoever orders you to do it. It's against the law and will get you in big trouble. I shall be coming past regularly for the rest of the afternoon to check that the situation has stayed peaceful.'

Two of the men immediately moved back to the lorry, looking distinctly relieved. The leader hesitated, then followed them, scowling at Mayne and Al. One of the other men, whom Mayne had known for many years, gave him a sly wink as he went round to the driver's seat.

'I'll leave you to get on with your work now, Mr Esher,' the young officer said once the trio had driven off. 'I don't think they'll return but I'll report it to Sergeant Deemer next time I go past the police station. He'll be the one to deal with Mr Thompson. I'll just take this back with me.' He picked up the crowbar, touched his helmet in a polite gesture and strode away.

'He's going to make a good police officer, that one,' Mayne said. 'He stood his ground well.'

'I wonder why those fellows did this?' Al said. 'They must have known they wouldn't succeed. They didn't even have any heavy digging equipment in the back of the lorry.'

Mayne looked at him, trying to work it out. 'I think they just wanted to get into the grounds.'

'Stake a claim, as it were.'

'That settles it. If we're going to have to fight them off every day, I'd better ask for an injunction from the local magistrate to prevent them from trying to force their way in. I thought Thompson would stop if we showed him we're on our toes, but clearly he was just biding his time.'

Al didn't reply, but he was chewing the corner of his lip and looking doubtful.

'What's the matter?'

'Well, it'd be OK if you got old Colonel Crayshore as magistrate, but if you got Mr Horton, he'd be on Thompson's side. I saw them going into the Order of Ancient Ravens' lodge together the other night. I wonder if Thompson's a member or has been invited to join?'

'That'd give him another arrow to his bow, because members of that society stick together like glue. I reckon Horton only got to be a magistrate because of the war.'

'And because he's got money. He's not liked in town but money talks and he's got enough to talk loudly.'

'What a tangle this country is in! I don't envy the government the huge task of trying to change back to peacetime ways of doing things. And in the meantime villains are making the most of the confusion to try to grab what they can.'

After a moment's silence, he added, 'Will you be all right on your own here, Al? I'd better check the front entrance.'

'I'll be fine. If you'll just hold the hinge in place while I put in the first couple of screws, I can finish fixing it quite quickly and then bar the gate. I doubt those fellows will be back today with Constable Waide patrolling regularly.'

'I've not seen the one with the crowbar before. Have you?'

'No. I don't think he's from Rivenshaw, and you have to wonder if he's even employed by the council.'

Mayne helped Al fix the hinge then set off at a brisk pace. As he passed the big house, he saw Daniel and Christa hurrying towards him down the main drive, looking anxious.

When they told him about Thompson's latest effort to force his way in, he pounded one clenched fist into the palm of his other hand a couple of times to vent his anger. 'That settles it. I'll have to get some legal advice about what steps to take.'

Just then he saw Ray walking up the drive with his lawyer friend Forrester. 'Good timing!'

Their partner greeted Mayne with, 'So you've found some paintings, have you?'

'Yes. There are several – big and quite old, I think – but we haven't been able to take a good look at them yet, because of where they're stored. I left Jan pulling the ceiling down in that bathroom. Glad you could come to look at them.'

'I'm looking forward to it.'

'Unfortunately there's been another attempt to break into the grounds by Thompson, at the front *and* the back.'

'Mrs Rennie told us about the one at the front.'

'Tell us exactly what happened at the rear,' the lawyer said quietly.

When he'd explained, Forrester frowned. 'Give me time to think about this. It's not as straightforward as you might think, not with the council involved. Some magistrates can be a bit difficult, too, always on the council's side, whatever the facts.'

Mayne suppressed a sigh. Nothing seemed to be straightforward at the moment. 'Very well. I'll wait to hear from you. Jan should have pulled down the false ceiling by now. Shall we go and see how he's getting on?'

They met Judith en route and all went upstairs together.

With his usual efficiency and tidiness, Jan had already finished the fiddly job of taking the bathroom ceiling down and was studying the pile of paintings still suspended above the room on a rough wooden frame. There were four, each wrapped in dusty canvas.

'I think I can edge them gently off the rack on my own, Mayne, but I'd like to bring a solid table in here and have someone standing on it to help lower them. That'd be more secure than a ladder for this job, I think, and gives somewhere to stand the paintings on the way down. Then two or three of you can lift each painting carefully out of the room.'

'Will we really need that many people?'

'I think it'd be safer. If all the frames are as large and ornate as the top one, they'll be quite heavy and awkward to handle. Better safe than sorry.'

'I know where there's a table,' Judith said. 'Just along the corridor in Victor and Ros's bedroom. It's not big but it's definitely solid. I'm sure they won't mind if we nip in and borrow it.'

Mayne, Daniel and Francis followed Judith and hauled the heavy mahogany table to the bathroom, where there was only just room to fit it in. Then, with the two older men watching from the doorway, Jan cut the ropes lashing the paintings to the framework and, to their relief, everything stayed in place.

Mayne got up on the table. 'Right, let's have the top one.'

They continued till all four paintings were down, leaning them against the walls of the corridor outside.

'Let's take them along to the window at the end of the landing and see what they're like,' Mayne said.

They put the first painting up on the window seat and Jan used a Stanley knife to cut the stitches at one corner. Slowly, carefully, he peeled off the canvas cover to reveal a lady in eighteenth century clothing.

Mayne gestured to Ray. 'You're the expert.'

The older man bent to study the painting, looking at the signature and frowning.

That didn't bode well, Mayne thought, and his faint hopes died.

Ray stood back. 'Is this one of your ancestors?'

'I doubt it. I've never seen the painting before.'

'Hmm. Could we uncover the rest before I come to any conclusions about value?' Ray asked. 'Perhaps they're by other painters.'

Mayne knew then that they hadn't uncovered anything of real interest to the art world.

The second painting looked even older and darker, and was of a gentleman in eighteenth century clothing, with his dog and gun.

Ray studied it, but Mayne knew already what he was going to say about it. Oh yes, he knew. His mother had been cheated if she'd thought she was buying valuable paintings. She had probably been going by size, thinking the bigger the better. Had she ever really looked at this one? It might be old and large, and the frame was beautiful, but the painter hadn't been at all skilful: the gentleman looked wooden-faced, and there was something not quite right about one of his arms.

Ray looked at Mayne and shrugged slightly. 'You can see it too, can't you? Yes. These two are not good paintings. And I doubt the others will be any better. The frames are more valuable than the paintings. I could get you over £100 for them, possibly more. They're in excellent condition.'

It was Mayne's turn to shrug and his voice was harsh. 'Let's look at the others and get it over with.'

Judith moved to stand beside him, taking his hand and squeezing it in sympathy.

One by one Jan uncovered the other two paintings. Ray stepped forward and examined the final canvas with a magnifying glass. 'This one's better than the others.'

For a moment hope flickered in Mayne, then he saw the sympathy in his partner's eyes, so saved him the trouble of pronouncing judgement tactfully. 'But not very valuable, even so.'

'I can probably get you about three hundred pounds for it, with frame.'

'What I don't understand is why my mother went to such lengths to hide them.'

'Perhaps she thought they were valuable and didn't want the soldiers stationed here damaging them?' Forrester suggested. 'Some of the big houses that were requisitioned during the war were very badly treated. Some paintings were even used for target practice.'

Mayne twisted his hand to hold Judith's more tightly. 'The sooner you can sell the paintings the better, Ray. And Judith, if you can find somewhere to store them where I won't have to look at them till then, I'd be very grateful.'

'I'll store them for you at my warehouse,' Ray offered.

'Thank you.' Mayne let go of his wife's hand and left the room.

'It would be nice for him to have some good news for a change,' Judith said quietly once her husband was out of earshot. 'He's faced nothing but bad news and problems since the war ended. One thing after another.'

'No, you're wrong,' Ray said quietly. 'He's also been granted one wonderful gift.'

She looked at him in puzzlement.

'He's found and married you. You're worth your weight in gold to a man in his circumstances, as my dear wife is to me.'

She flushed bright red, then gave him a wavery smile. 'Thank you for that compliment. I value it greatly coming from you.'

'I meant it.'

She nodded and said in a choked voice, 'I'd better go to him.'

Ray watched her hurry out. 'I feel sorry for the chap, Edward. He didn't deserve this inheritance of debt and deceit, and what he's trying to do, start a building company, is what our battered country needs. But everything seems to be conspiring against him. If I can help him, I shall.'

'I like him,' Forrester said. 'Count me in on that.'

'I wish my man had turned something up to discredit Thompson,' Ray said, 'so that we could remove one of Mayne's problems, at least, but there's been no news so far.'

Steph and Anthony stayed in London for several days, going out for short walks to build up his strength and, she soon realised, to increase his tolerance of open spaces and groups of strangers. He flinched sometimes when people got too close.

On their first outing he stopped to stare into the window of a bakery, seeming fascinated by the rows of fresh loaves. 'I'd forgotten how wonderful new bread smells.' He gave her an embarrassed smile and moved on.

She didn't think she'd ever forget the blissful expression on his face as he closed his eyes and breathed in the air from the shop.

On two sunny but chilly afternoons, after a rest from the morning outing, they took a taxi to a small park nearby. There they could sit in a sheltered spot and chat quietly before catching a taxi back from near the park entrance.

'Are you rich now, Steph?' he asked abruptly the second time.

'Why do you ask that?'

'Hailing taxis.'

'I can afford to pay for taxis, since it gets you out and about. I work for my Uncle Ray and live at their house, so I have no real expenses and my savings are mounting up.'

'Some men don't like the idea of women going out to

work, but it'd be a shame not to use that fine brain of yours,' he said after a while. 'What exactly do you do?'

'All sorts of things. Driving, office work, fetching and carrying, whatever my uncle needs. And I'm learning about antiques. That's fascinating.'

He seemed to enjoy listening to her, though he didn't say a lot himself, and certainly nothing about his years as a POW.

'My uncle says he can find you a job too once you're well again.'

'I'm not taking charity.'

She laughed. 'And he's not offering it. My Uncle Ray has a dozen irons in the fire and although he says he's half-retired, he'll never stop finding new things to do. I don't get on all that well with my parents, so I feel as if I'm more of a daughter to my uncle and aunt than a niece. One day they may need someone to look after them, and I'll be able to repay them properly for what they're doing for me now.'

Anthony nodded then fell into one of his silences and she didn't try to force a conversation.

Eventually he said, 'If he was offering me a *real* job I'd be grateful for it – only I don't think I'll be strong enough for a while to do something that needs me to stand up all day or work normal hours. I'm not sure I ever will be. I feel . . . faded and worn, Steph, love, like an old photo of myself.'

'You'll gradually recover, I'm sure. And there's no rush. If we get married you can share my room and help out here and there as you build up your strength.'

'You still want to marry me, then?'

'Of course I do, you fool.'

'I need your determination and help so much, Steph.' He gulped, struggling with his emotions, then pulled her to him and started sobbing against her shoulder, heedless of who might be passing by.

When the sobbing subsided he pulled back, avoiding meeting her eyes.

'There's no shame in weeping for what was done to you,' she said softly. 'But I *will* feed you up and get you better, I promise.'

He smiled, a genuine smile this time. 'Oh, Stephie love, *you* are the best tonic of all, not the food.'

'Good. Don't you realise that having you back has done me good too?'

'How can that be possible? I'm just a burden at the moment.'

'No, never that. I only felt half alive without you, you see.' She touched her chest to indicate her heart. 'Here, I felt cold and lonely. I've never met anyone I feel so comfortable with as you, my darling. Never. Especially not in my own immediate family. Well, you've met my parents. You know how bossy and narrow-minded they can be.'

'That's a wonderful compliment.'

'I mean it. Now, let's make some practical plans. When do you want to go to Rivenshaw?'

He didn't hesitate. 'Tomorrow. I've been putting it off, but I shouldn't be such a coward. And I *am* feeling better, thanks to your care and some decent food.' He stared down at his own body and added, 'Though I still look like a walking skeleton.'

She didn't say that he wasn't eating as well as she'd expected. It was as if he had to force food down, and could only take so much at a time. She'd been trying to find him tempting snacks and treats in the shops near the hotel, though this wasn't easy when almost everything was rationed. But when she explained that it was for a recently returned prisoner of war, most shopkeepers found her something.

She pulled him to his feet, happy with that decision. 'Wonderful! You'll like Rivenshaw, I'm sure. I'll go and book our train tickets while you're taking your afternoon nap.' But this upset him again. His spirits went up and down like a yo-yo.

'Fancy a grown man needing so many naps.' The laugh that followed this was bitter.

She gave him a mock punch in the arm. 'Fancy a grown man not doing what his body tells him it needs. You're like someone recovering from a long illness. You need time to heal.'

'And the nightmares? You're sleeping next door. You must have heard me shouting.'

'You won't be the only returned soldier who's having nightmares, darling. People understand.'

'Do they? On the way back to Britain one of the doctors told me to "Snap out of it, man!" Didn't he realise we can't control what we do in our sleep?'

'He was a fool. The nightmares will fade, I promise you.'

'How can you be so sure?'

'I just am.'

He grabbed her and plonked a kiss on each of her cheeks in turn, smiling again. 'I do love you. You're the star in my heavens.'

At the hotel he lay on the bed and watched her pack his things.

She was watching him too. There was a hint of colour in his cheeks today. She definitely wasn't imagining that.

He fell asleep after a while, the faint frown that often sat on his face smoothing out as his breathing slowed.

It was going to be hard to stay cheerful, she knew, but as long as he was alive, she could manage. She wiped away a tear, annoyed at herself. No weeping, she'd sworn. Just get on with it. Do whatever it took to help him recover.

The following morning, they took an early train and as it rattled northwards, Anthony said softly, 'It's lovely to be home in England again. There's nothing like the English countryside.'

'We'll go walking on the moors together one day,' she said.

'I can't imagine having the strength for that.'

'Leave the imagining to me then, but make sure you clear your plate every time I put something on it.'

He slept for the last part of the journey to Manchester and Steph had to wake him up to change trains.

He stayed awake, looking round with interest as they approached Rivenshaw.

When the train slowed, she stood up. 'I'd better get our cases down.'

His smile vanished. 'I should be doing that.'

'You will one day.'

As they were waiting outside the station for a taxi, a man strode across the town square, looking furiously angry.

Anthony frowned. 'I know that chap. Now where do I know him from?'

'Never mind him. Here's the taxi.' She had to tug him towards it, because he was still watching the man.

As the taxi set off, he twisted round to look back. 'Do you recognise him, Steph?'

'Yes. Unfortunately. He's called Thompson and he's in charge of the council's planning section.'

'Thompson. Yes, that name rings a bell, but I still can't remember how I know him. I only know I don't like him.'

She could have told him about Mayne's troubles with the man, but she felt he had enough to worry him. 'Never mind Thompson. Look at your new home town.'

He smiled and took her hand. 'I'd rather look at you. Anyway, the more I concentrate the less likely I am to remember who he is.'

When they turned into the circular drive in front of her uncle's house, Anthony whistled softly. 'Nice place. No wonder he has room for me. They'd have crammed a hundred FEPOWs into a building like this, if not two hundred.'

She watched what an effort it was for him to get out of the taxi and move towards the front door.

It opened and her aunt stood there, looking motherly and holding out her arms. 'Welcome to Rivenshaw, Mr Giffen.'

'Darling, this is my Auntie Edna.'

'I'm pleased to meet you, Mrs Woollard.'

Edna gave him a quick hug, but his face was chalk white now and she shot a worried glance at her niece.

Steph had no intention of letting him pretend. 'I'm afraid Anthony's exhausted. Can he go straight up to his room?'

'Yes, of course. It's the bedroom next to yours. I'll ask the taxi driver to bring in the luggage and I'll be in the sitting room when you're ready for a cup of tea.'

'I'll just see Anthony settled.'

'Sorry I'm such a crock, Mrs Woollard.' Anthony hauled himself up the stairs by sheer willpower. 'Sorry I'm so slow, love.'

'I think you did really well today. You couldn't have managed that when you first arrived.'

He brightened slightly. 'I couldn't, could I?'

'No. And this is your bedroom so you can have a rest while I chat to my aunt.'

He collapsed on the bed and she managed to tug the quilt out from under him, lift his dangling leg on to the bed and cover him up. As he sighed and snuggled down, she took a few deep breaths, summoned up a smile and went downstairs.

Anthony still hadn't woken when her uncle and Mr Forrester came back from Esherwood and joined the three ladies.

'How did it go?' Edna asked.

'Give us a cup of tea and we'll tell you,' her husband joked.

'This pot has only just been brought in, so you timed your return well.' She poured them all cups of tea then listened to what they'd found.

After that, Stephanie told them a little about Anthony. 'He's . . . a bit fragile still. Gets very down in the dumps about his own weakness.'

'I read an article about FEPOWs,' her uncle said. 'It warned that it takes a long time for the poor chaps to recover after such shocking treatment, and said what to watch out for as warning signs of major problems. One is called "barbed wire disease".'

'What on earth is that?' Mrs Forrester asked.

'It's when they focus inwards, are sad and apathetic, and find it hard to concentrate, as if they're surrounded by invisible barbed wire.'

Stephanie considered this. 'I think Anthony is bone-weary and physically weakened, but he's not that bad. He's worried about being a burden to me if we marry. As if I care about that!'

'I can help him with a job. But there's no rush, surely? He'll be getting his back pay for the years he spent in prison camp, so he won't be without money.'

She tried to explain her fiancé. 'He's a very intelligent man and I believe he needs something to occupy his mind, even though he's very weak physically still.'

'What did he do before the war?'

'He hadn't settled into any sort of career. He'd only just finished reading classics at Oxford when wham, bang, he got his call-up papers and had to go straight into the Army.'

'Might he be interested in antiques?'

'It's possible. He always liked looking round historical buildings and reading books about British history, anyway.'

'Good. I have quite a few books about antiques, so if he's interested in working in that area, he can read a few and start learning. Actually, I'm thinking of opening an antiques shop. I'd get an experienced manager to start off with but one day—'

'Do you call this retiring, Raymond Woollard?' Edna interrupted in a mock severe tone.

He grinned at his wife. 'I've tried to retire, only I can't bear sitting round twiddling my thumbs. I am working fewer hours, though, you have to admit that.'

She chuckled. 'I knew you'd never last as a man of leisure. Antiques sound interesting. I might join you in that. I particularly like old embroideries and samplers.'

They exchanged loving glances that for a moment excluded the other people in the room and Steph sighed. Would she and Anthony ever be that close?

'Now is a good time to buy things,' he went on thoughtfully. 'Prices are very low.'

'We're not going to cheat anyone,' Edna warned. 'We should pay fair prices, even when they don't know how valuable something is.'

'I agree. But I do plan to make a profit so we're not giving them the potential value.'

19

Sam watched the thin line of sunlight creep across the floor of his mother's attic as the day passed. He was sick and tired of spending his time in hiding, without even a window to look out of. He'd read the local newspaper twice already today, and what a load of rubbish that was. But he didn't intend to spoil things by getting careless. Oh, no. He wasn't risking going back to jail.

Since it had been a fine day, he intended to go out for a walk tonight. It'd be cold, but he'd go mad if he couldn't stretch his legs. He'd have to wait till past midnight, though, to be sure there was no one on the streets.

It seemed a long time until darkness fell and even then, there were hours more to wait before he would dare go outside. He couldn't even light a candle and read because the police had been keeping an eye on this house ever since he'd escaped from jail and might wonder if they saw a light in the attic while his mother was busy in the café.

They'd searched the house without warning twice, but the double hiding place had kept him safe. Thank goodness his grandfather had been a suspicious old sod and not trusted his money to banks.

His mother brought his evening meal up and sat with him in the moonlight while he ate it slowly. You didn't get as hungry when you were sitting around all day.

'What's up with you?' she demanded. 'You've a face so long your chin's nearly on the ground and you've left some of that good food.'

'I'm not used to having nothing to do.'

'Well, if you will go thieving, you'll have to pay the price. I shan't feel easy till I know you've left the country safely. You've got enough money for your fare and something left over. Why don't you just go?'

'Will you stop going on about that, Ma! I've got jewels and pieces of silver worth hundreds of pounds waiting for me at Esherwood and I intend to get them.'

'More thieving.'

'*Leave—it—be.*'

'Oh, there's no talking sense to you.' She whipped out her handkerchief and gave her nose a good blow.

He could see the glitter of tears in her eyes and reached out to squeeze her hand. The one thing he had no doubt about was that she loved him. Well, there'd been just the two of them for most of his life, with his father having been killed in the Great War. 'I'll be careful, Ma. I promise.'

'You'd better be. Now, if you've finished eating I'll go and wash the dishes, then I'll get things ready for tomorrow's meals in my café.'

'One day you won't have to work so hard.'

'What would I do with myself if I hadn't got something to do? I've never been one to sit around any more than you have. No, I'll find something to do in Australia. And it'll be honest work, too. I don't intend to be a burden on you.'

He watched her go. Eh, she was a good mother.

Then his thoughts turned back to the puzzle lock and what might be behind the huge old door. He thought about that a lot. The hidden cellar might contain something or it might have just caved in when the first Esher house was destroyed during the English Civil War and be full of nothing but muck and rocks. Either way, he intended to find out.

He hoped and prayed that Cuthbert would find a way to open the lock. After all, he and his mates had found the secret cellar when they were trying to bury poor Alf after the accident. They'd known better than to report an accident that happened while they were thieving at Esherwood.

Even the Eshers hadn't known about the cellar then, so it was only fair for him and Cuthbert to get a share of whatever it contained.

If it contained anything. He bet they kept wondering about that too.

It seemed everyone was waiting for old Mr Esher to find the instructions for opening the cellar, even Cuthbert's boss, who might be a master locksmith, but who was being strangely cautious about this.

After his mother had gone downstairs again, Sam leaned back in the worn old armchair and waited for time to pass. Time. So much of it on his hands. It was the strangest thing, time was. Sometimes it galloped; sometimes, like now, it crawled like a wounded snail.

Montague Thompson went to see his main ally, Councillor Draper, and had hardly got through the door when he was greeted with, 'Well, how did you go today? I hope that plan of yours worked.'

'We didn't manage to get into Esherwood, I'm afraid. That chain's too solid to be sawn through with an ordinary hacksaw. And when my men tried to get in at the back, that new young constable interfered and said he'd be patrolling there regularly.'

Draper sighed. 'I'm very disappointed with your progress, I must admit. I'd expected better of you.'

Thompson kept control of his anger. He needed this timid

fool's help – for the moment. 'It's Mayne Esher's fault. He can afford to pay men to keep watch day and night, damn him, and the Accounts Manager would throw a fit if we laid out any extra money! No, we're going to have to make this acquisition through the courts, after all.'

'We can't be sure of getting as much land as we want if we take that path, I've told you that. The Esher family's been living there for hundreds of years. They're part of the town's history and people are stupidly sentimental about that sort of thing.'

'Who cares about history? It's money that talks in the modern world, as you and I both know. The builder will see us right.'

'He'd better. And make sure you keep my name out of it when you deal with him,' Draper added.

As if the builder didn't know, Thompson thought to himself. He'd make sure he got what he wanted. He wasn't going to be bested, either by Esher's stubborn resistance or by Draper's cowardice about acting too openly – or too violently.

He was damned well going to show all the people who'd trampled on his career in the Army, both before and during the war, that he could be successful in civvy street. If he played his cards right, he might even get a medal from the King for his patriotic house-building. That'd show them!

Dammit, he'd got used to a certain style of living as an officer and it was hard to achieve this in civilian life if you'd only ever been in the Army. He would have stayed in if they'd let him, but there had been a bit of unpleasantness and it had been suggested that if he didn't want to get into trouble, he should accept an early demobilisation.

He realised Draper had said something. 'Sorry. What was that again?'

'I said, I don't think we've got the numbers to carry it at the council meeting.'

'Tell me who you think will definitely resist and I'll see if I can persuade some of them not to attend the next meeting.'

Draper sighed. 'Well, just make sure no one can connect it to me. I have a respected position in this town, you know.'

What a fool the man was! Just like Thompson's commanding officer when he'd first been made up to corporal. People like them needed a go-ahead chap who wasn't afraid to take a few risks. He had no respect for them, none at all. Why, he had more respect for Esher than for Draper.

Stephanie chatted to her uncle and aunt for a while then went upstairs to unpack and change her crumpled clothes. Hearing the sound of someone stirring in the room next to hers as she passed, she tapped on the door and heard Anthony call, 'Come in!'

She glanced over her shoulder before slipping inside, knowing her aunt wouldn't approve of her being alone with her fiancé in his bedroom. As if he had the strength to do anything immoral or they'd be so stupid as to make love here!

He was sitting on the edge of the bed, looking rumpled and slightly flushed. 'How rude of me to fall asleep like that! Were your aunt and uncle offended?'

'Good heavens, no. They understand the situation. But it's good that you've woken up now. Will you be all right to join us for dinner?'

'Yes, of course.'

'There's a bathroom at the end of the corridor if you'd like to wash and change.' She was unpacking his suitcase as she chatted, laying out a clean shirt, noting he only had three shirts and they were the poor quality demob ones half the young men were wearing. She'd speak to her uncle about getting him more clothes.

She'd also write to Anthony's family to see if they had any of his things left. She suspected not. They'd probably been destroyed when the house was bombed. And if any had been saved, when they heard he was dead they'd have donated them to a clothing exchange. You didn't waste good clothes in times of scarcity.

She put the last pair of socks away and stood the suitcase in a corner. He was watching her with a fond smile. She hoped that meant he'd be in a good mood this evening, because he'd not met her uncle and aunt before. She didn't blame him for getting depressed after what he'd gone through, but she wanted them to see him at his best tonight.

'I'll go and get changed for dinner now, love. This skirt is crumpled from travelling. Knock on my door when you're ready and we'll go down together.'

Anthony stopped in the doorway of the sitting room, thinking how cheerful and homely it looked. He smiled at the Woollards and Forresters then let Steph draw him gently forward.

They made him so welcome, it brought a lump to his throat. To have a family fussing over you once more was wonderful, just . . . wonderful.

The six of them enjoyed dinner in the small dining room next door. The meal wasn't lavish, which wouldn't have been possible these days unless you bought on the black market, but it was good plain food.

To his relief no one commented on the small helpings he asked for and he found himself eating more than he had for a while. He could see Steph nod happily when he cleared his plate. He was so lucky to have her still.

He did more listening than speaking, fascinated by Mr Woollard's description of the recent happenings at Esherwood and the way Thompson was trying to seize most of the land.

And that jogged Anthony's memory so abruptly he

gasped aloud. '*Thompson!* I remember Captain Montague Thompson now. Oh yes! I came across him when he was a corporal, working in the stores. One of those chaps with a finger in every pie, the sort you hesitated to cross.'

He had everyone's instant attention.

'Tell us what you know, lad. We've been trying to find out about his background ever since he started his nasty tricks at Esherwood.'

'Well, it was my first posting after training and though I'd been commissioned as a Second Lieutenant, I was still wet behind the ears and terrified of putting a foot wrong. I was working in the next office to the commanding officer and I overheard him and Thompson arguing several times. Thompson always got what he wanted, though, by threatening to reveal something. I never found out what. Well, everyone knew how weak the CO was, but even then I knew corporals didn't usually get away with things like that.'

He hesitated. 'There was nothing I could do but pretend I didn't know what was going on. I think Thompson was blackmailing him for a promotion to sergeant and asking for money too.'

He sat frowning for a few seconds, then added, 'Things were a bit chaotic at that place. Later on, Thompson got another fellow into trouble by claiming he'd stolen some goods from the stores, which he swore he hadn't. But he had upset Thompson. They transferred the poor sod to the front. Hmm. I think that's all I know. I was posted overseas a few months later, and never saw Thompson again.'

Mr Woollard beamed at Anthony. 'That information could be very useful. Tomorrow morning, I'll ask you to go over it all again and I'll pass it on to a fellow who's working for me, looking into Thompson's background. I was always sure there was something a bit "off" about him, but I couldn't prove it.'

'I doubt you'll find anything incriminating. When I had a drink with some of my pals from that camp before I was shipped overseas, they said Thompson had been posted elsewhere and after he'd left, the CO had a private bonfire. The whole group knew something was wrong, though. It was a small camp.'

'Well, my detective chap is pretty good, so let's hope he comes up with proof of misdemeanours. I'm not letting that blighter destroy Esherwood.'

Anthony didn't seem convinced. 'It's a long time ago now. It'll be hard to trace.'

'But not impossible. Now, you're looking tired, lad. Don't think you have to stay up for us. We know you need your rest to get better, rest and the company of my niece. She's a different lass since she heard you were alive.'

The look Steph gave him as she walked him to the foot of the stairs was so full of love, Anthony wanted to grab hold of her there and then, and never let go. But he forced himself to say goodnight and make his way up the stairs alone.

Someone had turned down his bed and laid out his pyjamas.

He didn't bother with them, just visited the bathroom, threw off his outer clothes and crawled under the covers, unable to stand upright a minute longer.

That night, for the first time, he didn't have any nightmares.

Reginald appeared at the big house early the next morning before breakfast, looking as if he'd slept in his clothes.

Mrs O'Brien was in the kitchen and looked up with a smile.

He didn't bother to greet her. 'Where's my son?'

'In the office.'

He rushed along the corridor, not knocking but bursting

straight in, brandishing some papers and the diary. A couple of pieces of paper fell out of the untidy bundle but he didn't seem to notice, just announced, 'I've done it!'

'Found out about the puzzle lock?' Mayne asked.

'Yes. I've transcribed the relevant diary entries for you. I think they'll give you all the information you need to open that lock, or rather for Dick Reston to open it.'

'That's wonderful!' Judith picked up the fallen papers and gave them to Mayne as he took the rest from his father. They both read the top page, but were soon frowning.

He tapped the piece of paper. 'Does this make sense to you, Dad?'

'Not really. It's a bit technical for me. But I'm sure Dick Reston will be able to work out what to do to the lock from it. You should give it to him straight away.'

'Is this the only copy?'

'Except for the original diary, and I've put that on a shelf with some books bound in the same way to keep it hidden.'

'I'll make some copies before we do anything else,' Judith said, 'then we'll send one to the locksmith. Do you have some carbon paper, Mayne?'

'Yes, but no proper copying pencils.'

'I've got two hard, indelible ones hidden away, in case they were mistaken for ordinary pencils and wasted. They were among the office supplies Ray gave us. If there was ever a time to use them, it's now, when we need to make sure we have some permanent copies.'

She paused at the doorway as Reginald suddenly grabbed hold of the desk, looking as if he was about to faint.

Mayne steadied him. 'Are you all right, Dad?'

'I didn't have time for breakfast and I'm feeling a bit dizzy.'

Judith turned back. 'I'll get you something to eat straight

away, Mr Esher, then I'll fetch Christa. She can make a copy as well.'

Mayne watched them go, worried about his father, who was as white as a sheet. The old man was getting on for seventy and hadn't looked after himself at all well physically, even without the privations of wartime rationing.

Which brought another worry to mind. If his father died before seven years had passed since he'd handed over Esherwood to his son, there would be full death duties to pay on it.

Mayne pushed that thought quickly out of his mind. He had enough problems to deal with, didn't need to go looking for others.

He got out the carbon paper and some sheets of blank typing paper, wondering for the umpteenth time if they really would find anything useful in that hidden cellar. No. He couldn't be that lucky.

Christa concentrated on the document she was copying, pressing hard with the pencil to get good copies on the pages sandwiched between the two sheets of carbon paper.

Judith had explained what it was all about and how important it was to get every single detail right. It was very exciting. She hoped she could be there when they opened the cellar. What might you see after several centuries? It must be something extremely important for people to go to so much trouble.

It took her an hour to finish copying the document which had been put on a stand between her and Judith. 'Shall I make another copy?'

Her companion looked down at what they were doing, head on one side, then shrugged. 'Why not? I've got other things I can get on with after I finish this one. It's always better to be safe than sorry with important documents. Give the copies to Mayne once you've finished.'

At the door she turned to add, 'And don't let anyone walk off with that copying pencil. Hide it at the back of the top drawer after you've finished. It's nearly worth its weight in gold until production starts again.'

Christa finished a second copy, gave the papers to Mayne, hid the pencil and went to ask Judith what she could do next.

'Go out and get some fresh air. You've been bent over that copying for over two hours without taking a break.'

'I'm fine, Judith, really I am.'

'Well, you'll be even finer if you go out for a stroll. But if you fancied going into town, you could get me some more wool to darn Ben's navy blue school socks with. Thank goodness darning wool isn't rationed. That boy wears out socks faster than anyone I've ever met.'

Christa set off, feeling free and relaxed. She knew she was useful at Esherwood, and with Daniel's love, she felt she could look forward to a good life from now on. She wasn't foolish enough to think everything would be perfect, no life ever was, but she had a chance of real happiness.

She hadn't quite reached the main street when a shrill voice called, 'There she is!'

She spun round, horrified to see Mrs Pelling's niece, Mavis Grayton, glaring at her from across the street. Mr Grayton was standing beside his wife looking uncomfortable.

What on earth was that horrible woman doing here in Rivenshaw?

Christa nearly turned and fled, because she definitely didn't want anything else to do with them. But that would be cowardly so she walked on, head held high, ignoring a second call of 'Hoy!'

They moved along the footpath on the other side of the street, keeping level with her. Just before she reached the corner, Mavis ran across the road, followed more slowly by her husband, and the two of them barred Christa's way.

She tried to walk round them but they continued to block her way, and there was no one else in sight to ask for help. She stopped moving about and said firmly, 'Please let me pass.'

'Not until I've had my say.'

'I don't wish to speak to you.'

'I'm not surprised. I wonder you dare show your face in public, you lying trollop! How did you manage to forge that will?'

'What? I didn't forge it.'

'You must have done. My aunt wouldn't have left her money to a *German*. She only took you in out of pity. I'm her closest blood relative and the money should come to me. Shame on you! Shame!'

People were walking towards them now, staring, slowing down to listen.

Mr Grayton tugged at his wife's arm. 'Mavis, leave it. You're showing yourself up and it'll do no good.'

'I'll show *her* up for the cheat and liar she is before I'm through.'

But when some people came near them, he hissed, 'Don't make a scene, Mavis!' He kept hold of her arm and after giving Christa a dirty look that threatened more trouble, she went with him.

Christa couldn't move for a moment or two, upset by the encounter.

At the corner Mrs Grayton turned round and yelled, 'I'll make sure you don't enjoy the money! You see if I don't.' Then the couple vanished from sight.

A woman stopped next to Christa. 'Are you all right, dear? Have those people hurt you?'

'What? Oh. No. I was just . . . a bit shocked at their lies. I'll be all right now.'

But when she continued into town, she saw the Graytons sitting on a bench in the main square, a bench from which they could see everyone who went in and out of the shops.

What were they waiting for? Did they intend to catch her on her own again? And do what? Why had they come here?

Christa hurried into the haberdasher's, bought the darning yarn quickly and set off home. At the corner of the street she paused to look back and to her horror, saw that the Graytons were following her again.

She quickened her pace but another glance showed that they'd speeded up too.

When she got to Esherwood, she didn't hesitate. She turned into the drive, leaped over the chain and ran towards the big house as fast as she could.

She stopped at the front door and to her relief there was no sign of her pursuers, so she continued round to the back. Pushing the kitchen door open, she went inside, but had to lean against the wall for a few moments to pull herself together.

She decided not to trouble her kind friends with this encounter, because what could the Graytons do, after all? And they weren't likely to hang around in Rivenshaw.

But Daniel was in the kitchen drinking a cup of tea and he took one look at her and stood up. 'What's wrong?'

His aunt said, 'Whatever it is, let the girl sit down. I'll make you a nice cup of tea, dear.'

By the time the tea was ready, Daniel had got the whole story out of Christa.

'Don't go into town again on your own till we're sure they've left,' he said.

'No. I definitely won't.'

'I can't imagine what good they think coming here will do.'

'Neither can I. She's a horrible woman, Daniel. She frightens me, she's so vicious.'

'Well, you'll be safe inside this house. You're not on your own now and if I have my way, you never will be again. We'll tell everyone to keep their eyes open for those two.'

20

A messenger took word to the members of the town council that a special meeting would be held the following evening to discuss the steps needed to deal with the crisis with the land next to Parson's Mead.

All over the town, the eight councillors – seven men and one woman – discussed it with their families and friends. They were well aware that this really meant Esherwood land.

Some felt that 'young' Maynard Esher had been very generous about selling the back strip of land to the council for building prefabs on and that no more land should be taken from him. After all, the war was over now.

As one man said to another, 'If we'd taken him up on that offer straight away, before that Thompson chappie came here, the damned prefabs would be nearly finished by now.'

The woman councillor talked it over with her husband.

'I don't think you should go to that meeting,' he told her. 'I get a lot of business from Councillor Draper and we don't want to upset him.'

'But I don't think they're being fair to Mr Esher. I have to stand up for him.'

'Damn the Eshers! We have bills to pay, Nora. There will be other people at the meeting to deal with this, you know.'

Another man had his kitchen window broken by a stone,

lobbed in from the back alley. It had a note tied to it, saying, 'Don't go to the meeting, for your family's sake.'

His wife promptly had hysterics and didn't calm down till he promised not to attend.

'Oh, very well. They'll have a majority against Thompson's proposal without me,' he said. 'It'd be different if I had the deciding vote.'

The emergency council meeting was held the following evening at the town hall.

Councillor Draper sat with his pocket watch on the table next to him. 'It's seven o'clock. I doubt the others will be coming if they're not here now. Let's get on with it.'

'Shouldn't we wait?' one man asked nervously. 'Give them a few minutes more? It's only just seven, after all.'

'They know what time the meeting starts and I want to get home, even if you don't. Anyway, this is a straightforward matter.'

'Exactly what are we here to discuss?'

'The town has been forced to subsume the land at Esherwood since the owner won't sell. If necessary, we need to get a legal injunction to allow us on to start the building work. There are returned soldiers desperately needing housing, you know. This is a question of patriotism.'

'Which land exactly are you talking about? It wasn't clear in the letter.'

'The rear half of Esherwood.'

'The rear *half*! I thought it was just the strip at the back that the town was buying from Esher, and he's agreeable to that. Why do we need more?'

'As you know, over a million houses were destroyed in Britain during the war. All towns are being urged to build more as quickly as possible,' Draper said. 'We all pulled together and made sacrifices during the war and we must do the same as we settle into peace. Besides, Esher will still have more land at the front than most people ever dream of, even after we've taken the rear part.'

'There's no need to talk to me in that tone. I know very well we need to build houses. I also know that Mayne Esher has offered a decent piece of land, so I'm not voting for this.' He folded his arms.

'You've lost my respect, then.'

'And your custom, no doubt,' he muttered.

Draper ignored this. 'Has anyone else got any other comments to make?'

One man opened his mouth but when Draper glared at him, he sighed and closed it again.

'We'll put it to the vote. All in favour?'

Three were in favour, two against.

'I have the deciding vote and I'm in favour, so I declare the motion carried,' Councillor Draper said. 'Since I oversee Planning and Buildings, I'll see this decision put into operation tomorrow. I hereby declare this meeting closed.' He left the room without another word.

Two men lingered. 'I'm not happy with this being rushed through,' one said. 'And where were the others tonight? I reckon they were stopped from coming. I'm going across to tell Esher what's just happened. Do you want to come with me?'

'It's too late now to stop them, so I'd rather not make a fuss.'

'We can at least let the poor chap know what they're going to do. That's not making a fuss.'

'If only the other two had come, we could have stopped this. Nora's my cousin and I'd have thought we could rely on her support. She doesn't like Draper or Thompson.'

On his way to Esherwood, he had to pass his cousin's house and found her waiting by the gate, her breath a grey cloud in the chill darkness of the evening.

'I thought you'd come back this way, love. How did it go? What exactly were they trying to push through?'

When he told Nora what had happened, he saw tears come into her eyes.

'Oh, no! I should have come. Only my husband . . . well, you know how things stand with him and Draper.'

She didn't have to explain. It was common knowledge that Draper made sure local businesses whose owners went against him didn't receive any custom from him or his wide circle of friends.

'I shan't stand for the council next time,' she said. 'It's a waste of time trying to make improvements to our town, given the circumstances. And my husband doesn't want me to stand, either. But if I don't, there won't be any women on the council at all and that doesn't seem right. Oh, I'm so annoyed at myself for giving in to my husband.'

He left her still standing there in the darkness. He was annoyed at his cousin too.

Mayne heard the footsteps even before the knock on the kitchen door. He was sitting chatting to his wife over a cup of cocoa, intending to get an early night. 'Who the hell's that at this hour?'

When he found a man he was barely acquainted with but who was on the town council, he was puzzled but invited him to come in.

The man shook his head. 'I have to get home or my wife will worry. I just wanted to tell you about the special meeting of the council.' He explained and left immediately.

Mayne stood at the door watching him hurry away. 'Damnation! I was counting on the majority protecting me from this. How did they stop the other two attending? That won't have happened by chance.'

'What are you going to do?' Judith asked.

'Thompson and Draper will no doubt be seeing a magistrate first thing in the morning. Well, so will my lawyer.'

She didn't say anything, but they both knew Thompson had scored a major victory with this. 'Surely no magistrate will allow the council to take so much land away from you?'

'Stranger things happened during the war, and some of the fellows on the council used their positions to push changes through that lined their pockets, war or no war. I hadn't realised how bad it was till I got demobbed.'

A few moments later, he said gloomily, 'I didn't think Nora would vote for it. She's always been one of the most honest councillors.'

'It's too late to do anything tonight, love. Let's get a good night's sleep and start early tomorrow.'

'Mmm.'

But he lay awake half the night, listening to his wife's soft, slow breaths and worrying about the future. If they didn't have Esher land available, their building company would find it a lot harder to get a start. They'd all been counting on that land at the rear of the house.

What sort of world was it where returned soldiers were cheated out of their land, and their jobs given to those who'd wriggled out of being called up or had used the war to line their pockets?

Mayne phoned Ray early in the morning, knowing the Woollards always got up early. He was immediately invited over to discuss the situation with Ray and Edward Forrester over breakfast.

To his dismay, Ray had further bad news for him. Colonel Crayshore, one of the local magistrates, had had a seizure, so Horton, who was a friend of Councillor Draper, was the only local magistrate until another could be appointed.

'Couldn't have happened at a worse time and I'm damned

if I know what to advise,' Ray said gloomily. 'How about we ask Miss Peters to contact her brother? See if he can do anything?'

'Even a judge can't go against the law,' Edward said. 'I've seen the problem before in small towns, lack of alternatives for people dissatisfied with the person acting as magistrate. You can rarely prove anything, so it's hard to stop.'

They were all silent.

'The only thing we can do is document what is going on and then appeal against the decision,' Ray said.

'You seem fairly sure we won't win.'

'Aren't you, Mayne lad? We get nowhere in life by refusing to face the facts. I must admit, I too had been counting on there being a majority of reasonable people on the council. But if two of them didn't attend . . .' He frowned. 'Might be worth looking into how they were persuaded to stay away and see if we can link it to Draper or Thompson.'

Edward looked at him in surprise. 'You think they were blackmailed into staying away?'

'I thought those two were beyond his reach because Nora usually stands up to people. As I said, I'll look into it. And this very morning too.'

At a quarter past nine in the morning, a messenger brought Mayne a summons to attend an emergency hearing at ten o'clock into the resumption of his land.

He went to the court with Edward and the hearing began promptly.

In spite of his lawyer's protests that they'd been allowed no time to prepare a case, Horton raced through the hearing, stating up front that this seemed to be an open and shut case.

He made sure of that by using his powers as a magistrate to cut short any protests. And the way he looked at Mayne betrayed his hostility towards the Eshers.

Thompson sat at one side of the room, smirking.

The verdict giving the council the right to take over the land and start building immediately was no surprise to anyone.

Two women who'd come in to watch immediately called out, 'Shame!'

The magistrate ordered them removed from the court.

'I give notice that my client will be lodging an appeal,' Edward said promptly.

'You can lodge as many appeals as you wish. By the time they're heard, the ground will have been cleared and the building work started. And if your client was as patriotic as he claims, he'd not stand in the way of this. The men who fought for this country deserve decent places to live.'

'I must point out that my client fought for the country too.'

'An office job,' Horton scoffed.

'*What?* It was no such thing.'

'Then explain what he was doing.'

'He's forbidden to reveal that. He signed the Official Secrets Act.'

'I have it on good authority that this means an office job – for which I have little respect. I declare this session closed.' Horton stood up and began to walk out.

'But the appeal—' Edward protested.

'—is no concern of mine.' He left the court.

Thompson stood up, smiling and moved across to stand in front of them. 'My men will start work tomorrow morning Esher, and I shall require access this afternoon to mark the preliminary layout, or you will be faced with a charge of contempt of court.' He laughed. 'And that ruined old garden you're so fond of will be the first to go, for safety's sake.'

'It's a seventeenth century garden, a historical treasure that people come from all over the country to see,' Mayne protested. 'Even the Army took care not to damage it.'

'I'm a modern man. As far as I'm concerned that garden is a ruin and what a few old fogies like your father with their heads always in books consider important is not going to stop the march of progress. And I shall bring Sergeant Deemer along this afternoon to ensure compliance with the magistrate's instructions.'

He turned to Constable Waide, who had been standing near the door, his face expressionless. 'Where is the sergeant?'

'I don't know, sir. He said he had urgent business and left straight after Mr Horton did.'

'Well, go and find him this minute. I need his help to see that the magistrate's judgement is carried out.'

'He said I was to go and take charge at the station and, anyway, I don't know where he's gone.'

'Well, the minute he returns to the police station, tell him to come and see me. And don't forget.'

'I don't forget things . . . sir. I'll give him your message as soon as he returns.'

Only once Thompson had left the room, did Waide betray his real feelings by scowling after him.

With a sigh, Mayne followed his friends out of the court. This farce of a hearing was the final straw. He was furious that villains like these had taken such a firm hold of various aspects of civic life.

Office job, indeed! His work had involved hazardous missions behind enemy lines and dealing with some very ticklish situations on the home front. But he couldn't speak about it, so they could say what they liked and get away with such lies.

He stopped a little way along the footpath and offered his hand to his friends. 'Thank you for your help, Ray . . . Edward. I need to tell Judith then have a think about what to do next. She wanted to come to court with me, but I didn't want her wasting her time. I knew it would go against me. I just knew somehow.'

'We'll see if we can come up with any way of hindering them,' Ray offered.

'I can't think of anything we can do without breaking the law, not in time to stop Thompson tearing my inheritance apart tomorrow.' Mayne sighed.

'I think you could get away with refusing to let him in this afternoon,' Edward said. 'Pending appeal might be a useful phrase to toss at him.'

'What's the point?'

He heard Ray murmur, 'We'll find a way, lad.'

Mayne didn't bother to argue. His life was being destroyed and he seemed helpless to prevent it.

As he turned along by Parsons Mead, he heard someone call, 'Psst!' and turned to see Miss Peters standing near the gate, beckoning to him.

'Come inside,' she ordered with her usual imperiousness.

Sergeant Deemer of all people was lurking inside Miss Peters' garden keeping out of sight of passers-by.

As Mayne took a hesitant couple of steps forward, not wanting to offend her but in no mood for a chat, she took his arm, pulling him more quickly towards the house.

Deemer had already gone ahead of them into the entrance hall. He gave the newcomer a cheerful smile and headed for the small rear parlour.

'Thompson is looking for you, sergeant,' Mayne told him.

'Well, he won't find me till I'm ready to be found.' The old man looked at him sympathetically. 'Don't give up, young Esher. I was wondering . . . Could you perhaps contact those people you were working with at Bletchley Park and get their help?'

'It seems immoral to do that for a purely personal reason. And I doubt anything they can do will prevent Thompson starting work tomorrow.'

'Don't underestimate them or the value of what you've done for your country.'

But Mayne shook his head wearily. 'Better leave well alone, sergeant. It's too late.'

'Well, I'm going to ring my brother,' Miss Peters said. 'As a judge he should be able at least to stop them until you've had time to appeal.'

'And I've got a couple of other ideas that might help,' the sergeant said.

But Mayne was so sick of it all, felt so helpless and betrayed after all he'd done for his country that he could only shrug, thank them for their kind thoughts and say goodbye. Even during the war, he had never felt as battered and defeated as this.

The slope that led up to the front gates of Esherwood seemed much steeper today.

Judith was waiting for him in the kitchen. 'Mr Woollard rang and told me what happened. I'm *so* sorry, darling. Are you *sure* there's nothing else we can do?'

'Nothing that I can think of and all the lawyer can talk about is appeals, which will take too long. We've been fighting a rear-guard action for days. Losing the land is not the end of the world, I know. I won't be the only man to lose my inheritance because of the war. It'll just . . . take a bit of getting used to.'

'I'd like to punch that Thompson in the face,' she declared fiercely, her hands clenching into fists.

That provoked a scrape of laughter, but his smile quickly faded. 'So would I, love.'

'You're not even losing it because of the war, which I

would find more bearable, but because of two villains and their chicanery.'

'I know. That's what galls me. Anyway, give me some time to get used to it and we'll find something else to do with our lives.'

'Something else to do? What do you mean?'

'Well, I'm quite sure Thompson will make sure my building company doesn't get any contracts from the council. I can't think why he hates me so much.'

'He envies you. He spent the war in Stores and no one admires that. But he's not the only one to deal with council business.'

'No. There's Draper. He'll be working against me too. Rivenshaw's a small town, so maybe all five partners will need to review the situation, move our company elsewhere even. Once I've had time to think it through, I'll talk to the others.'

He rubbed his temple. 'Sorry to sound so sorry for myself. I'll be all right when I get used to it. They're coming tomorrow morning to start clearing the rear part of the estate, but Thompson's going to survey the area and mark it out today. He made a point of telling me that he's particularly looking forward to destroying the old garden which he reckons doesn't fit in these modern times.'

'*What?* Surely they'll leave that alone? The President of the Rivenshaw Historical Society told me it's a valuable historic site. And I've just thought – do you think their earth works will affect the hidden cellar as well?'

'Who knows?'

It was so unlike him not to fight back, she studied him anxiously. 'Are you feeling ill, my darling?'

'Only soul-sick with disgust. Perhaps we should emigrate to Australia. Leave people like Thompson to destroy this country and help build a new one. Our children might have better, safer lives there. There's a lot of tension between Russia and the Allies. And I read an article by George Orwell the other day in the *Tribune* warning us that this is a peace that is no peace. In fact, he called it a permanent "cold war". I don't agree with everything he said, but some of it made a lot of sense. It upset me.'

She flung her arms round him, but he was as stiff as a board. You could push someone too far, she knew, and that's what had happened to Mayne. The war had taken more out of him than most people realised. He might not have shown that, as some men had, but keeping a stiff upper lip could take its toll on you too. She had done her best to support him in every way she could.

He would recover his fighting spirit, she was sure, but even if he'd been his usual self, she doubted he'd have been able to save his land, and that mattered so much to him.

There had to be something she and the others could do to help him cope with the situation.

But what?

21

When Thompson turned up that afternoon with two men to assist him, he didn't even have the courtesy to inform Mayne that he'd arrived.

Since Mayne had insisted on obeying the law and leaving the gates open, he simply walked in the back way and started measuring the ground and putting in markers.

It was Ros who noticed him from her bedroom window and ran downstairs to tell Mayne.

He avoided looking her in the eyes. 'Nothing I can do to stop him. I've got work to do.'

Surprised by his reaction, she went to consult Judith and the others about whether to let Thompson start work unchallenged.

Victor volunteered to go outside and keep an eye on the fellow and at least make sure he did no damage.

Ros had a sudden idea and called her husband back. 'I'll come with you and bring a notebook. I bet if I keep writing things down, it'll irritate him nicely. It did when the lawyer did the same thing.'

'Is it worth it?'

'Yes, I think it is.'

She proved to be right about Thompson, who grew visibly irritated. After a while he came across to where they were standing silently watching him, with Ros taking notes.

'What the hell are you writing down?'

'None of your business,' Victor said. 'But I think we need to agree about where exactly the land you're interested in ends.'

'There's nothing to agree about. It's already been decided. Come back later and you'll see by the markers.'

'Or you could show us now.'

'I'm not wasting my time on you effete fools.' He turned away and went back to work, ordering the men around brusquely.

He didn't come across to them again, but he glanced their way often and glared at Ros in particular.

An hour later, Francis and Diana came out.

'There's tea for you two in the kitchen,' Francis called more loudly than he needed. 'Freshly baked scones, too.'

One of the men stopped work for a moment, sighing enviously.

Thompson yelled at him to get on with it. As he turned, he kicked one of the low walls in the old garden, sending a few loose bricks tumbling.

Francis was across in a flash. 'You don't have permission to touch that garden until tomorrow.'

'What the hell does it matter?' He raised his foot to swing it at the wall again, but before he could do it, Francis grabbed him and yanked him away.

For a moment they stood face to face. It was Thompson who backed away from the fury in the other man's face.

Francis went over to Victor. 'Go on. Take a well-deserved break. And don't worry. I won't let him touch that wall.'

Ros passed the notebook to Diana. 'It doesn't matter if you scribble nonsense. It infuriates him just to see someone taking notes.'

Diana looked at the book. 'You've written down what he's said and done, so I will too.'

From then onwards, Francis and Diana kept watch in the

old garden, despite how chilly it was. Thompson glared at them from time to time, muttering under his breath. But at least he didn't try to destroy the walls again.

As the sun began to set on another short winter's day, he made a great play of taking out his watch and consulting it. 'That'll do for today. We can make a good start in the morning on levelling this place. As I have an important appointment, I'll leave you two to pack up. Make sure you don't leave anything lying around.'

Victor, back on watch now, saw him leave and muttered, 'Good riddance!'

One of the men came across and said, 'Tell Mr Esher we're all of us sorry about this, but we don't want to lose our jobs, so we can't refuse to do the work. Is he . . . all right? I thought he'd have been out with you today.'

'He's very upset.' Victor gestured round him. 'We're all upset – especially at the thought of the old garden being destroyed. It's hundreds of years old and rather special.'

'Yes. Really pretty, those old walls are, sir. It is a shame.'

That evening everyone separated after tea, as sometimes happened. Once the children had finished their homework, they often got out board games, but tonight they didn't bother. After some whispering Gillian took the sewing box with her, saying airily, 'Just got to mend my hem.'

Judith chuckled. 'That girl never mends anything unless I nag her. It's not long till Christmas. I bet she's making presents. I ought to be doing the same. There's been such a lot going on that I haven't made much of a start yet. I wonder if there will be anything special in the shops this year.'

'Not much,' Ros said. 'Have you seen the Ministry of Food's recipe for mock turkey? Ridiculous. They can call it "murkey" but it's still sausage meat, vegetables and breadcrumbs – and it won't fool anyone.'

'Never mind. We'll play games and still have fun. Do you have a few moments to help me with the hem on that dress I found in the attics?'

'Of course. Will you be all right, Christa?'

Christa nodded. Their conversation had stirred up memories. How long ago it seemed since her mother had made her a Christmas present! She glanced at Daniel, but he was still lost in the latest designs for prefabs, which he'd been sent by a friend, so she picked up a book she'd borrowed from the ample supply in Mayne's library and continued reading. She was nearly at the end and when she'd finished, she decided she'd like a breath of fresh air before she chose another book.

'I'm going out to stretch my legs,' she told Daniel. 'Do you want to come?'

'Just let me have a look at this first. It's the last of the new designs.' Her words seemed to sink in suddenly and he looked up and called after her, 'Don't go far. Why don't you walk up and down the back yard, where you know you'll be safe? I'll join you shortly.'

'I might go as far as the old garden. It's only just behind the Nissen huts.'

'Don't go any further than that! And watch where you walk. The ground there is very uneven.'

'Yes, sir!' She walked out, pleased by the way he cared about her. She knew he wasn't neglecting her. She'd learned that he hated to stop work in the middle of a task.

It was cool but beautiful outside and she breathed deeply, looking up at the star-filled sky, enjoying the peace and quiet. A few clouds were drifting across it, but she didn't think it'd rain.

She strolled up and down the yard a couple of times, but there was still no sign of Daniel, so she went a little further, tempted by the pattern of paths in the old garden. It had been so overgrown during the war that only Mayne had known about it. But it had been gradually cleared in the past few months.

Thinking she heard someone behind her, she stopped walking, pleased that he had come out to join her. She turned round. 'Daniel, I—'

But it wasn't him. It was a woman with a headscarf pulled down round her face, holding a big stick in her hand, raised to strike.

Christa jumped sideways but couldn't avoid the stick altogether. As it thumped down on her shoulder she cried out in pain and moved further away. But the attacker was between her and the house, the low walls of the garden prevented her from running away and her shoulder throbbed every time she moved her body.

The stick whistled down again, only just missing her head this time. It hit the edge of a low wall instead and broke off a chunk of the crumbly old brick, which went skittering away along the path.

'You'll not live to inherit that money!' the woman said in a low voice, clearly trying to disguise her way of speaking.

But Christa knew immediately who was attacking her: Mrs Pelling's niece. 'Help! Daniel, help me!' she called as loudly as she could, but there was no answer. Desperation gave her the strength to scramble over another wall and dive behind some bushes.

Here the ground was so uneven, she stumbled as she landed and instead of hitting the ground, she fell into a hole that was several foot deep. She cried out in shock and pain as she hit the ground at the bottom hard.

From close at hand she heard a yell of triumph and for a moment could only lie there, winded.

A shadow fell across the top of the hole and a brick was hurled in, just missing her head. As it hit her chest instead, she cried out in pain again.

'Christa! Where are you?'

'Daniel! Daniel, help! Stop her!'

Another brick followed the first one then the shadow moved away from the hole. She heard the sound of her attacker trampling through the bushes and called out to Daniel again.

'Christa! Where are you?' He sounded closer this time.

'I fell into a hole. Watch where you tread.'

This time the shadow that fell across her was accompanied by his voice saying her name and she sighed in relief.

'Christa. Are you hurt?'

'She attacked me with a stick. Did you see her?'

'I saw someone running away, yes . . . What's this?' He moved away and returned with something dangling from his hand. 'It's a scarf. It must be hers. It'd caught on a low branch.'

'I think she was trying to kill me.'

'*Kill you?* Why? Who was she?'

'I couldn't see her face, but I recognised her voice. It was Mrs Grayton.'

Clouds covered the moon and it grew darker. He shone his torch down on her. 'Let's get you out of there, then worry about her afterwards. Can you stand up and reach my hands?'

She managed to stand up, but when she tried to take hold of his hands, she found her shoulder too sore to use, and when he attempted to lift her by the other hand, that hurt her shoulder too. She couldn't help whimpering and letting go.

'Damn! I'll have to go and find a ladder. I won't be long. There's one in the old stables. Yell at the top of your voice if she comes back. I'll be within earshot.'

For a few agonising minutes, Christa leaned against the side of the hole, shivering with cold and praying the woman wouldn't return. The clouds passed and there was enough light for her to see her surroundings more clearly. There was a piece of wood showing in the side of the hole near her foot. She kicked at it and the earth round it fell away, revealing more wood. It looked like part of a door.

There was the sound of footsteps on gravel and for a moment she tensed, then she heard Daniel calling her name and Mayne's voice echoing him.

'Thank heavens!' she murmured. 'Oh, thank heavens.'

They lowered the ladder and Daniel climbed down to join her. He helped her on to it and steadied her as she climbed out, because she was still unable to use her injured shoulder. She called back at him. 'There seems to be a door in the side of the hole.'

He flashed his torch around. 'So there is. I'll just check it before I follow you up. It's easy to kick away the earth and . . . you're right, it is a door.'

Mayne helped Christa off the ladder and peered down into the hole. 'Did you say a door? Do you think there's another secret cellar or something down there? Christa, did you see any—' But he broke off as she swayed dizzily and if he hadn't put his arm round her for support she might have fallen.

'Don't try to do anything. Just lean against me.'

Daniel climbed out of the hole and took over, steadying her, kissing her forehead.

Mayne used his torch to examine the interior of the hole. 'I'll help you carry her to the house, then I'll bring some of the others back to check out what we've got here.'

'I don't need carrying. I can walk,' she protested, but he ignored her and they made jerky progress across the garden towards the house. She still felt a bit shaky and distant, and shuddered as she remembered how helpless she'd felt trapped in the hole. What if Daniel hadn't come out to join her in time? Would that woman really have killed her?

In the kitchen she was immediately surrounded by love and warmth. Mayne, Victor and Francis went back to examine the hole, and the women sent Daniel out of the room while they undid her clothes to examine her shoulder.

It was so painful she couldn't help wincing and they decided to call in the doctor.

While Judith phoned him, Mrs O'Brien put a cup of hot, sweet tea on the table in front of Christa, who used her good arm to lift it.

Now that she was decently covered again, Daniel was allowed back into the kitchen and as he came to sit beside her she said in a low voice, 'I'm sure all this fuss isn't necessary. I just need to rest for a bit.'

'Let us make sure, my darling. And once Judith's finished calling the doctor, I'm going to telephone Sergeant Deemer and tell him what happened. I've got the scarf of the woman who attacked you. Perhaps if he confronts her with it, she'll confess.'

Christa sucked in a shaky breath. 'It was definitely Mrs Grayton. I recognised her voice. She was trying to kill me, said I'd not live to inherit the money.'

'She must have run mad to attack you like that. She needs locking away or who knows what else she'll try to do?'

Judith came back, saying the doctor was coming straight away and Daniel went off to phone the police.

'You all right?' she asked.

Christa nodded, but she was still shocked that anyone would want to kill her.

As Judith put a blanket round her shoulders, she was warmed far more by the kindness of her new friends than by the tea and blanket. It felt as if she had a family again.

Daniel came back. 'Sergeant Deemer knows who the Graytons are and where they're staying because he saw them in town earlier today and thought they were acting strangely so followed them for a while. He's going straight there now and I'm meeting him with the scarf. Will you be all right, darling?'

'Of course I will.'

'We'll look after her,' Judith said and there were murmurs of agreement from the other women.

Mayne had gone back to the old garden with a small spade. First he examined the area round the hole and found a large piece of rotted wooden trellis to one side. 'This must have been over the top of the hole, covered with branches,' he said, thinking aloud.

The other men came to look. 'Christa must have knocked the cover away as she fell,' Victor said. 'Look, the ground's soft enough to show where she slipped.'

Mayne lifted up one edge of the trellis to examine the underside. 'It doesn't look as if it was attached to anything. I wonder why we didn't notice this hole before, though?'

'You've only been back for a few months,' Francis said. 'And it was behind the clump of rhododendron bushes.'

'Well, let's check that door.' Mayne climbed down the ladder and Victor passed him the spade.

It was easy to clear away the rest of the sloping heap of dirt that covered the door. 'This soil hasn't been here for long. It's too loosely piled.'

More use of the spade, then, 'It is a door, quite old, I think, and there's a padlock on it, a bright, shiny new padlock but not a very strong one. The door opens inwards. Well, no one's locking me out of my own property!' He lifted the spade and used it to smash the padlock, then pushed the door wide open.

'Well, I'll be damned! I'd expected a cellar for storing root vegetables, but there's a tunnel. My ancestors must have been paranoid, making tunnels and secret rooms everywhere like this.'

'They came out of Civil War. Wars make people do crazy things. I'd have been paranoid too to protect my own,' Victor said.

'Well, here goes.' Before they could stop him, Mayne had leaned the spade against the side of the hole and gone into the tunnel. All they could see was the faint light of the torch.

'Hey! Wait for someone to go with you,' Victor called. But there was no answer.

'We'd better stay here in case the tunnel collapses and we have to dig him out,' Francis said to Victor. 'He really ought to have been more cautious.'

'He doesn't have time. Thompson is coming tomorrow to clear everything away.'

'Oh, hell. I'd forgotten. Well, this settles it. If we all have to lie down in front of the earth mover to stop them destroying the old garden and all it contains, that's what we'll do.'

'They'd just drag us away. Thompson's bound to bring a lot of men with him, in case we cause trouble.'

They turned at the sound of a car.

'I'll go and see who it is,' Victor said.

He was back a few moments later. 'It's the doctor. No sign of Mayne?'

'No.'

'Where the hell has he got to?'

'We can't go after him without a light of some kind.'

'We'll give him a few minutes longer then I'll go for an oil lamp. My torch battery is running low.'

The doctor examined Christa's shoulder and said that while it was badly bruised there was nothing broken, thank goodness.

'You need to rest it and keep your arm in a sling for a day or two, young lady. How did it happen?'

'She was attacked in the grounds,' Judith said grimly.

He looked at her in shock. 'Who by?'

They explained and he shook his head sadly. 'I don't know what the world is coming to. There wasn't so much violence when I was young. Have you sent for Sergeant Deemer?'

'Yes. He knew where the woman was staying, so Daniel's going with him to challenge her.'

'Well, if anyone can sort this out, it's our Deemer. That man deserves a medal for how he came back to work during the war. Anyway, miss, you'd better get off to bed now. You've had enough excitement for one day.'

But when he'd gone she pleaded with them to let her stay up and find out what had happened, so they found her a chair and waited.

'The men get all the fun,' Ros grumbled. Then she looked apologetically at Christa. 'Sorry. It wasn't much fun for you being attacked.'

'No. I wonder how Daniel's getting on. I hope she doesn't attack him as well.'

She took a deep breath and asked their advice about something that was worrying her, explaining about bringing her mother's wedding ring to Britain sewn into the rag doll's stomach. She'd never taken it out, afraid of leaving signs that something was hidden there, but whenever she touched the doll, she felt it connected her to her mother.

'I think that's lovely,' Ros said.

'What I wanted to ask was . . . when we marry, do you think Daniel will mind me using my mother's wedding ring, instead of him buying a new one?'

'Of course he won't,' Judith said at once and the others nodded agreement. 'How lovely to have something of your mother's still.'

'Thank you. When all these troubles are over, I'll tell him about it.' She leaned her head back and soon was sleeping peacefully.

The other women exchanged smiles. 'As if he'd object,' Judith murmured. 'She's still feeling her way, isn't she?'

'Yes, but she fits in well, and caring for her is helping Daniel recover.'

22

When Daniel left Esherwood, he shoved the attacker's scarf in his pocket and hurried into town. He found Deemer waiting for him as arranged.

'Are you sure they're staying here, Sergeant?'

'Oh, yes. I make it my business to keep an eye on things in my town – all day, every day. I saw the couple you described sitting in the square, then they started acting suspiciously and I realised they were following Christa, trying to keep out of sight. So I followed them.

'They stopped at the gates of Esherwood, watched her go down the drive and had an argument, before going back into town. I followed them again, checked where they were staying and left them to it. I'm fairly sure they didn't notice me. Too busy quarrelling.'

He paused, head on one side as he studied the house. 'I'll check them out carefully now, especially if that's the woman's scarf you were telling me about. I know Mrs Walters, whose house this is. She's a good, honest soul and we can rely on her to tell us the truth. Come on. We'll go round to the back and wake her up, if necessary.'

There was still a light showing at one of the rear windows, however. 'Oh, good. She's not gone to bed yet.' Deemer tapped on the window.

A plump woman came to check who was outside then

smiled when she saw who it was and opened the back door. 'Is something wrong, sergeant?'

'I'm not sure. We've come about your lodgers. What's their name?'

Her smile faded. 'Grayton! And if they weren't already leaving tomorrow, I'd be asking them to leave. I've never had such a rude woman staying here before and I won't put up with being spoken to like that in my own house, as I told her. And quarrel! They've done nothing but argue, those two.'

'Did you happen to hear what it was about?'

'I couldn't help but hear, they were shouting so loudly. *She* wanted to go out again and confront someone; he didn't. Oh, and she kept talking about some money. It sounded as though she'd lost it. That wasn't quite clear, but she was in a right old state about it, my word she was.'

'What's kept you up so late tonight, Mrs Walters?'

'Them. She might have persuaded him to go out walking but she wasn't going to persuade me to give them a key to the front door – the idea of it, giving a house key to a complete stranger! – nor would I leave my door on the latch, not after dark. Things are not as safe as they were before the war, not even in Rivenshaw, despite all your efforts. So I stayed up. They've not long been back. I was just going to bed myself when you knocked. Are they . . . in trouble?'

'We think so.' He turned to Daniel. 'Show her the scarf.'

Daniel took it out of his pocket.

'That looks like the one Mrs Grayton was wearing tonight,' Mrs Walters said without prompting.

'Right. That settles it as far as I'm concerned. I wonder if you'd mind waking them up and asking them to come down?'

'It'd be my pleasure, Sergeant Deemer.' She went up the stairs and he went to stand at the bottom and listen.

She knocked on a door. 'Can you come down, please? The police want to speak to you.'

There was no answer, so she knocked again and repeated her request.

A door opened and a man's voice said, 'My wife's asleep. Can't it wait till morning?'

Sergeant Deemer had had enough of this and shouted up the stairs, 'No, it can't, sir. If you don't come downstairs, I'll have to come up and get you.'

Silence, then, 'Give us a few moments to get dressed.'

'Put your dressing gowns on. I'll give you till I've counted to ten to come down.'

Mrs Walters joined him as he began counting aloud, standing to one side. As he got to ten the Graytons came out of the bedroom and down the stairs. They were, he noted at once, fully dressed.

The woman gave him a furious look but the man seemed worried.

'Come into the dining room,' Mrs Walters said, throwing open a door.

Deemer didn't ask anyone to be seated. 'Where did you two go tonight when you went out?'

The woman folded her arms and said nothing, leaving it to her husband to reply.

'We just, um, walked round the streets a bit. My wife couldn't get to sleep.'

'You were seen, and not on the streets either.'

The sergeant didn't elaborate, but smiled as the man exclaimed, 'We couldn't have been. There was no one around.'

The woman gave her husband a vicious jab in the upper arm. 'You're a fool, Harry Grayton and always were.'

He moved a step backwards, rubbing his arm.

'He means we didn't see anyone on our walk,' she amended.

'That's strange, because you were definitely seen by the

young lady you attacked at Esherwood and by her fiancé as you ran away.'

'Must have been someone else,' she said at once. 'We didn't go to Esherwood.'

'The person they saw had a scarf round her head, hiding her face. This one! It got tangled in a tree branch.' He tossed it on to the table.

'That's not mine.'

'How can you say that? You were wearing it tonight,' Mrs Walters exclaimed. 'I noticed it particularly because I've been looking for one in that colour myself.'

'Well, that one isn't mine.'

'Perhaps you could produce your scarf for us and prove that?' the sergeant said.

She stood biting her lip and when he repeated his question, she snapped, 'I lost my scarf while we were out. Someone must have picked it up. The world's full of thieves.'

'I don't believe you. I'm going to have to arrest you on suspicion of assault.'

'It was my husband who hit her,' she said at once. 'But she deserved it.'

Mr Grayton gaped at her. 'Oh no you don't, Mavis! I told you last time I wasn't going to let you blame me for what you do in one of your fits of temper.' He turned to the sergeant. '*She* attacked that young woman and I won't lie to protect her, not after she's tried to shift the blame to me. I hope the young lady isn't badly hurt?'

'She's got her arm in a sling, so it's serious,' Deemer said. 'Why did you attack her, Mrs Grayton?'

Angry words poured out like poison. 'Because she stole from me. That inheritance should have been mine. I'm not letting her keep it, though. Oh, no!'

'I don't think you're telling me the truth—' But Deemer broke off as she suddenly started hitting out at anyone within reach, screaming and shouting hysterically, not seeming even to notice when she bumped into pieces of furniture.

In the end, she was so out of control the sergeant had to use his handcuffs to hold her in case she hurt someone.

'Is she often like this, Mr Grayton?'

'More often lately. She gets . . . out of control sometimes.'

'Well, I'm afraid I'm going to have to lock your wife up, for her own and other people's safety,' the sergeant said. 'I'll be charging her with assault when she's calmed down enough to understand. You'd better come down to the station with me as well, since you were involved.'

Mr Grayton stood with his head bowed for a moment or two, then looked pleadingly at the sergeant. 'She can't help it.' He tapped his forehead. 'I think she's gone mad. She's been getting worse and worse all through the war, but I wouldn't let the doctor have her locked away last time. I thought inheriting the house would save her, make her happier. I was wrong. I should have taken the doctor's advice.'

'Well, we'll get our own doctor to look at her and see what he says. Come along now, madam.' He had to drag her and she started sobbing loudly, accusing them of hurting her. As she passed her husband she spat at him.

Mr Grayton jerked away. 'Stop it, Mavis. Can I go up and get our coats, please, sergeant? It's cold outside.'

'Will you go with him, Mr O'Brien? Make sure he doesn't do anything but get their coats.'

Daniel nodded. He didn't think he'd have any trouble, though. There was something pathetic about Mr Grayton; it was as if he'd been beaten down by the situation. The sergeant had a firm hold on Mrs Grayton, who looked like a wild animal at bay, her eyes darting around, anger still shining fiercely from them.

'I doubt she'll even get to court,' Deemer whispered. 'Her husband's right. She's sick in the head.'

Although Daniel felt sorry for the poor woman, he was glad that it had all come out. He didn't think Christa would have to worry about the Graytons again.

Francis and Victor were starting to get anxious about their friend's safety and were just about to go for help when they heard a sound from the tunnel.

Soon they could see the light of Mayne's torch and then he appeared, covered in smears of earth, grinning up at them from the bottom of the hole.

Francis called down to him. 'Thank goodness you're safe! We were about to send a search party after you.'

'Let me get out of this damp pit then I'll tell you what I found.'

Once he'd climbed out, Mayne continued, 'This is another way into our cellar at the big house. Once I realised where I was, I had a quick look at how the tunnel is opened and closed, then closed up the entrance and came back. I didn't want to frighten anyone in the house by suddenly appearing up the cellar stairs. And besides, you were waiting for me. I know how to open the tunnel again from the house end.'

He stared round, studying the lie of the land. 'This tunnel entrance will be right in Thompson's way. He'll be even happier to destroy the old garden now because it'll mean destroying this as well.'

Victor put one hand on his friend's shoulder. 'Maybe this is the time to ring for help from our old commander.'

'I hate asking for favours.'

'You know he'll be glad to help you when he can. The country owes a lot to you.'

'I suppose you're right. We can't let that vicious fool destroy a piece of English history. Let's go back and I'll make the phone call right away. There's someone at the other end 24 hours a day. I'm not sure that even they can do anything to stop it in time, though. They have a lot of power but they can't perform miracles.'

'We'll lock the rear entrance gates and hire some men to defend the place,' Victor said.

'What, and ensure the men we hire will have difficulty finding jobs from now on? You know that the council provides a lot of casual work.'

'Nonetheless, we have to try to protect your land, not to mention that garden and tunnel.'

'I'll see what they say at the special unit.'

When they got back to the house they found the women, heads down on their arms at the kitchen table, fast asleep. Mayne woke them and explained briefly what had happened, then looked at their pale, tired faces. 'Why don't you go to bed and get what rest you can? Tomorrow is going to be an eventful day, one way or the other.'

'But you will phone your old commanding officer?' Judith asked.

'Yes.'

She reached up to kiss his cheek, then followed the others up to bed.

'The men like to keep their dealings with the SOE private,' she whispered to the other women when they got to the landing.

A big yawn escaped her. 'He's right about one thing. We need to get some sleep if we're to be of help tomorrow.'

Mayne rang the special number, gave his name and phone number to the woman who answered the call, then put the phone down and waited. A few minutes later one of his former colleagues rang him back.

'Something wrong, Esher?'

'Unfortunately yes.' He explained what was going on and asked if they could, at least, help save the historic old garden and tunnel complex. 'I feel such things are national treasures.'

'I agree with you. We fought to retain our heritage not destroy it. I'm sure everyone here will do their best to help, old fellow. Stay near the phone in case someone needs to speak to you. Sorry to disturb your night's sleep, but it may take me a while to get someone on to the problem.'

'I wish this weren't the only phone in the house,' Mayne grumbled as he put it down again. 'One by the bed would be a big help at times.'

He stayed behind the desk and the other two men found chairs.

After a while, Victor lay down on the rug. 'I may as well get a little shut-eye.'

Francis remained in the rather upright armchair, grimacing at its slippery leather upholstery. But the discomfort didn't stop him falling asleep almost as rapidly as Victor had.

Mayne wished he could do the same. His thoughts were in a tangle lately. He kept wondering if he was mad to struggle so hard to keep his land, if he really was as selfish as Thompson hadn't hesitated to tell everyone.

No! It was Thompson who was being unfair. He was clearly in Draper's pocket and the two of them were probably getting some nice bribes out of this from people anxious to get building contracts.

Resentment boiled up in Mayne, shaking him out of his lethargy and making him even more determined to make one last effort to defend his land.

They'd left the kitchen door unlocked for Daniel and when he returned, he saw the light and came along to the office. Mayne woke the other two so that they could find out what had happened with the Graytons.

'She's as mad as a hatter, poor woman,' Daniel told them. 'I'm so relieved Christa wasn't hurt badly. Now, tell me what you found in the hole.'

Mayne explained and then admitted that he'd asked for help.

'About time too.' Daniel yawned suddenly. 'You've more than earned their ongoing help, so don't be too proud to ask for it.'

Mayne shrugged and leaned back in his chair. 'So . . . you three could go up to bed, you know. I can answer the phone on my own.'

They all shook their heads.

'We'll stay with you in case there's something we're needed for,' Daniel insisted, 'but I may just take a nap. Why don't you put your head down on the desk and do the same, Mayne?'

'I will.' He knew he'd only sleep lightly, but anything would help.

Soon, all four of them were asleep.

An hour later Mayne woke with a shock as the phone rang right next to his ear. He sat up abruptly, snatching the handpiece. 'Esher here.'

He recognised the voice at the other end at once, his former commanding officer.

'We'll do what we can, old chap. But it'll take a day or so to sort out the official paperwork and find some people in the north to help you. Can you keep these people off your land for one more day?'

'I can try.'

'Do it. If you have to use force, do so – within reason – and I'll step in to make sure you don't get arrested.'

'Or bail me out.'

'Whichever is needed.'

Mayne put the phone down and looked at his wrist watch. Three o'clock in the morning. He didn't dare go to sleep again. They had to make plans for the defence of the old garden.

He looked across at the other three who had also been woken by the phone.

'How are we going to keep Thompson and Co out?' he asked. 'Anyone got any ideas?'

Something woke Judith. She reached out for Mayne but he wasn't in bed with her and her heart sank as she remembered the events of the evening. There had been one problem after another for her poor husband lately. She'd like to strangle that stupid Thompson. He reminded her of her bigamous first husband in many ways, a mean and spiteful bully.

It was still dark outside and when she switched on the bedside lamp to check the wristwatch Mayne had given her as an early Christmas present, it was only half past three in the morning.

There! She heard the noise again. It sounded as if people were working outside in the grounds. Had Thompson dared to sneak in this early? She flung back the covers, glad she'd slept in her clothes, and went to wake the others. None of the husbands was there, but the three wives got up, and so did the four children, even young Betty refusing to be left behind.

The men weren't downstairs in the kitchen, either. 'I think they must be out there. Let's go and see what they're doing,' she said. 'They might need our help.'

'I'll get a big stick,' Ben said.

'You'll do no such thing. I'm not having you getting into any fights, my lad.'

'We might have no choice,' he pointed out. 'What if people hit us first? We'll have to defend ourselves.'

He was taller than her now, his voice deepening, nearly a man.

'If you see me joining in a fight,' she said crisply, 'then you can too.'

He grinned. 'Up an' at 'em, Ma!'

Mrs O'Brien came into the kitchen, yawning sleepily. 'I'm coming with you.'

They could see electric lights shining near the rear gate and when they went round the stables they saw that emergency lighting had been rigged up from there.

They found Mayne, Daniel and Victor digging up the ground a little way back from the entrance, working steadily and piling the earth up behind the gates, presumably to stop them being opened.

When her husband looked up and saw her walking towards him, he grinned. Her heart gave a little skip of joy as she realised that he'd lost his miserable, defeated look.

'What's going on here?' she asked.

'We're trying to stop them getting in for at least one more day. My old commander is setting something up to help us, but it'll take him at least a day.'

'Where's Francis?'

'Doing something to the electrics. He said there was a problem.'

'I'm too old to go digging, but I can make some porridge and brew up some tea in that big urn,' Mrs O'Brien said. 'You'll all need some good hearty food to keep you going. Sandwiches as well, if you're still hungry. I'll need some help. Diana, how about it?'

'I can help too,' Christa insisted, 'even with one hand out of commission I could stir the porridge.'

'Good for you, girl!' Mrs O'Brien patted her on the back.

'I can take my turn at digging,' Judith told her husband. 'I may not be as strong as you but I can work during your rests. And I can fetch and carry. Whatever you need.'

'I won't refuse your help,' Mayne said. 'Give me five minutes.'

She started shovelling vigorously and he watched approvingly as he eased his shoulder and arm muscles.

Francis went to his tools and selected two or three very carefully. He had to be quick, didn't want Mayne to suspect what he was doing. His friend was altogether too honourable now that the war was over, and didn't want to play nasty tricks on his own countrymen. But this was a desperate situation and every hour they could buy would be vital during the coming day.

He hurried through the dark streets to the council depot, checking carefully when he got there that no one was on guard duty.

No. The fences were high, the gates were locked and the vehicles were parked neatly inside the compound.

Smiling in the anticipatory way his friends would recognise from various sorties they'd undertaken during the war, he found a place where it was easy to climb the wall.

He nearly laughed aloud when he came to the first vehicle. It was unlocked and the keys were in the ignition. He'd guess this was to facilitate a quick departure this morning. Well, they were in for a surprise.

Moving quickly from one lorry to another, not forgetting the cars, he used his wire cutters and snipped the leads from the distributor caps to the spark plugs. He didn't miss a single vehicle or a single lead.

Then he checked that everything looked as neat and tidy as it had when he got there, and climbed back over the wall.

He wouldn't tell Mayne, not yet. He didn't want his friend to feel guilty about this. And anyway, if Thompson accused Mayne of doing this, it'd be better if Mayne knew nothing about it.

He ran back to Esherwood and joined his friends on digging duties.

'Did you fix the electrical problem?' Mayne asked as he passed. 'You were a long time.'

'Yes. I got it sorted in the end. Bit tricky.'

★ ★ ★

By the time it grew light, no one was complaining that they were cold. Earth had been piled up behind the gates, reaching to a yard or so from the top and the men were now working to reinforce those areas of the perimeter wall that were weak and crumbling, robbing the rockery to put piles of big rocks behind it.

'What do we do if Thompson orders the whole wall to be bulldozed?' Francis asked.

'Pray his machinery gets bogged down.' Mayne grinned at them, his teeth shining white out of his dirty face. 'In fact, we might disguise a couple of trenches to catch him and his men unaware.'

They worked on, very tired physically now. After they'd dug some trenches behind the two weakest places in the wall, Mayne called a halt and walked up and down in the grey light of the chilly dawn, surveying what they'd done. 'Well done, everyone! We need to hold them for one day, but it'll be touch and go.'

Victor wiped his brow with his shirt sleeve. 'What about the front entrance? Do you think they'll try to get in that way again?'

'I can think of several ways the men could get in, but not the machinery.' He went to put his hand on his stepson's shoulder. 'Ben, you're probably the nimblest of us all. Could you go and keep watch there? Do not get into any fights. It's information I need, so run and let me know if he tries to send someone into the grounds that way.'

Ben nodded.

'I can run as fast as he can, so I should go too. I could bring follow-up news,' Kitty pointed out. She looked at her mother, hands on hips. 'And don't tell me to go to school, because I won't do it.'

Judith came and gave her a cracking hug. 'No, love. You're part of this.'

'Good.'

Mayne had remained steadfast about not involving any of the men from the town who depended on the council or on people like Draper for their living. She admired his sense of honour, as she admired so many things about him.

And it was wonderful to see him in charge, his usual vigorous self again.

She found herself murmuring, '*Please, please, let him win.*'

23

When it grew light, they waited expectantly for the council lorries and digging equipment to turn up. But there was no sign of them, not a single lorry.

Mayne began walking to and fro, clearly on edge.

The others exchanged puzzled looks.

Francis said nothing, not yet. But every hour gained pleased him greatly and he found it hard not to tell them what he'd done.

It wasn't until nearly three hours after dawn, by which time everyone's nerves were stretched tight with tension from waiting, that they heard the sound of vehicles moving towards the rear of the house.

'Here they come! The Barbarians at the gate.' This time Mayne didn't go outside to speak to them but climbed up the loose pile of earth to look at them over the top of the gates.

It looked as if all the council vehicles were there and each had at least two men in it. He and his defenders were well and truly outnumbered.

Thompson got out of the big black car that had led the procession and stood with his hands on his hips. For a moment he simply stared up then said scornfully, 'You're a fool, Esher. You can't keep us out and we have the law behind us.'

'An appeal will be lodged today, so I'll ask you to wait until it's been heard.'

He laughed. 'No one's going to overturn that decision. And why should we wait? There is important work to be done.'

He raised his voice and shouted even more loudly, 'And your little trick of last night might have delayed our start today, but I'll see you in court for it, by hell I will.'

'I don't know what you're talking about.'

'Cutting all the distributor leads on the council vehicles. That's wilful damage. We had to requisition leads from all over town.'

'I didn't go near your vehicles.'

'You're a damned liar.'

'And so are you.'

'I'll give you one last chance. Open those gates and let us get about our lawful business, and we'll forget about those leads.'

'I know nothing about your leads. And I have a right to defend my property till the appeal has been heard.'

'Rubbish. You have no rights to this property now. It belongs to the town and it's for *me* to decide what to do with it.'

'I've already offered the council a strip of land on which they can erect at least ten prefabs. You've delayed that work, not facilitated it.'

A few of the men standing there seemed surprised by his statement.

Someone called, 'When did you offer them the land, Mester Esher?'

Thompson whipped round and roared, 'Quiet in the ranks!' at the top of his voice.

Mayne answered anyway. 'I offered it several months ago and my offer was accepted.'

'It wasn't enough,' Thompson snapped. 'We're told that over a million houses were destroyed by the Germans.'

'Land for ten houses is a fair contribution from one man,' someone else called in a muffled voice.

'Who said that?' Thompson demanded, but there was no answer, so he turned back to Mayne. 'You'll regret this, Esher and it'll do you no good. You'll not keep us out and you'll wind up facing a judge.'

He turned to the man who'd been driving his car and even though Thompson lowered his voice, Mayne could hear what he said.

'Try again to find Sergeant Deemer. It's his duty to support us and if he doesn't respond this time, I'll report him to his superiors for dereliction of duty.'

After that he turned round and addressed the group of men who were standing waiting for orders. 'Break down those gates.'

They looked at one another then one man was pushed forward to act as spokesman.

'Um, how do you want us to do that, sir?'

'Drive your vehicles at the gates. They'll soon fall down.'

'But there's earth piled up behind the gates and our lorries won't be able to get through. Anyway, they're good solid gates, those are. Our lorries would come off worst.' He turned to the man standing slightly behind him. 'What do you think, Ken?'

'I agree. It'd definitely damage the council lorries to drive them at the gates.'

Thompson waved his arm at the line of vehicles. 'Well, get the bulldozer off its trailer, you fool, and use that to remove the gates *and* the pile of soil.'

The man stiffened markedly at being spoken to like that and moved very slowly along the line of six lorries to pass these orders on to the man driving the vehicle with the trailer behind it.

Getting the bulldozer off the trailer took a long time, since the other lorries had stopped so close behind it they'd hemmed it in. And the men didn't hurry, for all Thompson's yells.

Mayne was somewhat puzzled by this. You'd almost think the men had parked the bulldozer like that on purpose.

One of them winked at him as the lorries were moved out of the way and Mayne's suspicion became a certainty.

But who had cut the leads?

He stilled as he remembered Francis saying he had an electrical crisis to attend to if the house wasn't to be blacked out. When he turned to look at his friend, Francis grinned and spread out his arms in a shrug.

'Well, I'll be damned!' Mayne muttered, and he couldn't help grinning back.

He remained on top of the pile of dirt, watching, while Thompson strode to and fro like a little toy soldier.

He looked furious and kept saying, 'Hurry up there! Move more quickly, damn you.'

But the foreman said, 'We have to do it carefully . . . sir. The town's only got the one bulldozer. Can't risk ruining it.' And the men continued to work extremely slowly.

Once the big machine had been unloaded, Thompson gestured to its driver. 'Go on, then. Knock the gates down.'

The man pointed up to Mayne, who had stayed where he was, having decided there'd be time to scramble down if the gates looked like being breached.

'What about Mr Esher . . . sir? I don't want to injure him.'

'Damn Mr Esher. Get going.'

Victor came up to join Mayne. 'I could easily shoot out the tyres of those lorries, but I suppose that'd be a step too far.'

That brought a faint smile to his friend's face. 'Unfortunately, yes. Holding firm to our own property is one thing, damaging theirs is another. Pity, though. I like the idea of a bit of target practice.'

'You can't do much to stop a bulldozer with those solid tracks to run on. It's like a tank. This one's quite an early machine, isn't it, from the design of the blade?'

'Yes. I remember it being brought into town a few years before the war. It was such a novelty, few people had ever seen one before, so every man and his dog went to watch it in action.'

They fell silent and time seemed to pass slowly as the ungainly machine crawled round to face the gates.

Before it started on the short journey towards them, Ben came racing over to them and Mayne groaned. 'Oh, hell! Something must have happened at the front entrance as well. This is going to be over even more quickly than we'd feared.'

When he first got to the front entrance Ben had kept watch carefully, determined to play his part. He was joined by Mr Rennie, then a short time later by some of Mr Rennie's friends, until there were about ten elderly gentlemen standing there, chatting and joking.

How could they joke at a time like this?

A lorry came up the hill towards the Dower House and stopped at the front entrance to the grounds. Four men got out of it, joking about 'easy jobs'.

Ben didn't like the looks of them. They were young and strong, and they had brought some big cutting equipment. They'd be intending to use it to remove the chain that barred the drive.

'Here we go, lads,' Mr Rennie said.

Ben watched in surprise as the group of old men formed a line across the front of the chain barrier, and Mrs Rennie came running out of the Dower House to join them.

The young men laughed and one tugged the nearest old man out of the way, dumping him not too gently on the ground. His companion moved to do the same to the next old chap.

But every time one of the old men was shoved aside his companions edged closer together to fill the gap while he got up, and moved back to join the far end of the line. And the older men outnumbered the younger ones.

Ben moved forward, intending to join in.

'You stay out of the way, young 'un,' Mr Rennie told him.

'I want to help.'

'They're afeared to hurt us too badly, us being old, but they'd be a lot rougher with you. Now do as I've telled you. Your job is to run and tell Mayne what's happening here once I give you the word.'

'Shouldn't I go and fetch him now?'

'What for? We've made our plans. Let's give them a chance to work.' He gave a rusty chuckle. 'You just watch. Our bodies might be old but me an' my mates have still got our brains.'

As Ben stood watching, more older men and women came out of the huts on the nearby Parson's Mead allotments and walked up the hill towards the gateway.

The young thugs immediately turned round and threatened to bash them if they didn't stay back.

'You touch me and my grandson will beat you to a pulp,' one little old lady yelled.

'Him and whose army?' the young man jeered.

'He won't need any help. He's a boxing champion in the Army, my Larry is, and he's home on leave.'

They looked at one another as if the name rang a bell. 'Larry! Larry who?'

'Larry Swinson,' she yelled in her shrill, cracked old voice. 'Pride of Rivenshaw, they call him.' While they were gaping at her, she walked past them with her nose in the air to stand in the middle of the line of old people, arms folded.

There were now about twenty people there.

The young men held a quick conference, then got into their lorry and drove it at the line of old people as if to run them down.

'They won't dare,' Mr Rennie called out scornfully. 'Hold firm, everyone.'

Ben watched as the old people did just that, some leaning on walking sticks. The driver was forced to brake at the last minute.

Someone yelled, 'Hoy, you! What do you think you're doing, driving a lorry at people like that? You could have hurt someone.' Miss Peters had come up the hill from her house without anyone noticing. She was dressed in her best church-going clothes, which included an elaborate old-fashioned hat trimmed with soft pink feathers, and she was brandishing a very large umbrella in front of her, as if it were a weapon.

'Oh, hell! It's Judge Peters' sister,' one of the young men muttered. 'I'm not tangling with *her*. Last time I was up before him, he said he'd have me locked away for three years if I got into trouble again.' He tried to hide from her behind the others.

The other attackers watched her warily.

'My brother is on his way to Rivenshaw and will make sure this dispute is settled legally,' she said. 'In the meantime, please let me pass. I wish to have a little chat with my friends.'

She went to join the line.

The young men hesitated, then put their equipment back into the lorry and drove away.

'Now you can go and tell your new father what's happening here, young 'un,' Mr Rennie told Ben.

Grinning broadly the boy raced off up the drive.

The grins were equally broad on the faces of the people he left behind.

*   *   *

'There's another lorry just arrived,' Daniel called, watching two burly young men get out of it and hurry up to Thompson. 'It doesn't look like a council lorry, though. Who the hell are they?'

Mayne, who had been taking a break, joined him again on top of the pile of earth behind the gate.

Thompson seemed flabbergasted at what one of the young men was telling him. He stood stock still for a few moments, mouth open, then took a deep breath and turned round with an expression of renewed determination on his face.

Just then Ben ran up and gasped out his tale, solving the mystery.

'You should have seen them, Dad,' he wound up. 'They might be old but they're as brave as anything.'

'They are indeed. Grab something to eat then go back and join them in case they need a messenger again later.'

'Gillian's there and nothing's happening now. Can't I stay here?'

'Oh, very well.'

Heartened by the news from the front gate, the defenders managed to keep the 'Barbarians' out for the whole of the morning. The earthmover didn't manage to knock the gates down, only damage the wood and send a few splinters flying. Which was strange.

Was its driver particularly inept? Mayne wondered. Or was it possible these men were doing the only thing they could to help him by working slowly and inefficiently? When another one winked at him, he nodded slightly in acknowledgement.

Some of them were on his side, anyway. Not all of them, though, and a few low-voiced arguments erupted among the men as the minutes ticked past.

But would this keep Thompson out till the end of the day? He doubted it.

There was still no sign of Sergeant Deemer, but people from the town had gathered nearby to watch what was going on and more kept joining them.

Thompson tried to send them away, but they paid no attention to him, and occasionally one of the people at the back of the crowd would yell, 'Shame on you!'

This turned the angry red in Thompson's cheeks to a blotchy purple.

At half-past twelve the workers stopped for their midday meal and when Thompson tried to make them carry on working, they stood and argued with him about the rules, and how they had a *right* to their break.

In the end he threw up his hands in despair, gestured to his driver and had himself driven away.

It was turning into a farce, Mayne thought, but still a farce that could end in disaster for him. He left Victor on watch and went to grab a quick sandwich from a platter brought out from the house and a mug of hot tea from the urn.

When Thompson returned, he was smiling again. He snapped out orders and though resentful looks were thrown at him, there was a flurry of activity. The equipment was moved along to one of the weaker spots in the perimeter wall and the earth mover raised the wide straight blade before rolling forward towards it.

'I was afraid of this,' Mayne said. 'I'd hoped Thompson would abide by the law, because he has no right to damage my wall. But even if the police charge him for this, by then the damage will be done. I wonder how much effort it'll take to knock the wall down. I think that's one of the earliest parts.'

'We did leave a few surprises for them behind the wall,' Francis pointed out.

'Sadly, those will only hold them back for a short time.'
He sighed and glanced at his wristwatch. The day seemed
to have been going on forever already.

The wall took longer to knock down than anyone had
expected but at last the bottom part fell in a cloud of dust.
Fragments of the narrow old bricks flew everywhere and
the watchers let out a loud 'Oooh!'

Thompson yelled in triumph, but his yell was cut off
abruptly as he realised that he was the only person to have
yelled. He scowled round. 'What are you waiting for? Drive
those lorries through the gap and we'll start clearing the
ground.'

The first lorry hit the trench that had been dug and
concealed with loose earth. The vehicle got bogged down
and the driver's attempts to reverse out only sent it even
deeper.

Thompson ordered another lorry to tow the bogged vehicle
back out on to the road and when it had gone, the earth
mover was to smooth the way. He yelled at the driver, 'While
you're waiting to level the ground, you can knock down
more of the wall. That bit a few yards along looks ready to
fall. It's probably a danger to passers by.'

'Which bit would that be exactly, sir?' the driver asked.
'It all looks ready to fall down to me.'

Thompson marched along, or tried to, but stumbled on
the uneven ground and staggered sideways. He slowed down
and moved more carefully, then slapped the wall. 'From
here . . . to here.'

'You leave that old wall alone,' a woman yelled suddenly
from the crowd.

'Vandals!' shouted a man with a deep voice.

Several chimed in with more cries of, 'Shame on you.'

Thompson ignored them and gestured to the driver of
the bulldozer.

Before he could do anything, a woman moved forward from the crowd and went to stand in front of the next bit of wall. 'That's enough destruction,' she cried. 'The war is over and we've a right to a peaceful life. They'll have to drive over me to do any more damage to poor Mr Esher's wall. He fought for us, now it's our turn to fight for him.'

There was loud cheering, then a man yelled, 'This is *my* street and that old wall is part of it. I used to climb that wall as a child, and I want my sons to do the same.'

'If we don't stop you now, you'll be knocking down our houses next. We don't want men like you in our town, Thompson.'

'Get back to where you came from!'

'Yes. Get out of Rivenshaw.'

'Out! Out! Out!'

Two more women walked forward to stand beside the first one, then a man, then an older woman hobbling along with a walking stick. Suddenly half the crowd was standing protectively in front of the wall.

Some of the more nimble ones clambered inside the gap that had been made, in spite of Thompson's attempts to have them held back.

'Just look at that,' Victor said softly. 'Isn't it wonderful? I don't think you'll be struggling to hold the day, Mayne. I think you've got a whole army behind you.'

Mayne couldn't answer for the lump in his throat and he felt dangerously close to tears. All he could do was salute the crowd, who immediately began cheering, returning his salute and yelling more insults at Thompson.

Judith came to join her husband, waving to some women she knew and linking her arm in his. 'We've gained our day's grace, love,' she said softly.

Below them the other defenders had found vantage points from which to watch what was going on. Ben started the cheering and hurrahs on the inside and everyone outside joined in.

Thompson tried to address the crowd and a piece of dirt sailed through the air and landed smack in his face, followed by something wet and nasty flopping against the front of his white shirt and leaving a brown stain. He yelled in outrage and began brushing furiously at it, but only managed to smear the sticky stuff around.

In the end he turned tail and fled towards his car, followed by more lumps of dirt.

Mayne stayed at the highest point of the defences and held up his hands in a gesture asking to be heard. As the shouts died down, he thanked his impromptu army, who cheered him loudly.

They were in a rollicking good mood at having routed Thompson. The fellow seemed to have made enemies in the town more quickly than anyone Mayne had ever met before.

'You go and have a rest, Mr Esher,' one woman yelled. 'You were working half the night, I heard you. We'll keep watch for you.'

More cheering and shouts of, 'Just let them try to start again!'

As he walked back to the house, Mayne felt suddenly boneless with fatigue after his almost sleepless night and stressful day.

Francis stayed behind to show the watchers how to use the emergency siren in case they had to summon the defenders back.

Mrs O'Brien braved her former fear of speaking in public to promise them a freshly brewed urn of nice hot tea within the half hour, which brought more cheers.

★   ★   ★

The four partners, their womenfolk and the children went to sit in the front drawing room and have a breather, sighing with weariness but smiling at one another.

'Weren't those people marvellous? Rivenshaw is still a good town in which to bring up children,' Ros said. Then she flushed as Judith gave her stomach a speculative look, and added, 'I didn't tell you before, but Victor and I are expecting a baby in June.'

All the women hugged her and offered congratulations, while the men shook Victor's hand.

There were voices outside and Christa, who was nearest to the window, said, 'It's Miss Peters and an old gentleman I've not seen before.'

Mayne joined her. 'That's her brother, Judge Peters. I hope he hasn't come to tell us we'll have to let those sods destroy our gardens.'

'He wouldn't dare,' Judith said. 'His sister would kill him if he tried.'

'She's an amazing woman, but not a miracle worker. Let's pray that the law, in this case, is not an ass. I'd better go and let them in.'

Both visitors looked at them rather anxiously then relaxed at the sight of their smiles. 'How did things go with that idiot from the council?'

Mayne explained what Thompson had tried and how the townsfolk had stopped him.

Miss Peters said, 'Ha!' in tones of deep satisfaction. 'Sergeant Deemer said he was going to tell a few people what was really going on and drop a few hints about what might help you. I must say he's had more success than I'd expected.'

'I didn't hear what my sister just said,' the Judge remarked. 'We'll set up your appeal about the forced sale of your land as quickly as possible, Esher.'

'And the people at my old unit are going to help, too,' Mayne told him.

'He won't say anything himself, but they owe Mayne here more than we can ever tell you, because we've all had to sign the Official Secrets Act,' Victor put in. 'Trust me, he was a hero.'

The judge inclined his head towards Mayne. 'I've had a few hints.'

'It's worked out jolly well, hasn't it?' Miss Peters slapped one hand down on a small table next to her chair, making a china ornament bounce about dangerously.

'And we discovered something else of interest to this case last night.' Mayne went on to tell them about the new passage.

'I must say, I'm looking forward to finding out what's in that secret cellar of yours,' Miss Peters said. 'Don't forget to invite me to the opening.'

'It's a very small space. Only those actually trying to get inside will be able to stand near the door. And there might be nothing inside.'

'I'm going to wait above the cellar entrance, in the Nissen hut,' Judith said. 'You're welcome to wait with me there, Miss Peters.'

'Thank you. I shall accept your kind invitation.'

'I think there will be quite a crowd of us up above,' Victor said. 'Good thing we cleared out most of the stuff stored in the hut, eh?'

Judge Peters stood up. 'Well, I can't stay in Rivenshaw for more than a day or two, so you'd better take me to see your lawyer, Esher, and we'll discuss the appeal this very day. Then, if necessary, I'll send word to the council not to take any further actions till it's all settled.'

'Did you walk up here? I have a car parked at the Dower House, to avoid the barriers,' Mayne said. 'I can speed things up by driving you round to Mr Woollard's house. Judith, could you phone them and let them know we're on our way.'

Ray came to open the door for them as soon as the car stopped. After the legal niceties had been gone through with Mayne's lawyer, he invited them to take tea. 'I have some other news which may interest you.'

He waited till they'd all sat down, then said, 'My detective has found out a few things about Thompson.'

Everyone stilled.

'It seems he was asked to leave the Army as soon as the war ended, because they believed he'd been pilfering from the stores. They couldn't prove anything against him or they'd have prosecuted him. He'd set up various underlings to take the rap.'

Mayne let out a long, low whistle of surprise.

'Anyway, they didn't feel it fair to make the underlings take the blame, since some of them were working in stores because of war injuries, so they demobbed them *and* Thompson, who had been regular Army, and left it at that. He came out without any medals or letters of recommendation.'

'But he must have had good references to get the job with the council!' Miss Peters protested. 'I know how the system works because I sometimes serve on appointment commit- tees for the more important jobs. I didn't this time, because Draper organised it all—' She broke off. 'Draper again! That man is another who has been suspected of dodgy practices, but no one's ever caught him out.'

'He makes sure people are too afraid of him to talk,' Mayne said.

'I wonder if I should have a word with the Mayor about him,' the judge mused. 'Stan may listen to me. We go back a long way and I doubt he knows half of what's going on. Losing his youngest son in the Far East hit him hard. And now the war is over, various town councils are starting to clean up their nests in a few places round here.'

He grinned at Ray and added, 'No offence. If ever a black market trader worked honestly, you did. And I knew you were doing some undercover work for the government.'

Ray shrugged. 'I won't pretend I didn't earn some good money at the same time. People needed the occasional treat and I provided that.'

'We'll have to agree to disagree about that.'

'Anyway, back to the Mayor. I've already told him about Thompson,' Ray said. 'Let's wait and see what he does. If he doesn't act, you can follow it up. I want my town run honestly now the war is over.'

There was silence then he turned to Mayne. 'And now, lad, I have some good news for a change. My friend Reston wants to come and open up that cellar of yours as soon as things have calmed down at Esherwood. He thinks he understands the instructions your father found, but if that doesn't work, you'll have to break in somehow, dig down to it perhaps.'

'Trouble is, it's under the old garden. That's what's been stopping us from digging. It'd ruin the garden walls. We're caught in a cleft stick there.'

'Well, how about we have a go at it tomorrow?' Ray suggested. 'Might as well get it over and done with before Christmas.'

'Yes, Judith's been saying she hopes we get things settled soon. She wants to concentrate on preparations for Christmas. It's less than two weeks away now.'

He drove the judge and Miss Peters home, then returned to the Dower House.

His father came hurrying out to catch him. 'I've found out something else about the cellar.'

'Oh?'

'Yes. I went on reading the diary and it seems there's

another key. It was hidden where the diary said it would be, inside a book. They'd cut the centres of some pages to fit it. Shameful way to treat a book! But this key is much smaller and I'm not quite sure what it's for exactly. You'll have to ask Reston.'

He held out a small key that could have been any door key before Yale locks. 'You take it and look after it. It's so small compared to the other one I'm liable to lose it.'

Mayne stared at it, wondering if he was imagining the tingling sensation and the warmth as he touched it. Who had last used this key? 'Thanks. We're going to try to open the cellar door tomorrow. You'll want to be there for that.'

Reginald shivered. 'I don't like being shut in small spaces, so I'll wait at the top of the cellar steps till you and Reston say it's safe.'

'Reston wants to do it at ten o'clock in the morning. Don't forget!'

Mayne drove slowly back round the perimeter to the big house, glad of a moment or two on his own. He had been moved to the core by the support of the townsfolk and felt moisture well in his eyes as he remembered how they'd stood up to Thompson on his behalf.

He parked the car near the rear gates, looking forward to the time when they could remove that big chain for good and not have to live in a fortress.

But there was still one problem to solve. It was more than time to test that puzzle lock.

He wondered if they really would get into the secret cellar. He couldn't imagine it would contain anything valuable, but he was as eager to see it as the others.

He needed to tell everyone that Ray was bringing the locksmith round the following morning and indeed, they'd have to make arrangements for his family and friends to wait nearby as the locksmith worked on the massive old door with its metal strapwork.

Everyone had worked so well together at Esherwood. What a team they made!

They deserved to be there to see the secret revealed, whatever it was.

If there was anything.

And then, whether there was or wasn't any treasure, he'd throw a party. They had a lot to celebrate.

After his defeat at Rivenshaw, Thompson was driven back to the town hall by a smirking chauffeur – damn the impudent fellow. His shirt smelled of the dung thrown at him and he was so furious he could hardly speak. Thank goodness he kept a spare shirt at work.

Ignoring his secretary, he went into his office, but she came in to join him without being asked.

'Kindly wait until I summon you, Miss Beckett. I need to clean up this . . . accident.'

To his surprise she stayed where she was. 'I'm afraid I can't do that. I need to tell you something. When I was collecting the mail this afternoon, I found a letter for the Mayor mixed up with yours so I took it across to his secretary, who just happens to be a very good friend of mine, and—'

'For goodness' sake, I don't need to know that.'

'Oh, but you do. In fact, it gives me very great satisfaction to be the one to tell you. Not about that letter, but about another one the Mayor received in this morning's post.'

Thompson frowned at her in puzzlement. 'Tell me what?'

'That you've been found out.'

'*What?* What the hell do you mean?'

'The Mayor checked your references again – my friend typed the letter – and it came back with "Not known at this address" written on it.'

'How do you know that?'

She smiled. 'My friend told me. It's good to have friends. You should try it sometime. I suppose you must have answered the original reference enquiries yourself after you'd applied for this job, but there's no one to do it now at that address.'

He felt sick with dismay. He'd been so sure, so very sure, that he'd covered every eventuality.

'So the Mayor telephoned a contact at the War Office and found out some very interesting information about why you left the Army. My friend just happened to overhear the call – you really shouldn't have been so rude to her.'

Thompson sat down suddenly. He couldn't speak, could only stare at Miss Beckett.

'The Mayor has called an emergency meeting of department heads for this evening, and it seems *you're* not invited,' she went on. 'I wish I could be a fly on the wall at it.'

As she turned and sauntered out, smiling, he drew in a shaky breath.

Then, moving like a very old man, he jammed a chair under the office door handle to keep that harridan out and began methodically packing his things.

24

Sam heard about the momentous events at Esherwood and then got a message from Cuthbert, so knew it was time to act. At last the waiting was over. With his mother's help, he got a message to Cuthbert.

When he slipped out of the house at one o'clock in the morning, Cuthbert was waiting for him at the corner of the street. He'd brought a haversack with the few spare clothes he possessed, in case they were successful and could leave the country straight away.

Sam greeted his friend, feeling excitement run through him.

Cuthbert, never the most cheerful of men, just grunted and shivered in the cold night air.

'Good thing you found out they're going to open the secret cellar tomorrow, Cuthbert lad. No, it's past midnight, so it's today they'll be opening it, isn't it? I'm surprised you aren't part of the official opening party.'

'Keep your voice down, Sam.'

They began walking, but neither was able to keep quiet.

'Reston told me to stay behind and mind the shop,' Cuthbert whispered. 'Mean old sod. Likes to hog the glory, he does. Well, he's in for a right old shock when I don't turn up to work today and they find the cellar has been opened already. And serve him right, too!'

'Got the key?'

'Of course I have.' He brandished the huge old key. 'Think I'd forget this?'

'Big, isn't it?'

'Yeah. I made myself a copy a couple of days ago while Mr Reston was out on a job. The hardest thing was to pack some spare clothes without the wife noticing.' He jiggled his haversack and added, 'I'm leaving tonight whatever happens. I've had enough of it here, what with Reston bossing me around at work and *her* nagging at home. It's worse than being in the Army, because at least I had my mates to work with there.'

'It's more than time I got out of Rivenshaw,' Sam said. 'Pity you couldn't get hold of the key and the other stuff more quickly. Ma's been on edge in case they found me in her attic.'

'We couldn't have done it sooner. Reston only just got the instructions. Old Mr Esher found them. Took me two goes to finish copying Reston's set. Thank goodness he usually leaves me to mind the shop.'

As they turned a corner, he added, 'So, about tonight – how are we going to tackle it? What did you finally decide?'

'We'll check the entrance to the tunnel as we go past, but first thing we'll do is find out what Esher's ancestors hid in that secret cellar. We'll take anything small that's valuable, then we'll go and get the stuff we hid during the war.'

'*If* there's anything valuable in the secret cellar,' Cuthbert said. 'Don't build your hopes on it. I'm still not sure we should bother with that at all.'

'They wouldn't have gone to so much trouble, or paid for that big, fancy lock, if there hadn't been something worth hiding. I hope it's not only big objects like furniture. That'd be no use to us.'

'You're sure the car and Army uniforms are still there?'

'Of course I am. I popped out to the smallholding a couple of nights ago to check and slipped the owner a fiver to keep the car there for another two weeks. He was happy enough, so stop worrying.' He indicated his haversack. 'I've got some canvas bags in here to put the loot in. Did you bring any?'

'Of course I did. The wife will go mad when she finds her precious shopping bags missing tomorrow. Serves her right for being such a bitch.'

They met no one. At Esherwood, they moved very carefully, avoiding the guards at the front and rear gates, and stopping briefly in the old garden to check that everything was all right.

Sam peered down into the hole to check the entrance to the tunnel. 'Look at that! They've found the tunnel and opened it up. Thank goodness they've not set someone to keep watch on it.'

'Well, I know from Reston that they've not opened the cellar yet. Ah, stop worrying. We'll be gone from Rivenshaw before they get up tomorrow. I wish I could see Esher's face when he finds out someone got there first.'

Sam's only worry was whether Cuthbert was as skilled a locksmith as he'd boasted. Was he really as good as Reston? Well, they'd soon find out. But if they couldn't get into the cellar, he'd still be able to retrieve his booty. He'd still have the money to set himself up in fine style in Australia.

He led the way to the Nissen hut, where Cuthbert made short work of the padlocks on the doors.

The interior seemed darker than Sam had expected since a half moon was shining brightly outside. He stopped to stare round. 'I don't like it in here.'

'I don't, either. Let's go and get our things from the other cellar and leave this lot alone.'

'No. I dreamed about that secret cellar all the time I was

shut in that sodding attic, and I'm going to find out what's in it if it's the last thing I do.'

When they got down the stone steps and stood in front of the big, ancient door, Cuthbert hesitated again.

Sam nudged him. 'Go on. We haven't got all night to do this.'

He took out the key and the instructions. 'Keep quiet now. I have to hear every little scrape of sound.'

The silence seemed to throb with tension. Sam could feel his heart pounding.

Cuthbert worked slowly and meticulously, consulting the copy he'd made of his employer's notes. At one stage he heard a sound which didn't sound right, but he stopped that move just in time, going back and doing it all over again, listening, listening to the sounds inside the lock.

His fingers felt strange, as if they belonged to someone else or were the only parts of his body truly alive. At one stage he couldn't move them, not even to wipe away the sweat pearling his brow.

Then he realised with a jerk of shock that instinct must have stopped him, because he'd nearly made another mistake.

He went on, concentrating hard, and this time it all went well.

The next step was now to be taken, a very important one. What if it didn't work? What if . . . Oh, he didn't have time to let his imagination go silly on him. He made the last move quickly and surely, and yes, the lock clicked to the open position.

After that he took the final steps, turning the handle just so, two turns to the right, one half turn back and then two more turns to the right. And the door opened as smoothly as if it had been oiled only yesterday.

He took a deep breath. 'Told you I could do it.' He stayed in the doorway, shining his torch. 'Look at that! There is still a cellar and it's much bigger than I'd expected.'

Sam pushed past him. 'Yeah. A lot bigger.' He took a few steps forward and stopped with an exclamation of shock, shining his torch on the floor and shuddering. 'Ugh! There's a skeleton here. Come and look.'

Cuthbert moved reluctantly forward, away from the door. 'I don't like skeletons.' He shone his torch round. 'There are shelves and boxes and— Oh, no!'

'What's the matter?'

'Looks like there's another skeleton over there.'

Sam shone his torch that way and jumped in shock, because the skeleton seemed to smile at him.

'That one was a woman,' Cuthbert said. 'There are shreds of her bodice and skirt left. How did they die, do you think?'

'I don't know and I don't care. Perhaps they got shut in here by mistake. It goes a long way back – at least twenty yards, I'd say. Whatever's under those pieces of canvas at the back of the cellar is too big for us, so we should ignore them pieces and check what's on these shelves.'

No sooner had Cuthbert joined his friend than there was a grating sound from the door.

They both spun round. 'What's that? Shine your torch that way.'

They looked in horror to see the door start to close, swinging smoothly and easily back of its own accord to fill the gap.

Cuthbert rushed across the room, but didn't get there in time to squeeze through and though he tried to hold back the edge of the door, whatever was closing it was too strong for him.

'We're shut in!' Sam's voice was shrill. 'We're trapped.' He came to hammer on the door, nearly screaming in his panic. 'Open it! Open it, damn you!'

But Cuthbert was standing like a man frozen and it was a moment or two before he said. 'There's no way to open it from this side. There isn't a keyhole here and anyway the key's still in the outside of the door.'

'We're trapped?'

'I just said so.'

'You can't mean it.'

'I do. I thought it'd just stay open. The notes said nothing about it closing itself. I've even left my tools outside.'

Sam turned round quickly. 'What's that? I heard something move.'

'You're imagining it. We've not even seen any sign of rat droppings.' After a moment's silence, Cuthbert added in a dull, hopeless tone, 'Better put out your torch. It's a waste to use them both at once.'

'I did hear something move.'

'Be quiet and let me listen, then.' Cuthbert strained his ears but shook his head. 'Nothing. You're imagining it.'

'There's a light over there, where the second body is,' Sam said suddenly.

'No, there isn't.'

'Yes, there is. I can see it clearly. It's moving, coming towards us.' He clutched his companion's arm in panic, but Cuthbert shook him off.

'You're imagining things.'

In a whisper now, Sam said, 'It's a woman. In a long dress.'

And then Cuthbert saw her too. Not a skeleton but a lady, dressed all fine with jewels at her throat. She was holding a knife as if threatening someone. As she took a step forward, he saw who she was threatening, a man who was standing where the other skeleton lay. He heard Sam moan in terror beside him.

Cuthbert couldn't look away. It was like being at the cinema, only no film had ever frightened him as much as this did. There was no sound and the two figures seemed to move very slowly.

And he couldn't move a muscle, however hard he tried. Even Sam had stopped pressing against him.

The man became clearer, dressed in old-fashioned clothing, plain dark clothes like the Roundheads Cuthbert had seen in a film. The man was yelling at the lady, though you couldn't hear the words, and when she waved the knife again, he laughed and reached for something at his belt.

She jumped quickly forward, knife raised and stabbed the man in the chest. His mouth opened in a yell like they used to do in the old silent films.

The man started to fall, but pulled her down with him and in a last surge of strength stabbed her with the dagger he'd been fumbling for.

At first she struggled to get away from him, but he'd made his last move now, and as Cuthbert had seen happen in the war, his eyes rolled up and he lay still. Death was the same wherever you met it.

She was badly injured but dragged herself across to where she'd been standing and sat down on a box. She had paper and a quill pen there already on a bigger box. She picked up the pen, dipped it into an inkwell and began to write slowly and carefully, stopping to grimace in pain, then carrying on again.

As she wrote, she clasped one hand against the wound in her belly, trying to hold back the blood. But it seeped out in a thick, dark stream.

When she'd finished, she looked across at Cuthbert and his heart nearly stopped beating, he was so sure she could see him. Her lips formed the words, 'This will tell them.' He could make them out clearly, even though he still could hear nothing.

Then the light began to fade and she crumpled and fell sideways, turning into a skeleton once more.

He could move again, but Sam was a gibbering mess,

and nothing Cuthbert said or did would bring him to his senses.

In the end he gave up trying. All he could do now was wait. Reston and the others would open the door tomorrow and let the two of them out. But then they'd shut him away again for a long time.

He wondered why the door had closed, how its maker had managed that. There must be some way of keeping it open, only they hadn't known it was necessary.

It'd be strange if it did the same thing to whoever came in here, and they were all trapped together.

He should never have got involved with Sam, never have got into thieving. But during the war, they'd all done things they'd never have thought of in peacetime, and he'd married in haste, repenting it within a couple of months, and needing the money to get away from her after the war ended.

He made himself as comfortable as he could, switched off his torch to save the battery, and waited. No strange lights and ghosts now, just his own thoughts to keep him company. And the occasional whimper from Sam.

It seemed a very long time until he heard faint sounds outside the cellar.

Everyone ate breakfast quickly at Esherwood and didn't pretend they had anything on their minds except the opening of the secret cellar. Luckily it was a Saturday, so there was no worry about the children missing another day's school.

As they gathered outside the Nissen hut to wait for Mr Reston, the excitement in the air was almost palpable.

It was sunny, for once, if still cold, and Ben soon grew fed up of standing around. He produced a ball and started playing catches with Betty, then his two sisters joined in.

Ray, his wife and the two Forresters were the first to arrive, driving into the grounds by the rear gates, which had been newly liberated from their piles of earth by Jan and Al late yesterday, then left open under their keen eyes.

'You'll never guess what's happened,' Ray announced even before he'd helped his wife out of the car.

'What?' Mayne asked absent-mindedly. He was too tense about what they might find in the cellar to be interested in gossip.

'Give me a minute of your full attention, lad. It's good news.'

When he had everyone's attention, Ray said quietly, 'You might like to know that Thompson has done a runner.'

'What? When? How did you find out so quickly? He was here lording it over his men only yesterday.'

'Thompson's landlady found his bedroom in chaos this morning, all his clothes missing and her bill for this week unpaid, so she went straight down to the police station to complain. On the way she met our maid and told her about it.'

'Well, I'd never have believed it, even of him!' Judith exclaimed. 'I do hope the police catch him.'

'I'm sure they will. You see, my detective is still following him and, believe me, he never lets his prey escape. He hates bullies with a passion because he was bullied himself as a little child. He'll alert the local police once Thompson stops somewhere.'

Everyone cheered and Mayne shook Ray's hand vigorously. 'Thank you. I'd have hated Thompson to get away scot free.' He looked at his watch. 'Reston hasn't done a runner as well, has he? He was supposed to be here ten minutes ago.'

'Give him time. You wouldn't have a cup of tea handy, would you?'

'Mrs O'Brien always has a cup of tea to hand.'

When her uncle had gone to Esherwood, Stephanie took the books he'd found for Anthony to look at, to see if he could get interested in antiques, and went to join her fiancé in the little room overlooking the garden. 'You're looking so much better this morning, darling.'

'Thanks to you and your family. Ah, Steph, it's a joy to see you every day.'

Which was a happier start to the conversation than usual, she thought, offering him the books and explaining what they were for.

He took them from her, his face brightening at once. 'So your uncle did mean it about finding me a job?'

'Of course he did.'

'I shall enjoy reading these. I hate having nothing to do.'

'Don't try to pretend an interest if you don't have one. Uncle Ray would soon find you out. He's the shrewdest man I've ever met.'

Anthony laughed softly. 'I'd never lie to you or your relatives. But I like the idea of preserving old things. Don't you?'

'I love it. Uncle Ray is turning more and more to antiques since the war ended.'

'Come and join me. You haven't given me a kiss yet today.' He held out his hand and she went to sit next to him on the sofa, snuggling close. He still felt so thin and fragile she hardly dared touch him, but he was the one to kiss her this time, a long lingering kiss.

Then he held her at arm's length and surprised her by asking, 'How soon can we get married?'

'As soon as you like. We could get a special licence.'

'Don't you want a special dress and a big wedding party?'

'No. The last thing I care about is a fancy wedding. All I want is to be with you and make up for lost time. I'm like you. I feel joyful every morning when I wake up and realise you're still alive.'

She had to blow her nose hard then because that thought brought happy tears to her eyes.

'We'll speak to your uncle then. Will he still let us live here for a while?'

'He'll *want* us to live here permanently. Would you mind?'

He looked round, rolling his eyes in mockery. 'Would I mind living in this big, comfortable house after being stuck with fifty other men in a hut in the jungle? Do you really need to ask me?'

Reston still hadn't arrived when Mayne's father came hurrying round the corner of the house with an anxious expression on his face. 'You haven't started yet, have you?'

'No.'

'Thank goodness! I found some more instructions at the end of the diary. You have to insert a small gadget into a hole to keep the door of the cellar open. Look. I've got it here. It's not a key exactly. It's hexagonal. I don't think even Reston knows about it. You could have been trapped inside.'

'Not me,' Mayne said. 'I'd intended to wedge the door open.'

As he was about to go into the house to phone the locksmith and see what was holding him up, a small grey van chugged up the rough back drive and stopped in front of the Nissen hut.

Dick Reston got out, looking annoyed.

'Something wrong?' Ray asked.

'Yes. Cuthbert didn't turn up for work today, didn't send word either. So I've had to leave the shop closed.' He took a metal box with a handle in its lid out of the rear of the van and handed it to the nearest person, who happened to be Mayne, before getting out a much smaller Gladstone bag.

'Well, are we ready, Esher?'

'Not quite. Dad found something else about the lock. Show him, Dad.'

Reginald held out the little gadget and Reston studied it intently. 'What did the diary say it was for?'

'To keep the door open. I don't understand how it could do that.'

'I do. It'll stop a bar of some sort from moving. Good thing you found it. It's probably to stop thieves from taking anything away.'

'The maker thought of everything, didn't he?'

'Old Crosskey was one of the best locksmiths of all time, if not *the* best. Maybe one day we'll find out his real name and then we can give him the credit he deserves.' Reston looked round. 'Ready to do it?'

'Miss Peters hasn't arrived yet,' Judith said. 'And wasn't the judge coming?'

'Yes, and Sergeant Deemer.'

'I'm here,' a voice called and the sergeant turned the corner into the yard and came across to join them.

'This isn't a raree-show,' Mayne shrugged. 'If people turn up late they can jolly well find their own way to the hut. I'm dying to open up that cellar.'

He and Victor lit the lamps that were waiting to be used, since there hadn't been time for Francis to run electricity out here to the Nissen hut yet.

Mr Reston gestured to Mayne to lead the way down the narrow stone stairs and followed him. Victor, Francis and Daniel perched on the stairs, because there wasn't much room at the bottom, and the others either stood looking down into the hole or took a seat nearby and waited till there was something to see.

The door to the cellar seemed even sturdier this morning, somehow. Mayne stared at it. For three hundred years it'd been keeping its secret and nothing would get past it unless his father's research was right. His father was at the top of the stairs, because he suffered from mild claustrophobia.

He turned back to watch as Reston gave the door an affectionate slap.

'Right, then. I need absolute silence, if you please, so that I can listen carefully to the sounds the lock makes.'

He worked very slowly, so slowly that Mayne was aching to tell him to hurry up.

After each step of the process, Reston waited and nodded, then made another minute adjustment. Not once did he fumble, but neither did he try to rush the work.

'This is the last step,' he said after what seemed to the watchers a very long time. 'I have to listen even more carefully now.' He turned the key, moved it back, then turned it again, and the door swung open as smoothly as if it had just been oiled.

There was the sound of people letting out their breath in relief.

He moved forward to examine the door frame, muttered, 'Ah!' and inserted the small metal device into one of the top corners. 'I think that will keep it open.'

'We'll prop it open with this as well,' Mayne said and Victor passed him an iron fire grate which would make a strong doorstop.

Everyone exclaimed in shock as they heard a sound from inside the darkness of the cellar.

'It's not possible that someone's inside it,' Reston whispered. 'How could they have got in?'

Everyone gasped as Cuthbert stumbled out of the shadows at the back of the cellar muttering, 'Thank goodness! Oh, thank goodness!'

When Mayne stepped forward to support him, he said, 'You should help Sam. His mind's gone, I think.'

Mayne helped Cuthbert out to Victor, held up his lamp and peered inside. Someone was curled in a ball near the side wall, eyes tightly shut. For a moment he thought the man was dead but then he saw that he was breathing shallowly.

Cuthbert seemed dazed but kept gulping in great mouth-fuls of air. 'I'm out. I'm out.' He tried to push his way up the stairs.

'Don't let him get away!' Mayne called and his friends grinned and took hold of Cuthbert.

He didn't struggle but looked back down at Mayne and said, 'There are two skeletons in there and . . . there's a ghost. You can mock me if you want, but Sam and I both saw the scene where she and the man struggled. She killed him, but he managed to stab her in the belly with the last of his strength. It took her a while to die and she wrote something on a piece of paper.'

There was dead silence.

He laughed, a bitter sound. 'You don't have to believe me – you'll see for yourself.'

'What the hell were you two doing in there?' Reston asked.

'Waiting for you to let us out. The door closes automatic-ally after a few minutes.'

'We know about that. I've just fitted in the other piece of the puzzle. Why the hell did you do this? You're a good locksmith, could have taken over the shop from me.'

'Yes, well. I wanted to get away from Rivenshaw and my damned wife, so I stole a few things during the war.' His voice became shriller, 'I didn't even want to go into that sodding cellar last night, but Sam insisted!'

He was very close to tears. 'I've been trapped in there all night with two skeletons and a madman. I've not been able to get a sensible word out of Sam since we saw those ghosts.'

'Tell us the details later,' Mayne said. He called up to Sergeant Deemer. 'Did you hear all that?'

'Yes. I'll see to him.'

Cuthbert seemed to have lost all will to resist. He let them take him up and handcuff him to a metal strut, slumping on the ground.

They had to carry Sam out of the cellar and he seemed not even to notice their presence. He didn't uncurl from the tight foetal position in which they'd found him or make any sound.

Mayne had seen that happen occasionally during the war. Something broke inside a man and he retreated from a reality that was too much for him to bear.

After he'd handcuffed Sam to the metal strut too, just in case he was acting, Sergeant Deemer came back to the top of the stairs. 'I'll take them down to the station later, if you don't mind, Mr Esher. I don't want to miss the excitement.'

No one did. There was complete silence as Reston beamed at Mayne. 'This is going to cause a sensation in the Locksmiths' Guild. That door's a marvel, an absolute marvel. I've never seen anything like it. If you'll allow it, I'm sure it'll become part of a master locksmith's training from now on to study your cellar. Sorry. I shouldn't go on. You'll not care about that at the moment.'

He stepped aside and gave a slight bow to Mayne, flourishing one hand. 'It's for you to do the honours.'

Mayne stepped inside the cellar, taking one of the lamps. As Cuthbert had said, there were two skeletons. He was just about to examine them when the light grew brighter and he saw the two ghosts appear, transparent figures yet with every detail clear as they struggled with one another and died.

While this scene was being played out, he held up his hand to stop the others speaking or moving to follow him inside.

When the scene faded, he asked, 'Did anyone else see the ghosts?'

Ray answered. 'No, lad. Who did you see?'

'The woman was Margery Esher. No doubt about that. I recognised her from her portrait. And I think, though I'm not as sure of that, the man was Carolus, her husband's half-brother. He fought for the Roundheads and was regarded as a traitor, because the rest of the Eshers were royalists. No one ever knew what happened to Margery or where she was buried, but now the mystery is solved.'

Only then did he move forward to bow his head and say a brief prayer over her skeleton. He gave the other bones barely a glance, feeling a sense of repugnance after what he'd just seen played out.

After that he studied the surface of what looked like a small desk. A piece of paper lay on it, covered in scrawling spiky writing he couldn't read, with a smear of something that had faded across one corner. Blood, probably, poor lady.

Worried that the paper might fall to pieces in his hand if he tried to pick it up, he called out to ask Ray to join him.

Ray came down the stairs, whistling softly when he saw the size of the cellar. He studied the paper, then fingered one tiny corner of it very gently. 'Vellum. Lasts a lot longer than paper. I'd slide it on to a piece of card and put it in an envelope to carry it out. The less you handle it, the better, obviously.'

'I can't read it anyway,' Mayne said.

'Your father will be able to.' Ray shivered and looked round. 'It feels sad down here. She must have died all alone, poor lady.'

'Except for the body of the man who killed her.' He shrugged. 'I shouldn't care so much. It happened hundreds of years ago.'

'But she was your ancestor. Of course you should care.'

'Mmm. Anyway, can you come back with Dad another time and go through the objects in those boxes with me?'

He gestured to the shelves which lined the room then walked to the far end. The objects wrapped carefully in canvas looked like paintings. He hoped these were better than the ones his mother had wasted money on.

Reginald was already peering through the doorway, so eager to see what they'd found that he'd overcome his fear of enclosed spaces. 'Oh, it's quite big in here, isn't it? I can manage this for a while.' He walked in more confidently.

'Look at this. I think it's Margery Esher's last message.'

He took one look at the piece of vellum and said, 'Yes, that's definitely her handwriting. I've got her diaries, but the last one is missing. Can someone please get me a large envelope to put it in? We don't want to damage this.'

'I'll fetch one,' Judith called from the top of the steps and ran off to the office.

Reginald gestured round them. 'This was once part of the first Esher manor house, so the cellar would have been even bigger than this to cater for their food storage needs. They must have cut this off from the rest so they could use it to save their possessions. Margery was in charge while her husband was away fighting. She must have been a brave and intelligent woman. Her children always wrote about her very lovingly.'

He beamed at them all, fairly jigging about. 'Isn't it exciting? The family may be rich again.'

But Mayne didn't feel at all hopeful about that. Didn't dare.

He heard footsteps and Judith came back with a big envelope, then moved across to slip her hand in his. He felt instantly better and more hopeful.

'There's a light over her skeleton,' she said, not sounding afraid, but full of wonderment. 'Oh. I can see her. She's smiling at us.'

'I saw her too. She must approve of our marriage to show herself to you.'

'Yes. Oh, I do feel lucky to have seen her. And I'm dying to see what treasures are in those boxes.'

'They come a long way second to you, darling. You're my greatest treasure.'

'Oh, Mayne. What a wonderful thing to say!'

'I mean every word.'

As he looked at her, the light seemed to grow brighter for a moment or two, then fade.

It was as if everyone else had been standing frozen in silence and suddenly they came awake and began talking again.

But Mayne thought he'd never forget that moment, that sense that all was right with his world, whether there was treasure here or not. He put his arm round Judith, feeling suddenly optimistic.

Maybe there was room for a little more good luck in his life. Maybe . . . He didn't dare put that thought into words. Not yet. Not till he was sure.

But whatever happened he had his wife.

'Shall we just have a quick look at the paintings?' Ray asked.

'Why not?'

They sent for another lamp and Mayne hung it on a rusty hook at the end of the room. Dust lay thick on the canvas covers, but the shapes couldn't be anything but paintings. Reverently, with thanks to Margery for trying to save everything for her descendants, he tried to unwrap them. They were so firmly tied he had to take out his penknife and cut the cords, then peel off the canvas covers slowly and carefully.

His father came across to join him as he lifted the first painting from the pile. He set it against one of the walls of shelves and they studied it: a family portrait. Not a big one, but with a delightful family group in the middle. This one, at least, had been painted by someone who understood human anatomy and could paint silken skirts that looked soft enough to touch.

'Who are they? More ancestors?' Ray asked.

Reginald shook his head. 'I've no idea who they are. *I* haven't seen them before anyway. Not in any family painting or sketch.'

Ray moved closer, stood back, moved in again and let out a soft whistle of surprise. 'I may be wrong but that looks like a Van Dyck to me.' He bent to examine the signature, using a torch to see it more clearly and pulling out a magnifying glass to check the signature again.

'We'll come back to it,' he said eventually. 'Let's see what else there is.'

Mayne undid the wrapping on the next picture. 'Ah, now that's our family.' He pointed to the woman at the centre of the group. 'That's Margery. You know, she looks a bit like my wife, doesn't she, dark-haired and determined?'

They turned to study Judith who flushed.

Mayne smiled at her and went across to plant a quick kiss on her cheek. 'It's not so much a physical resemblance, as her expression and the way she faces the world, looking it straight in the eyes.'

Ray studied the portrait again. 'I think it's another Van Dyck.'

Mayne's breath caught in his throat. 'They're . . . valuable then . . . aren't they?'

'Very valuable indeed.'

Mayne closed his eyes and tried to stay calm. Had his miracle really happened? Would they bring in enough money for him to keep his home?

'Hey, are we ever going to get a look in there?' Victor yelled, standing in the doorway now.

Mayne suddenly realised he was ignoring everyone. 'We'd

better leave the other things till later and let people come down and have a quick look round the cellar. They've certainly earned it. We'll go through the items in more detail at another time, when I can . . . take it all in properly.'

Ray laid a hand on his shoulder. 'I just want to say that if those are anything to judge by, you're in for some pleasant surprises for a change. Even those two Van Dycks would bring you in a lot of money.'

Mayne could only nod. He had hoped for a small miracle. Was it possible that he'd been granted a big one?

He changed the subject, not daring to dwell on that, looking across at the skeletons. 'I'll ask Jan to knock together a couple of coffins. Margery at least deserves to rest comfortably.'

But Jan had guessed they'd need the coffins as soon as word went out that they'd found two skeletons. He'd slipped out of the Nissen hut and gone into the stables, where he'd seen some rough wooden coffins left over from the Army's occupation of the house. Well, coffins were kept at many of their camps, had to be, unfortunately.

With Victor's help he took them down the steps, helped Mayne lay Margery gently on a clean blanket and place her in the coffin.

Victor dealt with the other skeleton.

Meanwhile Judith had called the undertaker, who grew very excited about being involved and said he'd be round straight away.

Deemer stayed where he was. 'The police surgeon will have to give them a quick check to make sure they aren't recent murders, which is more than obvious to anyone with eyes in their head.'

'And after that,' Mayne said quietly, 'we'll give my poor ancestor a proper burial.'

'What about this Carolus?'

'His body can go in the rear section of the churchyard. He doesn't belong with the Eshers.'

He felt in his pocket, taking out the small key. 'I think this must be for one of the boxes.' He put it back as it all hit him suddenly and he sagged against the nearest wall. 'I didn't get any sleep last night and I think I've run out of steam. Let's lock up the cellar and have a quiet, peaceful afternoon.'

'If anyone's earned a rest, you have,' Ray said.

But he received no reply because Mayne was yawning again, which made Judith and a couple of the others yawn too.

'We'll go and sit down in the drawing room, in case we're needed,' Mayne said.

'We can deal with the police sergeant,' Daniel offered.

'Thanks.'

'Will you be all right?' Judith asked her children.

'We'll be fine, Mum, but you look exhausted. Go and have a rest.'

Francis yawned. 'I'm exhausted.'

It was left to Jan and Victor and Daniel as the least tired of the partners to lock up and post watchmen, then everyone else at Esherwood went to rest.

25

After a couple of hours dozing in a big armchair, Mayne woke up abruptly and found Judith smiling across the drawing room at him from another big chair.

'I just woke up too. I don't often sleep in the daytime.'

'Me neither.' He glanced at the clock. 'I feel better for the rest, though. I wonder if Ray is asleep? I'd like to have another look in the cellar. I'm not going to sleep well tonight until I solve the final part of the puzzle, which is—'

She finished the sentence for him. 'Whether you have enough valuable things to keep Esherwood in the family.'

'Yes.'

'Let's call Ray and see if he can come over, then just the three of us will go down to the cellar. I'll phone him.'

When she joined her husband, she was smiling. 'He's dying to see more and jumped at the chance to come over. In fact he said he'd set off "straight away". I'll just find a pad and pencil so that I can list the items we find.'

'I'd better find some sort of table to put things on as we sort them out.'

Victor had heard them talking and followed them down into the cellar with two folding card tables, he'd seen in the old stables. Then Daniel and Francis brought down some planks to lay across boxes, giving them rough display tables.

His friends seemed to understand that he didn't want an

audience as the contents of the cellar were revealed, so they left after that. And Ray had told Stephanie as they were driving over to go home to that nice lad of hers and he'd phone when he was ready to be picked up again.

'At last the uncertainty will be over!' Mayne said.

Ray patted his shoulder. 'I told Steph you wouldn't sleep for long and I was right, but I guessed you'd want to do this in private so sent her back. I'd have been the same as you, itching to check whether there are any other real treasures, besides the two Van Dycks.'

Mayne nodded. 'I, um, appreciate your help, and your understanding. I'd not sleep a wink tonight unless I got some idea of what was there.'

As they uncovered the rest of the paintings, they found landscapes and a few more portraits.

Mayne didn't dare ask.

'These are not Van Dycks but they're also very valuable,' Ray told them without prompting. 'You've unlocked a small fortune already.'

Mayne didn't need to tell him that it would take a large fortune if he was to have his dearest wish come true. And no works of art mattered to him when compared with Esherwood. He didn't need to say that, either. They both understood.

'We should check what's in some of the boxes as well, lad.'

Mayne turned to his wife. 'You choose one, Judith.'

She was drawn to a small box at the end of one shelf but when she tried to lift it, it was so heavy she looked at Mayne in surprise. 'What can be in it?'

He took it off the shelf and set it on one of the planks, rather than the flimsier card tables. The box was locked so he took out the small key and unlocked it, then lifted the lid. They all exclaimed in amazement at the sight of the gold coins it contained. They filled the box almost to the brim, so bright and shiny he couldn't resist running them through his fingers. 'Dear heaven, where did she get all these from?'

'The family probably kept all its money in the house,' Ray said. 'And this is it.'

'Will I have to declare them as treasure?'

'You would have to if you'd found them out in the fields, but these are part of your family legacy, stored safely inside your home.'

'They'll be worth a lot, won't they?'

'Yes. But you should let me sell them for you a few at a time. You don't want to attract attention to your findings here or you'll also be attracting burglars as well as taxmen.'

Mayne could only nod and reach out for his wife's hand.

'And this cellar makes a splendid place for keeping them safe, so you won't even need to lodge them in the bank vault in town.'

He stared at the gold pieces. Unlike the other items in here, these weren't dusty or tarnished, but shone serenely, catching the light. No wonder people loved gold.

'Let's try another box,' Judith suggested after a while. 'Ray, why don't you choose the next one?'

He did this, but let Mayne carry the box across to the table to be examined.

'Oh. It's only ornaments.'

Ray picked one up, took off the cloth it was wrapped in and laughed. 'Yes, but very old ornaments from the time before the English were able to make porcelain. This one came from China originally, probably via one of the Middle Eastern countries. That's why we usually call porcelain 'china', you know. This one is very valuable, all the more so because it's in perfect condition, which not many are. No wonder your Margery was hiding it from the Parliamentarians.'

He picked up another one. 'From China, again. There

might only be four ornaments in this box but they're worth a great deal of money.'

Mayne's voice was hoarse. 'How much?'

'Several hundred pounds each.'

Judith gasped and stared at her husband.

'If the other boxes contain similarly valuable items, then you're going to be a very rich man, Mayne lad.'

Six other boxes revealed silver and gold trinkets and items, a seventh revealed some exquisite jewellery. Ray said the pieces contained very fine diamonds and precious stones, even if they were old-fashioned in cut and style.

Mayne sat down abruptly on one of the planks. 'I can't take any more in today, Ray. Could we carry on with this another time?'

'I'm a bit overfaced with riches myself. I need to check up on gold jewellery in my antiques books, and I'd better find out what Van Dycks are fetching these days. I'll leave you two to it.'

'I'll phone your home for you,' Judith said.

'I know where your office is, if you don't mind me using the phone. You stay here and take stock.' He nodded and walked out.

Mayne drew Judith close, not saying anything, just holding her close. 'I know it sounds fanciful, but these feel like . . . gifts for our times from my ancestors. Such wonderful gifts.'

It was only when something wet fell on her hand that Judith realised he was trying to hold back tears – and failing.

'Let it out, darling. You've been keeping a stiff upper lip about losing your home for far too long.'

So he wept, strangled sobs and inarticulate mumblings. When at last he fell silent, he kept hold of her and she waited patiently till he moved his head back.

'What a fool I am. Weeping at good news.'

'Weeping for joy at keeping your home. Weeping out the

terrible stress you've faced ever since the war ended and you thought you'd be losing Esherwood.'

'Men aren't supposed to cry.'

'Well, they should. I've cried out my troubles many a time, and it usually did me good.'

He realised her cheeks were wet too. 'Why were you weeping today?'

'For you, my darling. For all you've suffered – and don't pretend you haven't suffered as you've tried to hold what's left of your family inheritance together.'

'I thought I'd hidden my feelings pretty well.'

'Not from me. And your partners understand how you feel, too. But what good would it have done for us to talk about it? You had no choice . . . then.'

'And now?' He pulled her to her feet and suddenly his face was lit up with joy as he led her into a slow dance around the edges of the cellar, weaving in and out of the boxes and tables until they were both helpless with laughter.

'Now, we're going to be able to save Esherwood, not only save it but bring it back to life. *And* plan how to invest the money so that the family finances are on a sound footing again.'

When Mayne came to a halt, he said, 'Let's go and tell the others. But not, you know, not *how much* exactly. I'll just say that it's going to be enough to save the house. Ray was right. Some things are better kept quiet. But I'm going to have this cellar door replaced. I wouldn't know how to deal with that lock, not to mention risking getting locked in.'

'Good idea. You can have a strong, secure door without all this fuss and give the old door and puzzle lock to Reston. He'll know how to make best use of it.'

'We'll put someone on guard over the Nissen hut until we can get a new door. Jan will arrange to keep that up.'

'What would we do without Jan? Or Al, come to that?'

'They've both been wonderful. As far as I'm concerned they'll have jobs at Esherwood, and good jobs too, for life.'

They paused in the doorway to the kitchen. Mrs O'Brien was busy cooking and the children had just finished laying the table for the evening meal.

'Where are the others?' Judith asked.

'In the sitting room, dear. The meal will be ready in ten minutes.'

'Could you turn the heat down and leave it a little longer?' Mayne asked. 'I have an announcement to make and I'd like everyone to hear it.'

'Yes, of course I can. A stew is very easy to leave on its own. One day we'll buy steaks again and then I'll show you how much I really love cooking.'

Mayne walked across the sitting room to stand to one side of the big fireplace. 'I have something to tell you all,' he announced.

One by one they fell silent, and the children and Mrs O'Brien came in from the kitchen to stand in a group near the door.

'From the expression on your face, it's good news,' Daniel said. 'Did you find some treasure in the cellar?'

'Treasure enough.' Mayne took a deep breath and said it aloud, 'Enough to save Esherwood and start our building company on a sound footing. We'll find other projects now we don't need to convert the house to flats.'

There was silence for a few moments as this sank in, then the room was filled with shouts and cheers, and people began hugging one another.

Judith's children ran across to hug her and she gathered them closely to her. They'd been through some hard times together until she met Mayne.

As he came and put one arm round her shoulders and

one round Kitty, a few tears escaped her and she faltered, 'I'm so h-happy.'

Ben laughed and Kitty said to Mayne, 'She always cries in that sniffly way when she's truly happy. I'm so glad for you, Mayne.'

'I'm glad for all of us. It means we can keep this house.' He smiled round the beautiful but shabby room, a lover's smile. '*And* we can let you three go to university or do whatever you want in life.' He smiled at them proudly.

Kitty gaped at him. 'I can train to become a doctor?'

'Ugh, who'd want that?' Gillian said scornfully. 'I'm going to be an actress and make a lot of money for myself . . . But I don't mind you helping me get started, Mayne.'

'I'm going to become an engineer,' Ben announced. 'A proper one, building roads and bridges and big things like that.'

'Is no one hankering after a lazy lifestyle?' Mayne teased.

'We wouldn't know how to be lazy,' Kitty said. 'What about you, Mum? What do you want?'

She put one hand on her stomach, 'To have this child and raise it here at Esherwood.'

'We're going to have a brother?' Ben gasped.

'Or a sister,' Gillian corrected.

Mayne smiled at his wife. 'I wondered when you were going to tell people.'

'You knew?'

'I'd guessed, yes of course, but I wanted to wait till you were ready to announce it. I think this child will be the best treasure of all to me, next to you and the children, of course.'

Ben rolled his eyes. 'Don't go all soppy on us.'

And the happy tears changed to even happier laughter.

Epilogue

The small church was crowded, the invited guests sitting at the front, other well-wishers staying at the rear.

Daniel stood in the entrance, easing his tie, which seemed too tight today. He checked that Anthony was all right, but his companion looked serenely happy not nervous like Daniel.

'Could you move down to the front of the church, please, gentlemen?' the verger suggested. 'Your brides will be arriving soon.'

The two men sat at the front, waiting as the slow minutes ticked past, until there was the sound of cars arriving and murmurs from the people sitting at the rear of the church.

When Daniel looked round, he saw Christa standing at the back, adjusting the skirt of her long cream silk dress, which had been retrieved from the attic at Esherwood. It was old-fashioned in style, he'd been told, but he thought she looked beautiful beyond belief in it.

Beside him Anthony sighed happily as Stephanie followed Christa into the church, also dressed in a gown retrieved from the attic. In her case, it was a pale pink in colour and he could hardly breathe at how lovely she looked.

The music changed and Mayne led Christa down the aisle, ready to give her away, walking slowly and in time to the rhythm.

Ray followed with his niece on his arm.

And then the marrying began with the time-honoured words that bind two people together in holy matrimony. The quiet sniffling of sentimental women and the fidgety sounds made by impatient children faded into the background as the four made their marriage vows loudly and clearly.

The couples vanished into the rear of the church to sign the register, and the organist played a happy, rippling tune, which changed to a triumphant peal of sound as the newly-weds came out into the church again, their faces alight with joy.

At Esherwood, a caterer hired by Ray Woollard had every-thing ready, and if the food was rather lavish for a country still tightly rationed, well, no one was going to complain or question where it came from. Not today.

Wine supplied from another hidden cupboard in Mayne's cellar flowed and speeches were made.

There was dancing for a while, then Betty went across to the musicians and another sort of music began – a conga rhythm. She jumped on to a chair and made her first public speech ever, one she'd rehearsed with her stepmother. 'We always dance a conga round the house when we're very happy. Please get up, everyone, and join the family.'

And they did, because who could deny a child so full of happiness? Who could refuse to dance at the wedding of two couples who were obviously deeply in love?

The line of people wound round the house with much laughter, jigging about, mostly in time to the music.

Judith turned her head to smile at Mayne, whose hands were on her waist as they moved round the rooms. 'Love you,' she mouthed.

'Love you more.'

He always said that. It made her feel cherished.

Victor and Ros followed them with his daughter Betty between them.

Francis and Diana were also stealing glances at one another, love shining in their eyes, fully together again in their marriage.

When the music grew quieter and people let go of one another, returning to their seats, still laughing, Mayne and Judith stayed in the big hall till they were alone there.

'Esherwood feels like a home again,' he said softly, raising both her hands to his lips and kissing them in turn.

'It *is* a home again, and we'll bring it fully back to life together.'

'As well as raising our children here.'

'Children?' she teased, placing one hand against her stomach. 'How many do you want?'

'At least three.'

'Sounds a good plan to me. I love babies.'

He put his arms round her. 'Ah, my darling, if they're all like you – and our other children – my cup of joy will overflow.'

As they shared a lingering kiss, they didn't see Kitty come looking for them, then go back and keep people away, giving them time together.

'What are you crying for?' Ben asked her.

'I'm not crying, well, not exactly. I'm just . . . so happy for Mum and Mayne. They were kissing one another.'

And for once he didn't scoff. 'She deserves to be happy. So does he.'

'Even the house feels happy today,' Kitty said.

CONTACT ANNA

Anna is always delighted to hear from readers and can be contacted via the internet.

Anna has her own web page, with details of her books, some behind-the-scenes information that is available nowhere else and the first chapters of her books to try out, as well as a picture gallery. You can also buy some of her ebooks from the 'shop' on the web page. Go to:
www.annajacobs.com

Anna can be contacted by email at
anna@annajacobs.com

You can also find Anna on Facebook at
www.facebook.com/AnnaJacobsBooks

If you'd like to receive an email newsletter about Anna and her books every month or two, you are cordially invited to join her announcements list. Just email her and ask to be added to the list, or follow the link from her web page.